HUNTING FOR WITCHES — SALEM'S BURNING

HUNTING FOR WITCHES — SALEM'S BURNING

BRIAN MCILROY

Trahor Fatis

Los Angeles

To Alex, Effy, Madimi,

and all my other muses

Part I

Ashton: One of my professors told me that Little Salem's the most haunted town in America. A lot of crazy business seems to have gone down here over the years, but I still haven't been able to dig up much information about individual hauntings, haunted places of interest—

Ada: That's because almost everything is haunted in Little Salem.

I

KILLED BY DEATH

When it comes to horror, some would argue that the most frightening type of horror involves an encounter with the unknown. A shadow creeping in the dark, contact with beings from another world. Fear of the unknown certainly has its place in horror, but it would be a grave error to ignore the fact that some of the most chilling and traumatizing scenarios come attached to a guise that is recognizable or familiar.

Professor Emmanuel wasn't expecting an encounter with horror that evening. A waxing crescent moon was glowing in the sky above him, and the night was quiet and still.

Emmanuel liked things that way: quiet and still. It was part of the reason he stayed on campus so late to finish his research each evening. His TA's handled most of the grading for his classes these days, which allowed him more time to indulge in his own personal devices, and that, for him, was perfectly fine. With every passing year, it appeared that his students were growing less attentive, less interested, and less capable when it came to wrestling with the challenges of "critical thinking"—a skill many would prove inadequate in when expected to apply this special talent upon graduation.

That was all fine with Emmanuel as well. He was aware that his occupation was mostly a novelty at this point—something to give him a purposeful role in society and a place to study how the newer generations were getting along. His real job was making sure his students weren't picking up any methods of thinking perceived as dangerous to the established order of things—an order to which he belonged.

Thankfully, there was no need to worry. Powerful, charismatic freethinkers were a rare breed to come across, leaving his life remarkably carefree and predictable for the most part, his nightly routine ending with a brisk walk that required him the same amount of time each and every class night until he arrived at his dependable vehicle—the only car that remained in the vast and empty lot.

On that particular evening, Emmanuel set down his briefcase as he searched for his keys. For an instant, he thought about how he could probably get home a few moments sooner if he started making a habit of crossing to his transportation with keys in hand.

How much time would he save by doing this? Three seconds?

It's no wonder he never cared to put forth the effort.

He would be home soon enough, and that, like everything else in his life, was perfectly fine.

Buzz. Buzz.

Emmanuel's face formed a curious expression. He wondered who could be texting him at such a late hour. Definitely not the wife. Their relationship was mostly a novelty at this point as well. Even if there was an emergency, he doubted she would feel the need to contact him specifically.

Hmm. This sealed the event as a perplexing mystery that could only be solved by reaching into his pocket. And with a life so effortlessly predictable and void of conflict, it was a unique surprise for him to discover a text from an Unknown Sender reading:

CHECK YOUR EMAIL.

Emmanuel pulled the door closed and hit the locks. His mind was racing, coming up with all the harmless reasons for why he would receive such a text. It appeared he would have to go along with the message's command to figure out why he was feeling so restless.

He clicked the mail icon on his phone and discovered "ONE NEW EMAIL" sitting in his inbox. The message was from an obscure email address from Czechoslovakia; a collection of random letters and numbers, along with the domain name "cz."

Could it be? No, perish the thought, he reasoned.

Emmanuel opened the message, which proved to be blank except for an attached MOV file. His heart was racing.

If the message was from Europe, could that mean...?

After a few more moments of hesitation, he tapped the file and watched the screen turn to black as the video began to load. Handheld footage appeared of what seemed to be a dimly lit basement, a man with an uncommonly majestic mustache tied to a chair in the center of the frame.

Emmanuel felt a knot start to form in the pit of his stomach.

The man looked familiar to him, but the room was dark, and his face was so horribly bruised and swollen, it was difficult to make out.

Could it be...? No, that would be...

Beads of sweat were forming on the back of his neck when his thoughts were interrupted by a voice that was chillingly apathetic.

"Name?"

The prisoner winced painfully.

"M-M-Malcolm Pryor..."

"And what do people call you?"

The man stuttered helplessly as the camera—a smartphone, probably—continued to record his mangled features. Clearly, the fellow was scared beyond all comprehension—and for good reason. He had already been beaten senseless, and who knew what unspeakable tortures might still lay in store.

"S-some people... Some people call me...*the Seventh Scholar*."

Emmanuel's jaw dropped at the revelation.

He knew this man! He really knew him!

As for the unseen videographer, the identity of that horrifying monster was still not exactly clear.

"The Seventh Scholar..." The unseen cameraman was obviously already aware of this information. "You must know many things to have earned that name."

The prisoner squeezed his eyes shut, trembling and sniveling. "I'm sorry. I'm so sorry..." His pleas were cut short as a black leather–gloved hand reached into frame, stroking the man's face with sadistic condescension.

"Shh-shh-shh... Let's try this again. You were about to tell me something. Something extraordinary. Tell me... *Where is the item I'm looking for?*"

Emmanuel watched the distressed captive resume his pitiful sniveling. He could sense the man's predicament, knowing he shouldn't answer, but the fear of what might happen should he refuse was too painful to imagine.

After a few moments, the man let out a desperate breath and forced a string of words through his cracked and bloody lips.

"It's... It's in... *Little...Salem...*"

Silence. Emmanuel leaned forward, waiting with bated breath.

All the color had left his face at this point. Not because of any empathy he might have felt for the victim, but because of the dread of having guessed the identity of the man's cold interrogator.

Confirmation came moments later as the unseen cameraman turned the camera on himself, revealing an abnormally pale young man who appeared to be his late twenties or early thirties. Dark fiery eyes, a shock of grungy platinum hair, his face partly shadowed by a black hoodie worn under a shabby black military overcoat.

Emmanuel felt a cold chill, his worst fear coming to fruition.

This was his son.

His son, McAllister. His flesh and blood.

But there was something different about him. McAllister had never looked so dementedly ghoulish and gaunt. The chalky, pale skin, the intense, razor-sharp features, and his eyes—his eyes were different as well. They seemed to have been stripped of anything close to resembling what could still pass for human and were filled with an irreparable strain of unbridled madness and cruelty.

Most disconcerting of all was how he appeared utterly at home in this transformation as he flashed a madcap smile for the camera.

"Hear that, Daddy-O?" McAllister grinned. "Europe was a blast, but it appears you'll no longer have to wait for the next family reunion to see me. *The new and improved me...*"

Emmanuel watched in horror as McAllister turned the camera back to the face of his captive and reached for the man's throat.

At the touch of his fingers, the face of the man began to change. The collection of blood vessels in the man's neck began to flame bright red, starting a chain reaction spreading throughout his face and the rest of his body. Within seconds, every drop of blood pumping through his system turned black as coal. The prisoner's life force was being drained, leaving a dark cobweb of blackened capillaries in its place—a feature that was all the more striking as all the color disappeared from the man's skin, leaving him a rotten and colorless husk as his terrifying executioner maintained a tight grip on him.

Emmanuel sat paralyzed as a spine-chilling cacophony of distorted screams rang throughout the vehicle, mutely watching as this man—the man with the distinctive mustache; a man he had known quite well at one point—sat dying before his very eyes. Murdered in a way too horrible and too unusual to put to reason. And he was watching it all play out on the smartphone cradled in his cold, clammy hands that for the bloody life of him would not stop shaking and could not release the object even if he had wished to do so.

* * *

Far away from Boston, a hooded figure stood across the street from the historic hotel where Tyler and Ashton had just arrived. A figure with a waifish, feminine form. Bright eyes, long dark hair, and innocent looks.

Ada's black-nailed, manicured hand pet the purring black kitten cradled in her arms as her gaze traveled up to Ashton's window.

She smiled impishly.

Nearly five years had passed since Ada swore her revenge on Little Salem, and she'd been preparing for her return to the familiar setting. He may not have known it, but Ashton had been selected to play a small yet important role in her schemes. So far everything was going according to plan—and not in a manner suggesting this was the result of chance or good fortune, but in the precise and exacting way that she and her cunning stepbrother had arranged.

Her stepbrother, McAllister.

2

PARANORMAL ACTIVITY

———————

Tyler stared at the faded wallpaper in his hotel room, still wondering where Ashton had disappeared. They were arguing in the local Chili's when Ashton excused himself to go to the bathroom, and he never returned.

The two amateur ghost hunters had only been in Little Salem for a little over a day, and Tyler was already getting the feeling his loyal amigo was growing sick of him. So far he'd found reasons to complain about everything: how the town they chose to visit was dull as dishwater, how the residents looked like they stepped out of a 1950s TV program. Most significantly, he complained about how there was only one place that served alcoholic beverages in the vicinity, and it closed at 11 (*Eleven!*). The contention that Little Salem was "the most haunted town in America" or the legend that Aleister Crowley had visited the hotel where they were staying offered very little consolation. He wished he could be anywhere else for a week, and that they'd chosen to spend spring break in Cabo instead.

For the past several weeks, Tyler had been looking forward to vacationing in Mexico, surrounded by hot babes in tiny bikinis pouring ungodly amounts of tequila down their throats. The plan changed once Ashton became convinced they should try spending the week in a more haunted locale instead, with the explicit goal of capturing prime footage for their fledgling paranormal YouTube channel. Tyler had been against this idea, arguing they should use the break to enjoy themselves. However, the fact that they'd been doing ghost hunts for over a year and still hadn't captured anything remotely mind-blowing was problematic, and there were two events that helped convince him to go along with the change of plans.

The first of these events involved a conversation the boys shared a few days earlier. They were enjoying coffees at a diner following a riveting ghost hunt that Tyler was certain had been their most successful investigation to date. He was smiling with excitement while reviewing the grainy night-vision footage on their camcorder—footage of him standing at the bottom of a stairwell while trying to coerce the stubborn spirits into revealing themselves.

"Dude—right here. I love this part," Tyler had said. "I just want to stay up all night, upload all this stuff to our profile on YouTube. Ghost Bros, bitch. Coming at ya."

Ashton looked more subdued, his earlier enthusiasm notably soured as he glared at an image on a digital camera—the supposed evidence that amounted to their long-awaited entry to the big time.

"Yo, what's wrong?" Tyler asked him. "It's the name, isn't it? You still don't like the name."

"No, it's not the—I mean, I still think it's a dumb name."

"Ghost Bros! You said we should pick a name that was, you know—"

Ashton grimaced with irritation. "The name was a joke! When we were talking about picking a name for ourselves, all I said was when you look at those long-running ghost shows, it's always a bunch of bros, and they're looking for ghosts. Ghosts, bros—it was an observation!"

"Right, and you want us to be successful, right? To turn this amateur ghost-hunting thing into a full-scale enterprise?"

"Yes, exactly. That's why I'm feeling a little disappointed—"

"Disappointed?"

"Yeah! Yes! Disappointed! With this. With this."

Ashton gestured impatiently to the digital camera and slammed it on the table. The viewscreen was displaying the image that had gotten Tyler so pumped.

"Dude, it's an orb."

"I know what it is, Tyler."

"Dude, this is legit paranormal stuff. Proof the investigation was a success."

"But was it? Was it?"

Tyler furrowed his brow, thinking this over.

"When we started doing these ghost hunts," Ashton recalled, "it was because you and I both know the supernatural is something real, right? It is seriously out there, and we wanted to get up close and show the world. But does what we captured do this? Us calling ourselves 'ghost bros' and running around haunted houses like a couple of fools—this is all we get from it? It's not enough."

"It was only one investigation," Tyler grumbled.

"Yeah, I know."

"It was our most successful investigation to date, but..."

Ashton stared out the window, looking introspective. "All these crazy stories you hear from people. Ghosts, demons, witches—"

"Yeah. Horror movie stuff."

"There has to be something to it, don't you think? Proof that those things are more than just stories and that they exist in the modern-day?"

"Dude, witches don't exist. That's just...cosplay for bored housewives and mallrats."

Ashton wasn't listening, still yearning for something more.

"I've always had the feeling there's something more out there. We've both had...experiences."

Experiences—this was something that Tyler couldn't argue with, and the conversation would be on his mind the following day. He agreed with Ashton on most things, but he refused to write off all of their minor successes. There was no question he was just as eager to capture something that provided conclusive evidence of the paranormal, but he didn't fully understand why his friend seemed so hell-bent on encountering something so horrifying. Like there was something Ashton wasn't telling him, and he was secretly seeking out this type of experience for highly personal reasons.

Despite the ongoing disagreements between them, Tyler had high hopes that their latest video would bring them one step closer to worldwide fame and celebrity. The footage from their investigation was still flashing in his mind when he arrived at the hotel in Boston—a posh metropolitan joint just a few miles from campus. After finding parking, he exited his SUV like a champion, as a tired and cynical voice droned on on the other end of his smartphone.

"Mr. Watts, I've told you a dozen times. Our company doesn't represent self-proclaimed YouTube celebrities."

"Well, maybe that's where your company's missing out, babe."

Phone pressed to his ear, he trekked across the lot with his chest puffed out and a slight bounce in his step. He was putting forth an extra effort that day to show off his inherent star quality.

Perception is reality, he recalled (he heard that in a movie once).

Not everyone held as flattering an opinion of the would-be paranormal superstar. To his surprise, he discovered he was being wall-eyed by every other posh and jaded hotel guest as he shuffled through the lobby in his ratty, dollar store flip-flops, cargo shorts, and a wrinkled baseball tee he pulled straight from the bedroom floor.

Geez, haven't any of these people seen someone who just pulled an all-nighter? he thought. However, he was more distracted by the weary tone of the publicity agent he called.

"I've seen your channel. You've posted a total of *eight* videos, all with under 10,000 views, OK? And with viewer comments I can only describe as...uniformly negative."

"Don't be so quick to brush us off, your babeness. 'Ghost Bros' is going to revolutionize the ghost hunting format. This is exactly how the Wright Brothers started!"

"I honestly fail to see any similarities."

"Just calling it like it is."

"Have a good day, Mr. Watts."

With that, the call ended—and not in the way he expected.

Oh well. One minor setback wasn't going to stop him. Tyler knew he was a star in the making, and it would only be a matter of time for the rest of the world to know this as well. The lyrics to a popular Taylor Swift song cycled through his head as he arrived at his destination—a large, spacious ballroom with a sign outside reading: PARANORMAL CONVENTION // ENTER HERE.

As Tyler navigated his way through a sea of empty chairs, a clunky video projector cast a dusty beam of light on a portable movie screen. He found a seat next to a burly neck-bearded fanboy, watching the footage of a film crew exploring an abandoned building. The young man was a paranormal enthusiast named Leon who was only a few years older than him but acted old enough to be a wizened Zen master with all of the vast knowledge of the world at his fingertips.

In other words, he was just as overly confident and arrogant as his Ghost Bro counterpart.

"Yo, what I miss?"

"Video on poltergeist phenomenon," Leon mumbled cynically.

On-screen, there was a loud crash, accompanied by a few choice expletives as a brick suddenly appeared out of nowhere and hurled itself at the film crew.

Tyler grinned with wry amusement. "Sa-weet."

After the fluorescents were flipped back to full, a frumpy-looking presenter in baggy clothing took his place at the podium. "As you can see, pretty heavy poltergeist activity on display," he muttered nervously. "Clearly possible demonic activity..."

Tyler was barely listening, still thinking about his successful ghost hunt from the previous night. "This is what I'm gonna do," he whispered. "I'm gonna have my very own TV show."

Leon frowned wearily, having heard it all who knows how many times before. He kept his eyes forward when the presentation was interrupted by a loud, booming voice from somewhere in the room.

"Shenanigans! You could see the friggin' strings!"

Tyler and the rest of the small crowd of audience members began to scan their surroundings, and his eyes eventually landed on a man in a black T-shirt. The man was a swollen, muscle-bound jock with short, dyed black hair and was accompanied by a scornful-looking posse of hanger-on bros all dressed in black as well. Their leader was clearly admired and respected, even if the company he kept was bargain basement, and Tyler knew the disgruntled bomb thrower and the reputation that preceded him.

"Holy crap. That's Eddie Specter from *Ghost Warriors*!"

Ghost Warriors was the show that sparked Tyler's interest in the paranormal when he was just a kid. Each show featured Eddie and his co-hosts exploring haunted hot spots and hellholes, trying to bully the resident phantoms into revealing themselves. There were several TV shows of this kind running on cable at the moment, but Eddie was the originator of this type of series—as well as the paranormal subculture's confrontational and controversial poster child, and a huge influence on Tyler in particular.

As the audience started to mumble in quiet recognition of the star standing among them, the frumpy-looking presenter awkwardly cleared his throat. He was no doubt feeling threatened by Eddie's high level of influence.

"Clearly—clearly, we have some disagreement with the, uh—"

"A disagreement? Is that what we have?" Eddie seemed to have reached a brand new level of moral outrage. "You posers will never make it to the big leagues with half-baked pretenda-vids like this nonsense! I'm outta here! Clowns!"

With that, Eddie made his exit, swaggering out of the room with his monochromatic ghost gang right behind him. While he was leaving, the presenter attempted to regain control of the disorderly setting, but Tyler's thoughts were somewhere else entirely. As the door was closing behind the infamous Mr. Specter and his sneering posse of cookie-cutter cohorts, Tyler and Leon exchanged muted expressions before jumping from their seats to chase after him.

"Ah, for cryin'—are you kidding me?"

Eddie was sitting at a giant computer monitor in his hotel room with Tyler nervously peering over his shoulder. Eddie's resident fan club, and also Leon, were gathered in the room as well, all of them glaring with collective disappointment at a digital picture of an orb displayed on the computer screen. The evidence that amounted to Tyler's crowning achievement as an amateur investigator and the *coup de grace* from his riveting ghost hunt the previous night.

"Dude! It's just a speck of dust!" Leon moaned.

Tyler scrunched up his face with disapproval. "Dust?"

"Look, I'll zoom in on it," Eddie grumbled. "You see those edges? Talk about amateur hour."

"Whoa! Who you calling amateur, Hollywood?"

Leon quickly tried to placate his incensed companion before a sudden interjection from Eddie forced Tyler to try to relax a little. His TV idol was facing him with a shining glint in his eye and a cold seriousness about him. Like he was about to take the would-be ghost hunter into his confidence.

"Look. I like you, brah," Eddie said. "You've got that fire in your belly like I did when I was first starting out with things. Because of that, I'm going to show you something you're not gonna get from those losers back in the convention hall. You know what that is? I'm talking about the real...*supernatural*."

Eddie clicked open a file on the desktop, and a homemade video began to play. It was the same type of video one would expect to see on any typical ghost show; a dark empty room, grainy night-vision footage. But right from the start, there was something different, and also palpably disconcerting.

The room the footage was shot in had a dreary and desolate atmosphere about it that was remarkably gloomy and unpleasant, the cramped and dilapidated space filled from floor to ceiling with piles of garbage and broken furniture. The environment reeked of tragedy and Tyler found it hard to imagine that anyone could subsist in such a setting. He assumed that whoever did must have had lives just like the furniture.

While pondering the disquieting state of the scenery, he suddenly observed the feature that Eddie had been so eager to reveal to him. In the corner of the room, a shadowy mist began to materialize. It was nothing alarming at first—Tyler had seen evidence just like this where something strange would appear and disappear just as quickly, and everyone would argue about whether it was something paranormal or just a glitch.

But the shadowy mist didn't disappear.

It continued to spread.

As the seconds passed, the haunting paranormal anomaly continued to flood the room, and Tyler found himself in a state of intense unease. He couldn't put his finger on it—whether his reaction was due to the apparition itself or the combination of the strange mist with the chilling environment. But whatever it was, the footage was definitively and without question the most unsettling piece of paranormal evidence he had witnessed.

"Whoa..." Tyler muttered, which was all he could manage.

Eddie seemed pleased, grinning widely as the eyes of his guest remained glued to the computer screen.

"You capture yourself a pretty piece of evidence like this?" he said proudly. "Everybody, and I mean *everybody... They're all gonna want a piece of you.*"

Back in Little Salem, Tyler sat on one of the hotel room's double beds, watching Eddie's video on his laptop. The video and the conversation at the diner had intensified his thirst immensely when it came to capturing a piece of the paranormal that would catapult him to the starry realms of celebrity. This was why he agreed to make the trip to Little Salem, still not yet knowing and not yet comprehending that the quiet and unassuming town he landed in would make both his wildest dreams and most terrifying nightmares a reality.

3

NEW FACES IN TOWN

Ashton glared into the bathroom mirror of the restaurant. Dark hair, gray eyes, a tall, athletic build that was tense as a bowstring.

Stupid Tyler. It was true: So far, Little Salem wasn't shaping up to be as perfect as he thought it would be. For a place that was supposed to be the most haunted town in America, it seemed exceptionally quaint and ordinary. The witch trials the town was known for were long in the past, and while the boys had already encountered a couple of odd experiences, they couldn't be rated as anything amazing. Nothing to do with the paranormal, nothing that would be of any use to pump up their fledgling YouTube channel.

Ashton remained determined to go all out in the hopes that Little Salem contained the strange, spooky experiences he was chasing.

So far, this outlook seemed overly optimistic.

Maybe Tyler was right. Maybe they never should have come to

this stupid town. Despite the weird, indescribable connection he had to the setting.

Feeling lost and volatile, his temper on a razor's edge, Ashton angrily grabbed one paper towel after another from the dispenser.

"*Ouch!*"

He cringed, noticing he cut his finger on the disposer blade.

Great. Some trip this is turning out to be.

Ashton grabbed another towel for his bloody finger and exited the restroom. He was so distracted with wrapping his injury he neglected to notice the smallish hooded figure passing him in the hallway, only beginning to pay any interest when he felt the warm breath from a pair of cherry-colored lips whispering: "You're cute."

Startled, Ashton spun around to address the figure, but no one was there.

"Hello?"

He turned and observed the empty corridor behind him and crept to the end of the L-shaped hall. Glancing warily around the corner, he spied a door swinging closed in front of him. He swiftly raced to it and pulled it open, stepping outside into a dark alleyway where a young woman wearing a gray hoodie was turning the corner at the other end—a girl he was sure he had seen once before.

"Stop! Wait!"

He rushed to the end of the alley to intercept her. But as soon as he turned the corner, he collided with a pedestrian.

"Hey, man! Watch where you're going!" the stranger exclaimed.

"Sorry. Sorry about that—"

Ashton watched the stranger dust himself off, noting he was a young Latino man. Late teens, maybe twenty. The young man was noticeably skinny, with expertly disheveled hair and was dressed in a flashy black pinstripe suit that gave off a rebellious rock 'n' roll vibe.

Not exactly the type of wardrobe one would expect to see in a small town. Definitely too cosmopolitan.

Feeling off-balance, Ashton glanced up and down the empty street. "Um, excuse me. Did you happen to see a girl in ... I think she was wearing a hooded cloak?"

"*Did I see a what?*"

Ashton frowned with embarrassment as the young man turned to leave. "You take care now, Mr. Rose," he said and took off skipping down the street.

Ashton's body stiffened. "Wait. How did you—?"

The young man turned around. In his hand was Ashton's wallet, his state driver's license with his name and picture on it shining in the moonlight. Snickering wildly, the thief started walking backward up the boulevard, and Ashton began marching straight for him with clenched fists.

"Hey! Hey! Come back here!"

The young man's derisive snicker turned into a maniacal laugh as he skillfully dodged his victim with ease, at one point juggling the wallet in his hands like a circus monkey while Ashton fruitlessly chased after him.

"Gimme back my wallet, you freak! Dude, I am not playing!"

Eventually, the pair reached the middle of the main drag, and the skinny hooligan ran to the converted Victorian home that stood across the street from the frozen yogurt shop. The place seemed much eerier and more disconcerting at night as opposed to when Ashton first caught sight of it during the day. This probably had to do with the fact that the establishment's massive handyman was outside on a ladder, painting the exterior pitch-black.

Laughing with glee, the shameless pickpocket ran up the steps, and Ashton gritted his teeth and followed. When he reached the doors, he came to a halt at the sight of what was waiting for him.

Standing between the twin pillars that lined the doorway was a waifish young woman who appeared to be in her late teens—she was nineteen going on twenty, to be precise. The girl had an unruly mane of dark, tangled hair that hung down to her waist and was dressed in a white tank top, gray hoodie, black pleated miniskirt, black stockings, and black combat boots. She held herself in a manner that projected poise and confidence and wore an impish smile, her thick, pillowy lips painted the color of dark cherries. But the thing that stood out the most was her piercing blue-violet stare; huge, haunting, otherworldly eyes like nothing he'd ever seen.

There was something odd about this girl—and wild and magnetic. Ashton didn't know it, but he just met Ada van Dreyer.

"Hi there, stranger," Ada said. "Fancy a drink?"

Ada guided Ashton by the hand as opera music played faintly in the background. The main room of the converted Victorian residence occupied the entire ground floor of the building and was larger than one might have expected, given the modest size of the historic dwelling. The humble tavern that resided within was about the size of a small bar or club and still partially under renovation. There were scraps of black carpeting still not fully tacked to the floor and black wallpaper gilded with gold leaf glued haphazardly to the walls in places. A large oak bar that looked like it had been sitting in a dusty basement for over a century adorned one wall, cardboard boxes containing expensive bottles of liquor stacked on top of it. And at the back of the room, a doorway led to the stairwell to the building's two upper floors, with the jukebox where the music was coming from sitting alongside it. The two remaining walls (minus the entrance that housed the building's front windows) were adorned with slick black vinyl booths. This was where Ada was leading him: toward a trio of young people sitting at a table tucked away in the far corner, and an experience he would rank as one of the strangest in his mostly uneventful life up to the present.

"So things are starting to get hot and heavy," a sultry and energetic voice exclaimed, "and the woman breaks free and says, 'Oh my! I need to get some air!'"

It was the redhead who said this as a petite young woman of indiscernible origins—gypsy or Romani, possibly—giggled at the passionate performance. The buxom ginger-haired beauty, who looked to be in her early to mid-twenties, was dressed just as provocatively as when Ashton and Tyler had spied her barreling into Little Salem behind the wheel of a flashy cherry-red convertible (a 1964 Cadillac DeVille), blasting riotous rock 'n' roll on the stereo. She was wearing a low-cut, partially see-through red blouse that showed off the red bra supporting her impressive freckled bust, which was accentuated with a selection of expertly chosen jewelry and hair and makeup that was picture-perfect. It was obvious she put a great deal of time and care into her appearance and was intimately aware of the jaw-dropping effect she had on both men and women alike.

The intriguing young woman sitting across from her was dressed in a manner that was equally eye-catching. The petite gypsy girl appeared to be in her late teens or early twenties (possibly the same age as Ada or a bit younger) and was dressed in a vintage leopard-print coat worn over a faded heavy metal T-shirt. The most striking feature about the girl's appearance was the abundance of sparkly jewelry she was wearing. She wore rings on every finger, her dark shoulder-length hair tucked behind her ears to show off her large dangly earrings that glittered in the lamplight. Ada was by far the most casually dressed of the three, but by the way her friends were carrying on, it appeared that some kind of celebration was underway. Ashton didn't know the reasons for the occasion, but it would only be a matter of time until he found out.

As Ashton warily took in the offbeat company and scenery, Ada pulled him beside her into the booth, sitting across from the final member of the party who was dressed a bit more modestly than his companions but looked exceedingly sharp nonetheless. The stranger was a young African-American man, most likely in his mid-twenties, wearing a black sports coat over a casual blue button-down shirt and black jeans. Ashton couldn't see much of the man's face, only viewing it in profile as his head was cast downward while he lazily scrolled on his smartphone. But just like the girls, he appeared to be fit and attractive, with pleasant features and enviable bone structure.

To Ashton, Ada and her friends were noticeably striking—but not in a conventional sense. Their appearances were almost...supernatural. And like Ada, whom he had only just met, they all seemed to be just as mysterious and were probably well past their first round of libations, based on the peculiar energies he was receiving from the gathering.

"So the woman scurries out of the room," the redhead continued, delicately swirling the glass of wine in her fingers, "and she rushes down the stairs, where she almost collides headfirst into her landlord, who's talking to a policeman. She turns her head and notices further down the hall a sight that makes her body shiver: A pool of blood oozing into the hallway directly outside the door to her neighbor's apartment..."

The petite gypsy girl cringed, completely riveted by the story. By contrast, the African-American gentlemen seemed much more disinterested, turning his attention to pouring some wine for Ada and motioning to pour a glass for Ashton, which he declined reflexively.

Noticing several of the guests were distracted, the redhead leaned forward, making her ample cleavage more visible. She seemed to be reacting to the fact that she was losing the crowd's attention due to the appearance of the party's newest arrival: a girl who seemed gifted with a presence that commanded everyone's notice whether she was doing anything or nothing at all. The strangest thing of all was that while Ashton was listening to the redhead's story, he began to feel somewhat light-headed—although, at this point in the evening, he was choosing to ignore the peculiar reaction.

"So, with her heartbeat quickening," the redhead grinned, "the woman creeps ever-so-slowly to the doorway. She peers inside and spies none other than the body of her lover lying dead and bloody on the floor. The very same lover she left in her apartment just a few moments earlier, kissing the woman's soft ruby lips."

This concluded the redhead's chilling tale, and Ashton watched as she leaned back with immense satisfaction at the silence that had come over the table.

"Mmm. That was a good one," the gypsy said, her dark eyes gleaming.

"That *was* good, wasn't it?" the redhead answered proudly.

"Do the one about the living portraits!" the gypsy pleaded.

The African-American gentlemen snorted dismissively, inspiring the gypsy to reach for her wine, pouting like a spoiled child.

"Oh, Miles," she moaned theatrically. "You hate all of my favorites."

Feeling confused and befuddled by the whole affair, Ashton turned to Ada. "What is this?"

Before she could answer, the redhead leaned forward, once again showing off her glorious rack for their special guest to admire.

"This?" the redhead grinned. "This is how we go about breaking in our new clubhouse. Care to join the fun, um—?"

"Ashton," he muttered, averting his eyes self-consciously.

It was curious—while the redhead addressed him, he felt a wave of strange sensations. Like his senses were being assaulted by a pow-erful fragrance that made his blood rush like crazy and his head feel dizzy. And yet, he was convinced it must only be his mind playing tricks on him, feeling more distracted by the sight of the three girls leaning toward him like hungry wolves.

"Know any scary stories, Ashton?" Ada asked.

"You like scary stories, don't ya?" whispered the gypsy.

"Me?" Ashton mumbled awkwardly. "Well, I have encountered a ghost or two. My friend and I are paranormal investigators. We hunt ghosts and stuff."

"My, how fascinating," the redhead exclaimed.

And once again, there it was—a perfumed odor attacking his senses, accompanied by the sound of tiny bells. Tinkling softly and euphorically every time she opened her plump and delectable lips.

"You should explore the town with Ada," the redhead said. "She knows all the sexiest, spookiest places."

Ada rolled her eyes as she reached for her wine. "Oh, Agatha..."

It was at this point that Ashton seriously started to question things. He wasn't entirely sure what was wrong or what was going on with him, but he suddenly felt very uncomfortable with being in the company of these strangers and was searching for an excuse to make his daring escape.

"Maybe another time," he said. "I really have to get—*ow!*"

Ashton winced, and the girls all stared at him in stunned silence as he removed a bloody hand from his pocket. His finger was still bleeding from the cut he received on the bathroom towel dispenser.

"My stars!" the gypsy gasped. "Are you hurt, baby?"

Ashton began to mutter a string of excuses, but these were all ignored. Without warning, the gypsy grasped his hand into her own, the three girls now fretting over him like a helpless child who had bumped his head on the jungle gym.

"It's just a scratch," he protested. "Really, I—"

Naturally, his arguments fell on deaf ears. The far-out-looking bohemian kept a firm grip on him and proceeded to blow warm breaths over the injury.

"Now, just think happy thoughts," she instructed. "You're walking in the sunshine, a pretty girl by your side..."

Feeling incredibly awkward, Ashton gazed helplessly at the girl as she rubbed his hand until a few moments had passed. When she was satisfied, she finally released him and let out a cheerful exclamation:

"And *voila!* All cured."

Ashton glanced at his finger and was surprised to discover the cut had not only healed but it was as if the wound had never existed.

"Wow. How did you...?"

The young eccentric winked and let out an amused giggle.

"Gypsy magic, baby."

Rendered speechless, Ashton glanced over to Miles, who shrugged his shoulders with indifference. He was about to pester Ada for an explanation when the flush of a toilet interrupted the gathering, and all heads turned in unison to a skinny young Latino man entering from the back.

"Whew! I feel ten pounds lighter."

"You! You're the freak who took my wallet!"

Before Ada could stop him, Ashton leaped to his feet as the young man laughed uproariously, mockingly holding up his hands with his accuser's wallet in one of them while the increasingly hostile victim of his cunning thievery began his steady approach.

"Yo, calm down, playa!" the smarmy pickpocket exclaimed. "I was gonna give it back. Say, smokin' hot picture of your girlfriend by the way. Yowzahs."

"Hey, Rudy. Hot potato."

The tension in the room was palpable, and there was no telling what Ashton intended to do to the sly thief. However, as soon as these words were uttered, he witnessed another odd event to add to his list. The seemingly innocent comment appeared to inspire Rudy to drop the wallet instantly, as if his hand was burning, with the skinny miscreant grasping his fingers and scowling with fury in the direction of where the remark was delivered.

"Ow! Not cool, Miles," Rudy hissed. "I'll put a hex on you, I'm warning you!"

Miles started to snicker while Ashton snatched up his wallet, still ready for a fight if it came down to it. Meanwhile, Agatha, the red-head, once again dissatisfied with not being the center of attention, yawned with halfhearted disinterest as she lazily flipped her hair and adjusted her cleavage.

"Did I hear you have a girlfriend, Ashton?" she asked casually. "Is she as titillating as the rest of us?"

And once again, as soon as she opened her lips, the sound of tiny bells began ringing inside of Ashton's head, making his body feel faint and woozy but also filling him with an urge for carnal lust.

The reaction was so extreme this time it was impossible to just ignore it. But before he had a chance to address this predicament, Miles raised his voice and cast a cold stare at his sultry ginger cohort.

"Agatha, that's enough," Miles said, before turning to Ashton. "It's getting late, stranger. You should be getting back."

Curiously, this innocuous comment had a strange effect on him as well. As if all the feelings he was experiencing had been wiped away and the only thought that was left was the desire to do what Miles suggested.

"Right. I should be getting back."

Ada jumped up from the table, like an actress who'd been given her cue. "I'll walk you to your hotel," she said, leaving her distressed companion with very little reason to argue.

Ashton felt he might enjoy a few extra moments with his newest acquaintance to help him come to terms with things. For the life of him, he couldn't understand what such an unconventional group of strangers was doing in a town like Little Salem. Or why every other voice at the table seemed to have such a bizarre effect on him.

And yet, it was funny—as he rose to his feet, he found he no longer remembered what was troubling him. He only felt that he best be off and on his way as Miles had recommended.

Ashton turned politely to the group and wished them well, but as he approached the entrance with Ada accompanying him, confident that the strange and unusual affair was over and whatever had been bothering him was ancient history, the last thing he heard was a woman's voice calling back to him:

"*The pleasure was all ours*," the voice said.

And once again, he heard the sound of tiny bells and his temperature began to rise unexplainably.

4

BARBARISM BEGINS AT HOME

For Nancy and Wilbur Truegood, life in Little Salem was practically perfect. They lived in a comfortable home in one of the town's most desirable districts, work at the frozen yogurt store they owned and operated was only a short drive away, and so was the safe and respectable high school their adopted Venezuelan daughter, Mary Sue, attended. The friendly couple knew all their closest neighbors, who they adored and socialized with regularly, and they attended church every Sunday (well, most Sundays) and engaged in activities as a family as much as their busy lives permitted. One couldn't ask for a happier middle-class existence, but recent events had left the Truegoods feeling worried and anxious. Something wicked was in the air in Little Salem, and they were starting to fear their comfortable way of living was under threat.

The sudden transformation of one of the town's most popular eateries was a surprisingly unsettling affair for the couple to witness, as was the appearance of several strangers who looked like they were present for more than just an innocent round of sightseeing—and right at the beginning of the annual "Season of the Witch" celebration. Throughout the day, several incidents had been observed that were disturbingly out of the ordinary. And for a town like Little Salem, where "simple and ordinary" was a way of life, these highly irregular occurrences didn't bode well for the community.

For the moment, the Treugoods seemed to be forcing themselves to ignore these matters while going through their normal nightly routines. Wilbur sat on the bed watching the sports recap and Nancy was in the bathroom, applying her lotion and complaining about the habits of their angsty teenage daughter who she just checked on.

"Fifteen years old and still sleeps with a night-light..."

"You should take it easy on her," Wilbur said. "The girl's had a tough life."

"Oh, don't start with me, Wilbur," Nancy groaned, crawling under the covers. "I still haven't forgotten the image of you drooling over that redhead like every other man on the street."

Nancy was referring to Agatha's grand entrance—a sight the couple had witnessed after introducing themselves to two tourist boys who were in town for spring break. Normally, they wouldn't be arguing this way, but recent events had left them increasingly tense and agitated, leading to an uncommonly hostile state of affairs that ran counter to their usual closeness.

"I just find it unusual so many strange people are showing up," Wilbur mumbled defensively. "It gives me a funny feeling."

"Yeah, I'll bet," Nancy said. "Are you going to be up for much longer? If so, I'm putting in my earplugs."

"I wasn't planning to. That is, unless you're in the mood for—"

Nope. Nancy had already reached into a bedside drawer and applied her earplugs and eye mask. "Goodnight, hon."

Only a few hours later, Wilbur would learn his earlier apprehensions were justified. It was the middle of the night when he first heard it: the sound of loud music (if one could even call it music). At first he thought he was hearing things, but once the music got louder and started reverberating throughout the home, he quickly sprang up and grabbed the baseball bat he kept under the bed for such instances, anxiously padding down the hallway and instructing his daughter to return to her room and lock the door behind her.

The whole home was dark when Wilbur reached the ground floor, creeping stealthily through the living room before reaching the den. While peering in, he noticed none of the lights appeared to be working. *A problem with the fuses, maybe?* Thankfully, no one else seemed to be present.

Nerves still in a tangle, he set aside the bat to fiddle with the seemingly sentient electronic system and breathed a sigh of relief after killing the awful racket. He was so thankful the strange occurrence was only a false alarm he'd already forgotten all the other disturbing peculiarities attached to the event, not noticing the shadowy figure sitting in the easy chair, watching him from across the room.

"You've redone the den, I noticed."

Startled, Wilbur retrieved the bat and faced the intruder.

"How 'bout putting that down, slugger?" the stranger added. "Before you hurt somebody."

Wilbur tossed the bat aside after concluding his visitor's identity. "McAllister. What are you doing here?"

The wiry young man rose to his feet and pulled back the hood of his hooded sweatshirt, revealing his shiny platinum hair and cruel angelic features. "Straight to the penetrating questions, eh, ol' buddy? After I've been gone for so long..."

He pouted his lips and held out his arms.

"Don't I get a hug?"

The conversation had only started, but Wilbur was already backing away with discomfort. Like Emmanuel before him, he was highly unsettled by how similar McAllister appeared since he last saw him—and yet so different.

"The Council went after you," Wilbur muttered. "Hunted you like a dog. Last I heard, they banished you from ever setting foot in Little Salem."

"Still eavesdropping on those old losers?" McAllister's predatory eyes shifted to the happy family photos on the mantle. "Some things never change."

"Word gets around."

"Didn't you hear?" McAllister asked facetiously. "The power of the 'old ways' is fading. Your former lords and masters won't be in charge for much longer." He began to mull over all the photos, turning them all face down. "Just a little something to think about the next time you wake up in the middle of the night. Your body covered in sweat, your poor little girl whimpering in the next room—"

Wilbur's fingers tightened around the letter opener sitting on the desk behind him. "If you even think of laying one finger—"

"You'll what? Old buddy?"

Standing motionless, Wilbur watched McAllister glance over at him while wearing an icy grin. This last statement was uttered with such a total lack of fear or cause for concern, it sent a cold shiver down the base of his spine.

"Anyhoo," McAllister said after neglecting to receive an answer. "I'd love to stay and chat, but hell's not going to raise itself. I thought I'd check in since I'll be hanging around for a bit. Don't worry—you'll be seeing a lot of me."

As McAllister crossed to the front door, Wilbur knew he had to do something. Unfortunately, trying to stab his visitor with the letter opener proved to be a horrible miscalculation. While barely even registering his assailant, McAllister swiftly demonstrated the superhuman strength he now possessed, shaking off his attacker like a pesky insect and tossing him like a rag doll across the room.

For a brief and surreal moment, Wilbur felt his body soaring through the air before crashing into a wall and landing on a coffee table that collapsed under his weight. *Was this a nightmare?* No, his whole body was aching all over. The pain shooting through him felt much too real—and this was only the beginning.

His head spinning like a whirligig, Wilbur watched a scruffy pair of combat boots slowly cross over to him, the fearsome, leering monster that was wearing them smiling ruthlessly at his victim.

"Impossible. McAllister... What...happened to you?"

Wilbur winced in agony under the pressure of his foe straddling his chest. Watching as he removed his black leather gloves to reveal the deathly whiteness of his hands and fingers underneath.

"More than you could imagine," McAllister grinned. "But my petty crimes and follies..." The villain released a chilling laugh. "They were not performed in vain. See, I've developed an obsession. To find the Engelander Diary."

Wilbur's eyes widened. "You fool. You'll kill us all."

His discomfort only amused McAllister further, clutching the face of his quarry and pulling it closer toward him.

"Them that die will be the lucky ones," McAllister hissed.

Wilbur felt a painful jolt as the blood vessels under his skin started flashing from red to black. Thankfully, the excruciating torment was mercifully interrupted.

"Daddy?"

McAllister looked up, spying Mary Sue at the bottom of the stairs. Wilbur panicked at the thought of what his attacker would do next, but McAllister only sneered and swiftly fled the premises.

"Daddy! What did he do to you?"

Wilbur was in a state of shock, barely managing to extend a trembling hand to caress his daughter's arm. Why she ended up chasing McAllister outside, Lord only knew. Perhaps it was out of curiosity, or so she could scold that nasty piece of work. But as soon as she reached the doorway, every motive seemed to leave her as McAllister stood stock-still with his back turned, breathing deeply before offering some final words of prophecy.

"Salem's burning once again," McAllister said. He pocketed a gold lighter and exhaled a cloud of smoke from a cigarette balanced between two fingers. "This time, the new school will be taking over. Watch and learn."

With a flick of the wrist, McAllister tossed the cigarette onto the grass, and the family's treasured front lawn burst into flames, the fiery blazes forming the shape of a pentagram. Eyes brimming with terror, Mary Sue cowered at the sight while the fiendish visitor used a small remote in his fingers to resume the pummeling music from earlier—right before seeming to vanish into thin air.

McAllister being back in town after nearly five years was no laughing matter. The situation felt cataclysmic, and the next day, the Truegoods organized a meeting with a handful of neighbors to discuss what to do in such a predicament. Once it was confirmed that McAllister and the other strangers around town were responsible for the business involving the tavern, all the typical questions were submitted given the shallow group of personalities that were present: whether the matter could be resolved by calling the authorities; whether the group they were dealing with was starting a satanic cult.

There was also discussion about whether the presence of these outsiders and the degenerate bar they opened would affect the neighbors' property values. This concern was especially uniform amongst the residents—the one thing that mattered more than anything.

Nevertheless, everyone started viewing the matter much differently once it was recognized that, in addition to having McAllister to worry about, along with his bizarre transformation, Ada was more than likely accompanying him. This made the situation even more troubling. Everyone knew about Ada's visit from five years earlier. And her curse against the town. And her threat that she and her brother would someday return. Most distressing of all was all the property damage she caused during the time of her previous stay.

And yet, despite these apprehensions, one neighbor tried to convince the group that maybe they were overreacting. There was no need to go losing their heads about things since, in reality, all they were dealing with was a group of messed-up stupid kids.

Nancy wouldn't budge. She remained adamant that it would be a mistake to underestimate the pernicious evil they were up against. "They terrorized my daughter," she said. "They terrorized my daughter, and they'll be coming for yours as well. She hasn't been the same since last night. We need to start taking things more seriously."

Nancy's outburst had a sobering effect on the meeting. After it was decided that a firm course of action was required, albeit begrudgingly, the neighbors determined the most proper thing to do was to visit that damn bar where those damn misfits seemed to be hanging out. That seemed to be the easiest way to get a better idea of what all the fuss was about. But it was also agreed that they should wait to do this until the following day. The Palmieri couple had to drive their little Nico to ballet lessons. Plus, they already had a roast in the oven, so...

Ruth, the most senior member of the group, tried her best to console Nancy as everyone hurried on their way. She stressed that Ada was a special girl, but she was no match for the Sisterhood.

Later, while the couple was alone and cleaning up, Wilbur lamented how he forgot to mention the crazy book McAllister was after and suggested maybe the Council would get involved.

"I can't wait that long," Nancy argued, snatching up her purse from the counter and heading for the front door.

For Nancy, the situation was crystal clear: Almost five years had passed since Ada swore her revenge on Little Salem, and the True-goods stood at the very center of her crosshairs.

Wilbur paused with the cleanup to call after her.

"Uh, Nance? What are you planning to do exactly?"

Nancy stopped and smiled, eyes shining with determination. Ada was a powerful adversary, but she refused to back down so easily. Not when everything she cared about was being placed in jeopardy.

"Only what any witch would do in these types of matters," Nancy replied assuredly. "You should know, hon. *You married one.*"

5

ATROCITY EXHIBITION

Ada leaned against the vintage Cadillac DeVille, parked a short distance from the Little Salem Grand Hotel. She was looking extra eccentric that day, in a black baby-doll Wednesday Addams dress, black stockings, and red sunglasses that complemented the color of her lips and the cherry-red hue of the convertible.

The night before, Ada had arranged to give Ashton a personal tour of Little Salem, following up on Agatha's suggestion back at the tavern. They agreed to meet first thing after breakfast, and she didn't have to wait long before spying two young men crossing down the street together, overhearing Tyler asking if she was friends with the redhead who was still on his mind since first seeing her.

Tyler's jaw practically hit the ground when he first noticed Ada, but she didn't take this reaction too seriously. A quick examination helped her conclude this was the normal response for him whenever he was in the presence of any moderately attractive young thing.

The sight was actually pretty amusing.

Ada noticed Ashton was making an effort to appear much more easygoing that morning. While he was making introductions, she saw that Tyler was trying to read the situation, ultimately wishing them well as he looked for a way to excuse himself.

"You're not coming with us?" Ada asked, cocking her head with curiosity.

"Me? Nah, I've got, um... Stuff. Lots of—oh! I have to go over the footage from that static night-vision camera we left in the attic!"

"Yeah, and you can do that later," Ashton noted with suspicion.

There was no convincing him. Tyler had made up his mind apparently. He seemed to have determined that giving his friend some alone time would be doing him a solid.

"Nah. I just want to...get it done. You know, while you get your thing done?"

Tyler gave Ashton a wink, which made him want to instantly die from embarrassment.

"OK, whatever," Ada said as she climbed into the driver's seat. "Have fun!"

"Thanks, dudes! Have fun raiding the Hot Topic! Or whatever!"

Ada hadn't been present for the conversation over breakfast, but the dynamic between the friends suggested that Ashton was trying to be a good boy while on vacation, whereas Tyler felt that nothing should be off-limits. Deep down, Tyler probably admired Ashton for being so committed to his girlfriend back in Boston, but there was also a part of him that longed for a partner in crime who was as shamelessly one-track-minded as he was. Ada noticed Ashton seemed more conflicted about spending time with her because of this. Throughout the day, she caught him checking his cell phone, forgetting it was dead. This would be a regular occurrence when he was in her presence, but he never seemed to catch on. Connecting with his girlfriend would always be impossible whenever he was in her company. Ashton had no idea she possessed the powers to influence such matters, but on that day, as she was showing him the sights, she was dropping more than just a handful of clues to pick up.

For Ada, all of this was highly amusing.

While driving through town, Ada actually said very little. Ashton may have suspected she would be pointing out haunted locales and telling him their stories, but she mostly directed his attention to various sights and local businesses—like she was giving him a tour of a setting that was perfectly normal in every way. It wasn't until they were driving along the road that ran alongside the massive forest that rested on the outer edges of Little Salem that he started questioning her about how despite the town's reputation for being haunted, his research hadn't been able to produce much when it came to specifics.

And yet he'd somehow been drawn to the place despite this.

How interesting.

Right away, Ada explained that the lack of specifics was because almost everything was haunted in Little Salem, but their conversation was cut short when she almost ran over a deer carcass. The sight brought back bad memories, and she had to pull over to collect herself. Once she had done so, they continued on their merry way.

Before he could question her further, Ada brought their conversation back to before the interruption. "A lot of bad blood has been sown out here over the years," she said. "During the Salem witch trials, many of the women that were hanged cursed this town with their dying breath. That curse remains to this very day."

"Yeah, I don't give too much credence to that whole witch trial hullabaloo," Ashton grumbled.

For Ada, this comment also amused her, and she glanced at her companion while flashing an impish smirk.

"Well, maybe you need to get some education, college man."

The Little Salem Witch Museum was a small four-room complex located on the west side of town. The red brick building was quite plain and unassuming and would have been easy to miss if it wasn't for the hopelessly tired and clichéd representation of an evil hag positioned directly out front. The statue was something Ada found to be more dull and unimaginative than offensive during her previous visit to Little Salem, but slowly her fascination with the museum began to build over time. After all, if a museum could get something so wrong right on the outset, she wondered what else it could be misrepresenting and had been looking forward to the day when she could finally visit and see for herself.

A middle-aged tour guide with a thick Boston accent and short, high school gym teacher hair led the way as Ada and Ashton joined the daily jumble of bored suburban thrill-seekers. Ada suspected the woman's job must get awfully repetitive, but she seemed to be having great fun with her occupation, treating the occasion as more than just a dodgy museum tour and more like a performance.

"The Salem witch trials occurred in 1692 and 1693 in various towns and villages in colonial New England," the guide said. "And the initial catalyst happened right here in the town of Little Salem."

Looking all around her, Ada noticed that positioned around the room were dozens of aging mannequins dressed in dowdy Puritan fashions, standing alongside conventional cartoon imaginings of stereotypical wicked witches. The sketches and paintings on the walls were slightly more impressive, though not by much. These served as the tour's major focal point, their guide gesturing to a portrait of two Colonial girls hanging on the wall beside her.

"It all started when two young girls, Betty Parris and Abigail Williams, returned from the woods one day with their family servant—a Caribbean slave named Tituba. Nothing seemed wrong with them at first, but in the middle of the night, the girls' families received the scare of a lifetime when they discovered them screaming for mercy while suffering from strange epileptic fits.

"As these were very superstitious and Puritanical times, the girls' parents believed the malady was the result of enchantment. So fingers were pointed at Tituba and two other outsiders—the widow, Sarah Osborne, and an elderly beggar named Sarah Good."

The guide next stood opposite three portraits of three different Puritan women. The first showed a modest-looking woman with a dark complexion, and the others showed two steely-eyed white women who both looked a bit mad and disheveled in appearance. None of this information was news to Ada, but she was impressed that Ashton was exhibiting a high level of engagement in the presentation. He was taking a particular interest in the portrait of Tituba as the group moved on to the next room with Ada among them.

So far, the tour had been relatively tame and predictable but all in good fun. Ada was already looking forward to telling the group back at the tavern about the experience, but this innocent perception would change once she entered the next room that awaited them.

The room standing before her was packed wall to wall with torture instruments from a long-forgotten era in history: the Witch Burnings in Europe. A period that was no laughing matter to anyone the least bit familiar with the violence and cruelty that were par for the course for those with the misfortune to live in those horrible times. Many of the instruments that were used to torture suspected witches were on display: an Iron Maiden, a Judas Cradle—a whole host of disgusting devices, the mere sight of which caused Ada to feel sick to her stomach.

As Ada averted her eyes, she found herself gazing humorously at the gaggle of visitors. They were huddled around a selection of paintings showing various aspects of the trials themselves: the accused sweating in front of hostile crowds of spectators, the doomed languishing in irons while awaiting their inevitable sentencing.

"The three women who were accused were sent to jail to await their impending trial," the guide explained. "Sarah Good and Sarah Osborne denied the charges, and Tituba was the only one of the three to confess to the accusations. It was Tituba's testimony, in particular, that was responsible for igniting the mass hysteria that followed, arousing the fevered imaginations of the townspeople with tales of dark supernatural forces and forbidden sorcery."

"Such as?"

Ada was impressed to discover it was Ashton who asked this.

"Tales included stories of riding broomsticks to the Witches' Sabbath, talking cats and dogs—things like that," the guide said. "Tituba also recalled an encounter with a man in black on the road to Boston, who asked the suspected witches to sign a special book. What was assumed to be the Devil's book."

The guide gestured to a painting depicting such a man: a shadowy figure, face hidden, holding out a worn and ancient text. For Ada, this was far and away the most evocative item in the exhibit. She studied the composition with fascination as the restless crowd of museum guests wandered into the next room, ignoring the disturbing artwork's critical significance.

"During the trial," the guide continued, "Tituba listed the names of many others that she saw written in this book, some of whom happened to be the most powerful and influential members of the community. They were the next to be put on trial. It was a very sensational time in American history. Even now—despite massive evidence to the contrary—many still believe there are witches living in Little Salem to this very day."

Ada watched the guide glance briefly in her direction, but

quickly turned back as if she hadn't seen her at all and no more than sensed an unusual presence. The reaction elicited an impish smile out of Ada, who remained confident of her ability to blend into crowds despite her offbeat appearance and eccentric manner of dressing. Interestingly enough, it seemed the guide had noticed her, which was rather curious. Perhaps she had witches in her bloodline, Ada pondered, which would make her employment at the museum all the more fitting.

With the presentation appearing to be wrapping up, Ada turned her attention back to Ashton as he explored the nightmarish gallery of atrocities in the room behind her, his eyes falling on a particularly intimidating piece of furniture gathering dust in the corner. This uniquely sinister and reprehensible contraption was a spiked metal chair with metal cuffs, the seat specially designed so the metal could be heated up before the witch was placed upon it, the burning spikes specially administered to draw whatever confession the torturer desired out of his poor victim.

It was this item in particular, out of all the other sordid and disgraceful objects, that perfectly encapsulated the outright horrors that were the order of the day during those times. And as with the majority of the items that surrounded her, Ada was deeply familiar with the lamentable history of this monstrous invention and the terrible times it was used in.

Ashton was much less knowledgeable about these matters, showing an intense regard toward the fearsome oddity that reflected a lot more than idle curiosity. Before he left the room, Ada watched him lean forward to get a closer look at the placard posted below it:

WITCH'S CHAIR—17TH CENTURY

"I don't buy it," Ashton said.

Ada smiled in turn as she walked alongside him. They were exploring the small garden area out back where more corny wax-works of prototypical witches awaited them—a soothing palate cleanser following the stomach-churning torture palace they left behind them.

"Don't buy what?" Ada asked innocently.

"Dude—witches today? You know what I heard? That those young girls probably just ate some moldy bread and had a psyche-delic freak-out. And those trials? It was all a political thing. The two most powerful families in town competing to rub out all of the dis-tasteful elements in the community."

"I don't disagree with you that the trials were political," Ada noted. "It's funny. Those things Tituba saw? All those powerful names in that funny little book."

"Who knows what that nonsense was about," Ashton moaned. "But you agree with me. You just think those girls were actually enchanted."

Ada watched Ashton glance over at her, only able to guess what she might be thinking. What she said next would be no help at all to him, no matter how plainly her words suggested she knew a whole lot more about these disturbing moments in history than what was revealed on their recent tour.

"All I'm saying," Ada said, "is those girls must've seen some crazy stuff in those woods."

After leaving the museum, the duo crossed to where the red con-vertible was parked on the street. Gray storm clouds were gathering overhead, and Ashton's mood hadn't improved since their conversa-tion back in the garden.

"So you believe in all that," Ashton commented. "In witchcraft."

"There are stranger things to believe in," Ada said.

"How exactly does one become a witch?"

Ada tilted her head slightly, as if she had to think about how to respond—although, in reality, she didn't have to think about it at all.

"Well," she replied matter-of-factly, "I think some witches are born, and some witches are made."

"Yeah. Interesting theory."

Ashton may have wanted to believe that witches were real, but the trip to the museum had failed to convince him.

This reaction didn't faze Ada in the slightest.

No, not one bit.

Such a naïve and sheltered young man, she thought as she plopped into the driving seat. He would be learning the truth about such things soon enough.

Ada was distinctly aware of how difficult it was to separate real witchcraft from the whole "pointy hat and broomstick" bit. The museum they spent the afternoon exploring was living proof of this. Ada knew all about witchcraft and that real witches weren't like how they were portrayed in fairy tales and horror movies—well, not the vast majority of them. She knew that real witches came in many different sizes and packages; that some of them aligned themselves with darkness or with light, but most were a lot more complicated than that. And they were into a lot more than casting hexes and singing praises to the moon or whatever, with the witches of Little Salem being a very special breed of witches in particular.

To answer the question, "What do witches do?"—well, the answer to that was, "Anything they liked, pretty much." They even saved the world in some cases. But all of this would have gone way over Ashton's head, and she wasn't in a rush to explain the whole enchilada to him.

That would come later.

His education was just beginning

In the meantime, Ada was deriving a great deal of amusement from watching her companion parade his cocksure arrogance about while clinging onto everything he thought he knew beyond a shadow of a doubt and avoiding what was so plainly in front of his face.

The boy definitely needs training, she reasoned. *An experience to leave him with something to think about.*

This was when she got especially excited, knowing the precise medicine to administer and just the place to take him.

"Here's an idea," Ada said. "Let's visit where they were hanged."

6

HELL IS ROUND THE CORNER

Lucy sat in the ground-floor café of the Little Salem Grand Hotel, fidgeting nervously. The centuries-old establishment was situated at the far end of the main drag, where many of the town's most popular businesses were located—a stylish and wholesome shopping district that was a boon for families and one of the most enjoyed facets of living in the idyllic community. Or, at least, it used to be, as right at the center sat the all-black tavern that was quickly becoming the talking of the town, and the bane of Little Salem's inhabitants.

Only one day earlier, the preserved multi-story Victorian residence had been a family restaurant: the local "Burrito Hut"—a beloved locale that housed a quaint, convivial charm and provided a friendly atmosphere with welcoming smiles and service. The hearty restaurant fit the mold of the renovated historical building perfectly and housed a comfortingly reserved design aesthetic that was tasteful and non-threatening. With its warm, pastel colors that instantly caught the eye of every passerby, it was the total antithesis of what the stark and imposing structure now projected. In just twenty-four hours, the setting's familiar and inviting appeal had been removed entirely, turning into its exact opposite.

Lucy had been present to observe the transformation, which started with Sanchez showing up to work at the same time he always did, his massive, gargantuan form squeezed into his customary blue overalls. Most of the locals seemed not to pay any notice to the sudden fury of construction, but those who stopped to take a closer look insisted that while Sanchez was hard at work, he appeared to be locked in a trance or a strange somnambulist state. At some point, after working from morning to well after closing, a new sign came out: "Black Death Tavern." After this, it didn't take long for the locals to register the district's newest addition for what it truly was. The name was a warning. A foul and abominable plague had arrived in their community, and just like with any other horrifying disaster, chaos and discord were expected to follow.

Lucy could tell the whole affair was deeply troubling to the townspeople as word of the tavern's malign presence began to spread. "There goes the neighborhood" was a popular refrain, along with the lamentation of how "people loved that Burrito Hut." These petty disagreements were hardly surprising. On top of the bad omen associated with the clever business name and the long, dark shadow the building now seemed to be projecting down the length of the street, Little Salem was a town that didn't take to change so easily. This was a distinct characteristic ever since the town's founding; a feature most prominently on display while the witch trials were taking place—even though they were still generally attributed to the much larger neighboring city of Salem.

Normally, the locals didn't mind that most people tended to overlook this connection. The majority of Little Salem's humble inhabitants just wanted to go about their daily business without being forced to adapt to any strange or distracting disturbances. That's what the tavern was, along with the group of misfits who were living in the rooms situated directly above it: a most disagreeable and troublesome disturbance that greatly threatened the pleasant neighborhood's treasured allure, along with the town's delicate balance of order and tranquility.

Word had yet to spread about McAllister's surprise visit to the Truegoods or the fear that the notorious Ada van Dreyer had returned, but as far as the tavern was concerned, Lucy thought the community's reactions were all a sick joke. With all the dark and distressing matters happening right under people's noses, and the stuffy locals only started getting hot and bothered once an aesthetically disagreeable bar opened its doors? The situation was a total farce that only intensified her shattering disappointment in the world of late—and with adults in particular. Especially when her own troubles seemed so hellish in comparison to what the residents were showing so much superficial concern for.

Lucy didn't come to the hotel to seek out the two tourist boys she spotted to voice her concerns about some stupid bar or any of the other rubbish her fellow citizens were getting their knickers in a twist about. She had much more pressing matters to discuss and was hoping she would cross paths with the boy called Ashton, who seemed like the more level-headed of the pair. She was completely unaware at the time that Ashton was being given a private tour by the dangerous outsider that the residents feared more than anyone, and it was the boy named Tyler who would ultimately be the one to notice her.

Lucy first spotted the stocky and uncivilized brute as he traveled down the stairs before having a dumb exchange with the giant Native American man who worked the front desk. Her gaze reflected disappointment, but when he finally noticed her, his eyes brightened and he started smiling from ear to ear.

The sight of this left Lucy feeling off-balance and irritated. It was true that she was one of the prettiest girls in town in a moderately fetching "girl next door" kind of way. She had shiny blonde hair and modest doll-like features, but she was also the daughter of the town preacher and always dressed very conservatively to ward off any boys getting funny ideas about her. Despite these precautions, her observer had clearly taken a fancy to her, and the ideas going through his head were hardly pure or virtuous.

"Sup," Tyler said after crossing over.

Lucy directed a cold stare at him that was worthy of an ice queen. "Is that your usual tactic for approaching a girl? Sup?'"

"Eh, I try to vary it up every now and then. Throw in a 'Hey, baby, come here often?' 'What's a cutie like you doing in a dump like this?' You know, the staples."

"Well, this might come as a total shock, but I didn't come here so you could practice your lame-ass pickup lines."

"Bummer."

Conversing with the cretin made her want to gag. For years Lucy had dreamed of when a handsome young stranger would arrive in Little Salem to come to her rescue, and he would be uncommonly dashing and suave. Tyler was none of these things. He could barely even pass for handsome—especially in the presence of Ashton, who was a total Adonis.

In comparison to Ashton with his dark hair, dreamy gray eyes, and chiseled features, Tyler was just your typical college inebriate. The kind of "winner" you would expect to find passed out drunk on Daytona Beach with one hand down the front of his swim trunks and a picture of someone's genitals drawn on his forehead. To characterize her current interaction as anything other than disappointing would have been an understatement. But Lucy felt inclined to carry on with what she set out to accomplish, swallowing her indignation before he provided her with an opportunity to become even more irritated.

"I came here to warn you," Lucy whispered after peering around the room.

"Ah. So you did come to see me."

"Shhh! You have to leave! Leave tonight while you still have a chance!"

Tyler suppressed a laugh, unable to believe what he was hearing.

"Wow. You're joking, right? OK, where's the hidden camera?"

"This isn't a joke! You have no idea what goes on in this town!"

Lucy's body became tense, her voice pained with distress.

"I've...seen things."

For a brief second, Tyler appeared to show genuine concern.

"Like...sexy things?"

The lewd comment rendered Lucy speechless, but she regained her composure in an instant.

"I'm leaving."

"No! Don't go!" Tyler laughed as she gathered her things. "This conversation just started getting interesting!"

"I don't even know why I came here!" she sneered. "I was just trying to be a good Christian and warn you out of the pure, shining goodness of my goddamn heart! I thought that maybe there was someone nice and thoughtful underneath that idiot frat boy exterior. But you're not a nice person. You're just an ass!"

The meeting didn't go at all how Lucy planned. Still, despite her passionate outburst, she was hoping he would take her words to heart. Deep down, what she wanted was someone to save her from the terror that was slowly whittling away her precious sanity—and if not this, to at least spare an innocent traveler from any future trauma that could be avoided. The disappointment she felt was overwhelming when she spied the dim-witted ghost hunter still hanging around town the next day. She was standing next to her father, the Reverend Palmer, outside the Truegoods' frozen yogurt shop while he was in deep discussion with the couple about the reviled "house of sin" directly across the street from them. This was when she noticed Tyler crossing down the street with a carton of instant ramen and a 12-pack of Mexican beer under his wing.

"What are you still doing here?" Lucy hissed after managing to sneak away. "I thought I told you to leave!"

"Maybe I've developed a certain fondness for the friendly, down-home atmosphere you've got here."

To back up the comment, Tyler turned and waved to the Truegoods, having already met the friendly couple the other day. The obliviousness of this gesture made Lucy's whole body tense up in agitation. Before her father had a chance to notice them, she shoved Tyler into the alley and kissed him hard on the mouth.

Lucy had no time to mess around or wait for her brain-dead associate to reach the panicked state of emergency she was currently stationed at. Thankfully, she was pleased to discover she caught him completely off-guard with her choice of actions, rendering him quiet and docile; like putty in her hands.

Good, she thought to herself. It was exactly what the situation called for and precisely the response she wanted.

Lucy wiped her mouth as she pulled herself away from him. "There! Did that get your attention? Are you going to shut up finally?"

Tyler nodded like a bobblehead in affirmation. With the boy now firmly in a place where he could actually listen, she placed his face in her hands, her eyes hard as steel to reflect how serious she was.

Lucy knew this would be her only chance to get through to him.

But where to even begin? She already tried to discuss all of this the previous day, and there was so much she wanted to say to him and wasn't much time. This didn't leave her much opportunity to explain things in detail, which meant she would just have to start talking and see where the conversation headed.

How did that quote from *Alice In Wonderland* go?

Begin at the beginning, and when you reach the end...

"Now listen to me," Lucy said. "There's an evil presence that's been poisoning this town for centuries. You don't know what I've seen. You don't—"

"Lucy!"

The distressed teenager started in frightful recognition of the voice, terror shining in her eyes like starlight.

It was her father calling out to her.

This was bad—no, worse than that.

Lucy secretly feared her father more than anything. His stern, commanding tone gave her shivers—especially when she heard him utter her name.

"Lucy! Time to go!"

She could sense that Tyler was finally looking at her with all the concern she'd been yearning for. This was hardly surprising; all the color in her face had disappeared. The moody, angel-faced teenager was no longer a charming assembly of contradictions, with her permanent, icy scowl attached to her sunny, conservative wardrobe and doll-like features. She looked like a scared little girl, unable to look her would-be champion in the eye as she struggled with all the fear and anxiety hollowing her out from inside.

But what could he ever do about it? she thought morosely. He was no hero, and it was stupid of her to even try to tell him anything in the first place.

Resigned to confront whatever horrible fate was coming her way,

Lucy hanged her head and slowly backed away. As she turned her back to him, Tyler pulled her back toward him, suddenly taking the entire situation with all joking aside for a change.

"Wait. Tell me," Tyler said. "Tell me what you've you seen."

If only he'd listened sooner, she thought. Now it was too late.

Lucy had lost all hope for the world or for a better tomorrow, leaving her with nothing to do but stare at the ground and struggle to find the words to explain herself. For a moment it looked like she lacked the courage to say it—like it was too awful to think about—until finally, she glanced at him with a somber, pleading look in her eyes, her voice shaking.

"*I see demons*," Lucy said. "*I see demons everywhere.*"

7

HOLLOW HILLS

———————

Ashton gazed skeptically at the scattered pockets of wilderness from the top of the grassy hill. The sun was setting on the horizon, and a cold wind was blowing—early signs that the skies would soon be darkening and a powerful storm was rolling into town.

"Gallows Hill, huh? Doesn't seem so spooky to me."

"Really? Place always gave me the super creeps."

Ashton couldn't exactly relate to the sentiment. He did recall the tour guide discussing how many people lost their lives at this setting back when the Salem witch trials were in full swing. More than two hundred women and men were tried for practicing witchcraft during those dark and hysterical times, and out of those, five of the accused died in prison, including two infant children, while nineteen others had been brought to Gallows Hill on the border between Salem and Little Salem to be "hanged by the neck until dead."

With so many innocent lives lost to what he was still thoroughly convinced was nothing more than a tragic case of mass hysteria, he could easily imagine the location where these poor victims met their end would be uncommonly dreary and morbid. But the tree where the accused were strung up had been chopped down many decades earlier, and from the top of the hill, one could see numerous examples of modern civilization dotting the landscape.

A nearby pharmacy. A red brick office building.

No sign of the dark follies of the past seemed to remain.

Not to his eyes, at least.

Ashton wasn't the type of person to hold it against Ada for possessing a more sensitive response to the setting. He had no idea that their location couldn't have been further from her mind and that she was presently occupied with other distractions—in particular, the colorful map of Little Salem positioned across her lap.

The item was a tourist map he retrieved from a kiosk at the hotel, filled with cartoonish images of Little Salem's most popular spots for sightseeing; an unbelievably silly and amateurish presentation that made the town look more like a colossally lame amusement park than ground zero for a significant piece of American history. For the past several minutes, Ada had been drawing circles around a selection of locations and placing heavily detailed notes and playful doodles next to them, smirking slyly from behind her sunglasses as she sketched a cartoon ghost next to one spot and a pointy witch's hat next to another.

Still in the dark as to what Ada was up to, her comment managed to conjure up a series of questions.

"What do you think is so creepy about the place?" he asked.

Ada pursed her lips in concentration and pushed her sunglasses to the top of her head.

"I dunno," she said. "Place just always has the faint smell of death in the air. And suffering. It kinda breaks my tiny little heart."

Ada changed gears in a heartbeat, sliding off the hood of the convertible and slinking toward him.

"If Gallows Hill doesn't get your motor running, maybe the places I circled on the map will do the trick."

Ashton reached for the object, but Ada hopped back, playfully keeping the meticulous work of art she created out of his grasp.

"Hey! Not so fast, cowboy. Don't you want to hear about some of your awesome choices? Like the haunted factory or the old church? Or the spooky asylum!"

Ashton's smile widened as he lunged for his slippery playmate.

"Little Salem has a haunted asylum?"

"More than one! But none of that compares to what's out there..."

A strong gust of wind whipped through Ada's hair as she gazed at the large stretch of woods on the outer edges of Little Salem: A vast medley of tall, skinny trees packed so close and tightly together the sunlight rarely touched the ground where a matted tangle of winding roots was submerged deep within.

"The forest?" Ashton asked her.

Ada nodded, face void of expression.

"Ever since the dawn of time, man has feared the things that go bump in the night. Ghosts, spirits, strange beings that defy reason and can't be understood by any ordinary means of comprehension. And most of all, man fears those with the ability to traffic with such beings."

Ada's haunting tone and her unusual manner of speaking were startling. The words she uttered were confusing—like they were somehow offering the key to a baffling mystery.

What could be the hidden meaning of this speech? And why did Ada feel compelled to say such things in such a strange and ominous fashion? There were so many things that were so exceedingly difficult to figure out about her—things that Ashton, who saw himself as a relatively ordinary and straightforward type of person, didn't understand at all.

"Are you all right?" he asked her. "What—what are you talking about?"

Ada cast her bright and captivating eyes upon him and took his face into her black-nailed, manicured hands. "Maybe you should walk back to town among the patches of forest along the main road," she said. "You can report back to me and tell me...what you see."

Ashton found himself staring, spellbound, into Ada's bewitching gaze, gradually answering in a monotone, surrendering himself completely.

"Good idea. I think a walk would do me good."

Without thinking, he plodded down the hill and started crossing to the main road, still not sure of why he felt compelled to do so.

"Ashton."

At the sound of Ada's voice, he turned around to face her, watching the wind whipping relentlessly at her dark and voluminous mane.

"Tomorrow we should explore the old graveyard," she suggested. "I'll see you around nightfall."

Yes, of course. He nodded obediently and headed on his way.

As he took off, Ada's eyes stayed on him until he vanished into the distance, and her cherry-colored lips curled into her token impish smirk. Behind her, five silhouettes arose from the other side of the landscape, creeping their way toward the hilltop until there were six figures standing together, all of them dressed in nightmare black.

Ada, McAllister, Agatha, Miles, Rudy, and Izzy—all of the members of Ada's coven were gathered and assembled as the wind lashed away at them like a beast that was impossible to tame. The new arrivals were all dressed in black sportswear with the exception of McAllister, wearing dark sunglasses and dressed in a black leather biker jacket with a silver ouroboros branded on the back. McAllister was also wearing a fashionable wide-brimmed hat that Ada had never seen on him—probably an item he borrowed from Agatha that looked a bit strange and out of place but totally shielded his face from the sun. Ada reminded herself she would have to talk to him about this intriguing choice of apparel the next time they were alone together. But at that moment, he was turning to address her as the sky continued to darken and the wind blew unmercifully.

"Let's do this," McAllister said.

Ada nodded, ready to execute the matter they were united to complete together—a task that would test the mettle of every one of them and determine the immediate future of their motley crew. With this mission firmly on her mind, Ada turned to face the dark and sinister patch of woods that lay beyond the hill, disappearing to the other side with the others following after her, the blood-red sun that was setting overhead signifying it was time for the fun to start and the game was about to begin.

* * *

Later that evening, Tyler would witness the strangers' return as they piled out of the convertible and headed inside the tavern to celebrate. He had no idea what they were up to, and even less of an idea why Ashton had returned to the hotel in a trance and headed straight to bed after this. There was something deeply unsettling about the tavern and those that had taken up residence therein, adding to his suspicions that something peculiar was going on and the boring old town he landed in was a lot more than it seemed.

8

BEYOND THE WALL OF SLEEP

The morning after his trip to Gallows Hill, Ashton was fast asleep in his hotel room; his eyes squeezed shut, a thin layer of sweat upon his brow. As the gentle rays of sunlight streamed through the curtains, his body began twitching erratically; an unsettling reaction to the stormy realization that he was drifting into the same dream he always had—a dream that hadn't visited him in some time.

In the dream, Ashton was a ten-year-old child sitting in the drawing room of his extravagant family home—a comfortable upper-class mansion he and his mother continued to occupy following his parents' unhappy divorce. The floor he was sitting on was slick and polished, made of the finest imported materials money could buy. The furnishings were elegant, the wallpaper old-fashioned and dignified; reflecting a history of affluence that stretched back generations.

The wealth in Ashton's family all came from his father's side, but his mother received a large portion of this after a separation that occurred when he was very young. Following the split, he didn't have much contact with his father and barely knew a thing about him. He had no idea how his father got his money or what he did for a living; only that he always smelled like expensive cigars and cheap hair oil, and when he visited him every year on his birthday, he was always dressed in an extremely expensive business suit.

Coincidentally, it happened to be his birthday that day—or at least, it was in the dream. From his place on the floor, the young boy observed his father sitting on a modest-sized couch that sat in the center of the room. Or, to be even more accurate, Ashton assumed the dark silhouette was his father. The opulent piece of furniture was placed in front of a large set of bay windows with the sun bleeding faintly through the curtains, so he only saw a hazy outline where the man was seated.

"Hello there, Ashton," the shadowy figure called out to him. "How's my favorite birthday boy?"

The young Ashton remained silent, staring at the man like a stranger; discomforted by how he was unable to see the man's expression due to the notable lack of light in the room.

The figure nodded at the board game at his feet. "Is that a new game Mommy gave you? How nice. How very… "

The dream appeared to skip forward, and another man now joined the dark figure on the couch. The man was sitting stiff as a mannequin and was dressed in a classy business suit that was a bit dusty—like it was emblazoned with the waste of the past. The man was also much thinner and possessed sharp, angular features, his withered, skeletal hands resting on a worn leather briefcase.

Ashton was exceptionally familiar with this strange visitor and found the man's presence acutely distressing. He couldn't see the man's face, but in his bones, he knew the man was smiling.

And this wasn't just any smile.

The man that accompanied his father had the habit of wearing a distinct reptilian grin that made any other smile appear remarkably quaint and ordinary by comparison. In fact, it was safe to say that the smile of this gentleman elicited the exact opposite effect that any other smile might provoke in a person—and the man never removed it. This was one of the reasons, among many, why his father's associate made Ashton feel iller at ease than he felt around anybody.

"Ashton, you remember my friend, don't you?" his father asked dryly. "My friend, Mr. Frau."

Back in the hotel room, Ashton began to toss and turn more violently, his body fighting the haunting fantasy as the dream once again jumped forward and his father was no longer present. The man who accompanied him was now sitting alone and by himself, his hands still resting on the briefcase.

"Hello again, Ashton," Mr. Frau coolly uttered (Ashton couldn't see it, but he was sure he was wearing that sickening smile of his). "Your father asked me again to drop by to read to you your yearly story. On today, the day of your tenth birthday."

Ashton felt a cold chill as he heard the brass snaps click open on the man's briefcase—right before his obsequious guest reached inside and removed an old book. It was a book he had seen many times and would have recognized anywhere. The worn and tattered item was in exceedingly poor condition, with a filthy yellow cover, a busted spine, and faded, tattered pages that were falling out. Ashton had already lost count of all the times he had listened to the contents. Surely, it was only ten, but it seemed like more. His recollection was blurry and as strange as it may have sounded, it felt like the story he was being subjected to was slowly becoming a part of him—something that disturbed him to no end.

"Let's resume where we left off," the man said as the young child watched anxiously from his place on the floor. And Ashton felt another chill as Mr. Frau let out a slight chuckle while searching for his place in the old book, the room suddenly appearing to get much colder and more hostile, compelling the boy to want to flee the room if only his body could move.

Back in the hotel room, Ashton's chest started heaving in desperation. But in the dream, the boy continued to stare at the silhouetted figure in front of him, eventually finding the page he was searching for and settling into his seat.

"Now," elucidated Mr. Frau, "when we last left our hero, he had just abandoned his familiar surroundings and wandered into the gloomy moonlit night. *'Past accursed and desolate places and numerous formidable hardships, journeying to the place beyond the pyramids...'*"

It was at this point that the horrifying visions started.

As Mr. Frau read from the dizzying contents of his tattered, yellow book, Ashton witnessed in his mind's eye the brief flash of the remnants of an ancient city—a bizarre and monstrous structure that appeared much older than anything described in history, the horrible and misbegotten setting dominated by a chilling, macabre palace of flesh and bone that could only have belonged to the likes of the most abominable civilization to have ever existed. The distressing visions caused the sleeping Ashton to toss and turn more violently as the presence of this horrific setting began to grow more vivid and magnify in intensity, the revolting sounds of bodily activities bursting from the landscape forming a painful knot in his stomach while the sickening smell of rotting flesh and tissue singed his shuttering nostrils. And simultaneously, while Ashton continued to suffer these reactions in real life, within the dream, his younger counterpart appeared to grow more panicked as well, the stony, silhouetted storyteller pausing briefly to crane his head and issue his sordid smile in the child's direction—yes, even right then he was wearing it.

"I see you're starting to remember," Mr. Frau calmly noted.

Another quick flash of the horrifying city lit up in high-definition in Ashton's TV vision, accompanied by the familiar gurgle of activity; sounds and smells that caused him to grip the bedsheets as he desperately struggled for breath. The maddening visions were almost unbearable, and Ashton didn't know how much more he could take. But just when he felt like his head would split open from the experience, suddenly, within the dream, time jumped forward, and Ashton's father was now standing in the room with Mr. Frau beside him, both their faces still indecipherable and looking like black, empty voids on account of the hazy darkness all around them.

"Well, Ashton, we'll see you again next year," his father said. "But before I go, I have a little gift for you. A simple token to herald my son's illustrious future."

A small package was presented to the young Ashton. He carefully tore off the wrapping to observe a hefty hardcover book with a fancy embossed title on the cover.

The title of the book was *Dictionnaire Infernal*, and the precocious and inquisitive child stared at the item with fascination. With the haunting cover illustration of a smirking demon gazing up at him, the boy perhaps wondered what this unusual object truly was and why it was being given to him, while back in the real world, his older counterpart gritted his teeth and tossed relentlessly; bombarded with horrifying visions once more.

* * *

A string of drool hung from Tyler's mouth as he lay sleeping in the bed opposite his roommate's. While blinking himself awake at the noises coming from close by, it took him only a moment to become fully alert and up like a shot after noticing Ashton was shuddering violently.

"Ashton? Ashton!" Tyler reached out, eager to stir his poor friend—but an unexpected voice interrupted him.

"You shouldn't wake him."

Startled, Tyler spun around to address his visitor and was ill-prepared for who he found: an abnormally pale young man wearing dark sunglasses, a black leather biker jacket, and a sly and icy smile upon his lips. Tyler recognized the intruder sitting in a shadowy corner of the hotel room as one of the residents from the tavern and knew he was bad news. He wasn't yet familiar with the man's name or the stormy reputation that preceded him, but he would find out soon enough that the dark and mysterious stranger was called McAllister. McAllister Kinneary.

"Holy—"

True to form, McAllister failed to show the slightest reaction to Tyler's surprise, shifting his stony gaze to the troubled sleeper across the room from him.

"If you wake him now, he'll never know how it ends."

This detached observation had a chilling effect on the young ghost hunter as he followed his guest's haunting glare to the thrashing limbs of his companion. However, his attention was quickly drawn to something equally unanticipated: McAllister retrieving his black wide-brimmed hat and slouching toward the exit, offering a deadpan invitation to an occasion where some of Tyler's most pressing questions might finally be addressed.

"Coming to breakfast?"

9

COFFEE AND EVP

"I'm sorry if I startled you," McAllister said. "I didn't know anyone was in."

Tyler chewed on his eggs, observing the pale young man sitting across from him. "Likely story, bro."

There was something about McAllister that didn't sit right with him. On the one hand, his slick platinum hair and all-black wardrobe were easy to write off as the standard garden-variety attributes of a conventional pseudo-goth weirdo. But unlike your typical teenage mallrat, there was something seriously off about him. There was the unnatural paleness of his skin, for instance, and his curious proclivity for wearing sunglasses indoors—even when there was hardly any light about. And there was the way that he smiled like he was in possession of a dark secret, and that he had the features of an angel.

But there was nothing angelic about him.

There was also the fact that McAllister wasn't eating anything, despite his invitation for Tyler to accompany him for the complimentary morning meal in the hotel's quaint ground floor café, and that he was pouring his fifth bag of sugar into his second cup of coffee. Putting aside the lack of any reasons for why McAllister would want to pick his brain in the first place, this is honestly what provoked Tyler most of all. More than anything.

"What were you doing in our hotel room in the first place?" Tyler grumbled.

"You're staying in Aleister Crowley's old room," McAllister said. "Didn't you know?"

"No," Tyler admitted. "I mean, Ashton pointed out the plaque that said the guy stayed here. He was that evil British occultist, right? The so-called 'Wickedest Man in the World?'"

Tyler was familiar with Crowley but didn't know much about the notorious magus. While fascinated by ghosts and other examples of paranormal phenomena, the occult was something that interested him very little. For Tyler, the subject was an intellectual dustbin better left for eccentric oddballs and lunatics similar to the freakishly off-putting young man sitting across the table from him.

The infamy of a person like Crowley wasn't lost on him completely. In his mind, Crowley was a faux satanist from the turn of the century who liked to dress up in kooky robes and have weird deviant sex with other weirdoes. Oh yeah, and he also inspired the Beatles for some reason. Maybe the Beatles also enjoyed dressing up and having sex with weirdoes, and perhaps McAllister would offer to elaborate on this. But McAllister's familiarity with such matters only made him even more difficult to figure out as he sat there sipping his coffee, his thoughts and opinions locked behind an impenetrable fortress of stony indifference.

"Who's the guy to you, pal?" Tyler asked.

"Just a fellow gentleman and scholar," McAllister said. "He was a bit on the vain side. I found this carved into your doorway."

McAllister removed a smartphone from his jacket and slid it across the table. Without enthusiasm, Tyler grasped the object, frowning cynically before glancing at the screen. The phone showed a photo of five V's carved into the doorway to his hotel room. What they were doing there he hadn't the faintest fucking idea. His face formed a sour expression as he furrowed his brow in confusion.

"Five V's. And it means?"

"Crowley's magical motto," McAllister said. "*Vi Veri Universum Vivus Vici*. '*By the power of truth, while living, I have conquered the known universe*.'"

Tyler suppressed a light-hearted chuckle.

"Seriously? Geez. The brass balls on this guy..."

The revelation was amusing but still meant very little to the wily amateur ghost hunter. Although it did prove one thing definitive: McAllister definitely knew a whole lot more than he was letting on.

While all that McAllister knew remained indecipherable, all this pondering about Crowley and high strangeness vanished from Tyler's mind once he had satisfied his hunger with a full stomach. The heavenly comfort that came from appeasing his taste buds prompted him to forget about the hidden secrets of Little Salem in favor of musing about things that were of a much higher personal value to him. Like the fact that he was on spring break and looking to party, and McAllister was acquainted with a certain bombshell, sexy redhead he couldn't get out of his head.

Those long legs, freckled skin, ridonkulous rack. Images of that tempting beauty had been infecting his every waking moment since he first laid eyes on the goddess. And why wouldn't they? The woman was built like a sassy heroine in a Russ Myer movie: danger-ous, seductive, and all curves. Tyler was convinced he'd murder his own grandmother for a piece of that action. But while his mind was being distracted by lascivious thoughts about the ginger siren, McAl-lister was continuing their conversation from the hotel lobby as they walked side by side down the hallway.

"Along with being my namesake, Crowley was also a collector of rare books," McAllister explained. "He traveled with a large trunk full of them."

"Yeah, large trunk. Got it." Tyler was pretty much ignoring what-ever was being said to him at this point. "Hey, you're staying at that creepy black house with all those other weirdoes, right? Think you could hook me up with the redhead?"

McAllister's smile widened after hearing the suggestion, stifling a short laugh before answering.

"Uh, no?" He paused briefly to face his clueless companion. "Find your own girlfriend. Bozo."

Ashton was still tossing and twitching when Tyler and McAllis-ter returned to the hotel room. Sure enough, the five carved-out V's were visible at the top of the doorframe.

Right where McAllister said they were.

"So you crept into our room looking for a rare book Aleister Crowley might have left here like a hundred million years ago?"

Tyler was really fighting hard to maintain his interest. What he was really trying to rationalize was how a beast like McAllister could land a beauty like the redhead when he would personally brave hell just to smell her dirty bathwater.

"I'll admit, it was a bit of a shot in the dark," McAllister said.

But the idea wasn't too far off the mark. A quick survey of the historical outlay suggested the room had been preserved to give off the appearance of when the charming establishment had been built almost two hundred years earlier.

"The idea's not too crazy," Tyler reasoned. "The thing is... If Aleister Crowley *did* leave something, it probably would've been moved into storage. Someplace like the basement. Or the attic."

McAllister cocked his head with curiosity, inspiring a mischievous smile to form on Tyler's lips. While hooking up with a stacked red-hot babe still ranked at the top of his list, he remained driven to learn what McAllister was hiding and was delighted to see he was getting somewhere.

Or, at least, that's what he thought.

After sneaking through a door marked "Staff Only" and climbing a rickety staircase, Tyler and McAllister entered the dusty hotel attic, which was dark as a cave and filled with clutter. At first glance, nothing appeared out of the ordinary—just a selection of old cardboard boxes, broken furniture, and forgotten suitcases. If something of Crowley's had been left there, it could have been anywhere. Even if chances were slim that anything of value still remained.

"Watch your step," Tyler warned, feeling his way across the room. "A lot of...interesting things up here."

McAllister remained close to the entryway, his eyes still covered by sunglasses even though the attic was almost pitch-black.

As Tyler pushed his way further into the chaotic setting, he caught McAllister staring stone-faced at an abandoned camcorder sitting on a tripod. "We tried to capture a ghost here the other night," Tyler explained. "Me and Ashton? We hunt ghosts and stuff."

Tyler smiled wryly and pulled aside the torn curtain covering the solitary window on the attic wall. A glimmer of sunlight proceeded to streak through the glass and illuminate the gloomy setting, and he watched McAllister shift his head reflexively to avoid the glowing, golden beam before stepping back to retreat into the shadows.

Before Tyler could comment on this unusual display, he noticed his companion tense up as he gazed at where the sunbeams had brightened the floor. Something was written there in what appeared to be faded white paint—and the writing wasn't just where McAllister stood. There were strange markings all over, most of them covered with boxes and abandoned bric-a-brac.

"What the... I didn't see this here before..."

Eager to explore further, Tyler moved aside a stack of boxes to reveal a collection of obscure occult markings he couldn't make heads or tails of. The drawings looked like strange words and planetary symbols. Something having to do with astrology, maybe? Or maybe something else entirely...

"What is it?" Tyler asked. "Something satanic?"

McAllister answered in his typical deadpan fashion. "Ceremonial magic. Someone was performing a ritual up here."

"Who? Aleister Crowley? Why would he be doing this all the way up here?"

McAllister remained silent while directing a vacant stare at the attic window, still avoiding the glistening rays of sunlight filtering into the room. "Tradition, probably," he noted. "Nostradamus used his attic for rituals. Under the light of the moon, he saw the past, present, and future, all reflected in a bowl of water."

McAllister shifted his gaze to the discarded video camera.

"Did you find any evidence of spiritual activity up here?"

"Nada, bro."

He pursed his lips before glancing at Tyler suggestively.

"Perhaps you should give those recordings another listen."

After parting ways with McAllister, Tyler crossed down the hallway, thinking over all of the information that had been presented to him. McAllister hadn't provided him with anything even remotely coherent, leaving him with more questions than ever; the most frustrating of these being why some glamour model of a super-babe would choose to shack up with a certifiable head case like *that*.

Tyler couldn't help but imagine the types of shenanigans they got up to. Whips, chains—they probably did everything. The thought of it! The relationship left him green with envy, and he tried to console himself with the idea that perhaps McAllister had met his current ladylove at a very strange place in her life. Without a doubt, the bond shared between them had to be as strange as they come.

Did this mean he still had a chance with her? Tyler would have liked to think so. But at the same time, if guys like McAllister were the redhead's type, it was almost a sure bet she was more trouble than a guy like him could ever handle. Not like this was enough to convince him to steer clear of the chick—or dispel his unbridled jealousy of the guy who got to her first.

"Frickin' weirdo," Tyler grumbled.

Back in the attic, McAllister replaced the curtain over the window and began to explore the massive drawing that was now visible. All of the objects and obstructions had been pushed away, and there, painted on the floorboards, was a large protection circle.

McAllister wasn't focused on the circle. His eyes were locked on one word standing apart from all the qabalistic names and words of power that had been scrawled there ages ago—a word inside of a triangle, with a strange, exotic symbol accompanying it.

With a calm and steady gait, he crossed over to get a better look at this discovery. His body crouched low to the ground, fingers gently brushing the inscription.

What was written there was a word he was more than casually familiar with. A word that brought things into perspective.

All the answers hadn't been revealed to him, but many of the missing pieces were falling into place.

The word that grabbed his attention was "Vassago."

10

GRAVEYARD GIRL

———————

Flashes of the city of flesh and bone assaulted Ashton's senses until he wrestled himself awake. A waxing moon was shining through the window, and Tyler was sitting at the hotel room table, listening to hour after hour of audio from the static night-vision camera they left in the attic.

Tyler noticed Ashton sitting up and removed his headphones.

"What time is it?" Ashton asked in a daze.

"Almost 10," Tyler said. "Pm. You slept for over twenty-four hours."

Ashton looked shocked and confused. He checked his cell phone on the nightstand only to discover the battery was dead.

"I have to meet up with Ada. Plug this in for me?"

He tossed his phone to Tyler and started stripping off his shirt, making a beeline to the bathroom while his fellow ghost hunter frowned with concern.

Ashton had only been up for a handful of moments, but he wasn't thinking at all about his loyal amigo. Or their paranormal YouTube channel. Or what Tyler had been up to while he was sleeping. Or why they had come to Little Salem in the first place.

For some reason, after sleeping the entire day away, his thoughts immediately went to the spirited young woman he recently met—a minor detail that should have been a huge red flag that something was amiss. Ashton didn't seem to think much about this. Not until he started musing about his girlfriend who he still had yet to contact since arriving in Little Salem.

While standing underneath the showerhead, his thoughts drifted to recent memories of his devoted sweetheart. The intimate times he spent with her, her silky black hair and chocolate skin.

Mercy was an underclassman he'd been dating for close to a year—a stone-cold fox who drove his heart crazy. While he was thinking of her, the steamy images suddenly turned to those of Ada, with her dark, tangled hair and piercing, blue-violet stare. The intrusion of this fascinating creature into his casual thoughts and fantasies startled him more than a little. So much so that when he left the shower and was drying off, he was still feeling rather unnerved by the experience.

When Ashton descended the staircase with his camera bag slung over his shoulder, he found Ada standing in the center of the lobby, smiling up at him with her token impish grin. She was dressed similarly from the first night he ran into her, in a gray hoodie, white tank top, pleated miniskirt, stockings, and combat boots. This time the skirt she wore was a blue plaid pattern to match her eye color, and her stockings were ripped and tattered, rocketing her defiant riot grrrl aesthetic to a whole new level.

"Hi," Ashton said as he approached her.

"Hello," Ada answered. "Looking forward to exploring the graveyard?"

"Totally. I just gotta call my girlfriend back home."

Ada nodded politely and he wandered several feet from her, his body turning rigid when Mercy answered his call in a panic.

"Ashton! What's going on? Are you OK?"

"Sure, babe. Is something wrong? My phone's been off, so I haven't—"

Mercy interrupted him, her voice shaking. "Ashton, listen to me. I think you're in danger. A lot of strange things have been happening, and... Have you met anybody new recently?

"New? Sure, what do you—?"

The line suddenly turned to static.

"Hello? Babe, you're breaking up!"

Ashton ended the call in frustration, thinking the crappy reception in Little Salem must have had something to do it. He completely missed the sight of Ada standing behind him, casting a piercing glare at the phone pressed against his ear.

"That's odd," he noted. "Guess I'll have to try later."

"The graveyard's not far," Ada told him. "OK if we walk?"

"Yeah, that's cool. Hope it doesn't rain."

The Wisteria Grove Cemetery was only a short stroll from the hotel. When Ashton and Ada arrived, they found it closed, with a heavy lock chained to the front gates. Ada was somehow able to pull away the lock with ease, but Ashton didn't think much of this. Soon they were walking side by side along the winding asphalt paths that stretched across the grassy scenery like giant serpents.

While traversing the premises, Ashton aimed his camcorder at the shadowy graves that surrounded them. It was no surprise Ada would think he'd get a kick out of the place. The general creepiness made it feel like something could jump out at any moment.

Ada was unusually quiet while they were exploring the lonely setting. She never even mentioned the events of the previous day, which, for Ashton, remained blurry. He didn't know her well enough to know if this quietness was a characteristic of her. Despite their riddled conversations about the history of witches and other spooky topics of interest, Ada had the habit of keeping much in the way of her own history relatively secret. Whether this reluctance to talk openly about herself was because she was being modest or for reasons that were much more severe, he could only imagine. This was why he was somewhat surprised when she smiled nostalgically and started talking about her family, of all things.

"Walking through graveyards always reminds me of my mother," Ada said.

"Your mother?"

"Story my mother once told me. An ancestor of mine was burned at the stake."

As if on cue, thunder started rumbling in the distance.

Ashton found her comments surprising, but he remained silent. Ada opening up to him was a new experience considering how tight-lipped she was about herself. Still, this should have been of no real consequence since he'd come to the conclusion that not getting to know her too well was probably for the best. He already had a loving girlfriend in Boston who was everything he wanted in a relationship. He was in Little Salem to look for ghosts and other spooky types of phenomena—that was it. Not to become closer to a strange and ethereal young creature that was the weirdest thing he had encountered on his vacation so far.

And yet, those earlier visions of Ada still bothered him considerably, and the revelation about her ancestor aroused his curiosity in a way that was unexpected. Secretly, he found himself hoping Ada would continue opening up to him and reveal more about herself.

"Are you close to your family?" she asked him.

"Not really," he answered reluctantly. "I only see my father on birthdays. Had a really bizarro dream about him last night."

Ada smiled coyly. "You should talk to Agatha. She's good at interpreting people's dreams."

"Nah. The less I think about my father, the better."

Ashton's body stiffened, noticing his camera seemed to be picking up something in the distance: the faint twinkling of tiny golden balls of light. "Do you see that?"

Ada turned her bright, oversized eyes to where his camera was aimed, and he started racing forward. Once she caught up with him, the lights seemed to have disappeared.

"What am I supposed to be seeing?"

"They're called cemetery lights. Weird lights that only appear—"

"—in cemeteries?"

Ashton turned his camera on Ada as she started laughing uncontrollably, amused and delighted beyond words at her companion's eagerness to assign a supernatural explanation for everything.

Ashton didn't mind. Ada's laughter was something he found quite stimulating, and it had a curiously intoxicating effect.

"I think it was just fireflies," he grumbled. "Dammit."

Ada glanced away from him, wearing a mischievous smirk. "Do you think your obsession with the unknown has to do with your father? How he remained so unknown to you while growing up?"

"Do you think your obsession with witches has to do with your ancestor being burned as one?"

Ada continued smiling, shrugging ambivalently.

"Obsession runs in the family."

Thunderclap!

Right on cue, the rain started pouring down in buckets, and the race was on to locate shelter from the sudden storm. It was strange—black storm clouds had been hanging over their heads all evening, but the massive downpour seemed curiously abrupt.

Once the rain started, Ada grabbed him by the hand, and the pair took off running like mad. While sprinting through the graveyard, Ashton noticed her grip had an unnatural strength to it. Ada was of small pixieish stature and thin as a reed, so this seemed to contradict the laws of physics.

Spying sanctuary up ahead, he pulled her toward a mausoleum, not giving a moment's thought to whose timeless sleep they might be disturbing while nestled in the concrete doorway.

"C'mon. We'll be dry here."

As he hustled toward their chosen place of refuge, she suddenly broke free from him, shedding her baggy gray hoodie and tossing it to the ground.

"Ada! What are you doing? You'll freeze!"

Curiously, Ada remained perfectly still as she stood underneath the heavy downpour, her eyes closed and her face turned up to the heavens. She was breathing deep, heaving breaths, feeling the fall of the rain on her eyelids. "No, I love it. I love it."

Thunderclap!

Ashton found himself mesmerized by the sight, gazing at his unusual guide as she stood underneath the endless showers that were soaking through her top and drenching her skirt, her stockings, her black combat boots. Despite the hostile conditions, Ada remained entirely still, as if caught up in the midst of a sacred ceremony—or a divine ritual that had been long forgotten.

Unable to resist the chance to document such an intriguing spectacle, Ashton clicked the Record button on his video camera and aimed the lens in her direction, right as she started to speak.

"They were burning witches in Germany at the time," Ada said. "My ancestor wasn't so much a witch herself, but she was...sympathetic to them. So she was tortured, thrown into prison, and condemned to burn with the others."

That's right—Ada said that graveyards reminded her of her family, Ashton recalled. Was this why she was telling him this story right now, of all times and places? And in the pouring rain on top of it?

Before he could question her, he noticed her slinking seductively in his direction, her eyes staring right at him—practically staring straight through him.

"They discovered my ancestor was pregnant," Ada said, "so her execution was temporarily postponed. But since she was destined for the fire, she was marked with the sign of the consecrated. A flower with thirteen petals. Burnt onto her flesh with a hot iron just below the left breast. Right here."

Ada pointed her black-nailed finger to where the spot would have been on her own person as a violent clap of thunder boomed directly above them.

Thunderclap!

Staring silently at where she pointed, Ashton observed the visible outline of a black bra worn underneath her thin white cotton tank top that was now soaking wet. But the top wasn't sheer enough to see any further, leaving the one significant and pressing question relating to her story left unanswered.

"She gave birth to the baby," Ada said, once again turning away from him, allowing the rain to drench her fragile figure. "A little baby girl. Three weeks later she was burned alive, along with sixty others."

Ashton felt a discomforting lump in the back of his throat.

"What happened to the kid?"

Ada directed her eyes to the heavens, wrapping her arms around herself before answering. "The child was taken into the care of a

French army commander, who discovered shortly afterward that the mother's stigma had mysteriously been passed on to the child. The red flower. Right here."

She pointed once again to just underneath her left breast before glancing at him and smiling impishly. "And to this day, all of the women in my ancestor's bloodline are born with the same cursed mark. The very same."

With that, it appeared that her story had reached its conclusion, and she shook the heavy sea of raindrops from her damp and unruly mane. Her whole body was soaked and shivering, but Ada's riveting performance wasn't quite finished. Spellbound, Ashton watched her approach him, wearing a crooked smile upon her lips.

"And do you know what is also said?" she asked him. "That every woman in my family will love once, and only once will she find true love within her lifetime. And that the man who loves her back will be doomed to suffer an early death."

Ashton paled at the grim suggestion. "So your father is—"

Thunderclap!

Ada nodded. "Dead. My mother's dead to me as well."

Her face became warmer, her smile more playful and natural.

"There," she stated matter-of-factly. "Are you impressed?"

It was curious. Ada had revealed some of her past after all—or something like it. And the story had left his mysterious acquaintance appearing more unusual and fascinating than ever.

One question was left unanswered.

"What about...the mark? Do you have it?"

Ada's smile widened, her rain-soaked body still shivering. She slowly leaned into him and pressed her slippery form against his muscular torso.

"I'll show you mine if you show me yours," Ada said.

Thunderclap!

Ashton gazed into her eyes, watching as she leaned in for a kiss while slowly pulling up her soaked shirt. He felt himself being drawn to her. His eyes closed, and his lips parted...

Buzz. Buzz.

Just like that, the spell was broken. At the sound of the vibrating cell phone, he pulled back, watching as Ada, suddenly looking very irritated, resecured her soggy tank top and answered the call.

"Yes, yes—hello?"

A panicked voice was on the other end.

"Ada! Something went wrong! The asylum! I can't find Izzy!"

Ashton recognized the call was from Rudy and watched Ada's eyes fill with distress, her cool confidence and acerbic wit disappearing in an instant. The transformation was quite a stunning sight to witness, as this was the first time he'd seen her looking so rattled and off-balance.

"I'll call you back." Ada terminated the call and turned to her confused companion, searching for what to say. "I have to go. I need to find my brother."

Ada grabbed her soaking wet hoodie from the soggy, flooded ground, and started on her way. Still in a daze, Ashton felt a string of words burst forth from his lips.

"Can I see you tomorrow?"

She stopped with her back to him, her body stiff, looking torn.

"Perhaps. I just really need to find my brother."

Once these words left her lips, she was off like a shot, her black boots stomping through the murky puddles now swallowing the asphalt path.

Ashton called after her and discovered that, despite any logical explanation for it, his body was now frozen to where he stood.

"Ada! Wait!"

There was no answer.

Ada had disappeared, leaving Ashton to stare after her in quiet bewilderment while the red light of his camera continued blinking methodically, the rain pouring down on the dreary headstones as the mysterious beauty that had so effortlessly captivated him during the short time he'd known her became lost in the bitter darkness of the unrelenting storm.

Part II

Miles: Ada told us we were coming out here to get even with the town that wronged you two. But you seem to have other plans. What exactly will you be having the others do for you?

McAllister: The same as I'll be asking of you. Inquiring about a man traveling on the road to Boston with a book.

II

SEDUCTION OF THE INNOCENT

Nancy and Wilbur stood outside the tavern, going over the game plan for how best to confront the menace that had taken over the trendy establishment. Wilbur was being looked at to play the role of leader for the mission—a role he wasn't particularly enthusiastic about. But it was vital to inspect the intimidating all-black building to get a better sense of the precarious situation that was unfolding. With things as they were, all he could do was force a smile and do a quick survey of the company huddled around him.

There was Jerry, a jovial outdoorsman type who managed the local hardware store and whose high school football years were long behind him; Priscilla, his modest homemaker wife; Steve and Cheryl, two Northeastern yuppies, their hands itching to check the electronic devices burning holes inside their pockets; and Ruth, a silver-haired no-nonsense type of woman—arguably one of the pillars of the Little Salem community. Not exactly the "dream team" for taking on a dangerous coven of witches. But it was all the support he'd been offered, so he would have to make the best of it.

"OK, here's the plan," Wilbur said. "I think only one of them's in there right now. I say we go inside, do our fake 'Welcome to the Neighborhood' bit—*do not mention Ada or McAllister*. We'll deal with those two once we figure out what's really going on with this place."

"Plan sounds good," Steve interjected, stowing away his smartphone but leaving his reliable Bluetooth where it was. "And let's hurry it up. Cheryl's gotta pick up little Nico from horseback-riding lessons before lunch."

The group all nodded and mumbled in agreement, and Nancy rolled her eyes with annoyance.

Once the neighbors crossed through the doors, they were greeted by the sounds of strip club heavy metal music. It was startling how many changes had been made in such a short amount of time. Gone were the pastel colors on the walls, replaced by strikingly decadent black and gold wallpaper. The inviting family-style booths had been covered with black vinyl; the sunny environment smothered by curtains, the bright fluorescents replaced with exotic chandeliers.

"Uh, hello? Anyone home?" Wilbur glanced anxiously to the bar where Sanchez was polishing glasses like an old-timey saloon owner, monitoring the group's activity. While taking in the scenery, the locals remained in a state of stunned passivity, coming to a halt after catching sight of Ada's hospitable welcoming committee.

Agatha was standing with her back to the group, dressed in a provocative red designer dress. Her body was hunched over a black felt pool table, rear end poked out suggestively, with her curvaceous hips twitching like a metronome to the beat of the lascivious music.

Ada was a crafty one, Wilbur silently conceded. The group had only been inside for a matter of moments, but the stunning creature had all the men hypnotized, their jaws dropping in unison.

"H-hello? Miss?" Wilbur received a quick jolt as Agatha slammed one end of the pool cue into a rack of billiard balls, with several falling into their respected slots. "Uh, we're just a few of your new neighbors—just a few of the local neighbors. Came by to say-ay-ay—"

"I'm Agatha. Charmed."

Crack! Agatha sank another ball while striking a seductive pose for her new admirers, and Wilbur was pained to notice that Steve and Cheryl now had their eyes glued to her every movement.

It was peculiar. The normally uptight and absentminded couple were now salivating over their hostess like a pair of dogs in front of a butcher shop. Something fishy was going on, but he couldn't put his finger on it.

Feeling increasingly worried, Wilbur did a quick head-count. Two out of the seven in their courageous group were already out of commission, and it was highly likely that others would follow. But for the moment, Jerry, Priscilla, Ruth, and Nancy seemed to be with him—although everyone appeared highly distracted, with all of them seeming to be losing this strange battle.

"So! Agatha!" Jerry heartily announced, appearing eager to leave the toxic environment. "We couldn't help but notice you've made some changes to the ol' Burrito Hut."

"Can't stop the winds of change from blowing," Agatha said.

Crack! Another ball sank into a pouch.

"True, true." Jerry patted the sweat on his forehead. "It's just that, well... People really loved that Burrito Hut."

Crack! Another ball sank into a pouch.

"We thought the town might like a fun bar instead," Agatha said. "Did you know this place used to be a brothel? Owned and operated by my great-great-grandmother. The family felt a bar would be more fitting for a place with such a colorful past."

Agatha leaned over the pool table, showing off her ample cleavage as she effortlessly sank another ball. Wilbur noticed that Ruth was now blinking her eyes rapidly, slowly succumbing to the seductive ambiance of the place while also being overwhelmed by the lithe and sensual movements of their hostess.

"Good Lord," Ruth muttered.

Sensing they were close to losing another member of their well-intentioned posse, Wilbur found himself burdened with a great deal of concern. Ruth was the most senior member among them, and usually the most levelheaded and the most serious. Once she was out of the picture, that would spell big trouble for the rest of them.

Luckily, they hadn't lost this mysterious battle just yet. And speaking of mysteries, why did his temperature suddenly appear to be rising? And what were these strange euphoric sounds he was hearing tinkling away in the back of his head?

"Well, Agatha," Priscilla chimed in nervously, still appearing to have some fight left in her, "this all might sound like a super-fun idea to you, but some of your friendly neighbors might have an eensy little problem with this scenario. I mean, a group of outsiders opening a fashionable bar in this district?"

"City doesn't have a problem," Agatha replied, strutting around the pool table like a show pony. "To them, we're restoring a historical monument and providing the town a brand-new attraction for the tourists. The permits have all been filed with the public record."

Crack! Another ball sank into a pouch.

"Well," Priscilla said, visibly sweating under the pressure as the captivating beauty struck another scandalous pose for the group. "You see, Agatha—it sounds like you've already given this a lot of thought, but this neighborhood is filled with local businesses that are catered toward families. Businesses that are quiet and respectable. Like Wilbur's and Nancy's, for instance."

"Then they really aren't going to like the stripper poles I just signed for."

The group all turned in unison to address the voice that had spoken. They were pained to discover that McAllister was now also present, signing a delivery receipt for several tall, skinny packages sitting next to the main doors. From that point on, the situation quickly went from bad to worse as McAllister steadily revealed that, yes, the bar was going to feature strippers—or "dancers" as he noted they preferred to be called—and invited all who were present to comb through a thick black binder in his possession featuring all the juicy headshots of the scores of beautiful girls who were applying.

This is where the dam appeared to burst, as Jerry and Priscilla, now both completely out of their minds, nearly tripped over one another to get a closer look at the racy contents.

So much for good intentions, Wilbur thought. All was lost. They walked straight into the mouth of the lion's den, woefully unprepared for what lay in store.

While Jerry and Priscilla were busy leafing through the binder, Wilbur glanced over to the pool table and noticed Agatha now giggling with Ruth, Cheryl, and Steve. All of them were nestled close to her like a slavering pack of groupies.

Well, she is a reasonably attractive woman, Wilbur silently conceded. *With those beautiful green eyes and pin-up figure, and the daintiest freckles imaginable over every inch of her—*

"Ow!"

Wilbur grabbed his arm where Nancy had pinched him.

"She's enchanting them," his wife warned. "Don't fall for it."

That's when it dawned on him.

It was witchcraft. That's why all of his neighbors were fawning over Agatha like a celebrity, and why he seemed hypnotized by the sounds of sensual sighs and tiny bells in the back of his mind.

Wilbur kicked himself for not realizing this sooner. But Nancy was already several steps ahead of him, asking for directions to the bathroom before turning back to her husband.

"Keep the witch talking."

As Wilbur proceeded to chat with Agatha about the sordid history of her ancestor's former business, Nancy disappeared into the back, bypassing the public restrooms and making a beeline for the tavern's upper levels. Once she climbed to the top of the stairs, she snuck down the hallway, peeking into all of the rooms that awaited her as the building's weary floorboards creaked under her feet.

Nancy's mind was racing. She was improvising, not quite sure what she was doing or what she was trying to find.

She passed two bedrooms. Probably Ada's and Agatha's, both empty, which meant... Yes, the private bathroom was where she would find what she needed.

She disappeared inside and searched the medicine cabinet—empty; then the drawers—there was a hairbrush, but all the bristles were clean. Shit, shit, shit—this was a disaster! She knew there had to be something!

Her heart was beating like a faulty jackhammer, and she would have to return to the main room before anyone started to get suspicious. She peered all around her in desperation, and her eyes lit up at what she saw.

The shower! Of course! She would find something in the shower!

Nancy dropped to her knees and bent her body over the rim of the tub, running her fingers around the drain.

Eureka! she thought. She quickly wrapped her discovery inside a wad of toilet paper and exited in a hurry. She was overjoyed she had proven successful at getting what she needed but was tragically unprepared for what was waiting for her on the other side of the door. When she pulled it open, she found herself face to face with Rudy, silently staring back at her while wearing a pair of strange high-tech night-vision goggles for some reason.

Caught entirely by surprise, Nancy let out a startled scream, and Rudy screamed back in reply, alarmed by the woman's response more than anything. He was just as shocked when she shoved right past him, racing down the stairs and into the main room; trying her best to act casual as she made her way to the exit.

"Wilbur. We have to go."

"Leaving so soon?"

With the front door only inches away, the couple turned to spy McAllister smiling like the devil from behind the bar. Agatha was by his side, their neighbors all hovering around the filthy black binder, fighting to get a better look.

"Hate to see you leave, Nancy," McAllister chillingly grinned. "But if you don't mind me saying, that ass is looking fan-tastic."

McAllister received a playful smack from Agatha for the comment. Keeping his eyes firmly held on the couple, he added, "She's a keeper, isn't she? Wilbur, ol' buddy?"

Not knowing how to respond, Nancy eventually managed to fight her nerves long enough to glare at her nefarious agitator. Once the couple had left, the rest of the group began shaking their heads in confusion. As if they'd just broken out of a trance and forgotten where they were and anything that had just happened.

The experience inside the tavern left Wilbur feeling more disturbed than ever. Ada and McAllister were dangerous enough on their own, but he had no idea that the others along with them might possess frightening supernatural talents as well. He was equally disturbed that his wife would take off into enemy territory without knowing who she might risk running into, voicing his concerns as they made their way across the street together to the safety of the frozen yogurt shop.

"What were you thinking? To go snooping around like that?"

"I was looking for something, and I found it—will you drop it?"

"Those kids are going to suspect something! These aren't just a bunch of punks horsing around in detention! These kids are smart!"

"I will do what it takes to protect my daughter! Don't you get it? This is all tied to Ada's grudge from five years ago! She wants to ruin us! To corrupt the town and turn us against ourselves!"

Wilbur knew this discouraging diagnosis was no exaggeration. But he still felt hesitant to take any action. A string of memories was still fresh in his mind: How worthless he was when squaring off against McAllister, and what Ada had shown them she was capable of during her previous visit.

Most of all, Wilbur feared the person he might have to become to rise and meet this challenge, still wanting to believe he'd left that regrettable part of his life behind him.

For Nancy, now wasn't the time for hesitation. Sensing her husband's apprehension, she glared at him with a fearsome look of dogged resilience.

"If you aren't prepared to fight to protect the things you really care about, then stay out of my way," she hissed. "I'm not about to have you dragging me down, mister!"

"Uh, what are you talking about?"

Wilbur glanced over to notice their adopted daughter watching them from the doorway to the yogurt shop. With Mary Sue, they were still trying to pretend that everything was fine and dandy, and Nancy deftly changed the subject after spying the Reverend crossing down the sidewalk with his pretty teenage daughter alongside him.

"Take five, Mary Sue. Reverend Palmer! Reverend Palmer!"

As Wilbur left his daughter's side to join up with his better half, his mind remained fixed on the harsh and discomforting words his wife had directed at him.

It seemed there was no way of getting around it: The problems in Little Salem were just beginning, and things would only be getting worse from here on out. As things continued to worsen, as much as it pained him to accept it, he knew he would have to leave his perfect life behind and play the role of the bad guy one more time.

12

ZODIAC THRILLER

————

Mary Sue had always suspected she preferred girls over boys, but this was proven the day she met Izzy. It was no question she always knew she was different from other girls. She was the only girl at school that had been adopted, and one of the few brown girls that lived in Little Salem—and a brown girl from Venezuela by way of Guatemala, to boot. When people asked her mother where she came from, Nancy would usually tell them she'd been adopted from Guatemala and leave it at that. But when Mary Sue questioned her father, he grumbled something about her originally being from Venezuela and that her adopted name was Maria Suzella, no last name, ending the conversation shortly afterward.

That was the curious thing about Mary Sue's history: She couldn't remember any of it. Everything that happened to her before the age of eleven, prior to her adoption from the orphanage in Antigua, was a total blank. When McAllister appeared and burnt a pentagram into her family's front lawn, the sight of the fire seemed to awaken a dark, distant memory in her. A horrible recollection that her mind was keeping locked away, preventing her from gaining access to her shadowy and mysterious past.

Feeling so different from everyone, Mary Sue had a difficult time growing up in Little Salem, and this was only made more difficult by the complication of having zero childhood memories to guide her in her personal development. Despite having two loving parents, they were no help at all in these matters, so while she always knew there was something about other girls that seemed to excite her more than boys, she never felt entirely comfortable about this preference. Sometimes this proclivity even made her question if there was something wrong with her, loathing the fact that her personal orientation made her feel more isolated and different from everyone.

This torrential flood of contradicting emotions predictably drove her to search for solace in a variety of creative outlets such as loud music, alternative comics, and art. Drawing was everything to her, along with horseback riding, which she probably loved more than anything. The feeling of the wind whipping at her hair with her legs wrapped tightly around the majestic animal as it galloped across the foggy hills—these precious moments always gave her such a thrill. At any other time, she felt distracted by the constant clashing of emotions doing a crazy dance number on her insides and never imagined there would be another time she would feel such a powerful surge of positive feelings. But, sure enough, this is exactly how she felt whenever she was around Izzy.

Mary Sue first came into contact with the young gypsy when Izzy visited her family's frozen yogurt shop, Ponies and Coneys. The popular dessert place sat right in the middle of Little Salem's main drag, directly across the street from where the Black Death Tavern now stood—prime real estate before Ada's hostile takeover. The name of the yogurt shop had been her mother's idea. She thought it would be a cute idea to offer their customers a pony ride to enjoy with their tasty cup or cone. That was why Mary Sue's pony, Baby Blue, was kept in a stable out back and was beloved by many of the friendly locals, both adults and children. The main objective for opening the shop involved a noble effort to help foster a positive family environment in Little Salem—something the whole community could enjoy, including the Truegoods' precious Mary Sue. But because their shy and introverted daughter felt so different, she always felt excluded from the happiness enjoyed by others—something that would disappear once she met Izzy.

Mary Sue had just entered from the back after spending the past hour moping next to the corral. She was still bothered by the sight of McAllister and the fire and felt frustrated that the incident seemed to be calling back memories she had no access to. She was regretting even bothering coming to work that day when she glanced to the front counter and saw a girl like nothing she'd ever seen—a stirring vision amid the shop's immaculate white scenery.

Like all of the members of Ada's group, Izzy was uniquely attractive. She didn't have the showgirl figure of Agatha or the strange, alien beauty of Ada, but was cute and adorable in her own particular way. In terms of appearance, she had a petite figure, soft, appetizing features, and enviable hair and skin. But her most notable feature was her inner radiance—something indefinable where she seemed to light up any room she walked through. Izzy was the type of person who could become fast friends with just about anyone, with many desiring to become close to the young gypsy after knowing her for only a matter of moments. She also had a particularly impressive personal style, mixing lots of sparkling jewelry with psychedelic fabrics and vintage T-shirts. She wore cool platform shoes that made her appear much taller, shredded fishnet stockings, and wild-colored nail polish on every finger.

To Mary Sue, Izzy looked like a rock star. Everyone in Ada's company did. They seemed much more like a cool rock band than a dangerous coven of evil witches, as the rumors around town suggested. For a small-town girl like Mary Sue, both things were so foreign to her that one could easily be substituted for the other and were equally as evocative. And of all the members of the band, Izzy was her instant favorite. She had dark hair and dark skin like she did, and that winning smile made her heart beat faster than anything—including riding on horseback through Little Salem's lonely, desolate hills.

"Oh, yay someone's here!" Izzy exclaimed after spotting the timid teenager. "Save me. I'm having such a snack attack. So... What's good here?"

Mary Sue was tongue-tied and awestruck. "You're asking me?"

Izzy let out a girlish laugh. "Oh my God, you're so precious. Don't you have a favorite?"

"Um, no?"

"Oh my God, you're too much! You're someone who likes to keep to yourself. I'll bet you're a Cancer."

"How did...?"

"But hold on, hold on. I'm also getting a strong Gemini vibe, and then there's a little, oh what am I talking about? Something to do with suns and moons, blah-blah-blah. Born on June 22nd, right?"

Mary Sue was in a state of shock. "How did you...?"

Izzy pumped her arm in victory. "*Yesss.* Still got it. Oh! And I think that means your favorite flavor is Vanilla Caramel Fudge. One of those, please!"

Izzy's words caught Mary Sue completely off-guard, issued forth in a deliriously bubbly and girlish manner one would hardly expect from someone suspected of being a dangerous witch. She was so stunned by this impressive and energetic display that the rest of the conversation was a blur. Mostly she remembered Izzy mentioning a special trial McAllister was having them perform and her nagging worry she would fail and be kicked out of the group as a result. Mary Sue could also recall the way Izzy beamed back at her when she shyly wished the witch good luck before she headed out the door. The smile was like a blessed beacon of sunshine poking through the clouds on an otherwise stormy day—something that had been dancing in her mind ever since.

Just thinking about her time with Izzy made Mary Sue feel warm and fuzzy all over. When she got home later that evening, she sketched a quick drawing of her new irresistible girl crush entirely by memory so she could gaze at that glowing smile before going to bed. Doing so made her feel flush with positive emotions and not so freakish and alone for a change.

But Izzy was no longer smiling when Mary Sue spotted her the next day. Since school was still off for spring break, she once again accompanied her parents to work at the yogurt shop, secretly pining for another glimpse of the dazzling gypsy while Ada and the others were camped out across the street. While her parents were distracted with talking to the Reverend about the troublesome doomsday-like presence of the all-black tavern now uglying up the neighborhood, she gazed across the street and saw her: Izzy, wearing a baggy black hoodie, long, flowing black skirt, and a colorful scarf wrapped around her head. Smoking like it was going out of style and pacing back and forth, her earbuds pumping loud music into her cranium.

Mary Sue frowned at the sight. With the young gypsy looking so lost and fragile, her mind drifted to the fury of gossip she'd been overhearing, and her parents' controversial opinions on the company Izzy was keeping. The presence of Ada and her spooky stepsibling was now a hot-button issue among the residents, and Mary Sue's introduction to one half of the fearsome duo led her to suspect her newest acquaintance might be in more danger than she knew.

Sensing an opportunity to connect with the object of her affection once more, Mary Sue glanced nervously at her parents, seeing they were still caught up in their conversation with the Reverend. After confirming they were distracted, she summoned all her courage and walked briskly across the street.

"Hey. Are you OK?"

Startled, Izzy removed her earbuds and spied Mary Sue. "Oh, hello. Sorry, I don't normally..." She quickly ashed her cig. "I'm just a little nervous about what's happening later tonight."

"Why? What's going on?"

"Oh, nothing. Another test of my abilities."

"Is that creep McAllister putting you up to this?"

"Not really. And McAllister's not a creep. He's a Leo, I told you."

Izzy's voice drifted off. She took a seat on the curb, staring fretfully into the distance. Mary Sue still felt starstruck around the eccentric beauty. She wasn't sure if she should continue her questioning to confirm if Izzy was in danger and got the feeling it might be best to temporarily change the subject.

"How did you do that the other day?" Mary Sue asked bashfully, gathering up the confidence to sit beside the young witch. "Guessing my exact birth date."

Izzy laughed softly. "Lucky guess? A little trick my grandmother taught me. She was a famous fortune-teller and—well, it's like this. You've got this cool and mysterious antisocial poet thing going on for you. Like a lot of Cancers."

Izzy glanced over and cast her winning smile at Mary Sue, causing her rapid heartbeat to rocket into outer space. "But I can also tell you're a bit of a chameleon," she said. "Maybe you secretly like to show off a bit. Which means you're a bit of a Gem as well. June 22nd is on the cusp, so..."

Mary Sue watched as Izzy innocently shrugged her shoulders and began to laugh nervously. The starry-eyed teenager remained frozen where she sat, not knowing what to do or how to react around someone she was so hopelessly infatuated with.

"Ada's a Gem," Izzy said. *This meant Gemini*, Mary Sue reminded herself. "She's the most amazing person I've ever met. But you see, there's really nothing to it. Sometimes I say things or predict things, and Ada thinks it's because I'm special. But I'm no one special. What I'm doing... It's just stupid birthday clown magic tricks. Just a pile of stupid luck. That's all it is."

Watching Izzy looking so downcast and beside herself made Mary Sue feel desperate to cheer her up in any way she could. She wanted to tell her that whatever negative emotions she was feeling were all just rubbish. That she was only giving herself a hard time and surely the remarkable truth of the matter must be something really awesome and spectacular.

While Mary Sue was normally shy and introverted, as Izzy had noted, she knew she had to fight against this to reveal how much she'd been affected by the brief matter of moments they'd shared. She wanted Izzy to know she gave her life hope and the courage to face the world all on her own. That because of their brief meeting, she no longer felt so alone, and she now longed to see that radiant smile of hers beaming brightly in her direction.

"Well, I think you're special," Mary Sue passionately declared. "Even if you're not a psychic. Maybe your gift is having lots of friends who love you and believe in you because you're really really lucky. And maybe being friends with these people makes all of them really lucky as well. And I think that's awesome, you know? I think that's a pretty awesome gift if you ask me."

Izzy took a moment to process this, and her face lit up like a summer's day. "You know, maybe you're right! Wow—you're like a walking anti-depressant. And so wise. Must be because you're a Cancer."

Izzy laughed and smiled, and Mary Sue couldn't help but smile as well. After this encounter, Izzy would remain on her mind for the rest of the day and long after, but in a completely different sense. It would be later that night that Izzy would suffer her ordeal at the asylum, and following this tragic event, she would never be the same.

13

HAUNTED HALLWAYS

───────────

On their third evening in Little Salem, Izzy and Rudy ventured to the crumbling mental hospital on the edge of town. The plan was to hold a séance to contact the ghost of a former patient—an unusual task, to be sure, although not without purpose. A purpose Rudy revealed when they were seated in the tavern earlier that morning.

"We've all heard the story," Rudy said. "During the Salem witch trials, a bunch of the women accused of being witches mentioned a man on the road to Boston carrying a strange book. The servant, Tituba, in particular."

"Right. The famous 'man in black' story," Izzy noted. "History tells us she was fibbing, but Ada insists she wasn't? My brain hurts."

"Here's the thing," Rudy said. "It just so happens this wasn't the only time people reported seeing such a man in the vicinity."

"Don't you think those descriptions are a bit vague?" Agatha was sitting nearby, more absorbed with filing her nails than listening to

Rudy's summary. "A man traveling to Beantown with a book? It's just the traditional legend of the 'Black Man of the Sabbath.' And we all know who that's referring to."

"Now hold on—here's where it starts getting interesting." Rudy referred to some notes on his laptop. "Back in 1692, there were reports of a chemist from Rhode Island named Sebastien Jedediah Bishop, who local colonial types actually accused of *being* the 'Man In Black.' He ended up going crazy and killing himself? The reports aren't clear. There weren't any sanitariums in the area until 1878. And check it out: In 1916, another man pops up, screaming about a 'Man In Black.' Some unsavory wackjob named Tom Thumb. Guess where he ends up?"

"Where?"

"At the abandoned asylum right here in Little Salem."

"Does he have any relatives or next of kin?"

"Fraid not. Poor sucker died at that place. And I don't think McAllister wants us to contact the relatives. I think he wants us to contact *him*."

The idea of visiting some creepy asylum to call up the dead was something that didn't sit well with Izzy. Clearly, McAllister saw some connection between the book the Man In Black was rumored to be carrying and the fabled diary that he was overturning heaven and earth for. But the mission filled her with a great deal of anxiety, and she didn't hold back on voicing her concerns while Rudy was packing up supplies for their later excursion.

"But I've never done a séance!"

"C'mon. You've done them lots of times."

"I mean, yeah—I've held those things for laughs at slumber parties. What teenage girl hasn't?"

"So you'll just be doing one for real this time."

Izzy was about to argue further, but Rudy cut her off.

"Izzy? Hey—I get it. You don't have much faith in your abilities, or whatever powers or abilities people other than you might think you were gifted with. And to be perfectly honest, neither do I, OK?

"But Ada does. She believes in all of your gifts and your potential and always has. Now I know you like to get down on yourself, and you can be one stubborn witch at times, but she's been trying to put those gifts to use for as long as I've known you. How about you stop making excuses and start giving her some credit?"

Despite her reservations, Izzy eventually surrendered to going through with the bizarre assignment. A plan was set in motion, and the investigation started out fairly pleasant and easy-going. Izzy and Rudy managed to break into the condemned institution with no problems and started scouring the gloomy basement archives for more information on their departed subject.

While searching the disorderly remains of the crumbling, tumbledown setting, Rudy shined his flashlight on a collection of tall metal shelves until it landed on a decaying box of files relating to the former resident in question.

"Can you imagine living in a time with no computers or internet?" Rudy asked.

"I imagine you'd have a harder time finding material to jerk off to," Izzy noted.

"I dunno. I've been known to be pretty resourceful."

Izzy sighed wearily. "You're such a Virgo."

After securing Tom Thumb's file from the basement, they discovered that while their target had spent his time institutionalized on the second floor, he died in the ground floor sick ward. With this information in hand, they relocated to this site to prepare for the main attraction. Izzy lit four white candles and broke out a witch's board (a common Ouija board), while Rudy set up a video camera to document the attempted evocation.

Once the preparations were set, they sat cross-legged on the floor, the board placed in between them. They each took a deep breath, absentmindedly forgetting to perform a banishing ritual just to be safe, and placed their hands upon the planchette.

Izzy was still feeling severe apprehensions for taking part in the divination, but she didn't want to disappoint McAllister or Ada. In the end, she decided to swallow her inhibitions and go through with it—even if this was something that gave her a great deal of discomfort, considering what she was being asked to accomplish.

"OK, focus. Focus." Izzy released a breath and squeezed her eyelids shut. She gradually felt her body relaxing, and once her mind was clear and free of distractions, she petitioned the spirits to show themselves and communicate with those who were present.

"Spirits, we reach out to you. We promise we mean no harm. Please come through and speak with us."

Following the respectful appeal, she sat with Rudy in silence.

But nothing stirred.

With the séance not going at all as planned, the pair continued sitting perfectly still for several moments until Izzy asked the room, "Are there any spirits here with us?"

Once again, there was no answer.

At this point, Izzy felt resigned to give up the damn endeavor. It felt like they were wasting their time and that the plan was a total wash.

All this changed in an instant when she suddenly felt a cold chill, holding her breath as she felt the planchette beneath her fingers moving across the board and slowly gliding to the word...

YES.

After opening her eyes to observe the answer, Izzy broke into an anxious grin. She noticed Rudy was gazing at her in astonishment, both of them baffled and amazed that they experienced a tiny sliver of success.

With the séance now off to the races, Izzy proceeded with her next question: "Spirits in the room, is there more than one of you?" And just as before, she held her breath as she felt the planchette move, the board offering a reply of...

YES.

Izzy and Rudy were more than just a little freaked out, but every response provided a surge of adrenaline. This emboldened Izzy to continue with her third question: "Is one of you Tom Thumb?" The planchette moved again, straight to the word...

YES.

Unfortunately, the interrogation was all downhill from here, and disaster and calamity were right around the corner.

Rudy stared at Izzy in anticipation as she released a nervous breath and uttered question number four: "Are we speaking to Tom Thumb right now?"

The planchette didn't move, and after several moments, Rudy frowned and let loose a cynical comment.

"Looks like the board's gone dead."

This would prove to be far from the case.

After a few more moments of idleness and frustration, Rudy released a heavy sigh. Izzy was shocked to notice that his breath was now visible, and the room had gone ice cold.

"Rudy. Your breath."

Suddenly, the candles snuffed out. There was a low creaking sound and the Ouija board went flying across the room.

Heart racing, Izzy screamed like a banshee and fled in a panic. Rudy was initially too shocked to move. When he finally emerged into the hallway, he couldn't find her anywhere.

It was as if the budding young psychic had vanished into thin air—or she'd been spirited to another realm. Rudy racked his brain for a satisfying explanation for the disappearance, the whole time unaware that Izzy was in another section of the hospital altogether, calling out his name in desperation.

Izzy had been screaming Rudy's name for what seemed like an hour, but it could have been only a minute. Time inside the abandoned mental hospital had gone all lopsided. Her head was throbbing, her voice was hoarse from yelling. She was falling apart at the seams, and all of her senses felt scrambled and disoriented.

When the panicked young gypsy fled the crumbling sick ward, she paid little attention to where she was going. Her only instinct was to run full speed from the presence that she and Rudy had contacted, expecting she would eventually come across an exit if she only ran long enough.

Izzy had no idea how long she had sprinted through the hospital's cold, labyrinthine halls, only to discover there was no exit to be found. It was like she was trapped in a maze, and the further she explored the abandoned setting, the more her surroundings appeared to change; the atmosphere growing darker, the environment much quieter and more affected by the ravages of decay.

The air seemed to have grown thick with a stale and suffocating heaviness, and the hallway was growing gloomier and more unwelcoming by the second. Izzy had to strain her eyes to see anything, barely making out the small amount of space being lit by the hazy amber beam of her flashlight.

To gain a more accurate assessment of her current location, she temporarily abandoned her thoughts of escape and shined her flashlight on a door to her side, providing her with yet another unsettling shock to the system.

The number on the door read, Room 237.

This was the room that Tom Thumb had once occupied—where he was placed while he was still alive.

"But I was on the ground floor," Izzy muttered. "I—this doesn't make sense."

As the poor girl's panic began to build, she suddenly heard a low, creaking sound. Eyes wide and swallowing short, terror-filled breaths, she spun around and directed her flashlight down the hallway. But there was nothing there.

Not being able to locate the cause of the noise that startled her provided very little reassurance. Her body was shaking, and her heart was leaping inside her chest like a cornered jackrabbit.

But the nightmare she was trapped in was only just beginning—something that only became more apparent as her flashlight started blinking before dying right on the spot.

"Oh my God, oh my God—"

Izzy's suffocating fear and uneasiness shifted into overdrive. As someone who was extremely knowledgeable about supernatural phenomena and the behavior of our incorporeal neighbors, she was distinctly aware that these types of difficulties were often a sign that something was draining all of the electromagnetic energy in the area in an effort to make contact with the living. And given her current set of circumstances, this was clearly not the most ideal scenario for her to be dealing with.

Before the darkness could overwhelm her, Izzy tossed the flashlight aside and pulled out her smartphone, using the camera flash to guide her as her eyes darted about. Breathing hard, she spun around to observe all three hundred and sixty degrees of her surroundings and was alarmed to perceive another startling discovery as the sound of an approaching thunderstorm boomed in the distance.

The door to Tom Thumb's old room was now wide open and beckoning for her to investigate. And while every fiber in her being was urging her to run like hell and quickly, she regrettably concluded that the only way out of this torturous predicament was to face her fears head-on.

Inside the old hospital room was nothing special. It was a modest room containing a rusty, abandoned cot and little else. If this was indeed Tom Thumb's former residence, he hadn't occupied the space for close to a century, so it wasn't likely for there to be anything present that was connected to the deceased patient. But the abundance of dark shadows within the damp and claustrophobic cell still managed to have a distinctly unnerving effect on Izzy—and to make matters even more distressing, it felt like she was not alone and that there was something in the room with her.

"Hello? Is someone here?" Her heart raced faster and faster. "Tom Thumb? It really feels like... Like there's someone in here..."

A loud crash rang out from somewhere deep inside the building, and Izzy spun around, her eyes wide as headlights. She was trying her hardest to keep it all together, disturbed to discover her body was now shivering and she could see her own breath. Sudden temperature drops were another sign that something was desperately trying to make contact, and Izzy found herself quietly lamenting her gross misfortune to find herself in such a mess.

"This stupid search," Izzy moaned. "Why did I come here? I don't care about talking to ghosts or stupid magic books..."

This was the honest truth, of course. She couldn't have cared less about the obscure magical text McAllister was searching for, or the special abilities Ada was convinced she was gifted with. It felt silly that a supernatural presence would be seeking her out due to these factors, and this inspired a sudden epiphany.

"Wait. It wasn't the book at all, was it? You're only here because someone summoned you. Summoned you back into—"

Tragically, this inspired realization came much too late. All of a sudden, she heard a low groan and spun around to face the intruder, immediately disheartened by what was nothing less than the most horrifying thing she could have imagined.

A clap of thunder accompanied by a burst of lightning that appeared for only an instant briefly illuminated the terrifying presence standing mere inches from her: a slender spectral figure with eyes hidden by a filthy medical bandage and skin so wrinkled and pale the texture was almost sponge-like. The figure looked neither alive nor dead, but closer to a living corpse than anything—and even closer to something that existed in the darkest depths of a paranoid's nightmare than anything that resided in the reassuring world of the living. It was difficult to say, but the emaciated phantom looked like it had been human at some point, which only made its putrefied appearance even more disturbing. Its decaying features were like shallow imitations of the real thing, except for the wanton, crooked mouth filled with black, rotting teeth that were grinding and sneering in her direction—taunting the frightened girl to do anything.

Unsurprisingly, there was little Izzy could do besides scream bloody murder, and her reaction was startlingly brief. Almost instantly, after emptying her lungs of all the screams she could unburden, an invisible force threw her body against the wall. After this, the poor, unfortunate gypsy who never wished to search the abandoned setting in the first place (and felt strong apprehensions not to) woefully lost consciousness.

A series of strange and chaotic events directly followed this disturbing encounter. Izzy's screams drew Rudy to her location, but when he arrived, he didn't find a body lying on the floor but Izzy's petite, fragile figure hovering in midair in a crucifixion pose before crashing to the ground in a dull, tangled heap. Rudy phoned Ada at the tavern to inform her of the terrible horrors he witnessed, and from the ghostly look on Ada's face, Agatha, who was anxiously lingering in the background, could easily observe that things were far worse than either she or Rudy could fathom.

None of this was as significant as what was occurring across town. Back at the Truegoods' cozy suburban home, Mary Sue found herself stargazing, peering out a second-story window overlooking her family's backyard. Izzy had been on her mind for days, and she'd been hoping to wish on a lucky star to bestow good fortune on their blossoming relationship. Unfortunately, as fate would have it, buckets of rain were being let loose from the heavens, blocking out any sign of starlight as thunder boomed in all directions.

After a quick burst of lightning, Mary Sue lowered her eyes, her gaze drawn to the sound of an eerie and unpleasant creak. It was her mother, exiting the garden shed. She was dressed in long white robes and appeared incredibly weary.

Mary Sue watched the worn-out woman sluggishly cross the yard, tensing up when she came to a sudden halt. Nancy cast her eyes upward and a burst of lightning illuminated her, capturing a sallow countenance that was eerily devoid of human feeling.

Mary Sue pulled back at the sight, frightened and confused as to why she would be witnessing such a spectacle. But she would receive no answer, watching her mother lower her gaze and slump through the rain. Back to the perfect home of those she was willing to fight for, no matter what the cost or sacrifice.

14

VOICES IN THE ATTIC

McAllister sat on the edge of the bed, mind racing, ready to burst out of his skin. Dealing with situations he had no control over had the habit of doing his head in, and he knew this often made him volatile and difficult to put up with. The times when he didn't feel this way were few and far between. Conversing with his stepsister had a soothing effect on him, as did his prurient activities with Agatha. All things weighed equally, killing people was what soothed his nerves most effectively—and since killing anyone right now was out of the question, he needed to broaden his horizons and search for another way to calm himself.

Agatha was sleeping next to him, dolled up and shagged out in a red silk nightgown that showed off her curvaceous figure. McAllister noticed she appeared to be dressing exclusively in shades of red these days, and her choice of clothing was more fashionable and upscale since their fortuitous meeting five years earlier. Ada seemed to have had a positive effect on the feisty redhead, and this pleased him considerably. He always hoped they'd get along, and during his five-year absence, they'd grown to be best friends.

McAllister's own transformation had been a bit more startling for Agatha to process, but she was quick to demonstrate how eager she was to pick up where they left off. It had been ages since they'd last seen each and she wanted to make sure he knew she was worth risking everything to come back to. To know that she still desired him and was just as insatiable and irresistible as ever.

It wasn't just physical attraction that drew them to one another. They also shared a lot in common. They were both wild and adventurous and shared a uniquely cruel and unusual sense of humor. Like McAllister, Agatha also possessed a fiery temper. There was no doubt she'd still be climbing the walls at present if he hadn't been there to comfort her.

Unfortunately, McAllister wasn't someone who could be calmed down so easily, and as a result, his mind kept on spinning. Feeling restless and unable to sleep, he eventually exited the bedroom, and his bare feet crossed lightly down the hallway. He was wearing only a pair of black skinny jeans, but it was springtime in Little Salem, so the temperature on the upper floors of the tavern was quite agreeable—even if temperature was something that barely seemed to affect him.

As he passed the room next door to his, he peeked inside, creating a narrow shaft of light that shone on the single bed that was positioned against the wall. There, Izzy lay sleeping, with an eclectic assortment of spirit traps hanging above her, still locked in the same sorry state from when she returned from the asylum. Sleeping next to her was Ada, her arms wrapped tightly around her cherished companion. Holding on for dear life as if the merciful action was the only thing keeping her from crossing over from one world to the next.

McAllister stared stone-faced at the heartfelt scene. He found himself humbled by the startling amount of compassion Ada appeared to possess. This special quality of hers didn't surprise him, but it had been so long since he'd last seen his stepsister, he'd forgotten about certain aspects of her. The depth with which she appeared to care for people, and her talent for accurately observing all that was happening around her. Still, it felt a bit silly to find himself still calling her that: "Stepsister." That was more of a private joke between them than anything, and lately, he was finding the term increasingly discomforting—especially considering his evolved feelings for his dear "sister" since their reunion two nights earlier.

He found himself focusing on the thin cotton T-shirt she was wearing, currently hiked just high enough to show off the smoothness of her navel, positioned right above a set of girlish hips molded into a pair of black briefs and attached to a pair of long spindly legs. But not high enough to show off the infamous mark she told him about years earlier; a mark with a legendary curse attached to it—something that didn't sit well with him.

In light of the awful tragedy that had happened, McAllister found it somewhat ludicrous he was allowing himself to be distracted by his nagging affections. But he also felt his blackened heart pulling him in a direction that brought with it a great deal of anxiety and trepidation. It was no wonder he felt so conflicted. He would just have to force himself to put these thoughts behind him, returning to the shadowy hallway and releasing the trap door above his head.

The rotting wooden floorboards creaked underfoot as McAllister explored the dark and dreary room. Inside, the air was dry and musty. The attic had been hermetically sealed for over a century and was presently empty save for one particular object: a battered black steamer trunk that sat bathing in moonlight from the one lonely window positioned on the attic wall.

With no time to waste, McAllister approached the item, clicking the brass snaps and opening the lid to reveal its inner contents: a meager selection of black clothing along with a collection of old books. There was John Dee's *Monos hieroglyphica*, Crowley's *Magick Without Tears*, and Austin Osman Spare's *Book of Pleasure*, along with over a dozen other worn and well-thumbed occult texts. The trunk also contained a copy of William Blake's *The Marriage of Heaven and Hell*, several trade paperback volumes of *The Invisibles*, and a red leather-bound book that had a distinctly sinister aura about it and appeared well over a century old.

At the moment, the books didn't interest McAllister in the slightest. He was still obsessing about the events from earlier—flashing in his mind for the past several hours. He recalled the sight of Izzy's body twisting and contorting as she was laid on top of the pool table, and the sound of Agatha's panicked siren call as she tore into Rudy, belittling him for abandoning Izzy at the asylum where the horrible calamity occurred.

McAllister may have been the one who sent the two novices to explore this hazardous location, but his current state of irritation wasn't due to any sense of guilt he felt about this. He was convinced there was something more at work in this situation, and he needed more information to allow him to determine what to do next.

After retrieving several items from the trunk, McAllister lowered the lid and began to prepare the space for his intended purposes. The first of these was a moderately-sized cloth tapestry that he hung on the far wall—a custom-made curiosity displaying the occult Seal of Aemeth over a black background, featuring a circle encompassing a pentagram surrounded by three heptagons, the image also littered with numerous obscure angelic names and occult symbols. The next item was a piece of chalk, which he used to draw a small circle in the center of the room. After the circle was finished, he pulled a torn, black sweater over his tightly toned torso, covering the tattoo of the Roman numeral for the number 13 on his right pectoral, and the Sigil of Lucifer that was inked on his left forearm.

With that, the stage was set. The perpetrations were complete, and he was ready to get down to business.

To begin, he performed a quick banishing ritual and sat in the circle in the lotus position; his eyes squeezed shut, body focused in total concentration

"*Thee I invoke, the Headless One,*" McAllister muttered. "*Thee, that didst create the Earth and the Heavens, that didst create the Night and the Day, that didst create the Darkness and the Light...*"

As he softly chanted this incantation, moonlight reflected off a Tibetan singing bowl positioned directly in front of him. The bowl had been placed outside of the protective circle, the interior painted inky black with the image of the moon appearing as a cold, glowing orb on the surface of the clear, motionless waters. As he continued, the water inside the bowl appeared to darken and become black as pitch with ripples forming upon the water's surface, and a soft, pervading hum of low vibrations started emanating from underneath.

The faint sound of white noise began to fill the room: a buzzing din that contained a swarm of chattering voices, as if the bizarre ceremony had allowed him access to a powerful cosmic radio dial that he was currently trying to tune. In his imagination, he visualized blurred, rippling images taking form on the surface of the water, and a shadowy figure taking shape: an aging, silver-haired patriarch with a long, ghoulish face and thin, colorless lips.

A disembodied voice addressed the figure amidst the crowd of whispers. "I tried to follow him," the voice said. "I think the rumors are true. About his transformation."

The ghoulish reflection frowned with irritation. "And?"

McAllister's eyes remained firmly closed, his face locked in a frigid disdain for the figure his cunning remote viewing happened to conjure. His hostile feelings for this man were far beyond the stony indifference he had for most people. He also had no love for the voice addressing his target, which belonged to a young, bearded man who tried to follow him earlier that evening before he managed to pull off a disappearing act that would have rivaled any of Houdini's.

These toxic emotions were an unwanted distraction while engaging in his current practice. He struggled to remain focused as he sat with his spine held perfectly straight. Listening with rapt interest as the voice addressed the apparition in the singing bowl.

"You're not...concerned?"

A brief moment of silence followed.

"I'll deal with that trash soon enough."

"*McAllister. McAllister, baby...*"

Oh, hell.

McAllister's face twitched disagreeably at the newest arrival. It was a voice he recognized instantly. The smoky quality coupled to the distinctly feminine sing-song intonation—all of this identified the owner as someone he knew quite intimately.

McAllister knew he should keep his eyes closed and try to stay focused, but his curiosity was getting the better of him. After all, if it was who he thought it was, the sudden appearance of this person (if he could call her that), was bound to bring about future challenges that one had best be prepared.

Wearing a blank expression, McAllister cautiously opened his eyes and bent forward to peer into the singing bowl. The clear, motionless waters had been replaced by the swirling image of a woman facing forward, her long chestnut-colored hair covering her face. The woman's physical presence was chilling, but even more striking was the twisted laugh that accompanied it. A laugh that was fiendish and bloodthirsty and not at all pleasant or comforting.

"Found you," the dark reflection cackled as the woman wistfully craned her head. "You know what's been killing me, baby? The way you could just leave me in Europe? Leaving me all by my lonesome when we were getting along so well. You don't want me to have to come all the way out there, do you? All the way to Little Salem to punish you for leaving a girl all on her own?"

Fast as lightning, despite any logical explanation for how it could be possible or what dark magic was being applied to allow it, two pale hands suddenly leaped from the waters, reaching for McAllister's face—and not the illusive watery reflection of such a thing, but real, actual hands that were deathly white in color and straining forward to reach right out and attack him.

The action startled him, but not to the point of total ruin. He launched his leg reflexively, kicking the bowl across the room.

As the water spread across the floor, McAllister sat back, breathing hard and staring wild-eyed at the harmless object while the mad, girlish cackle that lingered faded into nothingness.

Ah, yes. It was all coming back to him.

As if he didn't have enough problems. His suspicions had been confirmed, and things weren't looking optimistic.

While the forbidden ritual McAllister had attempted had been performed to spy on a man that he loathed with every bone and fiber in his body, his reckless and desperate actions had allowed the one fiend who was more trouble to him than anything to determine his current whereabouts.

Dakota had found him. She finally found him. No matter all he'd done to throw her off his scent and sever the ties between them, the unscrupulous hellcat had located him, and there was nowhere to run and nothing he could do about it.

Words felt trivial when addressing such a crisis, but one sarcastic and cynical comment felt more than fitting. While staring morbidly ahead of him, thinking of all the trouble he would be in now that Dakota was back in his life to torment him, McAllister sat back and lit a cigarette before expressing the one response that felt most appropriate, given his present circumstances.

"God. Dammit."

15

BLACK CELEBRATION

———————

When Ashton and Tyler rolled into Little Salem, one of the first things that caught their attention was the banner stretched across the main drag, reading, "Little Salem — Season of the Witch." The boys would later learn this annual celebration was held every spring to commemorate the town's history and the stormy events it was best known for. It was the one week out of the year where the residents didn't shy away from their controversial heritage but chose to honor it in a mostly superficial manner, hanging up tacky witch-themed Halloween decorations and holding light-hearted costume parties where anyone could don a pointy hat and even pointier nose and play at pretending to be a witch for one evening.

It was no secret the festivities were mainly a ploy to attract tourists, but the annual celebration was also held during the same time of year as one of the major holidays honored by witches across the world—and wasn't *that* a coincidence. With this special knowledge in mind, when the Truegoods learned that Ada and McAllister had finally returned to their fine community, the timing appeared eerily convenient. Regardless of any obstacles they might encounter, the troublesome duo seemed hell-bent to deliver their own imaginative take on what a proper "Season of the Witch" should amount to. One that the town would never forget.

Taking over the business directly across the street from the Truegoods' frozen yogurt shop was clearly part of a much grander and more elaborate scheme that hadn't been fully revealed, and Nancy and Wilbur finally learned what this clever arrangement was in service of two nights after McAllister burnt a pentagram onto their front lawn. It was during the witching hour when Wilbur first heard it: a faint, methodical thumping that seemed to come from outside. With the noisy racket announcing McAllister's shocking late-night visit still fresh in his mind, he jumped out of bed and rushed to the window to observe what was occurring out front. There, he was startled to discover a swarm of masked riders on BMX bikes, buzzing like locusts through the quiet, suburban setting as the monotonous thumping continued to echo from further down the street.

There was about a dozen of them, all outfitted in black hoodies and grinning skull masks, with small army surplus mail pouches slung over their shoulders. As they zoomed past the rows of picturesque houses lining the neighborhood, one by one, the masked riders jumped off their bikes and rushed to the front door of every home, dropping a piece of mail in the mail slot and sticking something to the door before scurrying away and peddling down the wet, glistening asphalt.

When one of the masked riders arrived outside the Truegoods', Wilbur felt a cold chill, gazing at the eerie skeletal grin being cast at the bedroom window before the rider made his delivery. Feeling increasingly anxious, he raced downstairs to intercept the message.

When he made it to the ground floor, he found the front door wide-open, with his daughter staring stiffly in front of her.

"Mary Sue! What are you doing? Get back upstairs and go to—"

Wilbur's voice trailed off, his words hanging in the air as he followed her gaze to what was making it so hard for her to look away.

Traveling down the street was a makeshift float accompanied by an intimidating drum line of sinister-looking clowns. An obese, painted-up monstrosity was beating time on a bass drum, while several attractive young women dressed in black cloaks, their cold countenances a mishmash of colored hair and eclectic piercings, all stood perfectly still on the slowly moving structure next to a hanged effigy of a witch and a sign, reading:

BLACK DEATH TAVERN. SPREAD THE DISEASE.

For Wilbur, the sign put everything into perspective. As the women returned harsh and heartless stares and the float continued creaking down the road, his eyes darted to the sticker the marked rider had posted on the front door: a fluorescent yellow circle featuring an Algiz rune with "lol" written over it.

Wilbur snatched a flyer away from his daughter's fingers—clearly the item that had been dropped off moments earlier. His hands were shaking, knowing all too well who was behind this and how the problems in town were now accelerating. He could already guess the flyer's message without even having to read the damned thing.

On the flyer was a single sentence:

"The Lords of Light invite you to the Black Death Tavern's Grand Opening."

Hours later, Nancy and Wilbur sat in the front pew of their neighborhood church as a tepid wave of middle-class suburbanites shuffled through the entrance. It was the end of the workday, and people were tired and distracted, many of them confused as to why their presence was requested. A sizable portion of the community showed up regardless, including the Reverend's teenage daughter, who, as usual, was looking stiff but respectable.

As the humble residents continued to file into the building, the shaky Truegood couple held hands in silence, contemplating all the disturbing events that had happened since Nancy originally convinced Reverand Palmer to organize the gathering. It may have seemed that Ada and McAllister were laying low at present to anyone other than the select few who witnessed the same alarming spectacle in the late hours of the night, but the news of the grand opening of the witches' decadent and racy bar was a matter that needed immediate attention. It was of the utmost importance to nip this in the bud immediately, and Nancy was thankful that the environment chosen to address the matter was the setting that was symbolic of all that was moral and decent in her community.

The Little Salem First Congregational Church was located on the northeastern side of Little Salem and was still a relatively new building, built in the middle of the last century. The humble residents that gathered here on a weekly basis weren't the type of folk who cared much for mega-churches or colossal, stone cathedrals, preferring to worship in spaces that were only as large as needed and moving into a roomier environment only when necessary. The current structure was built during a time when church attendance was on the rise, but it had been on a steady decline in the past decade. Whether this was because people were feeling overworked and too busy or that their faith no longer resonated with them was open for speculation, but the historic community once bound together by their religion no longer existed, and those who managed to show up to church every Sunday mostly did so out of habit and were the type of churchgoer that was prone to growing extremely antsy whenever the services stretched over the typical one-hour. Those who were present that evening all seemed to be particularly restless as well, not pleased with having to sacrifice another sixty minutes of their workweek to visit the hallowed setting. Nevertheless, tensions were running high among the normally quiet and reserved citizenry, so holding a town meeting was in order.

At five past the hour, it appeared that everyone was gathered together—or, at least, all those who were expected to show up. Reverend Palmer's bullish figure approached the pulpit, gazing at his congregation in a manner that was bluntly authoritative.

"Brothers and sisters," the Reverend said, "these are troubling times for the town of Little Salem. Under cover of night, a horrible plague rolled across our borders and has set up shop in what was once a prosperous Burrito Hut."

This was quite a bold and dramatic choice to initiate the assembly, but for the Truegoods, the introduction was pitch-perfect. They still feared that their friendly neighbors weren't taking the threat of Ada very seriously. Suspicions that were confirmed when a voice beside them whispered, "People loved that Burrito Hut."

"In its place," the Reverend continued, "these malicious outsiders have erected a palace of sin to disgrace this fine community, with the expressed intent of corrupting the hearts and minds of every citizen among us. Every one."

"When does this place open, exactly?" another voice inquired, and spirited laughter rang throughout the pews. But the Reverend was just as concerned about these developments as the Truegoods, refusing to allow his congregation to linger on the sidelines or turn a blind eye to the situation.

"Brothers and sisters, listen!" the Reverend pleaded. "Do not be tempted by these sinners! Take heed! For one does not gain access to the kingdom of heaven so easily! One does not gain access through the participation in vice, or through carnal pleasures and lust—"

The Reverend was only just getting started, but his passionate appeals were interrupted as Cheryl swiftly rose to her feet. Her husband was hovering beside her, his ever-present Bluetooth lodged into his eardrum.

"Is this bar going to affect our property values?" Cheryl asked with distress. "If our property values went up, that wouldn't be so bad, right?"

Nancy rolled her eyes as mumbles of approval rang out amongst the crowd. Thankfully, the Reverend remained persistent.

"Silence! Silence, brothers and sisters—do you not see? This is not a battle regarding property! It is a battle for our way of life! For the innocence of your children! For your very souls!"

This reasoning should have resonated strongly with the townspeople, but the Reverend's fiery words were quickly overshadowed by the sound of a minor chord playing on the church organ.

Nancy felt a discouraging sensation—as if a ghost just walked over her grave. She noticed the disturbance had startled Lucy as well. The troubled teenager turned her head to search for the cause for the interruption, but there was no one at the keys. The majority of the congregation looked baffled, but Nancy was much more mindful of what the bizarre event really meant, squeezing her husband's hand even tighter as she waited for the chaos to unfold.

The immediate follow-up to this unusual incident happened almost instantly as the doors to the church flew open and a group of hoodlums on battered BMX bikes poured into the sanctuary, speeding through the aisles like a plague of flying monkeys with menacing skull masks covering their faces and flags reading "lol" flying high above their seats. The motley skeleton crew was only an introduction as a dark masquerade of jugglers, acrobats, and fire-breathers came next, accompanied by the intimidating drum line of evil clowns. The clowns, in particular, looked especially gruesome when viewed in the full light. They were wearing crooked smiles made of false teeth and shuffling through the house of worship like the living dead, the obese clown with the bass drum beating time for the demonic procession as the throng of costumed monsters and circus freaks crowded into the main aisle, seizing control of the religious setting.

The sound of a whistle called the grisly spectacle to a halt, and the clown with the bass drum started beating his instrument in double time, inspiring the fiendish drum line to break into a funky and energetic dance routine. But all of these disquieting sights and disturbances paled in comparison to that of the figure leading the procession: Ada van Dreyer, her slender, pixieish physique all dolled up to resemble a gothic drum majorette, wearing a sparkly black leotard and fishnets. Her celestial features were transformed into those of a demented mime, with her face painted white, eyes black, and her thick, pillowy lips fixed into a black cupid grin.

Ada welcomed the unsettled response from her audience, the whole time smiling like a Harlequin as she marched to the front of the sanctuary. After striking a pose and holding her baton high in the air, the drumbeats ceased, and the gang of intruders fell still; all parties watching in silence as the magnetic monochrome bandleader cheerfully addressed the crowd of astonished church folk.

"Friends! Townspeople of Little Salem! Greetings from your new neighbors, the New Lords—or 'Lords of Light,' if you will. My name is Ada van Dreyer, and I've come to extend to you an invitation to Little Salem's newest and *nudiest* attraction: *the Black Death Tavern*."

The crowd gasped and murmured as Wilbur felt his blood turn cold, and Nancy's temperature turned feverish. This was the first time she'd seen her former protégé since Ada's fated return to the community, and what was once an uncommonly quiet and intro-verted young scamp had blossomed into something else altogether.

As anyone who'd known Ada when she was a child could have predicted, she had blossomed into a remarkably stunning young woman—but not in any way that was conventional. Some of her features still appeared too large for her face, and her bright eyes, unruly hair, and waifish form in combination with her more offbeat and eccentric proclivities seemed to meet a brand-new definition of beauty; a distinctive allure that was somewhat gawky and clumsy but also irrepressibly wild and threatening. For the cherry on top, there was also a new terrifying intensity to her; behind the impish smile and innocent appearance, something dark and dangerous was lurking. It was these traits, in particular, that took Nancy's breath away, her brow furrowing with worry as she waited for more signs to demonstrate how the witch had evolved during her absence.

"Quite a fitting name, don't you think?" Ada dryly stated. "Espe-cially considering the pleasant history of this lovely community."

Nancy glanced over to gauge how the Reverend was reacting to the incident, relieved to see he was showing no intention to tolerate the discourtesy.

"Devil!" the Reverend roared at the intruder. "Wretched, silver-tongued devil! Do you mock us?"

True to form, Ada remained markedly nonplussed.

"Mock *you?*" she delightfully oozed, strutting down the aisle and wiggling her hips suggestively. "I wish you no harm or malice. My only desire is to spread joy and good cheer. To shine like a beacon and put a smile on all your funny little faces."

"Cunning demon, I beseech you—" the Reverend implored.

But Ada had already grown tired of this exchange.

"OK, enough talking," she said, and the Reverend's microphone erupted into a loud burst of feedback.

The Reverend jumped back in a panic, and the crowd responded similarly, shrieking and covering their ears in discomfort. Things were quickly shifting from bad to catastrophic. Nancy stole a glance at Lucy and was surprised to observe the teen not looking anxious and fearful but gazing at the enigmatic young woman standing at the front of the sanctuary in what appeared to be total awe.

This was Nancy's greatest fear coming to fruition. It wasn't Ada's impossible magical abilities or her immovable grudge against the town that most filled her heart with dread. It was that her clever wits and charm would have a dangerously seductive influence on those who were most vulnerable. What Nancy dreaded most of all was it would only be a matter of time before Ada's bewitching influence spread to young girls like her daughter—a fear that appeared to be materializing right in front of her.

"So, if you've had enough of *this* three-ring circus," Ada cheekily announced, wrapping up her eccentric sales pitch, "the New Lords invite you to the best new game in town."

She paused briefly, suddenly remembered something.

"Oh! Free snow cones and balloon animals for all the kiddies. Ta!"

With her cheerful invitation concluded, Ada turned her back on her audience and marched to the front doors with her baton back in motion, signaling the ragtag gang of costumed percussionists to erupt into another riotous drum routine.

As the procession made its exit, the Reverend raced back to the pulpit in a final attempt to berate the meddlesome gatecrashers, not yet knowing it was a fool's errand to provoke his adversary or try to steal the final word from her.

"*Witch! Temptress!*" the Reverend roared. "How dare you mock this place of worship with a parade of freaks! To slither into God's house on Earth and expect God's children to—"

In retrospect, Nancy wished she could have warned him not to challenge her like he did. It was clear as crystal that Ada had already had enough of this sad little man. To illustrate this, without even bothering to turn around to face him, the dazzling misfit simply waved her fingers and ear-shattering feedback erupted from the microphone right before the pulpit burst into flames.

The abrupt fire predictably sent the crowd into a panic and Nancy watched shell-shocked as Wilbur rushed for a fire extinguisher and the entire congregation proceeded to flee the church *en masse*. The Reverend looked mystified, standing stunned and moribund as he watched his flock scatter like rats. Nancy was feeling just as distraught over the meeting's disastrous outcome but was equally disheartened to notice that Lucy was no longer present. She seemed to have snuck away at some point during the madness.

A mob was gathered, chatting and grumbling, as the Truegoods staggered outside to join the others. Their dependable neighbors were all present, standing amongst the agitated masses with each of them voicing their observations on what they just witnessed.

"I don't know about you, but caution be damned!" Steve vehemently exclaimed. "I want to check this new place out!"

"What was wrong with that sound system?" Jerry vented to his wife beside him. "I don't ever want to set foot in that place again!"

As her neighbors proceeded to nod and murmur in agreement, Nancy became filled with trepidation. Ada's strategic marketing campaign had done its business, and the residents were turning against the institutions that advised them to keep their distance.

Sensing further disaster lay waiting on the horizon, she squeezed past the unruly rabble and onto the sidewalk. She yelled at the crowd that was gathered, desperate to reason with them.

"Friends, neighbors!" Nancy pleaded. "Do not be deceived! Do not let yourselves be tempted by this cunning enchantress! As a community, we must stay strong! We must stay vigilant! We must stick together, so we do not lose what we care about most!"

But Ada's fun and trickery were not quite over. Directly across the street from where the crowd was gathered stood a young man wearing dark clothing with a battered boombox sitting at his feet. The young man was Rudy, smiling deviously as he crouched low to the ground and pressed a button on the shabby contraption and the sounds of heavy traffic, cars crashing and vehicles honking, mixed with random acts of violence, a boxing match, and other troubling noises proceeded to bleed through the speakers.

As the turbulent sounds blended with the din of the assembly's angry post-meeting gossip, the crowd started looking increasingly agitated. The townspeople began to argue, with the arguments turning into threats, the threats into shoves and, in no time at all, the Truegoods' friends and neighbors were gnashing their teeth and pulling each other's hair, throwing wild punches at one another.

Nancy found she could do little else than stand in shock as the violence continued to swell all around her, while directly across the street, Rudy was enjoying an entirely different reaction. His smile widened as he cranked up the dial on the boombox, watching gleefully as the innocent gathering turned into a full-on riot.

This change of events was more than Nancy could take. She shouted in despair for the crowd to calm themselves, but her voice could not be heard. The brutal escalation of conflict seemed to be drowning out her pleas for sanity and intensifying all around her—quickly and dramatically.

Fortunately, a police car pulled up in the nick of time before the mounting aggression got too out of control. The mob quickly dispersed like roaches at the flick of a light, leaving Nancy and Wilbur standing alone and at their wits' end on the church steps.

What on God's green earth was happening? Nancy's deepest and most nullifying fears were already being surpassed, and this was only the beginning. The beginning of the end to her precious utopia.

Ada and her cohorts were about to deliver a "Season of the Witch" they would never forget. One that was likely to have long-lasting and devastating effects. This shattering realization was being felt by both Nancy and Wilbur alike as they continued to stare at the departing throng of townspeople with Rudy smiling back at the couple while making his escape with the others. They were all walking in the direction of the tavern, everyone eager to see what the fuss was about after the successful presentation from Nancy's most formidable adversary: the notorious teenage witch, Ada van Dreyer.

16

WILD IN THE STREETS

––––––––––

When it came to the practice of witchcraft, Nancy felt she was gifted. She believed that the craft was ingrained deep inside of her and that, like all great witches, she was blessed with the power to see and to know what others could not. In nearly every culture across the world there were those who possessed such gifts, and in the past when one would seek a witch, it would usually be for one of three things: the first, an act of divination foretelling the future, tradition-ally performed with tarot cards or by consulting the stars or another similar method; the second, a charm for healing or good fortune or for cursing that was often performed using herbalism or sympathetic magic. The third, and most dangerous of these, was the request to petition the spirits for knowledge or favors, and to do so required a strong connection to the hidden realm beyond the veil. A world that was concealed from most and wasn't meant for normals.

Taking these three specific practices into consideration, this is where Nancy's perception of her abilities could be argued as being slightly exaggerated. It was true that she felt a special connection to the universe and was highly intuitive, but when it came to the art of divination, she was utterly useless. And when it came to spells and curses, utilizing whatever course was available, she wasn't very skilled at this either. But most significantly, when it came to spirit work, she was a complete and total failure. Despite her strong gifts of perception and kinship to nature, she had only a loose and almost nonexistent connection to the non-material world. With the exception of the one significant spiritual encounter that started her along the path of witchery, she had no contact at all with the spirits—at least not intentionally. She could often feel them whispering to her and pointing her in various directions, but this rarely amounted to anything, as usually, these signals were very dim.

Normally, Nancy was fine with this. She may have been a proud practicing witch, but still identified as a Christian. When these identities were in conflict, she felt more comfortable with having the faith she was brought up with take the wheel while letting the whole "pointy hat and broomstick" bit take the backseat. Trafficking with spirits was a messy business, so she offered her nightly devotions to her Lord and Savior and spoke her prayers aloud at every meal and had very little communication with the world beyond this one. She'd already accepted that forming a connection with the spirit world just wasn't for her, leaving her free to indulge in her preferred comforts and practices in the areas she felt most safe. The only problem with this decision was it left her woefully unprepared for the day she would cross paths with a witch who did have this type of connection. And the notorious Ada van Dreyer had it in spades.

Where Ada's powers came from Nancy wasn't entirely sure. She had some idea, but she didn't know the whole story, and Ada's gifts were genuinely inexplicable and not the slightest bit ordinary. Every so often, one would hear a story about a monk in Tibet who meditated every hour of the day for ninety years and somehow managed to demonstrate a fraction of the young witch's abilities. But even this comparison still came up short. At a young age, Ada had dazzled witches with generations on her, and had only proceeded to grow stronger and stronger, being able to perform the impossible without breaking a sweat—and she was still just a teenager. Whether Ada's abilities were tied to a special connection to the world that Nancy avoided and found utterly unexplainable or there was much more to this, she couldn't say. The one thing that was certain was Ada was ten times the witch she would ever be, which is what made her such a formidable opponent.

Ada's prodigious nature was one of the reasons why her return to Little Salem had Nancy feeling so terrified. She knew just how outmatched she was when it came to dealing with her former protégé. Of course, there were also much more complicated personal feelings attached to this fear as well. When Nancy first met Ada, she felt a strong kinship with the unique and remarkable girl and not only saw something of herself in the budding young witch but also thrilled at the idea of being regarded as a mentor to someone with such an unnatural level of potential. Regretfully, it didn't take long for her to realize that Ada had no need for a mentor, especially when it came to someone as lackluster with applied magical practice as herself. Ada had always been fated to be so much more than her so-called teacher, and now, after not seeing hide nor hair of her for almost five years, she discovered that in her absence Ada had surpassed her in every way. Ada was young, beautiful, powerful, and she charmed everyone in a manner that Nancy could only dream—even despite her own immense likeability. She remained convinced it would only be a matter of time before Ada would charm her beloved daughter. Just like she had charmed her former teacher five years earlier.

The fear of this potentially disastrous but highly probable outcome was racing through Nancy's mind as she stared at the recently renovated Victorian while listening to the rumbling bass beats vibrating from within. Following the disastrous town meeting, Nancy and Wilbur returned to the yogurt shop to check on their daughter and observe the unpleasant disruption that the tavern's opening festivities were having on the community. An unruly hoard of gregarious out-of-towners seemed to be showing up in droves, forming a long line down the street. And, just as was forewarned, Ada's circus of freaks was handing out free snow cones to the children who had snuck away to catch a glimpse of the curious spectacle.

Upon their arrival, Mary Sue informed her parents how Lucy had somehow hustled her way inside, driving Wilbur and the Reverend to take off to search for her. For Nancy, Lucy wasn't the problem. It was only Ada that concerned her. Ada, Ada, and nothing but Ada. On her mind like a scratch she could not itch; the dread of what would happen when her daughter met the witch eating at her like maggots on a rotting corpse.

Mary Sue would take a liking to Ada immediately, Nancy reminded herself. With her cool clothes and eccentric appearance—the bright-eyed skinny little thing. She would love Ada more than anything; more than her own mother, especially. That was what stung most of all about Ada's return to Little Salem: the reminder that in comparison to the irritating prodigy, Nancy would always be second-rate. As a mother and a woman in addition to a witch.

"I don't want you working at the shop anymore," Nancy said while staring at the ominous black building across the street. "Not while all of this..."

For a moment, Mary Sue appeared distressed to hear this but managed to hold her tongue as she watched Reverend Palmer exit the tavern while firmly clinging to his shaken teenage daughter.

Nancy's eyes widened considerably at the sight. As he pulled the poor girl away from the dark and hostile setting, her mind once again started racing, watching Wilbur stare despondently at the wild, hedonistic party that was raging in the bar behind him before turning back to face her and shrugging helplessly.

No. Nancy wasn't going to leave things the way they were. With her whole world crumbling around her, she knew it was now or never to make her voice heard. Not just to the group of renegade witches who were currently laughing and drinking themselves into a mindless stupor, but also to the entire town.

"*Ada van Dreyer!*" Nancy balled her fists while stomping forward. "This is Nancy Truegood! Come outside and face me, dammit! I demand that you show yourself!"

As Nancy's fierce and passionate words echoed in the air, the riotous atmosphere that surrounded her fell silent. The scary-looking clowns, fire breathers, and circus performers, along with those who were still waiting to join the party raging inside the tavern, were all quietly staring in her direction at the furious wild-eyed woman standing like a statue in the middle of the street.

For several moments, it felt like all time on the planet had come to a grinding halt; the only sound that could be heard was Nancy's fiery breaths. The silence was eventually broken as the soft creeping of a pair of boots came clicking across the tavern's front porch, and Nancy was suddenly facing the living embodiment of all her most horrible nightmares: Ada, standing by the entrance while stroking a tiny black kitten in her arms.

"Something on your mind, grandma?" Ada was still dressed in her goth drum majorette outfit, her sparkly black leotard shimmering under the moonlight. All of the mime makeup had been washed from her face, but the smile she wore couldn't have been more chilling if it had been painted on her lips.

"You think I'm going to take this lying down?" Nancy hissed. "Let you waltz into my town and watch you torment my husband, corrupt my daughter, and poison my community with your clever words and ways?"

Unsurprisingly, Ada didn't appear bothered in the slightest by these outbursts and proceeded to slink down the steps, her impish smile widening as her narrow hips swayed from side to side and a glaring intensity began to form behind her eyes.

"Aww. What happened to the love, Nancy?" Ada pouted. "I was like a daughter to you once. Before I saw through that clever mask you wear."

All of a sudden, a slight wind began to blow down the street, brushing against Nancy's hair and sending a cold chill throughout her bones. Deep down, she knew this was a warning she should keep her distance. But she was too fired up to take heed.

"Ada? You messed with the wrong witch."

With that, Nancy began to approach her former ward and protégé, but the poor woman should have known better. After taking her first step, an invisible force immediately pushed her back while Ada kept her unearthly blue-violet eyes held fast on her nemesis.

Incredibly, the more Nancy struggled to press forward, the more the wind picked up, pushing her further and further back with every laborious step. With her feet sliding clumsily about like she was walking on ball bearings, it didn't take long for her to realize that all of her efforts to reach the girl would be fruitless. Meanwhile, Ada was charming the crowd, winking and smiling like the dramatic confrontation was all part of the planned entertainment. The guests who were waiting in line were laughing, and so was the gathering of freaks. Even the children, with remnants of snow cones stained on their faces—they were all laughing as well. Securing Ada's status even further as an expert showwoman and entertainer, effortlessly demonstrating how at the end of the day, she would be the one to have the last laugh. Without even breaking a sweat.

No. Nancy refused to settle for this.

There was too much at stake.

For the good of the town, her daughter, and, perhaps most of all, herself, she refused to be Ada's fool. She continued to struggle forward, regardless of whatever humiliation she would suffer, her unbending stubbornness causing the wind to pick up even further, inspiring the spectators to shield themselves from the powerful gale that was so violent and forceful, it looked like it would tear the woman to pieces at any moment. She probably would have continued her useless efforts to the point of mortal injury if the one person with the ability to stop her hadn't suddenly stepped in.

"Mom! Stop!"

At the sound of her daughter crying out to her, Nancy's eyes widened, and her body stiffened.

"Please," Mary Sue begged. "Just let her be."

Nancy felt her spirits sink and her face turn pale at the request. Dear God, it was already beginning: her daughter was turning against her. With her perfect life of comfort practically shattered beyond repair, she backed away and lowered her head in shame.

With Nancy's reluctant surrender, the punishing wind died down, and her mood sank even further as her credulous audience erupted into a round of applause. The response was mortifying, but the distasteful reaction didn't bother her as much as the final words from the witch who continued to smile defiantly while petting the purring black kitten held snugly in her arms—a kitten that hadn't reacted at all during the confrontation.

"Your time in the sun is up," Ada said. "*Our time* has just begun."

Nancy remained silent the whole drive home and was still wide-awake long after the rest of her family had gone to bed. It was around the time of the witching hour, and she was sitting at the kitchen table with a half-empty wine glass in front of her, staring miserably at the walls while a decorative wooden cross looked down on her.

Ada.

Ada.

Ada.

Like a bug that had crawled underneath her skin, that name had bored its way into her brain.

How dare she make a fool of her? How dare she.

But what was she to do?

It seemed that all of her efforts had no effect on her opponent. As much she didn't want to acknowledge it, Ada had held true to her warning from five years earlier, and her curse against the town was coming into realization.

No. Defeat was not an option.

She too had the power to make others suffer—and if it was a curse that Ada desired, then a curse is what she would get.

Nancy had avoided petitioning the spirits for much of anything at this point, but right then and there she decided she'd be willing to traffic with the blackest and most horrifying of all of them to remove the vile pestilence that was feeding on her family and community and making her appear more useless by the minute.

Yes, if it was malice these witches wanted, then Nancy would give it to them. If it was chaos and disorder they worshipped, then she would create as much of this for them as well. With her mission firmly in place, she downed her glass of wine and retrieved her witch's kit, returning to the metal-paneled garden shed to engage once again in this wretched business. Only this time, she was willing to give up everything to make it stick.

17

DREAMS IN THE WITCH HOUSE

There was a good reason why Tyler and Ashton had no knowledge of Ada's appearance at the church and why they wouldn't hear about this event or any of the drama that unfolded until much later. For the Ghost Bros, the morning after Ada's masked riders delivered their invitations started very tense as Tyler struggled to convince his friend to finally start addressing the giant elephant that was in the room with them: Ada van Dreyer.

Ashton was sitting on the edge of the bed, looking introspective. "I don't know what comes over me. Being around Ada's like being on some crazy drug... That probably doesn't sound too healthy."

"No, dude," Tyler sighed. "Drugs like that aren't healthy."

Ashton's erratic behavior over the past couple of days had led Tyler to conclude that, despite his initial impressions, the incomparable strangeling his fellow ghost hunter was spending an increasing amount of time with was bad news. Ashton initially tried to dismiss these reservations, but he now felt inclined to agree with him. For one thing, he still couldn't remember how he arrived back at the hotel following his outing with Ada to Gallows Hill. The fact that he had slept for nearly twenty-four hours right after was equally bewildering. There was also the manic behavior he displayed at the graveyard once Ada rushed off to meet her so-called brother, with Ashton aggressively berating his fellow ghost hunter after Tyler accused him of developing an unhealthy obsession that was causing him to neglect what was going on with his girlfriend back in Boston.

The primary cause for these unusual acts of behavior remained a mystery, but Ashton was steadily growing more confident that the pretty young woman with the haunting blue-violet eyes and distinctly charming and mysterious personality was clearly involved in these matters. Meanwhile, Tyler remained stumped when it came to the hidden significance behind many of the bizarre occurrences they'd witnessed since their arrival. The sudden appearance of Ada's motley crew and their hostile makeover of the tavern, the strange occult markings in the hotel attic, the dire warnings from Lucy—Tyler was eager to get to the bottom of these things. More than anything, he felt driven to get himself and Ashton back on track in terms of addressing the purpose for why they made the journey to Little Salem in the first place.

After engaging in a highly necessary but difficult discussion about all the things that had happened, the boys decided they would work to avoid crossing paths with Ada and start devoting all their energies toward searching for noteworthy signs of paranormal phenomena, hoping to discover that one significant piece of evidence that would increase the traffic to their paranormal YouTube channel and propel them into the world of global celebrity.

There was one problem that stood in the way of this plan: Even though the boys had journeyed to Little Salem with ghost hunting on their minds and been in town for three days, they still had no clue where to search for the experience they were looking for. Tyler was the one to suggest they should use the map that Ada had marked up for reference, but once they were on the road, he grew to regret this. After driving a short distance, Ashton pulled up in his Prius to a seventeenth-century red saltbox home that sat on the south side of town—the historic dwelling of one of Little Salem's most infamous residents, a woman who'd been known as Rebecca Nurse.

Ashton carefully surveyed the landscape as they crossed to their destination. "Rebecca Nurse was one of the women who was executed during the Salem witch trials."

"Witches?" Tyler groaned. "Aw, dude—don't tell me we're back to witches!"

"Check it out."

Tyler momentarily swallowed his indignation as he turned to where Ashton was pointing: to a collection of weather-beaten graves within a stone's throw of the building.

"Ada writes that after Rebecca Nurse was hanged, her body was thrown into a shallow grave next to the gallows because alleged witches were forbidden a Christian burial. Her family had to steal her body away in the middle of the night so they could bury it at the family home."

For Tyler, this information triggered a profound emotional response. If he'd known the full story, he would have known that Rebecca Nurse was one of the most beloved inhabitants in Little Salem prior to the accusations made against her at the height of the Salem witch trials. He also would have known that while the trials were taking place, many of the locals remained convinced she was the spitting image of a God-fearing Christian woman and that the wild allegations against her were a total farce. Unfortunately, many of the accused's closest friends and neighbors were much too fearful of voicing their disagreements, but historians would later argue that Rebecca Nurse's execution marked the decisive moment where the townspeople finally turned against the trials and the pack of deceitful girls pointing fingers at the community.

Not the most avid student of history, Tyler was unfamiliar with these details, but the brief info provided by Ada was enough to move him to quiet contemplation. For several moments, the boys examined the grave in silence before turning away and heading to the household's front entrance.

"Hello? Anybody home?"

The home of the accused witch was a collection of small rooms containing a modest assortment of period wooden furniture. The furnishings were sparse and simple, as was the tradition in those days, and Tyler filmed the empty spaces that littered the ground floor while Ashton located the ancient wooden staircase and took off to explore the upper levels.

As Ashton climbed the stairs, his eyes glanced at his EMF meter, checking for signs of abnormal electronic energies. Everything appeared normal—that is, until he reached the master bedroom; a room that was almost bare save for a couple of old wooden beds. He noticed the needle on the device suddenly spike and crossed further into the room, thrilling at the possibility of genuine paranormal activity taking place somewhere in the vicinity.

"Yo, Tyler! Get up here!"

The prospect that the first location they visited housed a spiritual presence gave Ashton a rush of excitement. A silly grin spread across his face. One he was still wearing as he turned to get a better look at his surroundings and spied an elderly woman standing in the corner, silently staring back at him.

"Oh. Hello. We didn't know anyone..."

The woman's appearance was perplexing. Ashton couldn't recall anyone standing there when he entered, but he initially wrote this off as the result of being distracted. While adjusting to the surprise of discovering he wasn't alone, he took a closer look at the woman, noticing she was of average height and quite slender. She had long, silver hair that was parted in the middle and was dressed in what appeared to be an old-fashioned white nightdress.

There was a look of disturbed bewilderment in the woman's bright and soulful gaze, and Ashton became worried he had barged unknowingly into someone's current residence. A fear that intensified as Tyler rushed into the room, with Ashton signaling for him to lower his camera as he attempted to communicate with the stranger.

"Sorry. Do you live here?" Ashton inquired with embarrassment. "We thought this was a museum. We didn't mean to—"

"Are you...film students?" asked the woman.

Ashton exchanged a cautious glance with his associate.

"Uh, yeah—we're students. We're also paranormal investigators. We hunt ghosts and stuff."

The woman appeared to smile with open amusement before Tyler started chiming in with his own pressing questions.

"Do you live here? You haven't had any spooky experiences in this house, have you? Any ghosts or anything...strange?"

"Can't say I have," the woman answered, appearing to have dropped her guard as she wandered out of the bedroom and into the hall. "Although this house does hold a troubling history. You can almost feel the weight of it."

Ashton and Tyler once again exchanged cagey glances before hurrying after the stranger. After catching up to her, Ashton wasted no time in resuming the lead role in the questioning.

"Rebecca Nurse—the woman who lived here. You think she was a witch?"

The elderly woman chuckled light-heartedly. "Oh, heavens no, far from it. She was just a simple woman who got caught up in something much larger. Larger than anyone could have predicted."

The woman smiled warmly, her face becoming bashful and self-conscious. "Please, forgive me. I'm just an old woman rambling."

"No, we're interested," Ashton said. "There's something super weird about this town. We've both noticed it."

Despite their initial reservations, Ashton and Tyler were now in agreement: There was something uniquely strange and off-putting about Little Salem. With each passing day and every unusual discovery, they became more convinced that beneath the setting's pleasant small-town exterior, something sinister was hiding under the surface. But regardless of their convictions, they weren't prepared for the words that the woman was about to deliver.

"My poor dears," the woman said, "there are *dark forces* at work. Fighting for the hearts and minds of all who are living in this town and places much further. And they will stop at nothing to achieve their goals."

Ashton felt his blood rush at the revelation while Tyler glanced up at the wooden cross hanging above the stairway. It appeared they had stumbled upon a goldmine. One that held the keys to all the unsettling secrets involving the impossibly ordinary community they'd chosen to visit.

As Ashton stared in all earnestness at the woman, he made sure to maintain a composed demeanor, masking his determination to receive more answers.

"Tell us more about these dark forces."

The elderly woman sat with Ashton at a small wooden table while a patter of footsteps creaked across the floorboards, his fellow investigator exploring the other rooms.

"So is it true?" Ashton asked the woman. "Were the Salem witch trials brought about because of a political war between two families?"

Surprisingly, the woman shook her head. "This wasn't a matter of two families," she said. "What happened in Little Salem was part of the age-old battle between good and evil."

Tyler was in another room when he decided to add his two cents to the conversation. "You can't be serious," he said. "A handful of Puritans accused of being witches and suddenly it's a holy war?"

The woman remained unfazed by the comment, her soulful eyes gazing at Ashton with intensity.

"Young man, Little Salem may look like an ordinary town from the outside, but underneath...there are dark machinations at work.

"Those mysterious events that happened back then—mysterious and marvelous, astonishing events. These events made some very powerful people very worried indeed. An evil faction with unsavory levels of influence secretly manipulating things from behind the scenes. Oh, how they wish they could have made those mysterious and marvelous events *unhappen*.

"And so there were the trials and later the hysteria, and even much later special safeguards were put in place should anyone ever wish to confront this collective of ruthless and treacherous..."

The woman's confession had Ashton riveted, but his face shifted to one of concern as he watched her wince in agony, suddenly appearing light-headed.

Moving quickly, he reached out to assist her, but she relented, holding up a shaky hand to dissuade him.

"I'm sorry. I think I may have talked myself out for the time being."

As soon as she said this, Tyler entered the room, pointing to his watch—a move that inspired Ashton to frown bitterly and rise to his feet. As much as he wanted to continue the discussion, he accepted it was probably best for them to leave. But based on the woman's statements, it appeared that his suspicions were accurate.

Something was undeniably rotten at the heart of Little Salem.

The purpose for their being there now seemed crystal clear. The boys had stumbled onto a timeless mystery, and the plot was thickening. Ashton was fired up by this information but knew they needed more answers to get to the bottom of things.

"Thanks for the chat," Ashton told the woman. "If it's OK, we'd like to pop by at another time. Maybe talk to you some more?"

The woman smiled warmly. "You young men are just lovely. Yes, that would be fine. Be wary of who you meet out here. Friend and foe can be very hard to tell apart at times."

The two investigators crossed to the exit and Ashton turned back, wearing a solemn expression. There was one last question he needed to ask her, his curiosity getting the best of him.

"Who are these people? The ones plotting from the shadows."

The directness of this query caused the woman's smile to fade away before it was forced once again upon her lips. Her overall composure suddenly appeared much frailer and had taken on a troubled air of heavy uneasiness.

"They have been called many things across the years," she said. "Today, they call themselves *the Scarlet Council*."

* * *

The investigation of the Rebecca Nurse Homestead may have been unsuccessful, but Ashton and Tyler eventually agreed to return to the residence later that night. The goal was to search for an explanation for the sudden spike on Ashton's EMF meter while he was exploring the house's upper levels. But when the boys returned, they found the home locked and bolted, and a roving security guard explained that nobody had lived there since the 1920s and for the past few months the property had been closed for renovations.

Feeling incredibly shaken by this information, Ashton did some further research on the internet after Tyler had gone to bed. There, he discovered several illustrations of Rebecca Nurse that were similar to the woman he had conversed with—although he never found out for certain who he had met...

18

THINGS FALL APART

The Black Death Tavern's grand opening festivities were in full swing when McAllister slumped down the stairs and into the main room. The music was loud, the drinks were strong, and the bar was packed with an eclectic selection of goth and industrial types, bikers, thrill-seekers, and other assorted shady characters, drinking and partying with a small selection of wide-eyed locals thrown in for good measure. The stripper poles were in full use, and tattooed, scantily clad go-go dancers of various sexes and orientations were bopping, jerking, and twerking to sleazy electronic music being spun for a crowded dance floor filled with wild inebriates.

Throughout the riotous assembly, most of Ada's coven was present. Ada, still dressed in her goth drum majorette outfit, was sharing one of the stripper poles with two dancers, wiggling her hips and smiling with total abandon while Agatha was busy tending bar, receiving oodles of attention while flirting with the customers to her own delightful and devilish amusement. The grand opening was a hit, and the party was raging. But despite the high spirits and the cheeky vocals attached to the current churning musical selection proclaiming "*this sh#t will f**k you up*," McAllister saw no cause for celebrating, and his mood was grim.

McAllister's mind was poring over the information recovered from the asylum; in particular, the death certificate of Tom Thumb—the patient who was rumored to have gone mad after an unfortunate encounter with a "man in black." The certificate listed the man's former employment as a butler, and his burial was paid for by the ancestor of a man McAllister knew quite intimately—information that didn't sit well with him. There was also the matter of the protection circle in the hotel attic along with the word, "Vassago"—the name of a demon one would contact when looking for something that had been lost or stolen. McAllister was convinced that Tom Thumb and the ritual had some hidden connection to each other, and a bizarre picture of events was coming into focus. But despite these findings, the location of the diary remained elusive—and to make matters even more frustrating, he was feeling physically ill due to a complicated personal issue he'd rather not think about.

There was also the matter with Izzy, who continued to suffer from violent physical attacks and hallucinations. McAllister had spent the whole day looking after the poor girl, and during this time concluded her attacks were the result of something following her home from the séance. Izzy was convinced the ghost of Tom Thumb was tormenting her, and in the wake of suffering a particularly brutal attack from the spirit, she revealed the deceased mental patient had never recovered from the shock of something he saw while he was still living. The violence against her always seemed to occur when she was all alone, and to make matters even more complicated, the spirit apparently seemed hell-bent on trying to possess her (as if McAllister and the others didn't already have enough on their plates).

And the hits didn't stop there. There was also the business with Dakota, along with a string of other mildly vexing problems and irritations that needed some serious sorting out *tout suite*. And all of these things were out of McAllister's control—the one thing that annoyed him more than anything.

The toxic accumulation of mounting anxieties assaulting McAllister's restless headspace was enough to drive a person totally bats. To help his body cope with this tireless storm of obstacles, he grabbed a bottle of rum off of the tray of a passing waitress as he crossed to a booth marked VIP. With the way things were going, he wanted nothing more than to enjoy a stiff drink and fade into the scenery. But on his way to his destination, he had one more matter to deal with, intercepting Rudy, dancing with two hotties, and shouting at him over the loud music.

"Izzy. You're on deck."

"Aw, but McAllister—"

McAllister shoved Rudy away from him before he could finish his sentence. *The nerve of him,* McAllister thought as he slumped into the empty booth. As if he didn't have enough troubles. Tom Thumb, Dakota, Vassago, Izzy, and now Rudy. And then there was the matter of the enchanting young women in his life.

Agatha was the first to catch McAllister's eye as he observed his stunning girlfriend perched behind the bar, smiling like a movie star and flirting with a growing cluster of lovesick clientele. Things had been going well between them, but after only a few days, he was starting to feel distracted, and he could tell she could sense this. There was no use trying to keep secrets from a witch, after all.

The reason for this current state of restlessness rested with his sweet and irrepressible stepsister. For nearly five years, McAllister and Ada had barely spoken, and he was still having great difficulty in finding any comfort in how he was being drawn to the young woman she had matured into. Even at that moment, he found his eyes longing to look at her, becoming hypnotized by her movements as she laughed wildly and without restraint; shimmying next to the dancers to the side of her, her body gyrating seductively to the music.

The curve of her serpentine hips, the nape of her enticing neck, the sparkly black leotard hugging her breasts and every inch of her dainty torso. McAllister's eyes were drawn to all of these things but always eventually landed on the slope of the left side of Ada's ribcage, knowing what was branded there and the terrible curse attached to it. There was no question he had strong feelings for her, but he felt depressingly certain he couldn't ignore the fiendish mark, no matter how hard he tried. This wasn't something someone could forget about and naïvely hope for the best. The mark was perpetual and inescapable—like the hunger festering inside of him.

What a pain. Such bitterness accompanies these wretched feelings, McAllister thought wearily. As he continued to dwell on all the things eating away at him, he caught Ada's striking blue-violet eyes locked onto him; seeming to invite him to watch her further and devour her sensual movements free of any inhibition whatsoever.

For a moment, McAllister found himself becoming lost in the seductive allure of the charming solicitation. But he forced himself to look away when a pretty waitress with a distinctive assortment of facial piercings approached the booth and presented a note to him.

"Yes?"

"Man told me to give this to you."

"Who?"

"I didn't catch his face."

McAllister maintained a stony expression as he unfolded the peculiar article. The message inside was brief:

BEWARE THE IDES OF MARCH.

McAllister tensed up, his eyes darting around the room.

The sender's identity—was he still here? No, trying to locate the man was pointless. The tavern's entrance, the crowded dance floor, the back exit—there were strangers everywhere. The only faces he recognized were Ada, Agatha, Rudy—wait. Rudy?

McAllister's rabid gaze drifted toward the ceiling. Over the loud music, he could barely make out the sound coming from two floors above him—the worst thing he could hear on this occasion: the sound of muffled screams. As Rudy continued tearing up the dance floor, still sandwiched between two beauties, he felt a cold hand grasp onto his shoulder—a sight Ada and Agatha both witnessed, watching as McAllister, now aggressively hostile and livid, dragged the skinny hooligan out of the room.

Inside one of the guest rooms on the tavern's third floor, Izzy sat up in bed, screaming her aching lungs out with what little voice she had left. What she saw before her was like something out of the most traumatizing and disturbing of nightmares: the outline of a dark shadowy presence sitting in a chair across from her; not quite standing but not quite sitting either, appearing like it was about to pounce at any moment.

The terrifying vision now torturing her every waking moment was different from her glimpse of the figure back at the asylum. It seemed like the decaying mortal form she contacted had since deteriorated, and the only feature now clearly visible was the entity's gleaming crooked scowl. With the spirit continuing to direct its sights on her specifically, it appeared increasingly consumed with the attempt to feed on its target's life force, no doubt looking to gain a more permanent footing in the material world. To defend herself, all Izzy could do was scream until Ada rushed into the room, pulling her into her arms, knowing that whatever had her friend so frightened was something she alone could see and only had designs for her.

Ada had her suspicions for why this was happening but had little knowledge of what she was supposed to do in such a crisis. Spells and spirit traps had failed to remove the presence, leaving her with little else to do than grasp Izzy tightly and hug her close.

"Izzy, it's OK," Ada said. "I'm here. I'm right here."

Outside the bedroom, Rudy stood in the hallway with McAllister only inches away, exploding with uncontrollable fury.

"You're on thin ice with me, Rudy," McAllister snarled. "When I ask you to do something? When you have a responsibility to perform? It means it needs to be done *now. Now! Not* after you're finished talking to girls, *not* sometime next week, I'm talking *now! Right now! Fucking immediately! Do you hear me?*"

McAllister pounded his fist against the wall as Rudy cowered before him. It was probably not entirely fair of him to be unleashing his personal frustrations on the poor fellow, but Rudy had flaked on one of his duties and failed everybody.

"Yeah—yes, I'm sorry," he whimpered. "I'm—"

Agatha stood nearby witnessing the dramatic episode, woefully incapable of caring any less about the humiliation her fellow comrade was receiving. She was much more preoccupied with her troubled relationship with his accuser.

As McAllister predicted, Agatha had noticed him becoming increasingly attentive toward his estranged stepsister, and the situation was becoming grating. But there was another item that had her feeling some cause for concern—something about McAllister's appearance that she hadn't noticed until that moment.

While standing in the hallway waiting to speak to him, she happened to observe what looked like a rash upon his neck. And not just any ordinary rash but a deformed spiderweb of infected blood vessels, some of them bright red in color and some bruised purple and inky black. Evidence that something deeply disturbing appeared to be happening to him internally—as if his blood had been poisoned and was thirsting for a cure.

Putting this strange ailment aside, Agatha had other matters she wanted to address. Once Rudy fled to the bedroom to check on Izzy, she approached her tempestuous sweetheart, eager to move their thorny relationship to a more stable footing.

"We need to talk."

"Not now."

"Dammit, McAllister! You've been dodging me all day!"

"Deal with it."

Wearing a frigid look of irritation, McAllister turned away from her and slumped down the hallway while rubbing the mark on his neck. He wasn't blind to what was going on with him but was hoping he could spare the others from all that horrible business.

As McAllister departed, Agatha watched as he pulled down the trap door and disappeared into the attic. She was so fired up she wanted to scream, but the sounds of sobbing drew her attention away from her noxious emotions to Izzy's bedroom. Rudy and Ada were embracing their unfortunate colleague as a heartrending ocean of tears poured down Izzy's cheeks.

"When will it end? When will the nightmare end?"

Agatha felt her spirits sink even further after witnessing these words. She hoped that Ada would provide a miracle to save their shattered friend. But Ada, looking lost and alone, her bright, uncanny eyes now cloudy and dim, could only frown with dismay.

19

WALKING WITH A GHOST

———————

Ada and her gang weren't the only ones suffering from problems involving the paranormal of late. Ashton's girlfriend was dealing with her own share of unpleasant experiences, ever since her boyfriend left her in Boston to seek out the supernatural in Little Salem. For the past few days, Mercy had been cat-sitting for Ashton at his swanky upscale apartment in the ritziest part of town. It was the part of urban Boston where all of the multi-story apartment and condo blocks were brand-new—or refurbished to appear as such—with all of the household fixtures catering to the most discerning of tastes and containing high-class lobbies wired with top of the line surveillance and CCTV to scare off any unwanted solicitors and the occasional low-class riff-raff.

The apartment was paid for by Ashton's father, likely as a token in exchange for being so absent in his son's life, and was mostly sparse except for the bare essentials and the occasional object relating to Ashton's ghost hunting hobby or his obsession with cult horror DVDs. But despite the preference for ghoulish entertainment and the excess of ghost-related paraphernalia, this wasn't the type of environment that was known to be haunted or where spirits would frequently visit—which is precisely what made Mercy's present predicament all the more shocking and difficult to deal with.

It was three nights earlier that Mercy first saw the distressing figure—on the night following Ashton's arrival in Little Salem. She was playing with her tarot cards and just received an especially unsettling reading when she spotted Ashton's orange tabby, Max, growling into the darkness of the open bedroom closet. Mercy had never seen the cat act so strangely, so to put her mind at ease, she rose from the bed and crossed to the doorway, gazing into the void that awaited her. It almost felt like the cold, shapeless darkness was daring her to investigate further, but when she hit the light, there was nothing there—or at least nothing that had no place being there to begin with. Just clothes, books, a selection of shoes. The usual.

With the matter seeming to be settled, Mercy switched off the light and frowned at the tabby, feeling embarrassed for thinking anything could be wrong in the first place. She headed straight to bed, believing the disturbance was behind her, not knowing that this hasty appraisal couldn't have been further from the case. It was the middle of the night when a noise suddenly awakened her—a noise that upon later recollection, she curiously couldn't remember. When she opened her eyes, that's when she saw her, receiving the warning that had been echoing in her head for the past several days:

"Your friend is in danger."

The ghost left several additional messages but had only shown herself as a full-bodied apparition once more—and only to express the same unsettling warning, disappearing quickly afterward. Mercy had been having trouble sleeping ever since. The fact that it was becoming increasingly difficult to get a hold of Ashton while he was away only increased her sense of discomfort.

Mercy had placed several phone calls to her boyfriend but received no reply. She did manage to briefly communicate her growing apprehensions to Tyler, knowing nothing of the girl that Ashton had been spending time with and who was wholly responsible for why his phone ceased to function whenever she was present. Since Tyler was in Little Salem as well, there was little he could do to assist her, and he ended up ringing up Eddie Specter to check on the apartment in his absence.

"The glare off these walls doesn't make me look too pale, does it?" Eddie was addressing two black-T-shirted members of his TV crew as they tested the light and the acoustics in all the different rooms. "It's cool. We can dress it up. Fix it in post. Whatever."

Mercy was only slightly familiar with the popular TV personality. As the girlfriend of an aspiring ghost hunter, she mostly humored her boyfriend's obsessions and left them to be enjoyed in the exclusive company of his fellow "Ghost Bro." But Mercy didn't live under a rock and was aware that Eddie was the star of the popular paranormal reality show *Ghost Warriors*. She knew he was something of a cult icon and a notable inspiration for her boyfriend's amateur investigations. Even with this knowledge, she wasn't the type of girl to go all starry-eyed and breathless in the man's presence. For her, the dude glancing at the EMF reader balanced lazily in his palm looked closer to the standard imitation of a typical muscle-bound jock with a fetish for black T-shirts, black hair dye, and spooky pseudo-religious tattoos than anyone who could ever hope to be taken seriously by someone of her fine caliber.

"So how long have the spooks been knocking?"

"Spooks?"

"The little blonde girl who's been haunting you."

"Um, I don't know—a few days? You said Tyler called you?"

The sudden attention gave Mercy quite a start. Moments earlier, Eddie had arrived unexpectedly while she was already on her way out the door. All her nerves were still shot and slightly on edge. She had no idea Eddie would be the one Tyler would enlist to address her situation and had been hoping that the information would get back to Ashton, driving him to finally reemerge. Unfortunately, Ashton was miles away and still avoiding her calls for some reason, so she had no choice but to accept whatever help she could get at this juncture—which included tolerating the bold and buffoonish charlatan smiling at her like a strange animal of some kind.

"Tyler. That's right," Eddie noted. "Must feel nice to have a guy looking out for you like that."

Noticing his comment didn't appear to reassure her, he added, "Hey. Don't stress, dollface. We're professionals"—a statement ironically followed by a loud hiss as one of Eddie's flunkies barely avoided stepping on Ashton's cat.

"Pretty much getting normal readings right now, which means it's probably nothing serious. Here's what we'll do. You eyeball those release forms, then maybe we'll stop by tomorrow and put on a little show for you and the spooks. Sound good?"

One of Eddie's goons shoved some documents into her paws.

Mercy glanced at the papers in confusion. "Put on...a show?"

"In the meantime," Eddie stressed, "lock your doors, burn some white candles, and, um, put up some wind chimes."

Eddie flashed a cocky grin as he leaned toward her.

"Ghosts hate that shit."

And with that, Eddie and his crew were out the door, leaving her feeling just as anxious as if they'd never shown up.

"Adios, babe! Eddie Specter has left the building!"

Slam!

Several hours later, a set of wind chimes glittered in the moonlight as they swayed above the side of Ashton's bed. Mercy had reluctantly acquired the item following the conversation from earlier, along with an assortment of white candles that were positioned at various places around the apartment.

Before readying herself for sleep, Mercy went about lighting the candles and testing the wind chimes. The preparations seemed pointless and made her feel more than a bit foolish but also had a surprisingly soothing effect. Once she changed into a T-shirt and pajama pants, brushed her teeth, and washed off her makeup, she discovered she was able to fall to sleep almost instantly; in large part due to the wave of relief from doing something productive to ward off the ghostly presence, but in an even larger part due to the massive sleep deprivation she was still suffering. She still found it curious that all of this was happening as soon as her boyfriend had left town and remained eager to discuss the matter with him personally. She wanted to learn if there was an unknown variable that could be responsible but would have been just as satisfied for the haunting to wrap itself up so she would no longer have to address it.

At first, it appeared that she might have gotten her wish. Throughout the evening, everything remained quiet and peaceful. But in the middle of the night, the wind chimes appeared to vibrate ever so slightly, and the two white candles positioned on the bedstand suddenly seemed to snuff themselves out.

Mercy next found herself awakened by the low, spine-tingling growl of Ashton's cat, urging her to jerk her head up from the pillow as she cast her sleepy eyes all about the apartment. As her eyes adjusted to the lack of light, her gaze fell on the open bedroom closet and the tense orange tabby sitting right in front of it. Staring into the disarming pitch-black abyss that was silently gazing back. The cat emitted another low growl that seemed to reverberate throughout the room, and she slowly sat up, staring into the open doorway...

But nothing stirred.

After lying awake for several minutes, she finally accepted that nothing out of the ordinary was going to happen and eventually fell back asleep. Similar to her previous experience, she was still sleeping peacefully when her eerie, unearthly visitor finally reappeared. Just like before, she didn't know exactly what awakened her, but around the time of the witching hour, her eyelids started to flutter. Once they were fully open, she glanced over at the corner of the bed and became instantly chilled to the bone by what she saw.

The apparition was sitting in the very same spot it had appeared previously: on the far corner of the bed, with her back to Mercy. Everything appeared exactly the same as her last materialization. Long blonde hair, about thirteen years of age; a small, slender form wearing a white nightgown that was perfectly spotless.

It wasn't easy for Mercy to put her finger on what was so alarming about the girl's appearance. In many ways, she looked just like an ordinary little girl, except for the unnatural paleness of her skin. There was also something else. From what she could remember, she recalled that the girl's dark pupils looked disturbingly larger than normal when she glanced in her direction. Plus there was the matter of the nightgown, which was uncommonly old-fashioned and appeared much older than any clothing that was worn in the modern-day. Upon closer examination, everything about the girl presented the appearance of a thing not entirely of the modern world, and the sight of this strange figure made Mercy feel nauseous and short of breath, her hands unconsciously grasping the bedcovers.

Still not facing her, the little girl spoke in a voice that was quiet and vacant. "I tried to warn you. You didn't listen."

A single tear rolled down Mercy's cheek as she felt a stifled scream become caught in the back of her throat. Why she was reacting like this, she hadn't the faintest idea. The fact that this was happening made no sense at all.

There was something about the apparition that not only troubled Mercy but left her feeling extremely melancholy on account of the incomprehensible amount of sorrow the tiny figure seemed to be carrying. A special type of heartache that was too much to bear, especially for a little girl. Whether this sadness was the result of secret knowledge or the remnants of a tortured past, she had no idea. She didn't even know if this was a ghost or something else entirely.

Was it even common for ghosts to communicate this way? Or to manifest so clearly? Mercy would have been the first to admit she was out of her depths when it came to these things. As a result, no matter how much the idea upset her, she felt she had no choice but to try to communicate with the strange being—that is, if she wanted to know why she was being haunted in the first place and why the fate of her boyfriend seemed so significant.

"Warn me about what?" Mercy muttered. "I don't understand."

After receiving this confession, the little girl turned her solemn, taciturn gaze to face her inquisitor. Just when Mercy felt sure she was going to disappear, leaving her questions unanswered, the ghost raised her hand and offered it to her.

"I'll show you," the little girl said.

Mercy had trouble recalling what happened next. The next thing she knew, she was standing outside Ashton's closet with the little girl standing beside her. The girl's freezing chalk-white fingers were wrapped tightly around her own, and after pushing aside the clothes that were hanging limply in the narrow enclosure, the ghost turned her haunting stare to her companion, checking one last time to make sure she wanted to continue.

It was no secret that Mercy was feeling terribly uncertain. After turning her eyes to face the dark and gaping void that seemed to be gazing back at her, she felt her heartbeat start to quicken, and her mouth turned dry, all of her senses ringing like alarm bells. Nevertheless, she thirsted for answers. After shaking off the initial goosebumps and taking a deep and focused breath, she bravely fixed her sights upon the heavy, hollow emptiness and crossed into the darkness that had been waiting for her all this time.

20

STRANGE LOVE

────────────

The Seal of Aemeth was hanging on the attic wall, and McAllister sat in the center of the protection circle, chugging a bottle of rum. More than anything, he was fiending for distractions—searching for something to divert his attention from the hideous rash stretching across his neck like a midnight-colored sea anemone, and the persistent and intolerable hunger that came with it.

The emotional aftermath of his petty squabbling with Agatha and his conflicting passions for his ethereal stepsister weighed heavily on his mind. But these matters seemed trivial when compared to the hunger blinding all of his senses, and the message informing him they were all in great danger.

With everything appearing to be spiraling out of control—and quickly—there was no better time to address this danger head-on. To do so, he once again adorned his tattered black sweater and blazed through the necessary preparations that would allow him a better glimpse at what he was dealing with.

But on that night, things were predictably off.

The voracious hunger burning McAllister's insides, along with the torrid fury of emotions and maddening string of challenges piling up all around him—all of these obstacles were making it harder for him to concentrate and filling him with doubt in terms of how much longer he'd be able to hold it all together. Life was so much simpler when he could just kill his way out of a problem and be done with it. But he had sworn to try to be a better person now that he and Ada were back together, and even if he could fix his problems with mass slaughter, he wouldn't know where to start.

For McAllister, freeing himself from years of bad habits and destructive forms of behavior had been an incredibly rocky road to travel. It left him feeling completely alone in the world most days, with only his preferred ritual of choice to turn to—and he was now drinking excessively just to get through it.

Focus, McAllister thought. *Bloody focus!*

Determined to ignore all distractions and get on with the damn thing, McAllister slammed the half-empty bottle of liquor to the floorboards and leaned forward, pressing his knuckles against the floor to keep his body steady. After squeezing his eyelids shut, he visualized the dark waters within the singing bowl, and a buzzing cacophony of noise began to overtake his eardrums. As usual, he started to tune into a series of chattering whispers overlapping one another, but the voices seemed to prey on his countless insecurities; savagely mocking his efforts at rending the veil asunder.

"*Failure.*"

"*Fail like all the others.*"

"*You can't win.*"

"*CAN'T. WIN.*"

No, this was intolerable. It was unacceptable.

He needed answers—desperately needed answers.

But the answers? The answers weren't coming.

Drowning in frustration, McAllister let out a torturous bellow from deep inside his chest. Screaming like an animal, he swept the bowl away from him.

As the useless object flew across the room and wobbled to a halt, he shed his tattered sweater. The blackened capillaries staining his neck were pulsing, going from black to bright red amid a hideous spiderweb of bruised and discolored purple spreading throughout his arms and chest.

He dropped his fists and pounded the floorboards. All his efforts were leading nowhere, and he had nowhere else to turn.

McAllister wasn't the type of person to give in to failure so easily, but at the same time, he knew that in his degraded condition he was walking a fine line between the edge of sanity and the brink of total madness. The hunger was taking control, and he didn't know how much longer he could hold out. If he had no hopes of keeping Ada safe from danger, what was the point of fighting it? If his search for the diary risked forcing a situation where he might lose her during the process, what was the point?

What was the point of even going on anymore?

What was the point to any of this?

Waves of anxiety were overtaking him, and he felt about ready to give up the ghost. He balled his fists and squeezed his eyes shut while breathing through clenched teeth.

"I can't do it," McAllister groaned. "I can't...take it..."

That was it. He was finished.

He felt entirely spent.

He felt certain no one would hear him, but as soon as he muttered this hopeless confession, he received a shocking reply.

"What's the matter, baby? Has something got you down?"

His eyes burst open.

The attic was empty save for his crumpled body in the center of the circle and the battered black steamer trunk on the other side of the room. But he recognized this voice. It was Dakota.

After listening to deafening silence for a modest trickle of moments, McAllister let loose a maniacal chuckle, and his lips curled into a bemused smirk. He was so far over the edge at this point it only felt natural to shrug off every last shred of common sense he had left to give. He stifled his laughter and addressed the cold, claustrophobic walls surrounding him.

"Dakota...what the hell did we do to ourselves? I thought I'd be strong enough. That I wouldn't have to regret our sacrifice. But it wasn't enough. It wasn't enough..."

His words drifted into nothingness as his lean, sinewy shoulders slumped forward and his spirits continued to sink into the darkening abyss of his decaying physical condition and mental state. But if anyone knew what it was like to stand on the border of total insanity, it was Dakota. The two of them had a history together—a violent and bloody history he was still trying to run away from and was best not reflected on. In that desperate moment, Dakota's smoky, effervescent voice must have sounded like music to McAllister's ears. He seemed calmer—playful even—and his face lit up like a neon-soaked carnival after a moment of silence had passed and the voice chose to address him once again.

"Go on."

McAllister rose to his knees. With a shaky hand, he unfolded the terrible note he received.

"BEWARE THE IDES OF MARCH." That was all the note had said. The message's cryptic contents were troubling, but he found something darkly amusing about the unusual dispatch.

"Oh, Beloved. There's a traitor among us." McAllister released a chilling laugh. "Can you believe it?"

"Mmm, don't give up so soon, baby," the soothing voice replied. "That's not the McAllister I know. The one who declared all-out war on the Council? The one who murdered the Seventh Scholar in cold blood? This isn't you, baby. *Someone needs to let you off the leash.*"

McAllister's lips folded into a twisted grin. He felt the hunger egging him on, the urge for violence taking control. With Dakota by his side, there was no reason to feel guilty about these demented feelings. After all, she was just like him—a walking horror show. In his current, wretched state, he could almost weep for joy for being visited by someone he didn't have to hide from. Someone who knew all of his darkest and most sinful secrets.

"I always understood you, didn't I?" the voice continued. "It sounds like you could use a sympathetic...ear."

Yes. More than anything, McAllister thought.

And what was this? It could have only been because he wished it, but when the disembodied voice sang these words to him, he felt the sensation of someone breathing into his earlobe. Followed by two blood-red lips whispering:

"Or maybe a woman's...touch?"

Yes. Yes, maybe just this once. He pinched his eyelids shut and felt the brush of a hand slide down his torso and claw his bare chest. Five long nails digging into his skin just deep enough to add a sharp jolt of pain to the sensual pleasure of the gesture.

"It sounds like you could use...a friend."

With this observation, the will to fight abandoned McAllister completely, no longer rebelling against the bizarre visitation or his wicked memories. As a result of his surrender, he felt two hands reach out to caress his face, and he leaned forward, too enraptured in the moment to give his actions a second thought. He burrowed his head into the warm, inviting bosom of the figure sitting before him and found himself folding his arms around her, relishing the impression of the exquisite fabric now tickling his fingertips and gripping the enticing torso of the heavenly presence enveloping her arms around him.

But two figures were now present to observe this scene.

When Mercy entered the darkness inside her boyfriend's closet, she suddenly found herself miles away. She was crossing down the hallway of one of the upper floors of an aging Victorian, the little girl guiding her by the hand.

Mercy found the decaying decadent atmosphere quite curious. On her way down the dimly lit hallway, she spied a sleeping redhead in one room and two dark-haired beauties dozing in another. But nothing was quite as shocking as what she saw once she was led up a rickety stepladder into the gloomy, shadow-infested attic.

Kneeling on the floor, with McAllister's head lovingly pressed against her chest, was a breathtaking young woman dressed in an unusually old-fashioned but highly flattering floor-length violet dress. She could have been the most beautiful woman Mercy had ever seen. She had the body of a pop idol with long, flowing, chestnut-colored hair that a Disney princess would envy, along with deliriously inviting red-painted lips that were the color of fresh blood—a color magnified in intensity by her unnaturally pale skin.

Most startling of all were the woman's eyes. Large, doting doe eyes surely blessed with the power to seduce any man or woman they came across, except they'd been polluted by a harsh and disturbing strain of madness that would chill any prospective suitor to the bone. Within these eyes was a quality one could also find within the eyes of McAllister when he wasn't fighting to restrain the murderous thirst for destruction that was devouring him—and he was far from fighting these urges at present.

That was why Dakota seemed to be admiring McAllister with a level of fondness found only in those who discovered someone who was exactly like them in their most profound and personal attributes. After all, it was this unique quality they shared that had first drawn them together—and it now bonded them forever.

However, the fortuitous reunion between these two beautiful monsters was destined to be short-lived. As Dakota raised her paralyzing gaze to the intruders, a devilish and disturbing smile spread across her face.

"Mmm, we have visitors," Dakota sang.

At this remark, McAllister's eyes popped open, and he spun around to face the attic's entrance.

But Mercy and the little girl had disappeared.

While temporarily disoriented by the interruption, when he turned back, he noticed his former acquaintance had disappeared as well. It was as if she'd never been present, and this unfortunate discovery unleashed a tidal wave of mixed emotions—a toxic alchemical concoction of self-loathing and shame.

McAllister's relationship with Dakota had long been severed, but there was a part of him that still yearned for her and felt closer to her than anyone. It was the part of him his loving thoughts of Ada kept at bay but was also where the hunger lived as well. The hunger that would endanger every person he cared about if he didn't succeed in fighting this affliction and get a bloody grip on himself.

Tragically, the disturbing brew of doomed and desperate thoughts only continued its brutal onslaught, weighing heavily on McAllister's cursed and blackened soul. He slumped to the trap door and closed it behind him, abandoning the failed ritual along with the terrible note still lying where he had left it, now steadily collecting dust at the edge of the protection circle.

As he was leaving, he noticed he now felt more bitter and disgusted than ever. After an already stressful and disheartening evening, he now had another item to add to his unending list of troubles: that for a moment, while he was embracing that infernal temptress and feeling her arms wrapped around him, he felt the glimmer of an emotion that had been long absent. A feeling he thought he might never hope to experience ever again.

For a brief and fleeting moment, McAllister had felt relief.

Part III

McAllister: Be cautious. Our enemies are watching us.

Ada: Our enemies can't stop us. No one can stop us.

21

BETTER LIVING THROUGH CHEMISTRY

It was a sunny day in Boston as Miles approached the entrance to the Boston Athenaeum, one of the oldest independent libraries in America. He'd been in town for several days at this point, on an assignment to research a book at the center of the notorious witch panic that had seized the provinces of New England many centuries earlier. Or, at least, so was the story according to McAllister.

At first, Miles had been surprised to learn he was being sent away, but in retrospect, it was something he could have predicted. Once McAllister had joined the coven following his lengthy exile overseas, he reaffirmed the necessity for the group to be limited to five members, with one member representing each of the five magical elements. This meant one of them had to go and to determine who should stay and who should leave, a special trial was arranged to test the members' abilities—"The Trial of the Blind Witch." Miles easily outperformed all of the others in this evaluation, with the exception of Ada and McAllister, who stood impassively nearby to watch as observers, and he was shocked to discover that his prize for winning was being sent away on a field trip McAllister had arranged for the one who had proven most qualified.

It's safe to say that Miles wasn't exactly pleased with this outcome and disliked being separated from Ada and also from Izzy, who he enjoyed a special intimate send-off with before going away. But his mood had sobered considerably since becoming rabidly consumed with his assignment, and he was now making great progress. This pleased him a great deal since libraries were kind of his thing; Ada first discovered him in a library several years earlier while she was still a moody teenager in high school. Miles still found it ironic that she pulled him away from one library only to eventually be sent to another, but it turned out McAllister's suspicions about one thing had proven remarkably prescient: Miles was without a doubt the one most qualified for this assignment, and he was confident he would have all of the necessary information desired of him within the next twenty-four hours.

After entering the stately stone building, Miles crossed the slick, slippery floor to the library's front counter, waiting patiently as a stern older woman completed checking out items for a visitor. In terms of other libraries he visited, he found the timeless atmosphere of the setting quite impressive, possessing a distinguished air of polished respectability and seductive old world charm in its presentation. The librarian, however, was less than charming and observed the young man with suspicion as he approached the front desk.

"Good afternoon," Miles said. "I'd like to see the records for all the books checked out in 1896, 1897, and 1898."

"And you are?"

"Ronald McDonald. Pleasure."

Miles extended his hand, receiving an icy frown in response.

"Those records are confidential, Mr., um, McDonald, and visitors aren't—"

"Aren't allowed access to confidential library documents. Yeah, a colleague of yours gave me the same speech earlier this week."

"I'm afraid you can't see them."

The glare he received was stubborn and unyielding, but this didn't bother him. There was no way the curmudgeonly gatekeeper could have known it, but the argument between them had already been won. Such was the nature of his exceptional gift of persuasion—a gift he was about to put into practice as he returned the librarian's stare, his eyes gazing at her unblinkingly.

"But you'll let me see them anyway," Miles calmly asserted.

With this statement, the librarian tensed up like she'd been hit with an electric shock. Her eyes glazed over, and her mouth dropped open to answer his subtle inquiry—as if by suggestion.

"But I'll let you see them anyway," the librarian mumbled and slowly turned away to search for the items he requested.

Miles struggled to repress an amused chuckle. He'd witnessed this type of response many times, and yet it never ceased to entertain him. He couldn't remember when he first discovered this unique ability—something he suspected had to do with his connection to the Loa, his unique family lineage tying him to a long line of Voodoo priests back in Haiti where his family originated. But the undeniable impact his stirring words had on others was always satisfying. It was true that his gift appeared to have zero effect on Ada and a few others, which was disappointing, but for the moment, he was feeling immensely pleased with the talent that he was blessed with. He was grinning in a manner not so dissimilar from the impish smirk that

Ada had the habit of wearing as he watched the librarian go about completing the task she'd been given.

Three thick leather-bound ledgers were dropped onto the table in one of the Athenaeum's impressive reading rooms as Miles helped himself to a seat and proceeded to get to work. Thanks to his research, he knew exactly what he was looking for: titles of specific alchemical literature and the names of the persons who'd taken an interest in this material over a century earlier. At this stage in his assignment, he was keeping a keen eye out for one specific title in particular. When he arrived in Boston earlier that week, he secured himself a list of books reported lost or stolen from the Athenaeum, and the one that stood out the most was a book called Item # QD418, aka *Unknown Alchemist's Journal circa 1585.* A wealthy Bostonian political family known as the Danforth family had donated the book to the institution, along with a broader collection of rare alchemical texts and documents. But in 1898, the book suddenly disappeared from the collection, having mysteriously gone missing.

The significance of this discovery would have been lost on Miles completely prior to a conversation he shared with McAllister on the night before his departure. According to the strange yet highly illuminated young man who Ada had always spoken of as uniquely brilliant, there was a lot more to Tituba's infamous confession at the beginning of the Salem witch trials than was commonly accepted. How McAllister had come to this conclusion was not entirely clear, but it was well known to anyone the least bit familiar with him that McAllister was an apt collector of rare books, and while in pursuit of one book in particular, he adopted the belief that the "Man In Black" Tituba spoke of was more than just a clever euphemism for the Devil as most people tended to assume. For McAllister, the dark and accursed book the man carried, what the Puritans believed to be "the Devil's book" where all the names of those who signed over their bodies and souls to the Evil One were written, was something much more extraordinary.

McAllister was convinced this book was a legendary lost grimoire that various armchair occultists had dubbed "The Engelander Diary" and was confident the item had been in Little Salem before mysteriously going on walkabout and disappearing. He was also convinced that by finding out who was in possession of the diary during the years following the Salem witch trials, along with any information pertaining to who might have brought it back home to the original site of its first mention, he would finally be able to confirm if he was correct in his wild assessment and be one step closer to discovering where this priceless treasure was currently hidden.

Rudy and Izzy had played their own specialized roles in this search, scouring the asylum for information on the deranged maniac known for screaming about maddening hallucinations involving a "man in black" and a bizarre "book" during his final days at the institution. But for Miles, his task was simple: first, to find the names of those in the library who'd shown an interest in alchemy and other occult subject matter during the time that Item # QD418 had gone missing. Then, all he would have to do was research these names to see if any of them had any connection to the town of Little Salem. It was a lengthy process of elimination that was also quite tedious, but with all the information needed at his fingertips, he was certain he'd find the identity of the culprit and discover whether McAllister's disturbing claims were real or only flights of fancy.

Hours later, the sun had disappeared below the horizon, and Miles was still seated at the table. He'd made a great deal of progress, but his task was far from complete. After rubbing his eyes and stretching his limbs, he gathered up the ledgers along with the yellow notepad he was collecting his notes in before returning to the lobby and smiling widely as he waved to the librarian and pointed to the three ledgers under his wing.

"I'm taking these to my hotel," Miles casually stated.

The librarian smiled predictably without making the slightest fuss. "Goodnight, Mr. McDonald."

After grabbing a quick dinner, Miles returned to his hotel—a classy joint only a few blocks from the waterfront. He entered the room and tossed the ledgers onto the bed, heading straight to the bathroom to splash some water on his face. He stared at this reflection and took a deep breath, preparing to step into the breach once more, readying himself for the long night ahead.

With victory in his sights, Miles sat down at the hotel room table and returned to his assignment. While flipping through the pages of the third and final ledger, his mind started drifting to thoughts of what the others might be doing, thinking about Ada mostly but also of Izzy. It had been clear to everyone for a long time that Izzy had something of a crush on Miles, but he'd always chosen to ignore this. It had always been his fantasy that his relationship with Ada would someday evolve to a place beyond a simple friendship, but Ada's confusing obsession with her so-called stepbrother created an immovable barrier that prevented this.

Ada's intense admiration of McAllister was something he could never understand, no matter how many ways he tried to look at it. It was true that McAllister was a fascinating specimen and highly intelligent, but so was he. And Ada's dark and troubled stepsibling always seemed so temperamental and unhinged and was already romantically involved with Agatha, who was a much more suitable partner for him than Ada in Miles's humble opinion.

Still, it was undeniable that Ada and McAllister shared a special connection—probably the result of their experiences from five years earlier. These events not only helped refine who they were but also created an unbreakable bond between them. A bond that was so significant, he knew he had no hopes of competing with it—something that frustrated him painfully to no end.

Hours later, Miles awoke at the hotel room table with his face in his arms and the sun already risen. He couldn't remember falling asleep but flipping through his notepad revealed he accomplished a great deal, working straight through the night before eventually succumbing to drowsiness.

While sluggishly rubbing his face and reviewing his work, inspecting the list of names drawn up from the ledger, he noticed that while his notepad listed several guests at the library who'd taken an interest in the subjects he was researching, there was one name in particular that easily surpassed the others in accordance to the individual's devoted obsession to this material.

And there it was—one name on the yellow notepad that had been circled: ALFONSE MASTERS, with a list of eighty alchemical titles listed underneath.

Miles's heart started racing at the discovery. He booted up his laptop and typed the name into his web browser, pulling up a short bio for this odd figure:

ALFONSE MASTERS
Occupation: Inventor/Industrialist
Born: 1872, Boston
Died: 1916, Little Salem

Back in Little Salem, the dark storm clouds enveloping the skies had disappeared, and the sun was casting its blissful rays on the now legendary late-night party spot sitting at the center of the main drag. Inside, the tavern was still trashed from the night before. Empty bottles, glasses, and confetti covered every smooth surface in sight while two cute female dancers remained passed out in one of the black vinyl booths and a male dancer wearing ass-less chaps lay snoring face-down on the pool table.

In sharp contrast to the opening festivities, things were now quiet and peaceful. A faint buzzing broke the silence, and a pale hand bolted up from behind the bar, feeling for the smartphone vibrating on the surface and grabbing a pair of Ray-Bans sitting beside it before McAllister inevitably revealed himself, phone to his ear with dark sunglasses obscuring a face that was only just barely awake.

"Yeah?" McAllister slurred sleepily.

The voice on the other end suppressed an amused chuckle before answering, eager to share the exciting news of their success.

"We got it."

22

KILL THE LIGHTS

While Ashton and Tyler agreed it was best to distance themselves from Ada due to the bizarre string of events she appeared to be playing a role in, all of this changed on the day directly following the Black Death Tavern's grand opening.

It was still early in the morning when Ada appeared at the door to their hotel room with a proposition to accompany her on a ghost hunt that seemed much too good to pass up. The investigation was discussed over breakfast as she presented a series of printouts concerning a wealthy industrialist named Alfonse Masters, explaining that he'd resided in town at the beginning of the last century and owned a lucrative chemical plant that was the site of many strange occurrences following its sudden closure many decades earlier.

"The AM Chemical Plant," Ada cheerfully announced. She presented a faded photograph of the intimidating industrial setting. "Closed down in 1916 shortly after Masters passed away due to some rather curious circumstances. Lots of unfortunate accidents at the plant, along with unusual deaths. Thought you might want to tag along. Do your dialogue with the spooks bit."

The proposal felt highly promising, and Ashton was ready to join in without any hesitation. But Tyler had entirely different thoughts on the matter and wasn't afraid to speak his mind once he and his fellow ghost hunter were alone together.

"Dude. What are you thinking?"

"Dude. What do you mean?"

"I thought you were finished with this girl!"

"Are you crazy? This is a golden opportunity—"

"*Golden opportunity?*"

"For us and the show! Hunting ghosts in a haunted factory? We'd be chumps not to do this!"

"Chumps? We'd be chumps? Are you suffering from amnesia, you blockhead? That Ada chick is a black widow!"

"Oh, c'mon—"

"And what about our unanswered questions from yesterday? Salem Witches? Scarlet Council? What about the spooky business happening with your girlfriend? I mean, I know it's a separate issue..."

Ashton threw up his hands in frustration. "Why you gotta be such a Debbie Downer? Like, where's your sense of adventure?"

Tyler wasn't budging. He knew he had to put his foot down.

"You wanna do this thing? Your little date night at the amusement park with Wednesday Addams back there? I'm not going with you. You hear me? You're going to have to choose. Ada or me."

Unfortunately, Tyler proved a bit hasty in assuming his amigo's alliances and Ashton ended up choosing Ada instead. At the time, Ashton was still trying to convince himself his decision was in the best interests of the web channel, but there seemed to be an unknown variable that was drawing him to this mysterious girl. He knew if he had any desire to figure out the reasons for this, he needed to spend more time with her to find out.

It was later that evening when Ashton took off with Ada and her spooky stepsibling, Ghostemane cranking on the stereo of the vintage convertible. They traveled to the edges of the neighboring town of Middleton where their destination awaited them: A colossal industrial setting that looked more like a sprawling graveyard of broken-down warehouses, rusted pipes, and deteriorating turn of the century machinery than what was once a bustling factory that had ever mass-produced anything.

The investigation proved interesting—and not in any way that was expected. But it was what happened right after that would prove to be genuinely astonishing and would cause Ashton to feel the need to rethink everything.

Ashton and Ada had just left one of the old machinery buildings after receiving a shout from McAllister over their walkies, currently exploring another part of the factory and recommending they should leave. Ashton was confused as to why they were abandoning the investigation so prematurely when there was still so much to explore. He was expressing these concerns while crossing the garbage-strewn courtyard when a folksy self-important voice called out to them.

"Well, what do we have here?"

Standing in the courtyard and blocking the path to the exit was Little Salem's very own Sheriff Bucky Gates, accompanied by what looked like a dozen bloodthirsty good old boys, all of them grinning maniacally and armed to the teeth. The New Lords had already survived one run-in with the Sheriff while he was following up on a report filed by the Truegoods regarding their damaged lawn. Agatha had used her special talents to diffuse the situation, but since this last encounter, it appeared the cocky and resolute lawman had gotten his mind right and was now all geared up and ready for war.

It's official, Ashton thought to himself while surveying the mob standing before them. These "honorary deputies" looked way past the introductions stage. And the exact opposite of the friendly and good-natured citizenry he'd met so far in Little Salem.

As Ashton stood frozen in place, dumbfounded as to why such an overpowered ensemble would be taking an interest in his activities, the Sheriff flashed a simpering grin before nodding to one of the multiple "No Trespassing" signs posted around the property.

"Didn't you see the sign?" the Sheriff lazily drawled. "Back in Alfonse Masters' day, he used trespassers for target practice."

"We were just leaving," Ashton said, with the lawman's rough and tumble murder brigade cocking their shotguns and assault rifles and snickering in reply.

"You know," the Sheriff smugly grinned, "our town don't take too kindly to lawbreakers. Town don't take too kindly to witches neither. Unofficial policy is to shoot a witch on sight."

"Hold on," Ashton objected. "You don't seriously believe that she—"

While gesturing to Ada, his whole body froze at what he saw before him: a skinny girl with long, dark hair and haunting blue-violet eyes, fearlessly staring down her swaggering opponent as she took a defiant step forward.

"Take your best shot, Tex." Ada gestured to her face and chest. "But try to aim away from the merchandise. It would break my mama's heart if my funeral wasn't open-casket."

"*Ada!*"

McAllister was yelling from the other side of the plant, desperately signaling to them to get their attention. Ashton turned his head to address him and noticed the dark silhouette of a sniper on the roof of one of the utility buildings. A young bearded man wearing a black business suit, armed with a machine gun.

By the time Ashton realized the man had Ada in his sights, it was already too late. The sniper pulled the trigger, unleashing a hail of bullets at his target, and Ada cried out in pain. Luckily, the man didn't have much experience with his particular choice of weapon that evening. Firing wildly, he was nearly knocked off his feet by the recoil, preventing him from getting a straight shot.

Regardless, a spray of bullets had been launched at Ada with two rounds hitting her side. She dropped to her knees as blood splattered the ground, her face morphing into a mask of sheer agony.

Ashton watched the whole scene like a deer in the headlights, calling out Ada's name but he was too shocked to move. He remained in this vexing state of immobility as Ada lay helpless several feet away from him, breathing short panicky breaths.

While Aston was staring aghast at the sight, the Sheriff was enjoying an entirely different reaction, smiling with satisfaction at the gory outcome and turning to the goon beside him.

"Finish her."

"No!"

At the sound of the powerful objection, Ashton glanced over and watched McAllister come sprinting forward like a man possessed. In response, the Sheriff's handpicked executioner shifted his aim from the girl writhing on the ground defenseless and fired two shells at the man running toward her, hitting him square in the chest.

Blam!

The shot was enough to kill anyone, but McAllister just dropped to his knees before standing right back up. Wincing with stubborn persistence as he limped to his fallen stepsibling.

"Ada..."

The goon that fired glanced over to the Sheriff in confusion. Everyone seemed amazed by their target's resilience, but the plucky lawman briskly shook off his astonishment and snarled impatiently at the loyal pack of discount assassins behind him.

"Don't just stand there lollygagging! Fire at will!"

Dozens of shots rang out in succession, with hot metal searing into McAllister's body and wardrobe and tearing both to shreds. His body jerked like a fish on a hook with each painful new bullet that passed through him, with a splash of inky black blood bursting forth from every wound. This was a sight that Ashton was unprepared for and startled him to his very core.

Black blood? Was it really black blood he was seeing?

What kind of monster was this?

And Ada? He had no idea who she was either. Not anymore.

Eventually, the shooting stopped, and McAllister dropped to the ground, only a few feet from his injured sibling. While listening to the sound of their enemies reloading, McAllister coughed up a gob of black blood, and a single tear glided down Ada's cheek. Right before the badly wounded waif squeezed her eyelids shut and released a terrifying ear-splitting shriek.

The sound of Ada's cry was like nothing Ashton had ever heard. Like the entire Earth was howling at the revolting tragedy of the spectacle. The sting of her torturous siren call slammed her unsuspecting audience with a blast of hot air and an all-out sonic assault on the brain and nervous system of every bystander standing within earshot. And it wasn't just those who were gathered that were affected. When Ada cried out, all of the floodlights surrounding the property exploded into a violent shower of sparks and shattered glass that rained down on the startled spectators like jagged ash.

Panic was running rampant, but as shocking as all of this was, the real surprise was yet to come. After shielding their eyes from the lights exploding above them, the crowd turned back to where Ada and McAllister were located, discovering they'd disappeared.

No, that's impossible, Ashton thought. *There's no way. No way they could have made it out of here in their condition.*

"What in Sam Hill..." the Sheriff muttered. Before he could address this development, a loud chirp interrupted him.

"Hey, Sheriff?" The lanky, bearded sniper was sending a shout over the walkie. "I think the higher-ups want us out of here ASAP."

The Sheriff frowned with irritation and ordered his men to pack up. As they did, he glanced over to Ashton, staring at the dirt where two bodies had been lying moments earlier; a small pool of red blood on one side and a dark stain of black oily sludge on the other.

"Best run on home, boy," the Sheriff said.

Ashton was still in a state of shock when he left the factory, trying to piece together everything he had witnessed. The accusation that Ada was a witch, the presence of the armed thugs, the black blood that poured out of McAllister after being shot multiple times while somehow managing to survive. Most distressing of all was Ada's deafening cry and disappearance. It was all so unbelievable, and he didn't have answers for any of this.

Ashton was drowning in these thoughts and emotions as he slumped toward the convertible, parked on the side of the lonely road outside the abandoned facility. A faint noise suddenly grabbed his attention and directed his eyes to a sight that couldn't have been more surprising if it had been accompanied by a punch in the face:

McAllister, holding Ada close, their broken bodies huddled next to a telephone pole. Like they had materialized out of the shadows.

"McAllister!"

Ashton raced over to assist them. While observing the young man's battered body, he found himself still struck by the fact that the blood spilling out of him was inky black instead of bright red like for normal people.

"Help...her..." McAllister wheezed. "She...needs..."

His whole body was shaking, trapped in a losing battle to remain conscious.

"Can you walk? Hey. We need to get you to the car," Ashton stammered. "I'll drive you to the hospital."

McAllister grasped Ashton's arm firmly.

"No...hospital... They'll...kill her..."

Ashton could sense that McAllister was deathly serious, starting with surprise when he heard a noise close by. The giant Native American man who managed the front desk at the hotel was standing several paces up the road from them, tossing discarded pieces of metal and roadside debris into the bed of his pick-up.

"Excuse me! Hey! My friends need help!"

The giant silently glanced over to Ashton before casting a stern look at the two bloody bodies behind him.

"Follow my truck," the giant said. "I'll take you someplace safe."

Moments later, Ada was lying semi-conscious in the back of the convertible as Ashton set her wounded stepbrother's shattered frame beside her. McAllister was still coughing up blood, or whatever it was, a hideous tapestry of blackened capillaries spreading across his face.

"Dude, are you OK?" The sight had Ashton cringing with discomfort. "You don't look so good."

McAllister ignored the comment, finding his sunglasses and placing them on before pulling Ada close.

"Just...drive..."

Ashton didn't waste his breath trying to argue and got behind the wheel. He had no idea where he was headed, but one thing was certain: When he arrived at his destination, he would be expecting answers.

23

NO EXIT

There was no question that powerful forces were at work in the retaliation against the New Lords and the disturbances they caused in Little Salem. Everyone close to Ada and McAllister was fair game, and what became of Agatha was connected to an incident involving her and Lucy at the Black Death Tavern's grand opening.

When Lucy left the church, she had strong personal motives for visiting the coven's headquarters. She already tried talking to Tyler. Since their run-in on the street, her life had become increasingly difficult to tolerate, and she sensed that things were about to come to a violent head. Turning to a girl not much older than her who was rumored to be a powerful witch was an act of desperation. But that's what the situation was for Lucy, and she was willing to turn to anyone if there was even the slightest chance they could save her from all the troubles that were pursuing her.

The first obstacle she encountered was having to talk her way past Sanchez, who was acting as bouncer and doorman that evening.

"Let me in, Sanchez," Lucy scowled impatiently.

"No can do, girly. Place has rules."

"Oh, just move aside."

"Hey! You can't—"

Lucy muscled her way past him and nearly lost her breath upon observing what was happening inside. As the daughter of a small-town preacher and a self-identified "good Christian girl," she had never witnessed such a spectacle of outright debauchery and hedonism in all her life. The sights and sounds were overwhelming: exotic dancers sweating under flashing lights, wearing next to nothing, while loud, aggressive music throbbed out of the speakers. The squeaky-clean teenager found herself surrounded by a dark mob of intoxicated revelers, laughing and partying like they'd landed at Happy Hour in hell and tomorrow was a day that would never arrive.

Lucy was shocked and appalled by the riotous anarchic environment, but she also felt mesmerized and found herself being drawn into the middle of the main room...

That's when she saw her.

Agatha entered from the back like someone looking for a fight—or, even more accurately, like someone who just had a heated argument with an increasingly temperamental lover she'd just about lost all patience with. After all the drama involving McAllister and Izzy, she was looking for a distraction, and as her eyes met Lucy's, she felt a sudden change of mood. Her face softened, her pupils dilated, and her lips curled into a delicious smirk.

In Lucy, Agatha saw a fortuitous opportunity to have a bit of devious fun, along with a chance to turn the tables on those who were trying her patience. At first sight, Lucy was immediately hypnotized by the redhead's striking beauty, becoming lost in her alluring emerald eyes, unable to look away. These curious emotions she was feeling—her body felt hot all over, and her pulse was racing furiously; like it was trying to break a world record. Her mind now seemed incapable of thinking about anything other than that Agatha was the most exquisite creature she'd ever seen and that she was being drawn to her like a fly into a spider's web and there was nothing she could do to change this.

With her eyes locked onto the ravishing enchantress, all other sights and sounds seemed to fade into nothingness. Lucy felt her body moving, one leg after another, her limbs seeming to be operating entirely on their own volition and only coming to rest once they reached the enticing, statuesque beauty. It felt like all time had stopped, her lips quivering with anticipation for what was about to happen next.

Unable to break eye contact, Lucy found herself becoming lost in the witch's magnetic gaze. She felt her body tremble as a hand reached out to caress her darling face.

"Are you lost, little girl?" Agatha cooed.

Lucy gulped, not knowing how to answer. "Please, you have to help me. I—I don't feel safe."

For Lucy, what happened next was a total mystery. The only thing she could remember was before she knew it, she was upstairs in Agatha's bedchamber, feeling the taste of her lips and the exhilarating touch of her caresses. Lucy had never felt so turned on in all her life. She never had a serious boyfriend and grown so adept at concealing her secret urges behind a finely crafted image of perfect chastity and purity that the illusory nature of this highly calculated façade even fooled herself at times. Free from any judgment or criticism, it was impossible to betray all the powerful emotions she was feeling. With the lusty ginger siren beside her, she forgot all about why she had visited the tavern in the first place and wished that the blinding euphoria she was experiencing could last forever.

Alas, this infinitely arousing experience was unfortunately brief. It felt like she'd only been with Agatha for several moments when she suddenly found herself hurrying to adjust her hair and re-button her blouse as the bellow of her father rang out while accompanied by the frantic sound of footsteps racing down the hallway.

"Lucy? Lucy!"

When Wilbur and the Reverend burst through the door, the first thing they saw was the teenager looking disheveled and disoriented, sitting next to Agatha on an antique brass bed. Lucy was mortified to find her father catching her in such a state, but Agatha was wickedly unperturbed; smiling like a Cheshire while dressed only in a flimsy robe purposely left loosely open for a tantalizing glimpse at the stirring bounty of treasures underneath.

"Daddy? What are you—?"

Her father grabbed her by the arm. "Get your hands off my daughter, you succubus!"

"Couldn't keep her hands off me a minute ago," Agatha joyfully quipped, unable to suppress her satisfaction at having so infuriated the Holy Roller.

To cap off the witty response, Agatha smiled and winked at Wilbur right before the two men fled the room with Lucy accompanying them, the joyous afterglow from the wealth of boundless pleasures that had set her body on fire now being replaced with the painful arrival of guilt and shame.

Lucy spent the whole drive back home drowning in these emotions while at the same time struggling to understand why she felt so embarrassed. She couldn't put her finger on it—whether her feelings were in response to the knowledge that what she'd been doing was wrong or the result of being conditioned to believe that any other reaction was strictly forbidden. Regardless, her inner torment provided a useful distraction from the other more stress-inducing emotions she was struggling with. Like the anxiety inspired by the realization that she was alone again with her father and dared not look at him for fear of what she would see when she did.

Later that night, Lucy was still fighting to ignore these distressing visions as she wrestled with the nails on the bedroom window—precautions that were taken to prevent her from leaving except while under her father's supervision. She worked the battered fork clenched in her grip until her hands were sore and her fingers bled. The situation looked hopeless, and what made matters even worse was she was locked inside the family's vacation home—a two-story duplex that was secluded from any other property for miles around.

Lucy's father had been unusually moody since Ada's return to Little Salem. As a way to keep their distance from not only the witches but also a community that was growing more and more impatient for something to be done about them, the family was now spending more time on the outskirts as a result. Lucy hadn't seen her mother in ages. She wasn't sure if she'd returned to their home near the church or if some terrible fate had befallen her. All she knew was she had to escape before something unspeakable happened. This was the only thing she could think about as she continued to grapple with the window while listening to the muffled sound of her father, speaking on the phone from the confines of his study.

"Listen, Godfrey," the Reverend said. "This situation is getting out of hand. I want to know what's going to be done to these troublemakers."

Lucy wasn't paying much attention to the conversation and couldn't hear the reply. If she had, she would have heard a man's voice insisting that a course of action was already in motion, advising her father not to worry because *everything was under control.*

A faint beep alerted her when the call ended, and she felt a wave of panic wash over her. She knew her father would be checking in on her, and in a last-ditch effort to free herself, she struggled with all her might to pull the window open before giving up in frustration, stashing the fork and hiding under the covers.

The sound of footsteps treading lightly across the carpeting was what she heard first, followed by the jiggle of a deadbolt and the spine-tingling creak of the door being opened as a narrow sliver of light shone upon her trembling body.

As she waited for her father to speak, Lucy was surprised to discover she was fighting back sobs.

She'd been crying for hours and hadn't even noticed.

While her father stood in the doorway, silently staring down at her, the same rabid thought kept cycling through her head:

Don't look at him. Don't look at him.

This was the most important thing of all for her to remind herself—more important than anything.

"We'll have no more running away now," her father said. "Or there will be...consequences."

Lucy nodded profusely with her back to him, hoping that a speedy show of obedience would inspire him to leave.

Don't look at him. Don't look at him.

Sadly, she was forced to acknowledge that he would only depart after she had turned to face him. She saw no other way around it.

By all normal accounts, there was nothing remarkable about Lucy's father. While the Reverend was a rather striking man in his youth, nowadays his hair was thinning, he carried a lot more weight around the middle, and he occasionally wore glasses to improve his failing eyesight. In fact, he was wearing his glasses just then. But when Lucy turned to look at him, she found the shadows of the doorway not only shielded her father's eyes from her but also the strange haunting smile she knew he was wearing.

"Goodnight, Lucy. Sleep tight."

Following these words, the Reverend turned his back to her, and her heartbeat started quickening, her eyes widening in horror.

The wretched thing her eyes had been avoiding was about the size of a small baby riding piggyback along her father's spine; a hideous demon with dark red skin and hungry yellow eyes, its razor-sharp claws pressed deep into the man's flesh.

The demon gazed back at her and offered a crooked smile that made her want to scream to high heaven. The wretched thing seemed to be taunting her; reveling in the level of influence it had on her fallen guardian and delighting in all the trauma she was forced to endure because of this.

She felt her entire body revolting as the door swung closed and the lock was replaced. But the terrors were far from over. As she listened to her father's footsteps padding down the hallway, she thought she heard a faint laugh—not her father's laugh but a shrill nerve-wracking cackle that sounded like nothing of this world, the horrible racket compelling her to burrow deeper under the covers, fighting to smother the tears that wouldn't stop flowing no matter how hard she tried to make them.

Even with the demon no longer in her sights, Lucy remained in a state of intense torment. If she knew what lay in store for her, she may have wished to transform into an angel right then and there. Because in terms of how things were looking from her perspective, hell was empty, and the devils were all there—thriving as prowling permanent residents of the deceptively idyllic town of Little Salem.

24

RUN RUN RUN

Agatha scrunched up her face in disgust as she crossed through the muddy cow pen. The light of her smartphone was being used to guide her as she scoured the ground for what she had come all the way to the outskirts of town to seek.

Earlier that day, Ada revealed to the coven her theory that Izzy's condition was worsening because she was hexed. Dark witchcraft was at work, and to make matters even more terrifying, she suspected it wasn't a ghost that was haunting Izzy but a malevolent wraith.

"At first I assumed that what we were dealing with was purely paranormal in nature," Ada had said. "Now I believe that something has been escalating her condition. A powerful spell has been cast on her. A curse. And we need to start taking steps to reverse it, or we're going to lose our friend forever."

Agatha didn't know much about the difference between ghosts and wraiths, but one definitely sounded more threatening than the other. On the chance that some horrible entity was trying to possess their beloved gypsy, they had to act fast, and she accepted the assignment of securing the ingredients to craft a potion to cure her.

To accomplish this, Ada presented Agatha with her personal Book of Shadows—a small hard-covered copy of *Aradia – the Gospel of the Witches*. Inside, Agatha found the margins littered with Ada's magical thoughts and musings, along with a page dedicated to the instructions for concocting a special potion and the eclectic list of ingredients one would have to acquire to brew it.

"Mugwort, devil's snare, *panaeolus sub—sub-balt-eatus?*"

Agatha had great difficulty pronouncing this word when she stumbled across it. She racked her brain as to what it could be referring to until McAllister chimed in from where he was lounging on the other side of the room. He was nursing his hangover with a cold one while studying Tom Thumb's file from the asylum.

"It's a mushroom," McAllister said, "that grows in cow shit."

"Gross," Agatha groaned. She set the book aside and stared into the mirror above her makeup table before taking a long sideways glance at the lover who had fallen out of favor with her. "You know, while we're on the subject of loads of crap, you've been acting pretty shitty lately. I think you might be forgetting how lucky you are. To be liked by a woman who is as patient and devoted as me."

It would have been so easy for McAllister to clear the air between them. Just one little apology. So far, he was playing the fool and giving her the silent treatment. Pretending like nothing had happened to place them at such odds with one another.

Sensing her man needed more persuading to help guide him back into her good graces, Agatha rose from the makeup table and crossed over to him, snatching the file and straddling him seductively.

"I can be very nice when people are nice to me," she said. "But when I feel like my lover's acting cold and distant..."

The sound of footsteps interrupted the exchange. Agatha caught McAllister watching Ada as she swished her way down the hallway, his eyes still hanging on the doorway long after she disappeared.

"Hey. Eyes up here, cowboy." Agatha grabbed his hands and placed them upon her chest. "Why does *she* get all your attention?"

"Agatha—" McAllister started to say.

"*Agatha Agatha,*" she replied mockingly—and things only proceeded to get even more explosive when she asked if he screwed around with anyone during his time in Europe and he was momentarily hesitant to respond.

Unsurprisingly, Agatha left the tavern that day in a fury—and much too dolled up for someone who would later be digging through manure once the sun had dipped below the horizon. Sadly, her petty irritations were still not fully behind her. After stepping out the door all draped up in a blood-red designer dress and a set of killer heels, she ran into the tavern's normally bashful handyman, and their conversation only infuriated the quick-tempered redhead even further.

"Mistress Agatha—"

"Not now, Sanchez. Can't you see I'm in the middle of something?"

"I want my reward."

"You want..."

"I did what you asked. I want what you promised."

What a world-class stooge, Agatha thought. Whatever he was babbling about probably had to do with some empty contract she made—some idle pledge when she was seducing the gullible simpleton prior to taking over the tavern. Her unique gift did wonders with convincing him to assist in the preparations.

Agatha had a full dance card that morning and turned her back without a second thought. At the time, she thought if she just ignored the situation, it would be quickly forgotten about.

"In good time, lover," Agatha replied facetiously. "But right now I'm in such a hurry. I need to find the nearest 'Cauldron Kitty' or 'Wizard's Alley' or—"

"If you refuse," Sanchez muttered, lips quivering. "If you refuse to give me my reward...then I might have to take it."

OK, the shy and insecure thing had been cute, but this was too much. Did this nitwit really have the gall to suggest if she didn't give her body to him, he might have to take it?

The comment sounded like a threat, but Agatha wasn't intimidated. She made this clear as a bell as she spun around to face him, absolutely livid.

"Did you say you might have to take it? Oh heavens, I'm shaking in my boots, Sanchez. Honest to goodness, I think I just wet myself."

She got up close to him, her lips curled into a sneer.

"You don't have the balls."

He probably got the idea to confront her from someone else, she reasoned. Since there was no way he'd be brave enough to stand up to her on his own. Nevertheless, she felt pretty good after putting him in his place like she did, and with Sanchez looking like he'd been punched in the gut and the exchange properly concluded, Agatha resumed with her mission and took off in a taxi.

The mushrooms were the final item she had to acquire by the time the sun had disappeared. It had taken her most of the day to secure the other ingredients, so by the time she showed up to the slaughterhouse the moon was shining above her and a light fog was pouring down from the hills.

After pushing her way past the murky, inhibiting atmosphere and finally locating the cow pen, she began to search the muddy terrain while instantly regretting her annoying habit of never leaving the house looking like less than a million bucks. Agatha was the stubborn type and not one to give up so easily, so she gritted her teeth and continued to press forward, the blank eyes of the cattle watching her with disinterest as mud splashed against her dress and her heels struggled to wade through the dark and syrupy muck.

"Disgusting," Agatha grumbled miserably. "Izzy's going to owe me the longest lap dance in history."

Just when she thought her search would be fruitless, she finally saw it: a pile of cow dung in the far corner of the pen with a distinctive-looking mushroom growing right on top.

"Jackpot," Agatha exclaimed. With the end of her quest in sight, she proceeded to get to work, placing the fungus inside of her picnic basket and searching the pile of excrement to see if there was any more to pilfer.

Her job was complete, and she was eager to be on her way but still wasn't looking forward to confronting McAllister when she returned to the tavern. She knew she was stubborn, but he could be as equally proud and difficult. Then again, maybe he could still surprise her. And regardless of McAllister's feelings, she knew Ada would always be fond of her—even if the relationship between them was growing increasingly complicated.

Agatha was actually looking forward to seeing Ada's reaction after showing off her success for the day, but the most important article on the agenda was to get the items to Izzy. She was feeling the thrill of victory when she was startled by the horn of the taxi, beeping erratically for some reason before abruptly falling silent.

"Geez, driver. Impatient much?" Agatha decided to take this as her decisive cue to leave, but when she made it to the edge of the cow pen, she was treated to another unwelcome surprise: Sanchez, standing like a statue about fifty yards away from her. As usual, the towering juggernaut was dressed in his customary blue overalls, but there was something different about him. His body was a dark silhouette underneath the moonlight, broad shoulders slumping menacingly.

Right away, Agatha assumed the handyman had followed her to continue their conversation from back at the tavern. This behavior was unusual, but rather than starting to panic, she simply grimaced and scoffed with annoyance.

"Sanchez?" Agatha yelled. "Did you really follow me all the way out here to the boonies? Can't you just stalk me on the internet like a normal person?"

The situation may not have disarmed her acerbic wit, but Agatha would be quick to discover her suitor was present for more than a harmless chat, watching as he maintained his imposing stature while pulling a long kitchen knife from his back pocket.

The gesture was alarming, but Agatha remained fearless. Guys like him were all talk, no action—she felt totally assured of this.

"Ooo what's the knife for, Sanchez?" Agatha jeered. "Planning to get your Michael Myers on? I'm shaking so hard my tits are about to fall off! You think I'm scared of a little knife?"

Sanchez appeared startled by this response, but not deterred. He searched for a way to make his presence more persuasive, his eyes landing on a discarded ax in a tree stump, a hatchet, and a pair of garden shears. Working quickly, he duct-taped all of these items together, along with the kitchen knife, to form a makeshift "super-ax" that was absolutely monstrous and medieval in appearance.

"Shit," Agatha said, now seeing he meant business.

Once these words left her lips, Sanchez started heading straight for her. She took off like a rocket on a mad dash to the cattle trap, her insane wardrobe once again delaying her as she fought to retain her footing and trudge through the slippery mud.

After making it to the metal chute that would direct her to a place of safety, she followed the long, iron passageway to the end, and a wave of panic began to overtake her when she discovered a degraded latch barring her way forward.

Things weren't looking good for the fiery redhead—but she refused to give up. With her heart beating savagely, she forced her fingers through the bars and nervously glanced behind her, watching her insane pursuer getting closer.

Luckily, after only a moment, she managed to free the latch. She rushed like the devil into the dark and empty slaughterhouse where she discovered that she wasn't out of the woods just yet.

The dark recesses of the degraded abattoir were filled with countless metal cabinets and ghastly-looking hooks and chains hanging from the ceiling. Agatha rushed by all of these things, clumsily knocking over a water cooler and spilling gallons of water onto the floor while searching for a way out.

The foolish accident left the witch surprisingly shaken, but her spirits suddenly lifted when her eyes fell on a red door not far from where she stood. Unfortunately, her relief was only short-lived. When she arrived at the door and attempted to push her way through, she discovered a rusted lock keeping the exit firmly shut.

"Mistress Agatha..."

Nerves in a tangle, Agatha glanced behind her. She noted the massive shadowy figure slouching at the entrance to the cattle trap, his grimy stubby fingers gripping the super-ax.

"I told you I'd take what's mine."

The voice of the murderous stalker was cold and without emotion—nothing like how Sanchez normally sounded at all. But once again, Agatha refused to give up. As her deadly pursuer started to slump toward her, she threw herself against the door with all the fury she had to muster; slamming her body at the exit over and over as she struggled to break the rusted lock.

As the frame of rotting wood finally started to splinter, Sanchez steadily quickened his stride, watching his target heave her body at the unyielding obstruction until the stubborn lock finally gave. One more shove is what did it, and a beam of glorious moonlight streamed through the crack in the doorframe. With that, Sanchez picked up the pace and broke into a run, so focused on catching up to his victim his eyes blocked out everything else around him—including the wet and hazardous ground beneath his feet, causing him to slip on the pool of water that had gathered and lose his grip on the super-ax.

His back hit the ground like a ton of bricks, but the pain felt like a sloppy wet kiss when compared to when all of the blades on his custom-made killing device pierced his precious face. Later, Agatha would remember that while Sanchez struggled to remove the object, his shrill and stabbing scream sounded like a dying animal—something that felt ironically fitting given the morbid setting. But Agatha wasn't the type of girl to stand around to see what happened next. She threw open the exit in a heartbeat and hustled her way outside.

Agatha's energy was running on empty as she raced through the open field that greeted her. Chest heaving, she felt a second wind driving her forward after noticing an SUV parked on the road nearby. She sprinted toward it at top speed, spying the shadowy form of the driver with his body bent over, checking under the hood.

"Help!" Agatha cried. "Please! A man's trying to kill me!!"

After coming so far and surviving so much, it was a shame the stranger turned out to be the last person she'd ever want to meet under such circumstances. Once she reached him, he revealed himself to be the Reverend. The moral voice of Little Salem and father to the pretty teenage girl she corrupted.

"Something wrong, little lady?" the Reverend grinned.

"*You!*"

Agatha's eyes widened in terror, but it was already too late. As she turned to flee, she felt the pointy ends of a stun gun sending 50,000 volts straight through her, causing her body to shake like an earthquake until she tragically lost consciousness.

25

REDNECK ROULETTE

While the town of Little Salem could easily be categorized as an exceedingly idyllic type of place, at least on its exterior, the world that existed on its edges was something else entirely. It was here where the territory became much more rural and isolated, and even though the majority of those who lived on the outskirts were just ordinary people going about their daily business, there was also a much more savage and dangerous element lurking about. The residents of Little Salem mainly referred to these foul-looking weather-beaten types as "rednecks," but this was largely a misnomer. These weren't the types of folk whose main interests were activities like hunting, drinking, and fishing. Their interests were of a much crueler and more vulgar nature; namely rape, crystal meth, and murder. Most of the residents found it fortunate that this hidden horde rarely showed themselves around town because nothing good ever happened when they did. But, at the moment, things were far from normal in Little Salem, and Tyler was just as stunned as anyone when he saw the rabid crew of wired degenerates no longer roaming the shadows and now on the loose and patrolling the streets.

The retaliation against the New Lords was in full swing and Ada, McAllister, and Agatha weren't the only ones being targeted. After the Sheriff and his trigger-happy wrecking crew had seen to Ada and her stepbrother, they took off to descend upon the town's newest addition that had ruffled so many feathers of late. It was right on the heels of the Black Death Tavern's grand opening, and the place was packed with strangers from all over. But the rowdy activities would come to an end once the Sheriff's squad car and a dozen rundown pickups pulled up.

When the Sheriff exited the vehicle, he swiftly barked some orders for his bloodthirsty army of outlaws to close off the street. He entered the tavern while accompanied by the meanest and downright surliest of the bunch and fired a warning shot into the ceiling, announcing the establishment was being shut down permanently. At the sound of the gunshot, the patrons tried to flee but were stopped by the door so the Sheriff could take down their names and addresses, discouraging any pesky outsiders from revisiting. And while this was happening, the Sheriff's hand-picked mercenary assault team explored the tavern's upper rooms with explicit orders to shoot any witch on sight, making it extra fortuitous that Mary Sue had issued a warning to the remaining members of Ada's coven after witnessing the arrival of the lawman and his merry band of psychopaths.

By the time Tyler had shown up within earshot to observe this unnerving spectacle, the street outside was blocked off, and total mayhem was breaking out. The rednecks' pickup trucks were parked in the middle of the road, forming a perimeter around the venue, and a dozen of the nastiest jacked-up amphetamine-eyed hooligans you'd never want to meet was patrolling the area with their vast arsenals on display.

Tyler didn't know what to make of this. It appeared that these types of strong-arm tactics were a bit severe for any disturbance. His scattered thoughts were interrupted when he heard a voice calling out to him, and he turned around to spy Mary Sue, crouching in the doorway to the frozen yogurt shop.

"Mary Sue! What's going on?"

"Get down! We don't want them to see us!"

After ducking inside the shop while avoiding the Sheriff's posse, Tyler followed the distressed teenager to the pony corral out back.

"Izzy and Rudy were ambushed by the Sheriff," Mary Sue explained. "The three of us escaped. We don't know what happened to the others."

"So Ada and McAllister—aw dude! They were with Ashton!"

While they were conversing, Tyler saw he was being led into a stable where he found Rudy, typing on a laptop while using a phone tracker program to determine his comrades' whereabouts.

"Agatha's missing too," Rudy said. "I got a bead on her cell phone. Chilling at some slaughterhouse for some reason. I haven't been able to locate Ada's phone or McAllister's."

"Dammit," Tyler grumbled. "I should call Ashton."

"You can call him later," Mary Sue said. "Right now, we need to help Izzy."

Tyler's eyes shifted to the sickly-looking gypsy in the corner, noticing she was wrapped in a blanket and shivering uncontrollably. To say Izzy didn't look good would have been an understatement and Tyler ultimately decided to set aside all other concerns for now and play the game as they were calling it. He wasn't pleased with being expected to play the role of star quarterback all of a sudden but was determined to make the best of it.

"OK, uh... You."

"Rudy."

"Whatever. You're with me. Let's go take an assessment of the current situation or whatever."

Moments later, Tyler and Rudy were sitting behind the counter as armed thugs passed by the front window.

"OK, current situation is...not so good," Tyler bluntly acknowledged. "Got about a dozen trigger-happy goons out on patrol, both sides of the street closed off. We need a distraction."

While racking his brain trying to determine their next course of action, Tyler took notice of the collection of items Rudy had on him: a laptop, a small carrying bag, headphones, and what looked to be some obscure portable vintage recording equipment.

"Dude. What is all that stuff?"

"This? It's nothing. It's...stupid..."

Rudy appeared eager to change the subject, but Tyler declined to look away. After a while, he finally let out a sigh and began to fidget anxiously. He was about to drop some highly specialized esoteric trivia on his companion.

"Do know what sympathetic magic is?" Rudy asked. "There's this story about William S. Burroughs—the famous author? There used to be a deli close to where he lived. Horrible service, was owned by a bunch of creeps. Burroughs thought the neighborhood would be better off without it, so one day he decided to cast a magic spell to, you know...get rid of it."

Tyler stared at Rudy like he was a crazy person.

"OK..."

"Right—so, aside from being a famous author, Burroughs was into creating experiments that played with our perceptions of reality, OK? Him and this guy, Brion Gysin, invented this thing called *the cut-up method*, which experimented with cutting up words, sounds, images; and then piecing them back together to produce a magical effect. It's a technique used by artists. Writers, musicians—I'm talking David Bowie, Mick Jagger, Kurt Cobain—"

"OK, I get it! Enough with the pop history lesson!"

"OK, so—no need to get all—so one day Burroughs cuts up a bunch of sounds with some recording equipment. Sounds highlighting the general chaos of the city. He pieces them together—catfights, traffic jams, neighbors arguing in the street. Burroughs then goes and walks back and forth in front of the deli playing what he recorded, creating this invisible soundtrack that was consciously...unsettling. Weeks later, the place closed down."

Rudy glanced weakly at Tyler to check on his reaction to his story, dismayed to find him still staring at him like he was certifiable.

"This was because of the recording, not because the deli had poor service," Tyler offered skeptically.

Rudy released a long sigh. "See? I told you it was stupid. But I thought I would...you know, try it out and see for myself. The other night I played a recording I made in front of a crowd of people, and they all seemed to snap. Everybody lost it. Went completely off the hinges without ever knowing why."

Tyler frowned dourly, considering their lack of options.

He glanced toward the ceiling.

"Does this store have a PA system?"

As Tyler was setting a plan in motion, across the street from them, the Sheriff continued taking down names of visitors who were leaving the tavern. He was interrogating several of Wilbur and Nancy's reliable friends and neighbors, all of them dressed in painfully unflattering goth fashion staples and looking more like a bad middle-aged cover band of Switchblade Symphony than a group of hip suburbanites out for a whirlwind night on the town.

"Let us go!" Jerry pleaded. "We're local small business owners!"

"Names?" the Sheriff inquired, frowning humorlessly.

"Mr. Sheriff? This is a big misunderstanding!" Steve protested.

"Honestly, we just came here to use the bathroom!" Cheryl added.

The Sheriff took a beat before looking up and sneering.

"Get out of here."

"Thank you, Sheriff. You won't regret this!"

Meanwhile, back at the frozen yogurt shop, Rudy had unplugged Wilbur's iPod from the sound system and hooked up his recording equipment to the PA. Mary Sue had joined Rudy behind the counter with the shivering Izzy still wrapped in a blanket, watching expectantly as he made the final adjustments.

With all the preparations finally complete, Rudy nodded to Tyler, crouched next to the door and observing the activity out front. It was now or never if they had any hopes of getting Izzy to a place of safety, and Tyler swallowed his nagging cynicism and gave Rudy a hesitant thumb's up. His cagey associate released an anxious breath before pressing Play on the recording equipment, slowly cranking up the volume by twisting a dial on the PA.

Outside, the chaotic sounds of Rudy's noise collage started to fill the air, playing softly and imperceptibly on the loudspeaker on the roof of the shop. So far, it appeared that no one on the street was taking notice. Armed rednecks continued to patrol the area, the Sheriff continued his interrogations, and Jerry, Steve, Cheryl, and Priscilla stood restlessly next to Steve's parked Mercedes, currently blocked in by the throng of rundown pickup trucks.

"Um, hello?" Steve inquired. "We seem to be blocked in?"

"*That ain't my problem is it?*" a redneck barked impatiently.

"No—no, definitely not," Steve stammered, trying his best to avoid a confrontation. The humble suburbanites' outlandish outfits had caught the attention of several of the murderous outlaws patrolling the area, and one of them turned to another while wearing an unseemly snaggletooth grin.

"Well, looky here," the snaggletoothed redneck exclaimed. "Hey, Bear Claw! Them two are dressed like a pair of gay-boys!"

While this was occurring, Rudy slowly turned up the volume on the PA. Mary Sue held her breath, and Tyler continued to peer forward from his place next to the door, watching the street expectantly. Rudy's noise collage was getting louder, and at least one of the rednecks was beginning to appear increasingly bothered by something. His face was turning sour and starting to twitch.

This was the reaction from "Bear Claw," a steroid-fueled bulldozer of a man who the snaggletooth redneck, a meth-mouthed degenerate named Ezekiel, was addressing. Tyler and the others had no way of knowing it, but the man known as Bear Claw would prove to be the spark to ignite the chaos that was about to explode.

"Woo-ee! Them boys are dressed like they're a-visitin' from San Francisco!" Ezekiel continued to jeer.

Bear Claw wasn't having any of it, suddenly looking agitated.

"What yew grinnin' at, dumbass?"

"I'm grinnin' at what I feel like, yew ugly sonuvabitch!"

"That right? I reckon yew better wipe that smile offa yer face if yew know what's good for ya!"

Ezekiel spat on the ground, not taking kindly to the threat.

"Woo-ee! That sounds like somethin' yer momma told me when I was givin' it to her up the back door!"

Once this comment was uttered, both men raised their rifles and pointed them at each other. It looked like a bloody showdown was about to erupt at any moment.

"Yew take that back now, ya hear?"

"Yew take it back!"

"No, *yew* take it back!"

Tyler could barely believe what he was seeing.

Was the noise collage really working?

With their opportunity to flee fast approaching, Tyler signaled to Rudy to turn up the dial even more to assist them, and the anger of the two inbreds appeared to rise dramatically.

"Listen up, ya scrawny peckerwood." Bear Claw cocked his weapon, staring daggers at Ezekiel. "And y'all listen good cuz I'm only gonna say this once, ya hear? I'ma give yew to the count of *five* to wipe that stupid candy-ass grin offa yer face or so help me—"

Ezekiel cocked his weapon as well. "And I'ma give yew to the count of *three* to stop a-hecklin' me! Or are yew a-wanting s'more hollow space between yer ears?"

By this time, both had reached their boiling point, so the deadly countdown began.

"Five!

"Three!"

"One!"

Bang!

At the countdown's abrupt conclusion, both men fired their rifles in unison, blowing each other's faces clean off. Blood and pieces of brain sprayed out of the back of their skulls and into the street—a gruesome sight exceeded by the fact that both men died while still standing on their feet, making it appear that their argument might have even stretched past death as both bodies seemed to struggle to be the last to drop to the ground before finally falling in unison.

Tyler gasped aloud at the sight, wholly astounded by the senseless act of carnage. But he quickly returned to his senses as he watched the Sheriff eyeball the two corpses and signaled to Rudy to crank up the volume to the max.

Without missing a beat, Rudy obeyed as instructed. Sure enough, just like outside the church, the inventive cut-up seemed to inspire a full-on riot as all of the rednecks went into attack mode, throwing punches and kicking up dust.

Even Nancy and Wilbur's neighbors appeared to be affected by the sounds. Jerry and Steve were slap-fighting like a pair of school-girls while Cheryl and Priscilla were engaged in their own immature tussle, pulling each other's hair and shrieking like a pair of hellcats as the noise collage played at full volume.

As the Sheriff stared in stunned silence at the giant street brawl intensifying in front of him, Tyler signaled to Rudy and Mary Sue to commence their escape.

"Go! Go! Go! Go!"

With their enemies distracted, Rudy and Mary Sue rushed to the doorway with Izzy cradled in Rudy's arms. Miraculously, the group managed to flee down the boulevard while the Sheriff was busy addressing the all-out pandemonium erupting all around him.

Later, while reminiscing about this event, Tyler was never entirely certain that the inventive noise collage had been the decid-ing factor in their getaway. It could have just as easily been made possible by having so many violent personalities gathered together—something that made the vicious spectacle inevitable. But the growing list of strange occurrences was now forcing him to con-sider that this thing that what for lack of a better word was called "magic" might actually be real.

26

BLACK MAGIC 101

———

Tensions were running high at the Nipmuc Nation Reservation with the sight of McAllister's wounds proving as much of a shock for those who greeted them as they'd been to Ashton. When the visitors pulled up outside the reservation's general store, a solemn gathering of tribal elders was assembled. One look at the slaughter-soaked backseat of the convertible was all it took and an elder began yelling angrily at the giant who led the wounded to them, voicing his outrage in a tribal dialect Ashton couldn't make any sense of.

To his surprise, Ashton found himself and McAllister being dragged by a pair of men in one direction while Ada was carried off in another. The two male outsiders were hauled up the road to a cabin that served as a communal meetinghouse and muscled into a large room decorated with a modest selection of furniture and hallucinatory tribal imagery. Ashton expressed a marked sense of indignation at the gesture, demanding for a doctor to see to his injured associate.

Glancing to where McAllister was laid out on a table, he saw a body that was twisting and contorting, but while he was distracted, the two men made their exit and the next thing he heard was the sound of keys and a heavy deadbolt being turned.

"You're locking us in? No. No no no no—*what are you doing?*"

Ashton rushed to the door, trying the knob to discover he was trapped inside. He banged on the door and tried to plead with his stony-hearted captors, but it was no use. Once this was understood, he hurried back to McAllister, who was groaning in agony, his body shaking and convulsing, and when Ashton attempted to grab his shoulders to hold him steady, the wounded firebrand shoved him away with a disturbing display of human strength that sent the amateur ghost hunter flying across the room.

Ashton was struggling to regain his senses as he witnessed McAllister falling off of the table. He watched the young man howl like a crazed animal, his entire body tense with inner torment. The pain he was experiencing must have been excruciating, but it was what Ashton saw next that he found utterly unexplainable and about as haunting and mystifying as anything he'd ever seen: McAllister crouching on his hands and knees as bullet fragments started dropping out of his chest and falling to the floor, along with sticky globs of the unsettling black ooze coursing through his veins.

Unsurprisingly, the sight sent Ashton into a panic.

"What the fuck! Holy fuck! *Holy fuck!*"

With the spent ammunition clattering to the floor like pennies from heaven, Ashton spun around and banged his fists on the door.

"Help! Somebody help!"

No one responded, leaving him to face these unspeakable horrors on his own. Locked in a room with something not entirely of this world with all the windows barred and grated and no visible means of escape.

While Ashton frantically racked his brain for what to do to flee this awful predicament, he heard the sound of heavy breathing. He turned to see McAllister slowly rising to his feet, a dark puddle of black ooze now staining the floor beneath him, with a healthy pile of bullet fragments resting on top of it.

"What's the matter, Ashton?" McAllister sneered. "Afraid I'll bite?"

Fearing for his life and sanity, Ashton instantly turned white as a sheet. But something unexpected happened: the monster showed little interest in him. After suffering a painful coughing fit, McAllister staggered to a dark corner of the meetinghouse and fell to the floor in a heap. To Ashton's surprise and relief, his fellow prisoner made no attempt at all to challenge him, exerting only enough effort to nestle into the shadows before offering a few weak words in an attempt to console his distressed companion.

"Relax. I'm not going to hurt you," he muttered. "For now."

Eventually, the giant came to retrieve Ashton and accompanied him to check on Ada, who was recovering in a large tent. There, he found her positioned on her back with her eyes closed and a blanket placed on top of her. He found it comforting that she seemed to be recuperating, and the sight instantly reignited his endless curiosity in the ethereal waif.

After leaving the tent, Ashton started voicing all the questions nagging away at him. He chatted briefly with the giant and asked if it was true that Ada was a witch. The giant confirmed this but stressed she didn't choose to be born this way. He also asserted that she wasn't as bad as some of the other dangers in Little Salem, all while staring at the bonfires blazing in the distance where a ceremony was being performed to ward off the presence of evil witches.

Ashton asked the giant about McAllister and watched him pause before delivering an answer that proved to be even more cryptic.

"My tribe doesn't have a word for what he is," the giant said. "If we did, it would probably translate to 'he who walks at night.'"

This explanation failed to offer any satisfaction to Ashton, and after parting ways with the giant, he returned to the meetinghouse to confront Ada's spooky stepsibling, finding him in the same place he had left him: slumped over in the corner with his back against the wall, face hidden by shadow.

Upon his entry, Ashton gazed apprehensively at the poor bastard, still wary of being in the same room with such a frightening and unsettling anomaly. But Ashton remained hungry for answers. As a peace offering, he crossed over and set a bottled water a few feet away from him, watching McAllister ignore the gesture and search his bullet-ridden getup for a pack of smokes instead.

It took several moments for McAllister to find what he was craving, pulling several items from his pockets in the process. For Ashton, the lengthy quest was a welcome distraction. He used the opportunity to find a seat on the other side of the room in a place of safety before executing an awkward and heedful attempt to converse with the creature.

"I can't believe you're still alive."

"Am I?"

A short silence followed.

"Why'd they try to kill you?"

"Must not have liked the new titty bar."

McAllister lit a smoke, struggling painfully not to cough.

"So, it's true," Ashton expressed warily. "Ada's a witch, and you're... Dude, I don't even know what you are. How did you even get like this?"

McAllister exhaled a cloud of smoke before answering.

"Well, one night, after enjoying some drinks, my parents were feeling a bit randy..."

"Uh-huh. So no straight answers."

McAllister started coughing profusely. When the painful hacking stopped, several moments passed in succession before he spoke again. "That depends. Tell me..."

The battered, roughed-up oddity leaned into a shaft of moonlight, and what Ashton saw before him chilled his very soul.

McAllister's eyes were still hidden by sunglasses, but his entire face was now a spiderweb of blackened capillaries, the darkened blood vessels a sharp contrast to the stark whiteness of his skin and teeth, grinning eerily while asking: "Do you believe in black magic?"

In all honesty, Ashton didn't know what he believed when it came to this subject. It was true that he was a lot more fascinated by the topic than Tyler, but he was also very skeptical when it came to things like witchcraft and superstitious hocus-pocus. For Ashton, the supernatural was one thing, but the dark arts seemed to be the stuff of warped minds and paranoid fantasies. Something invented to explain things that were highly dubious and couldn't be understood by standard lines of reasoning. However, what he had seen in the past twenty-four hours was enough to inspire him to start to question everything, so he listened intently as McAllister settled back into the shadows and began his explanation.

"In the Middle Ages, medieval magicians started composing special books containing all the forbidden knowledge collected from across the centuries. Strange...incantations and magical symbols that had been smuggled out of Egypt and preserved in Spain and in Byzantium before being passed on to the heretics in Southern France and Italy. Some of the oldest magical knowledge was believed to have been given to us by angels. And some of it was believed to have been given to us by much darker forces."

Ashton's eyes widened.

So McAllister was talking about angels and demons. Ashton believed in demons, but angels were something he wasn't so sure of. It was pretty rare to run into an angel while investigating a haunted house or building, but demons were another matter completely. A demon was something you had a much better chance of running into whether you believed in one or not. Angels? Not so much.

Still, while Ashton's interest was piqued, if he'd known what McAlister was really talking about, he would have known the angels that he was referring to were a huge leap from his own personal interpretation of these things—as well as a far cry from the benevolent celestial beings of the harp and halo variety.

"The knowledge in this...material," McAllister continued, "can teach a person many things. How to create magical objects. How to cast spells or curses. But above all, a grimoire contains the knowledge of how to summon and communicate with powerful supernatural entities. Magicians in the past who conversed with these beings were often granted special gifts. Wisdom. Immortality. There are rumors that one magician was given information on how to launch the Apocalypse itself."

Ashton's eyes widened even further, but he was still feeling apprehensive regarding whether he was ready to believe any of these tales. Looking at McAllister, he questioned whether this was the type of person where anything he said could be taken at face value—this mysterious abnormality speaking amid a cloud of cigarette smoke.

"Magic. From the angels."

"Stranger things exist. And stranger days ahead."

McAllister took another drag from his cigarette while suppressing a cough. The awkward silence that followed presented the perfect moment for Ashton to voice his unwavering skepticism.

"You expect me to believe all this? Angels, demons—people communicating with these things? That's what you believe?"

McAllister didn't answer right away. It wasn't clear whether this was due to any personal apprehension on his part or because his body was too weak. However, after another few moments had passed, he finally addressed the question as he stared forward vacantly, his voice tired and forlorn.

"I believe that when you're young, the people who try to raise you, who try to explain to you how the world works, why things happen, what's '*going on...*'

"I believe that after a while, as much as you might try to accept the things they tell you, *you know*—in the back of your mind, something haunts you and tells you, and *you know that it doesn't add up.*

"And I believe there are certain *tools*. Things a person can *do*, lengths a person can *go* to receive a clearer picture. That's what I believe."

McAllister took another long drag before Ashton questioned him again.

"That's why you're like this? By playing with...?"

Ashton never completed the inquiry, watching McAllister's head take a slight dip like he was about to pass out.

"McAllister?"

"It doesn't matter," McAllister mumbled, briefly rousing himself to wakefulness. "I knew what I was getting into. To protect the others, I had to sacrifice my..."

Regrettably, McAllister never completed his explanation, appearing to have worn himself out. That is, until another few moments had passed, and he finally spoke once more:

"*You see... To practice magic... To practice true magic, you have to embrace the dark side. You must make a friend of darkness and chaos. Yes, always make a friend of chaos...*"

After that, McAllister fell silent, likely passing out from all of the blood loss or the loss of whatever it was that was pumping through his system.

Ashton left to check on Ada shortly afterward, and after having a brief but unnerving conversation with her, he sought out the giant and discussed with him how, in light of recent events, he no longer knew what to believe. When asking him whether Ada and McAllister were evil, the giant said there were definitely those out there who desired for him to see them as such. He told him an ancient Navaho story about two siblings who traveled to the ends of the Earth to rid the world of monsters, but his words failed to offer any comfort to Ashton.

Meanwhile, McAllister continued to sit in the shadows, his body drifting in and out of consciousness. The cigarette in his fingers had burnt to a nub, and on the ground were the items he emptied out of his pockets: a cracked smartphone, the thin hardcover book from the chemical plant, a gruesome ceremonial dagger sheathed in black leather, and a folded scrap of paper that read, "BEWARE THE IDES OF MARCH."

McAllister and Ada seemed to have encountered some of the hidden hazards this ominous message predicted. But rather than rack his brain trying to guess the identity of the deceitful traitor lurking among them, McAllister found himself too tired and physically exhausted to think. He almost found this relaxing, given how his mind tended to overwork itself to the point of reckless instability.

For the moment, McAllister was too burnt out to think about anything. Or to worry about how his mortal end might soon be upon him. He felt so utterly at ease on account of the blissful halcyon haze his body was swimming in, it allowed him to ignore the disembodied voice taunting him from the darkness mere seconds before he once again blacked out.

"Poor baby. You really messed yourself up this time."

"Go away, Dakota."

...

"Meanie."

27

ANGELS AND VISITATIONS

After escaping from the Sheriff's goons, Mary Sue and Rudy brought Izzy to Tyler's hotel room, and there was no one more amazed that they were able to evade the threat of catastrophe through the use of "magic" than Rudy himself.

"Woo! It's a celebration, bitches!" Rudy yelled, bouncing around the room like a pinball. "I can't believe it worked!"

Tyler remained more subdued, still floored that Rudy's noise collage appeared to have initiated both a double murder and a riot. "That was insane. Did those dudes really kill each other?"

"Oh, who cares? They were scumbags. They would have murdered us without a second thought. And raped our pretty corpses."

"Would you keep it down? I'm trying to take care of Izzy!"

Mary Sue's passionate outburst was entirely justified. Despite the group's successful escape plan, Izzy wasn't looking good. Her fever hadn't subsided, and she was too weak to keep her eyes open.

This notable lack of progress made it no wonder Mary Sue was so consumed with looking after the poor thing. To anyone with a pair of eyes, it was obvious she had strong affections for the young gypsy, and Tyler decided it might be best to go off with Rudy for a bit to give the girls some space to be alone together.

"All right. Cool your jets, Mary Sue," Tyler said. "We all have our own way of coping with things. C'mon, Rudy. I want to get your opinion on something."

Tyler tossed Rudy his laptop bag and gestured to follow him, glancing at the markings carved into the doorway. Aleister Crowley's magical motto: "*By the power of truth, while living, I have conquered the known universe.*" Or so McAllister had claimed.

Crowley was a subject Tyler assumed he wouldn't be returning to anytime soon, but after following McAllister's advice to review his ghost hunting footage from the attic, he'd been shocked to discover something he overlooked during his initial review of the material. At precisely 4:18 am, for only a few seconds, the faint sound of chanting could be heard—clear evidence of Electronic Voice Phenomena that seemed connected to a residual event from the distant past. The strangest thing of all was the language was like nothing Tyler had ever heard. He emailed an excerpt of the recording to his fellow amateur investigator, Leon, and earlier that evening received a phone call that made the whole matter even more mind-blowing.

"That spooky language? It's called Enochian."

"*Enochian?*"

"Yeah," Leon verified. "It's this occult so-called 'antediluvian' language that two sixteenth-century magicians happened upon. This was during months of magical scrying sessions with a group of entities claiming to be angels.

"The magicians would stare into a black mirror and ask the spirits... Well, everything I guess. And these beings—'angels' or whatever—gave them this crazy angelic language along with all these crazy chants and spells.

"The communications contained a lot of things. A unique mythology, wild prophecy. Some really insane and out-there shit."

"So a pair of magicians came up with it?"

"Well, that or some type of weird supernatural intelligence. Dude, there's not a lot of people who know how to speak this thing, let alone know donkey tits about it. Magicians mostly, other occult types—"

"Aleister Crowley?"

"Yeah, for one. Wish I could tell you more."

"It's cool. I know a guy who can shed some more light for me."

This discussion is what led Tyler to visit the tavern before noticing the Sheriff's thugs were raiding the place. He was hoping to gain a private audience with McAllister, the eccentric Creepshow weirdo who seemed to know more about Aleister Crowley than anyone and that Tyler's ghost recordings contained residual evidence of a ritual Crowley performed over a hundred years ago. Inexplicably, McAllister was also the guy with a dynamite redhead for a girlfriend that Tyler still couldn't stop thinking about.

In light of his resident Crowley expert being missing in action, Tyler decided to consult Rudy for whatever info he could give him, with the skinny miscreant studying the giant protection circle on the attic floor once they reached its location.

"Huh. Looks like an evocation ritual for the demon, Vassago," Rudy casually stated. "Ceremonial Magicians usually call on him to help locate something that's been lost or stolen."

"Ceremonial what? How do you know these things?"

Rudy lit a spliff he removed from his pocket.

"From grimoires."

He exhaled a cloud of smoke as Tyler continued to stare dumbfounded at his unusually knowledgeable associate.

"Want a hit?"

These weirdoes from the tavern are really something else, Tyler thought. He didn't want to think about the type of mischief they got up to when the moon was full. Or all the crazy things Agatha and McAllister took part in whenever the lights were—*dammit! Stop thinking about her, you stupid cretin!*

Still, it was no question that despite their odd behavior and eccentric appearances, Ada's wacky rock band of fellow misfits all seemed to know a great deal when it came to the occult—and not simply in a spooky dress-up kind of way.

"The blueprint for this thing comes from a grimoire called *The Lesser Key of Solomon,*" Rudy said. He gestured to the strange phantasmagoria of occult images and incantations painted upon the floor. "It's basic textbook demon stuff. Demon Magic 101 really. Magician says a spell, tells the spirit what he's looking for. Spirit tells him where to find it. Ba-da-bing ba-da-boom. Nothing to it."

Tyler nodded ambivalently while exhaling a cloud of smoke.

"Wow."

He glanced at the smoldering spliff between his fingers.

"This is some good shit."

Yes sir, these kids sure seemed to know a lot about this type of stuff. But was he really expected to take this seriously? I mean, hell, this was the occult they were talking about. A subject for antisocial losers and college history professors. Last time he checked, the occult was all just superstition. Wasn't it?

On the other hand, a lot of the strange things happening all around him would suddenly start making more sense if the secrets of the occult were factored in. It could explain how a spell performed in a language passed down by strange spiritual beings could leave a residual presence, for one. And if this was actually the case, what was he to make of the curious practice of contacting demons to locate lost objects and so-called "angels" that were handing out magic languages like cereal box prizes? These were just a few of the thoughts that were cycling endlessly through Tyler's restless headspace as he sat next to Rudy, staring attentively at the screen of his laptop, both of them sufficiently blazed at this point.

"Right—so this Enochian stuff? The language was, like, written on these crazy tablets, OK? Crazy mathematical tables arranged into a graph pattern, basically, with a bunch of squares that were filled with the crazy Enochian letters. And from all these crazy tables came the crazy incantations the angels gave to these guys called the Enochian Calls."

Tyler squinted at the screen as Rudy's fingers scrolled through an obscure web page on Enochian Magic. Displayed in front of him was a set of primitive-looking images for what was apparently the Enochian Alphabet.

Rudy clicked on a link that revealed the image of what was apparently the Enochian "Great Table of Earth"—a 25×27 magic square with all of the boxes filled with the peculiar letters.

"There was something like forty-eight of them," Rudy said. "Forty-eight calls or keys to break open the forty-eight gates of understanding."

Rudy's fingers continued working away, closing the image of the square and bringing up an image of the Sigillum Dei Aemeth; the strange occult seal that McAllister had the habit of hanging on the wall prior to performing a ritual—although Tyler would have no way of knowing this. And at that moment, he would've had no idea of how to even process this particular detail even if he did, accepting another drag as he made a valiant effort to organize the foggy contents dancing inside his head: the strange Enochian language; forty-eight Enochian Calls passed down by angels in order to accomplish...something; forty-eight keys and something about forty-eight different gates—is that what he said?

"There was rumored to be a forty-ninth," Rudy added. "The Forty-ninth Enochian Key. But if you chanted it, you would jump-start the Apocalypse or whatever."

Tyler coughed violently, exhaling all the smoke inside of his lungs. "*The Apocalypse?* Dude! This shit sounds dangerous! Who would wanna mess with this?"

Tyler already knew the answer.

McAllister was up to something, and you didn't need to be a math surgeon to put it all together.

McAllister had come to Little Salem in search of something specific. Whatever it was, it had something to do with this crazy Enochian mumbo-jumbo Rudy was laying down for him.

It may have merely been the herb talking, but in light of the information that Rudy was providing, internally, Tyler was now freaking out more than just a little, becoming more and more alarmed by the idea that the occult might actually be the real deal. Tyler's belief in the paranormal may have been inflexible, but he was, by nature, a skeptic. And while his mind was working overtime trying to rationalize his thoughts and observations concerning all of the incredible information Rudy was presenting to him, with every new morsel being offered and every hesitant shred of doubt being struck down, he could feel the walls of reason crumbling all around him, and this terrified him immensely.

And the daunting revelations kept on coming as Tyler sat in silence, staring at the dazzling collection of images being pulled up on Rudy's laptop—complex magical tables with wild names like "The Ensigns of Creation" and "Liber Logaeth"—while Rudy took what little was left of the spliff and slipped it into his pocket before blowing Tyler's mind with yet another stunning confession.

"It's hard to believe, I know," Rudy said. "Who knows what those old magicians were communicating with. Malevolent spirits, aliens from the star system, Sirius. Hell, it coulda just been their own subconscious nervous systems.

"But regardless, there is some crazy scientific knowledge hidden in this shizz. Scientists have scanned certain sections of the Angelic Conversations and found all these crazy mathematical concepts that no one would have known about in those days. It's, like, proof they were communicating with at least some form of higher intelligence. And we're talking about something with mad crazy-crazy intelligence..."

Rudy began typing furiously, and a kaleidoscope of obscure occult images flooded the desktop. One of them was an Enochian table that was smaller than all of the others; 8×8 squares with a title above it reading, "The Round Table of Nalvage." Rudy pressed a key on his laptop, which seemed to be running a program of some kind, and all of the strange primitive letters inside of the table began lighting up one by one, the letters shining brightly and returning to normal as a complex four-dimensional geometric image appeared, rotating on the screen. A series of hypercubes that seemed to be encoded within the secret language sitting inside the square.

"Dude," Tyler softly uttered, staring in slack-jawed awe at the rotating image.

Could it be true? Was this proof that some kind of bizarre superior intelligence was attached to the strange language? And if that was the case, was it really that much of a stretch to consider the code to launch a global apocalypse could be planted there as well?

Something else was on Tyler's mind, and he wasted no time with voicing this important realization.

"Hey. Are you hungry?"

Several minutes later, Tyler and Rudy were sitting in the ground floor café, munching on bowls of ice cream. They helped themselves since the staff had already turned in for the night, and the building was quiet as a tomb.

The insides of Tyler's mind were as active and busy as ever as he continued to contemplate the unsettling information Rudy had revealed to him. He positioned this with McAllister's unholy quest to discover an item that was undoubtedly linked to this odd material in a town that held a haunting history of witch-hunts and obscure secret societies—not to mention the growing list of events that had a distinct aura of magic and high strangeness attached to them.

"Whole lotta witchcraft goin' on in this town," Tyler stated.

"You don't know the half of it," Rudy said.

"But why here? Why Little Salem?"

Rudy tensed up at the question, averting his eyes and staring at the tabletop. Tyler knew the skinny misfit knew way more than he was letting on, but he wasn't going to push it. Ada and McAllister were clearly calling the shots in the group, and it would be a cold day in hell before he got any clear answers from those two weirdoes.

Still, if McAllister was in town for some reason other than getting his rocks off with his busty ginger lady friend and this had something to do with locating the missing Forty-ninth Enochian Key, could it be that Ada was just along for the ride or was she in pursuit of her own agenda? Was that why he didn't know the half of it as Rudy had so bluntly indicated? And what about the redhead? How was she involved in all of this? And did he just maybe have a shot with her or was his mind just telling him this because he was somehow doomed to continue thinking about her until he inevitably blew his brains out to silence this maddening obsession?

Tyler was finding it hard to concentrate as he struggled to confront these questions. At the time, he had no way of knowing that, in a matter of moments, he would be receiving some guidance to help resolve these puzzling mysteries, and that the terrible encounter would leave him totally shaken.

28

A TRAGIC HISTORY

———————

Lucy had her eyes closed and her hands tightly folded as she mumbled a shaky prayer under her breath. It had been several days since she'd been imprisoned in the basement of her family's vacation home, and several hours since she'd been locked inside of a discarded wooden cabinet.

It took less than a week for her father to demonstrate just how far his sanity had deteriorated since Ada van Dreyer's return to Little Salem. Word spread like wildfire about Ada's presence after McAllister's disturbing visit to the Truegoods and the unsettling introduction of the Black Death Tavern. What Lucy had no knowledge of was that in the midst of these events, her father was becoming consumed with worry due to the heavy burden placed upon him to address the situation—a situation where to help coerce the good reverend in the right direction, a mysterious package was left for him to discover on his way to retrieve the daily paper.

Inside the package was a book called the *Malleus Maleficarum*, also known as "The Witches' Hammer"—the infamous witch-hunting manual from the fifteenth century. The notorious volume was the first of its kind to elevate the practice of sorcery to criminal status, and throughout its many pages, it offered a detailed examination of recommended procedures for identifying a witch, along with various methods for torturing her to gain a speedy confession.

One of the most significant aspects of the work was the claim by the authors that witches were almost always known to be women; that women were inevitably more prone to diabolism due to their connection to Eve, who was tempted by the devil so easily, and also due to woman's abnormal insatiability when it came to carnal lust.

Lucy would remain ignorant that it was the argument regarding the irreparable frailty of women that her father began to obsess over. For several nights, he stayed up late reading the book from cover to cover, memorizing the contents and allowing the material to consume his daily thoughts and meditations. She would also remain unaware that the book was instrumental in her father's recent cold and hostile treatment toward her, keeping a watchful eye on his sheltered teenage daughter at every possible moment and locking her in her bedroom at night for no discernible reason.

Another thing that Lucy was initially in the dark about was that she wasn't the first victim of her deranged guardian's recent obsession. When she was dragged down to the basement and chained to the wall after a failed attempt to escape her harsh imprisonment, she found another body already present—only this body had been dead for days and was lying under a filthy white bed sheet.

The body was revealed to be Lucy's mother. Her mother had always been timid and submissive toward her husband, but her pleas to treat Ada with mercy had been all the proof he needed that the devil had gotten a hold of her. Once this was acknowledged, he saw it as his sacred duty to punish her. The Bible stated, "Thou shalt not suffer a witch to live," and this was his newly adopted mission statement. But the Reverend's devoted wife was only to be the first victim in his new outrageous crusade against the sinful, and it wasn't until after Lucy had been locked in the basement for over a day that she was fully introduced to his newly awakened cruelty.

It was late at night when her father returned home and ventured down to the basement, with Agatha knocked out cold and thrown over his shoulder. There was little Lucy could do to prevent the heinous travesties that were about to take place, watching helplessly as her father bound the witch's wrists and gagged her mouth with duct tape before hanging her body from the ceiling.

Once Agatha was secured into place, the Reverend recited his intentions to his two captives. He called their attention to the papal bull issued in 1484 that recognized, for the first time officially, the existence of witches all across the world, so as to allow the Church's followers the authority to prosecute and exterminate said witches.

"The pope at the time? He called witches 'the enemy of all mankind,'" the Reverend recalled dramatically. "Said 'they do not shrink from committing and perpetuating the foulest abominations and filthiest excesses to themselves and others.'"

"Well, I think two can play that game. Don't you?"

This proved only to be an introduction, and it wasn't until the following morning that the Reverend finally revealed his horrifying plans to them. After dragging Lucy kicking and screaming to the cabinet, the whole time insisting his demented actions were for his daughter's own benefit, the maniacal zealot turned his attention to Agatha, still bound and gagged with her arms above her head, her red designer dress shredded to pieces.

Wearing a sickening smile, the Reverend made it clear it was best for her to abandon all hope if this was something she still possessed.

"Don't want all those cries for help distracting us from our fun." He looked Agatha up and down, ignoring the sounds of his daughter's desperate pleas as she banged on the door of the cabinet. "You're a piece of work. You know that? A witch like you. One who with but a glance can bring a grown man to his knees.

"Were you born with that trait? A special scent that runs in the family? Well? Cat got your tongue? You're not denying you're a witch, are you?"

With one swift move, the Reverend ripped the duct tape from Agatha's mouth.

"I deny nothing," she said, eyes blazing with hatred.

The Reverend seemed pleased with this response, relieved to see there was still some fight left in her.

"Good," he replied. "Then let us begin."

The Reverend next retrieved a selection of items—a towel, a water pitcher, a noose, and a box of matches. He explained to Agatha how during the days of the Holy Inquisition—what witches lovingly referred to as "The Burning Times"—that while interrogating his suspect, the inquisitor would often first put the witch to the question. This usually involved a lot of torture, discomfort, and misery, and the Reverend was hoping to move past this section quickly to get to the sentencing, which would always be death, unfortunately.

"I say we should run the gauntlet," he said. "Death by as many measures possible until that slut-sewer of a body gives up. The three most popular witch-killing staples of the period! Death by drowning, death by hanging, and my personal favorite, death by burning. What do you say?"

When Lucy heard her father's scheme, she was horrified. Tears streamed down her face as she whined at him in protest. Agatha remained much more apathetic, her voice taking on a detached and cynical quality.

"There's no amount of torture you can do to me that life hasn't put me through already."

The Reverend bristled at the challenge.

"Yes, well, we'll see about that."

The next series of events, despite Agatha's convictions, was arguably just as alarming as Lucy had imagined as her father first subjected Agatha to water torture. He placed a towel over her face and poured a pitcher of water over the cloth, forcing the water down her throat to simulate the experience of drowning. As Agatha's body began to quiver and shake while she endured the horrific punishment, Lucy's screams grew louder and louder, her trembling fists pounding on the door to her makeshift prison while observing the witch's suffering through a small quarter-shape hole just above the lock. Sadly, Lucy's father ignored his daughter's pleas and continued the torture session with sadistic glee.

"Repent! Repent of your sins!" the man barked while forcing more water down the back of the witch's throat. However, the Reverend soon grew tired of this and decided it was time to move on to the hanging portion of the activities, tossing the pitcher aside and releasing the rope suspending his victim from the ceiling.

Once Agatha dropped to the ground with a violent thud, he threw a noose over her neck and pulled it tight, cutting off all the oxygen to her system before she even had a chance to catch her breath. The sight of her father's iniquity proved much too terrible to bear for Lucy, and she tightly closed her teary eyes as he basked in his personal Crusade against the sinful. As the torture continued, the hapless teenager thought she heard the same discomforting laughter from the frightening demon that she saw every time she was in her father's presence, the dark red monstrosity smiling sinisterly with its fiendish claws gripping the madman's back, showing no intention of ever surrendering its precious host.

But the Reverend soon tried of the hanging portion as well. After he had exerted himself and observed that Agatha's eyes were wet with tears, he decided to move to the next bestial punishment.

"Are those actual tears you are crying?" he mockingly observed. "The old witch-hunting manuals tell us a witch will only cry false tears when the Lord's justice has been put to her. Maybe you're not a witch after all."

When the noose was released, Agatha gasped for air as Lucy continued sobbing from the confines of her claustrophobic wooden cell. With the second torture completed, the Reverend crossed to the wall and re-suspended his victim from the ceiling.

"The Holy Inquisitors believed witches to be the greatest evil in all of humanity," he said, "and I agree with them. Some Christians see the Holy Inquisition as a black mark on the Church's history. I see it as a *golden age*."

"You're a sick, sick man," Agatha gasped.

The Reverend stifled a short chuckle.

"I'm sure there are some who would agree with you. When you and your degenerate companions came rolling into town, my wife tried to argue that you should be treated with mercy.

"But such is woman—weak and corruptible. Just like her predecessor, Eve, the devil's harlot. Woman is responsible for all the many sins of this world for it is she who first tempted man to sin. And there is no woman more wicked than the woman who gives her body and soul to the devil in the guise of witchcraft.

"So, where were we? Ah yes, death by burning."

For the grand finale, the Reverend pulled a sheet off of a covered object in the corner of the room. It was a gruesome piece of furniture covered in spikes: a precise replica of the Witch's Chair, the grisly medieval torture device that Ashton had observed in the Little Salem Witch Museum.

After retrieving a portable heater from the other side of the basement and placing it underneath the cold iron seat, the Reverend explained to Agatha the benefits of employing the contraption after the spikes had first been heated.

"Gives a brand new meaning to the term, 'hot seat.' This should only take a few moments. See you in a bit."

The Reverend left his two victims alone after this while Lucy continued to sob uncontrollably. She listened to the sound of his departing footsteps as the portable heater buzzed innocuously, emitting a cozy orange glow and slowly warming up the cold metal surface of the barbaric torture instrument.

Hours after the torment began, Lucy desperately turned to prayer to console her, begging for any type of assistance. While remaining disheartened by her own terrible fate, she was even more concerned for the unfortunate woman who was receiving the brunt of her father's punishments. In her mind, there could be nothing more un-Christian than the abominable tortures she witnessed.

"Please, Jesus," Lucy pleaded. "Please have mercy on us in our darkest hour. Please open your heart to us and deliver us to safety."

"Hey. Blondie. What are you doing?"

Lucy started at the voice and turned her attention to the small hole inside of the cabinet. Peering through it, she spied the tired and battered form of Agatha. The whole basement had gone deathly quiet with only the faint buzzing being heard from the heater, the seat of the chair in the corner now glowing bright red.

Agatha's voice had taken on the eerie calmness she used when first responding to the Reverend's schemes. Lucy found it curious she could appear so laidback in light of all the misery she suffered. To a simple, sheltered girl like herself, it made no sense.

"I'm praying to God to help us," Lucy answered. "To set us free."

"Your god will do no such thing," Agatha replied coldly.

Lucy wiped the tears from her eyes while gazing at her fellow prisoner. "How can you say that?" she asked. "You know, not all of God's servants are like my dad. God loves all his children, and if you open up your heart to him..."

Agatha chuckled wearily. "Open up my cursed heart? Your god doesn't care a pot of piss about me."

Lucy fell silent. She thought that maybe if she demonstrated her ability to listen, the witch would reveal the reasons for her cynicism.

"It won't be long now," Agatha muttered. "I always knew this day would come eventually..."

From the confines of the cabinet, Lucy watched Agatha issue a wry smirk, and steadily, all the answers for her dispirited outlook came pouring out:

"It's funny... I grew up not far from here. A small backwater town. Lived in a trailer, dad was a drunk. Typical, right? Lost my innocence at twelve to one of the neighborhood boys. Not by choice, FYI. When my dad found out, he called tons of names. He even threw an iron at my head. I still have the scar to prove it.

"I fled home at fourteen with my mom and little sisters. But it wasn't long before my mom traded up for a brand new disaster. A baby-faced cocaine dealer named 'Pretty Boy Lou.' Lou had me after I turned seventeen and after that... Well, Lou threw my mom aside, and my dumb jailbait ass was shacked up with him. Snorting a bag a day and turning tricks on the side for some extra scratch.

"Then one day, good ol' Lou sold me in a card game to a pimp named Hercules, and soon I was working the local truck stop. Now, Hercules—he used to wear these big gold rings on his hand, right? Loved to give all his little ladies 'love taps' is what he would call them. But I barely felt them. I was just so messed up all the time.

"I would fall asleep at night dreaming I was making love to an angel. The angel of death. I was a lost cause, and I didn't think I was much longer for this world. That's who I was before I met McAllister and Ada."

Agatha sniffed at the mention of her two companions, fighting back sobs. "They were the first two people to ever treat me like a human being and not some worthless meat puppet. They taught me how to love myself. And they loved me. They truly loved me.

"They saved my life, and I really mean that. I wasn't saved by a man in a pulpit or some invisible super-dad in the sky. It was two remarkable human beings who saved me. But they won't be saving me this time."

Lucy found herself steadily growing more emotional while listening to Agatha's story. She waited expectantly for the stunning conclusion as the sullen redhead turned to admire a pretty green bracelet around her wrist before staring into the darkness.

"Evil came for them like it's come for the two of us," Agatha said. "Because there's only so much goodness in the world, but evil? Evil is as plentiful as the stinking air. So you know what I would do? If I were you and wanted to do something useful? I'd save my breath."

Lucy shuddered as tears silently streamed down her cheeks. There was so much about Agatha that was a total mystery, but to hear even a little about the heartbreaking experiences she suffered made her feel more sympathy than ever for the unfortunate witch.

This dark and disdainful view of the world that Agatha possessed seemed all too fitting given the girls' current set of circumstances. It was easy for Lucy to see how Agatha could lack the faith she had—especially when considering the tragic and difficult life she'd been dealt. Even at that second, she felt her own faith being tested, finding that, in the absence of a miracle, it was growing more unlikely that they would make it through the night.

29

IN A LONELY PLACE

———————

As Ada lay recuperating at the Nipmuc Nation Reservation, her foggy mind thought back to the events that had brought her there, starting with the memory of accompanying Ashton and McAllister across the dimly lit yard of the chemical plant and back to the conversation with her stepbrother from earlier that morning.

Persuading Ashton to join their investigation had been no contest. Based on how she had dressed for the invitation, this was to be expected as she had chosen the perfect combination of sweet and sinful to present herself in: a black long-sleeve Pictureplane T-shirt and an ankle-length red velvet skirt with a long sultry slit running up the side, her inventive ensemble topped off with a pair of black thigh-high stockings and her customary combat boots.

Ada smiled whimsically as she returned to the tavern following her successful sales pitch. *Marketing and public relations: the real dark arts of the twenty-first century.* No hypnotism or spellcraft was even required.

When she arrived, she found McAllister in one of the black vinyl booths, drinking Bloody Mary's with a pair of strippers. The girls gave up their seats once they heard Ada's heels clicking across the dance floor to the beat of the noisy old-school deathrock playing on the jukebox, her slender hips swaying to the rhythm as she made her steady approach.

McAllister's present company was of no concern to her. All she cared about was enjoying the pleasure of her stepbrother's company for a brief spell and was feeling much more distracted by the bruised purple rash on his neck, steadily darkening to black.

"Did you convince him?" McAllister asked as she took a seat beside him.

"Would I ever let you down? McAllister, what's wrong with—"

He swatted her hand away from him and quickly turned up his collar. "It's nothing. You didn't mention the diary, I'm assuming. Having 'Ghost Boy' with us will be good cover, but he doesn't need to know everything."

The purple rash was highly disconcerting, but Ada chose to mask her concern for the time being. She knew she wouldn't be getting anything out of her stubborn stepsibling if that was his intention and wanted to savor what little time they had together before becoming consumed in their larger schemes. Tragically, they hadn't had many chances to enjoy many moments alone together since their reunion, and she wasn't sure if this was because he had been avoiding her or if it was because they'd been so busy. Lately, it felt like these questions were chattering away non-stop in her habitually overactive headspace, and she wished that he would stop hiding his feelings for once and open up to her for a change. Nevertheless, she decided to avoid a painful confrontation by keeping their conversation on topics that were safe, limiting their discussion to subjects like Alfonse Masters and the missing diary.

"You're sure Alfonse Masters had this thing," Ada carefully inquired. "It's strange he didn't go cuckoo crazy like the others."

"Oh, Fonzi had it," McAllister remarked while chewing on the celery stick that came with his beverage. "That corn-fed simpleton didn't make all those science-y breakthroughs on his own."

After completing her own research on this odd figure, Ada had come to the same conclusion. Miles had provided her with a wealth of information where she learned that Alfonse Masters had been a filthy rich industrialist during the early years of the last century and owned a lucrative chemical plant located just beyond the borders to Little Salem. The plant produced various paints and corrosive chemicals used by the Allied Forces during the First World War. Before this, Masters had become wealthy after discovering a way to use ionized mercury as a cure for various sexually transmitted diseases. Modern science had long since moved on from his findings, but he was quite the man of his field in his day.

What was especially curious about Masters was he made several brilliant discoveries and secured an absolute fortune without ever showing signs of possessing a mind for research or obtaining a college degree. This was why McAllister was convinced he was either a bona fide genius or a total charlatan and strongly suspected the latter in this situation.

Being one step closer to locating the diary was exciting, of course. That there was a connection between Masters and Crowley that McAllister was still trying to figure out was equally compelling. But while discussing this information, Ada found her mind wandering to much more personal matters. She found herself staring fixedly at her handsome platinum-haired companion, her bright, oversized eyes studying him intently.

"Tom Thumb, Alfonse Masters, Aleister Crowley," Ada mused.

McAllister leaned toward her, grinning devilishly. "They're all connected. And you and I are so close I can feel it."

Their conversation had been cut short by other pressing urgencies, but at least they were able to share a smile together.

Human feelings—what a nuisance, Ada thought to herself while reminiscing. But, in actuality, Ada loved feelings. The rush of emotions while enjoying a brand new experience or while experiencing joy or excitement or love. Feelings were what reminded her she was alive and directed her in her special magical relationship with the world. At the same time, being extra sensitive to all that was going around her often felt like an immense burden, and she wondered if this happened to be another quality that she and her crafty "stepbrother" both shared.

"I was reading online there was a gray figure spotted in the underground tunnels around here."

Ada followed her memories back to snapping out of her reveries as she looked to where Ashton was pointing: a position on the map of the plant's facilities that listed the entrance to a series of subterranean tunnels up ahead. The dark maze of tunnels underneath the plant was likely used for moving things below ground during the war, and if Ashton wanted to explore them, well, she would be game for that. After all, what they did together during their investigation was of no real consequence. Not when taking into account the real reasons for why she and McAllister had come there.

And at that very moment, McAllister appeared to be on the exact same page as she was, smiling slyly at his clever stepsister and stating:

"You two go ahead. I'll meet up."

After this, Ada cautioned her brother to be safe, and the group split up and went their separate ways.

Getting into the locked warehouse was no problem for Ada. The tricky part was looking convincing while pretending it had been unlocked all along. At this point, Ashton was still unaware of the full extent of her special abilities, and it felt unwise for her to reveal these to him until the timing made perfect sense.

After entering the large building thanks to her unique skill set, the pair found themselves in what looked to be a blower room filled with giant rusted compression engines. Treading lightly, they proceeded to use their night-vision cameras to guide them and help them navigate their way through the quiet and musty darkness.

"This place is sick," Ashton noted. "Tyler doesn't know what he's missing."

"He's like family to you, isn't he?"

"Tyler? I guess."

Ada's question about family seemed to briefly kill the conversation as they searched for the metal staircase that led to the tunnels beneath them. The subject was a keen topic of interest for Ada despite her own family relationships being somewhat complicated. For the longest time, McAllister was the person she thought of most when it came to this subject—even though they could hardly even call themselves such a thing. And now, with their relationship becoming increasingly complicated, she wondered what it would be like if their association was much different. The very notion of such a development caused her body to shiver at the thrill of it.

It was only natural for her to feel like this.

They'd always been so much more than siblings.

Ada had known their fates were connected the very instant their eyes first met. But the thought that McAllister could be destined to be struck down by some horrible malady on account of her hidden feelings made her immensely fearful of what awful tragedies would happen if she failed to keep these feelings in check. The whole situation felt so impossible no matter how she looked at it. She was left with no choice but to try to distract herself from these reflections, continuing to film the darkness in front of her until Ashton interrupted the heavy silence that surrounded them.

"I've been having those weird dreams again. About my dad."

"That's...weird."

"Ada, does the name 'Scarlet Council' mean anything to you?"

The questions surprised her, but she didn't show it.

"You should ask McAllister about that," she answered quietly.

"Why? What does he—holy..."

At the sound of his surprise, Ada directed her camera on him and caught him spinning in circles erratically.

"What? Did you just...?"

"I felt a—whoa. It felt like someone was following me. Did you hear footsteps?"

Ada smiled uneasily. She was already aware there were no signs of spiritual energy in the area but was keeping this to herself.

"Let's keep going."

McAllister's connection to the Scarlet Council. That was another topic that Ada didn't feel like pursuing, so her mind went back to contemplating his claims from earlier that day.

Tom Thumb, Alfonse Masters, Aleister Crowley; McAllister had said they were all connected, and the connection he discovered between Alfonse Masters and Tom Thumb had been quite chilling. And there was another name that could be added to the equation: Magnus M. Godfrey. The man who paid for Tom Thumb's burial and possibly hired him to engage in acts of treachery they were still only in the midst of discovering.

What a cruel and crooked web enshrouds this mystery, Ada thought as she crept deeper into the darkness that enveloped them—and as dark and winding as the underground tunnels that she and her charming ghost hunter friend were currently exploring.

Along their journey through the twisted labyrinthine setting, Ada and Ashton happened upon a furnace room and decided to search this, shining their cameras on the cold concrete walls as they scoured the bleak and lonesome atmosphere for any signs of misfortune left over from the distant past.

While Ada busied herself in her search, she could feel Ashton watching her, filming her movements as she explored the decaying furnaces that were looming all around them like expired metal monsters. The special treatment she was receiving wasn't particularly bothersome, but it did surprise her a little. Physically, Ada knew she had game and wasn't a troll or anything, but she often found her appearance awkward and cartoonish. She also tended to avoid interaction with normal boys due to her complicated personal history, which made receiving so much attention from one a relatively new experience.

"You and your brother seem pretty close."

The comment was unexpected, but she provided a speedy answer.

"I haven't seen him for almost five years."

"How long have you been stepsiblings?"

"Almost five years."

Not interested in going into any additional details, Ada's fingers began searching the ashen contents of one of the abandoned furnaces. She wasn't expecting to find anything, but given the chance the room proved to be the final resting place of the item McAllister and herself so passionately desired, it felt only natural to provide due diligence to determine whether this was the case.

"What are you doing?" Ashton asked her.

"Checking to see if anyone burned something."

"Burned something like...a hundred years ago?"

Ada remembered her brother's words about keeping the details of their quest to a minimum and remained silent. She listened to the sound of Ashton's shoes scraping the dirt as he sat down next to her, watching her with rapt interest as she pulled from the ashes what looked like a person's finger bone.

"Don't worry. It's probably not human," he said. "If any zombie cannibals show up, I'll protect you."

Ada couldn't help but smile at this comment.

"Feels nice to have a big strong man to protect me."

Her reply was facetious, but there was also some truth to this. In another life, Ada could see herself being fiercely attracted to someone like Ashton, with his dashing movie star looks and the build of a star athlete. But in this life, her heart was already being hopelessly drawn to another—no matter how doomed and ill-fated the situation appeared to be. And yet, despite her steadfast assuredness in these emotions, as she felt Ashton gazing into her, becoming lost in her eyes and her strange alien beauty, she turned to him and watched him slowly lean forward, and felt herself doing the same. Leaning toward him as their lips both parted, moving in for a kiss...

Ada wouldn't know the details until much later, but when McAllister went off on his own, he made a beeline for Alfonse Masters' former office in the main building. The door still displayed the former titan's name on the name plaque and was covered in tattered crime scene tape that had been there for over a century.

After making his way inside, McAllister stared stone-faced at the taped outline on the carpeting. Wearing a blank expression, he squatted down close to the ground to observe the exact position Masters' body had laid when the man's untimely murder was discovered. He instantly noticed one jarring peculiarity about the scene: Masters had been lying on his side with one arm raised over his head and the arm appeared to be pointing to something.

Shining his flashlight across the room, McAllister noted that the arm seemed to be gesturing to a steel safe behind a pair of accordion-style doors. The safe appeared empty, but there was a small amount of space on top of it before it met the underbelly of the wet bar directly above it. This seemed as good a place as any that one would use to hide something, and when McAllister rubbed his fingers along the dust-ridden surface, his suspicions were proven accurate as something sturdy toppled to the side and fell to the floor.

McAllister's eyes narrowed inquisitively at his discovery, not wasting an instant as he reached to the side to retrieve a thin hardcover book. He flipped to the cover page to confirm the contents, verifying this wasn't the book he was searching for, but an interesting and illuminating find nonetheless. A discovery that strongly supported certain powerfully held suspicions while further deepening the mystery of the priceless treasure that eluded him.

The book was a rare edition of *Tannhauser* by Aleister Crowley.

As Ada closed her eyes and Ashton's lips moved closer, her walkie-talkie went off with a loud *chirp*.

"Ada, you there?"

McAllister.

Ada opened her eyes and turned away from Ashton to answer.

"Yes, I'm here."

"We should leave."

"Roger."

After voicing her reply, Ada rose to her feet and headed for the doorway. Thinking back on this memory, she knew that Ashton was sifting through a number of conflicting emotions as his eyes continued to follow her every movement. Confusion, irritation, disappointment. It was no secret he felt frustrated that he was still unable to read her—and it was easy to see why due to the irregular displays of affection she showed him that had the routine habit of disappearing whenever something interrupted their steamy affairs.

Ashton didn't know that Ada's actions served a much more serious purpose—a purpose she intended on keeping hidden for at least the foreseeable future. Only a few hours earlier, her desire to keep her intentions private all hinged upon the prospect of whether her secret mission went successfully according to plan. Regretfully, the harrowing assassination attempt at the AM Chemical Plant threw an irritating monkey wrench into all of this, and her ignorant associate became wise to another particular matter she had no desire to reveal to him: that she was a powerful witch.

As vexing and ill-timed as this was for Ada, while she felt her mind becoming tired and being lured toward the seductive comforts of sleep, she imagined it would still take Ashton a bit longer to learn the true startling nature of her identity: that the spritely young thing he was spending an increasing amount of time with wasn't only a powerful witch but the most powerful witch of her generation.

30

BLASPHEMOUS RUMORS

It had been twenty-four hours since Mercy's last encounter with the ghost that was haunting her boyfriend's apartment. Things had been quiet all day, but she hasn't slept a wink, still profoundly affected by all that had happened and everything she had witnessed.

After following the little girl into the dark recesses of the closet and observing the mysterious dwelling on the other side, Mercy had woken up back in bed with her heart racing and her body covered in sweat. She knew it hadn't been a dream; all of the details were much too vivid to be anything but absolutely real, no matter how unlikely or impossible it sounded. This realization left her wanting, yearning for an explanation for things, and she found herself waiting in her boyfriend's bedroom as the minutes ticked by—waiting for her pale, blonde-haired visitor to appear to her again.

Mercy wasn't someone who would have categorized herself as dogmatic or particularly religious, but she was definitely superstitious. She believed in magic and the existence of supernatural phenomena and was quite adept at reading tarot and other methods of divination. Her cards had predicted some of the trouble Ashton would be facing long before he made the trip to Little Salem, so she took the little girl's warnings and everything she showed her with the highest degree of seriousness while also remaining extremely cautious, no matter how captivating these visitations happened to be.

The day after returning from her strange journey, Mercy wasted no time and searched her boyfriend's closet for clues for how such an experience could be possible. Despite all she had seen, everything appeared to have returned to normal. There was no longer a dark preternatural heaviness attached to the location or a hungry cosmic hell-mouth that opened to another world. She continued to feel certain this was more than just a fantasy, so when Eddie showed up with his ghost crew to perform their investigation, she ultimately decided to reject the offer. She wanted to avoid any contact with anyone who might cause the ghost to disappear. Tyler apparently received an earful from Eddie in light of this decision, but she would never hear about this; her only interest was in finding out why this spirit seemed to be visiting her and why it was so obsessed with the fate of her boyfriend of all things.

After twenty-four hours of no sleep, while being pressed perilously close to the borders of total delirium, the little girl finally reappeared. The visitation occurred exactly as the night before, around the time of the witching hour—only this time Mercy was sitting on the floor of the bedroom and staring into the murky blackness of the open closet. Predictably, she found her mind wandering as she waited—it was very hard for her to concentrate in her restless sleep-deprived state. While taking account of how it suddenly appeared that the inside of the closet had gotten much blacker, a moment later, she heard a quiet voice calling out to her.

"All is lost."

Mercy started at the sound. She spun around to spy the little girl once again sitting on the corner of the bed, her visitor appearing exactly as when she'd shown up to greet her previously. She was wearing a simple white nightdress with her long blonde hair trailing loosely behind her, sitting with her back to Mercy.

"I tried to warn you," the little girl said. "Now it's too late."

Staring timidly at the apparition, Mercy sought to answer her but felt her body retracting. She spent the entire day preparing for the interaction, but now that the tiny blonde phantom had reappeared, she found herself consumed by a sense of crawling unease in response to the spirit's unsettling piece of prophecy.

"W-What do you mean?" Mercy stammered. "I don't understand."

The little girl turned to face her and Mercy was once again blown away by the haunting blackness of her dark, sorrowful eyes—the only part of the girl's porcelain visage that retained anything close to a human expression.

"All...is lost," the girl repeated.

Again, the little girl turned her back to her tortured hostess as Mercy gazed at her in confusion. Everything she said or showed to her was veiled with an impenetrable air of mystery that pointed to a gathering storm of indeterminate horrors just beyond the horizon. But the warnings were so vague it was difficult to know what to make of them, and in response to the mounting ambiguities, Mercy felt like she was on the verge of a panic attack.

Despite her wishes being fulfilled by receiving another appearance, the ghost wasn't making things any easier. Nothing about the current situation was getting any clearer, and Mercy still expected the girl to disappear at any second. This made the pressure to make conversation painfully urgent, so while the girl appeared hesitant to provide any details to back her wild claim, Mercy decided to challenge her on this. She felt like she would lose her mind if she didn't receive some deeper insight and coherent answers for a change.

"Does this have to do with what you showed me last night?" Mercy asked. "That...man in the attic? And the woman...? I don't understand. What was that about? *What did it mean?*"

The little girl offered no response. Seconds passed, and she released a long dramatic sigh before the room once again fell silent.

Perhaps expecting a bit of clarity was too much to hope for. But the absence of a satisfying answer for why this was happening was driving Mercy to loose ends. So much so that when she finally leaped to her feet to face the girl, she'd already overlooked the fact that this was the longest amount of time the ghost had appeared to her and the most she had to say.

"First you tell me my boyfriend is in danger and now all is lost," Mercy stressed. "Why don't you tell *him* that? Why do you only appear to me?"

"Because my spirit is tied to this place," the little girl said. "I can only communicate with those who live in this building."

"And why's that?"

"My family and I used to live here. When we were killed."

Mercy was deeply shaken by this revelation.

"That's why you haven't moved on? Because of the violence suffered by you and your family?"

She was convinced that had to be the reason. Mercy had picked up various tidbits about ghosts and spirits during discussions with her boyfriend, so she knew that a spirit could be tied to a specific location due to a tragic event from the past. Knowing these things didn't make the exchange any easier, and the little girl's next confession would take her breath away.

"My parents died quickly," the little girl said. "I wasn't so lucky.

My death was part of a blood sacrifice to grant others strong magical powers."

The little girl turned her dark, mournful eyes to gaze at her reluctant associate, her voice eerily void of all emotion.

"I died at the hands of witches."

"*Witches?* Is that who's trying to harm Ashton?"

The little girl didn't answer and turned her back.

"Please! I want to understand! I need to know!"

What Mercy heard next sent a cold shudder throughout her bones. It was the sound of the rack of clothes inside Ashton's closet shifting to the side; as if an unknown presence had been listening and a doorway had suddenly opened.

As Mercy stood frozen in fear, the little girl rose from the bed. Without saying a word, she extended her hand to her.

* * *

Several miles away from his apartment, Ashton remained a cautious guest at the Nipmuc Nation Reservation. He stared listlessly at the late-night sky and listened to the perpetual sounds of chanting and drumming. Still bothered by his exchange with McAllister, he found himself wandering his surroundings, eventually pointed in the direction of where the vibrant sounds were coming from: the ceremony to protect the tribe from witches.

Ashton was still confused about the difference between someone like Ada and what the giant had alluded to as a much more troublesome breed of witches in Little Salem. With Ada and her cohorts having already been branded *personas non grata* for their shenanigans involving the tavern and other various misdeeds, he wondered how it could be possible for a much more dangerous strain of witchery to survive in such a climate and who those witches might be.

The presence of witches in the general area seemed to be a very disconcerting matter to the community, and the tribe was taking their protection ritual with the highest degree of exactness and urgency. Huge bonfires were raging, and crowds of people were gathered—chanting, drumming, and dancing furiously.

This wasn't a celebration. The looks on the faces of those participating were looks of firm resolve and solemnity. And Ashton appeared to receive another clue concerning the identity of the threat the tribe was up against when, upon his arrival, he noticed a young man nod over to his companion before using a stick to inscribe into the dirt the initials, "SC."

While continuing to feel immensely uncertain about everything he had witnessed and all that was discussed with him, Ashton still knew of one way to confirm whether this veritable landslide of disturbing and forbidden knowledge had at least a small measure of truth to it. On his way back to the meetinghouse, he stopped by the large tent where Ada was convalescing, taking a moment to brace himself before entering.

Inside, Ada was still lying flat on her back with her eyes closed, her slender body covered by a thick blanket. Ashton was surprised to find himself mesmerized, entranced by the hallowed expression of Ada's resting features and the way the flickering firelight danced like wanton fairies upon her skin. But he was a man on a mission. He didn't waste his time dawdling in silent veneration of the vixen, quietly approaching the ethereal young woman and pulling away the protective covering to observe what was underneath.

Ada was dressed only in her undergarments: a black lace bra and black briefs. This wasn't what Ashton was prying to get a look at. His eyes traveled to the left side of Ada's ribcage, and his body froze at what he saw.

There it was. The cursed mark, right where she said it was.

The strange aberration appeared to be a birthmark, but its shape was odd and unnatural. The mark was shaped like a thirteen-pedaled flower—just like in the story of her ancestor. The one who was branded with this disfigurement after receiving her sentence for the crime of witchcraft, with the wretched mark being passed down to the child she later bore.

Ashton found himself staring at the blemish in quiet awe, his thoughts racing. With the evidence that Ada's stories were more than just pieces of embellished history, he began to recontextualize all of the conversations they shared—their talks about witches, witchcraft, and Ada herself, combining these with the disturbing revelations from McAllister regarding black magic.

Was it all true? All of these claims about witchcraft and the occult? Witches—real witches—were more than just a myth? And the dark powers that were attributed to them—the stuff of bedtime stories and fairy tales. Could these all be real as well?

As Ashton continued to stare at Ada's side in wonder, he suddenly noticed she was wide awake. Watching him with her unearthly eyes that also contained a deep sadness now that he had learned her dark secret and their relationship would never be the same.

"Ada..."

Ashton was at a loss for words. He hastily repositioned the blanket, and she grasped his hand and stared at him beseechingly.

"Don't hate me," Ada said.

The heartfelt appeal inspired Ashton to smile and gently squeeze her palm in consolation.

But the two of them were not alone.

Standing a short distance behind the pair were Mercy and the little blonde girl, both of them unseen in their current incorporeal incarnations. Mercy was in a state of shock, stunned by all she was seeing and not sure how to deal with it.

"There. Do you see?" the little girl asked plainly.

"Who is she?"

"She is their leader. The dark witch who has enchanted your boyfriend. It won't be long until her evil plan for him is complete."

Mercy gulped, gawking in bewilderment at the odd couple.

"How am I supposed to help him? What am I supposed to do?"

Once this was uttered, the little girl turned her dark, sorrowful eyes to Mercy. There was now a harsh earnestness attached to her gaze—a look that seemed too cruel and too unnatural to be fastened to such a small thing.

"*You must travel to Little Salem to confront the witch and kill her,*" the little girl said. "*Kill her before it's too late.*"

Mercy gazed at the girl in astonishment, the horrible demand filling her with so much gut-wrenching horror she felt like she was burning up. But before she had a chance to process this, she found herself back in her boyfriend's apartment, thrashing under the bedsheets as she desperately gasped for breath.

After opening her eyes, Mercy hastily peered all around her, finding she was back inside the bedroom, and she was all alone.

The little girl had disappeared, but not before giving Mercy a mission to serve as her private executioner after showing her events and sharing information where regardless of how unbelievable it was, she knew it was all completely and terrifyingly real. The girl's discomforting words to her were an entirely different matter. According to the spirit, if she didn't act soon, Ashton would be lost to her forever.

As her mind continued to dwell on the spirit's daunting and sinister request, Mercy's eyes fell on the puzzled face of Ashton's tabby staring up at her from the bedroom floor. She was hit by the strangest feeling she was being watched—observed by something feeding off of her crushing sense of doubt and indecision. Her skin crawling, she continued to avert her eyes from the dark impenetrable void inside the closet, knowing deep down that even though whatever was present would disappear at the first ray of daylight, something would continue to be watching her until the deed was finally complete.

Once the witch was killed, the darkness would go away.

That was the real bargain the girl was offering to Mercy.

But the offer made her exceedingly wary because she knew these types of contracts rarely ended well or in the client's favor.

Knowing this didn't make the situation any less challenging. The void inside the closet may have appeared as dark and unfathomable as things could get, but she knew this was only her perception. Things could always get darker and often did. Some might say it was always darkest before the dawn, but Mercy knew this was merely a deception, and that, in reality, it always appeared darkest right before everything went pitch-black.

Part IV

Izzy: The pain—there is so much pain inside of him—

McAllister: Inside of Tom Thumb? Is it because of the book?

Izzy: No! Because of what he saw when he tried to steal it!

McAllister: Steal it from who? Steal it from who? *What did he see?*

31

A WITCH SCORNED

It should come as no surprise that following Mary Sue's first contact with Izzy, she started looking for every excuse imaginable to be close to the tavern, hoping to catch a glimpse of the young gypsy. Izzy was the reason she was suddenly able to get out of bed every morning looking forward to the day ahead, and meeting the charming and charismatic young woman had changed her normally gloomy outlook on not just life but also herself.

Naturally, Nancy was against her daughter having anything to do with anyone even remotely connected to her despised nemesis and firmly stood her ground with not wanting her anywhere near the family business until those meddlesome witches and their seedy degenerate bar were dealt with.

"But mom—"

"I don't care if you want to go to work or not. I don't want you near the shop while all those horrible kids are still around!"

"This is such crap! So you want to just hide me away! Hide me away from the big bad world behind lock and key!"

"When you have kids someday—"

"Oh! When *I* have kids? When *I* have kids?"

"—then you might finally understand how I always did everything for *you!*"

"*I hate you!*"

Mary Sue's parents left for the store following this conversation, which happened on the morning after Nancy's humiliating confrontation outside the tavern. She was left all alone with nothing to do but scowl at the walls in frustration. But her face softened when she saw her drawing of Izzy smiling back at her, which reminded her of the brief encounters they shared.

Mary Sue knew she just *had* to see her—especially after all the things Rudy had told her following a short run-in with the skinny miscreant. He was wandering the streets while recording the noises that surrounded him with some portable recording equipment.

"Hey. Hey you. What are you doing?"

"Nothing. Class project."

"Liar. You're not in school."

"How would you know?"

"You just moved into that old house with Izzy and those other weird kids."

"So?"

"So I haven't seen her around today. Is she OK?"

Rudy paused before answering.

"Izzy had a late night."

That was all Mary Sue was able to get out of him, but she could see the concern being masked upon his face. She knew deep down he was holding back something.

It was the remembrance of this expression that motivated her to leap out of bed and race down the stairs to where she kept her trusty BMX—in the shade of the family's garden shed. After hopping on her bike, she pedaled to the center of town, determined to locate Izzy and discover what had become of her.

As Mary Sue approached the main drag, she stealthily leaped off her bike and walked it toward the tavern, glancing across the street to make sure her parents didn't see her from inside the frozen yogurt shop. She was formulating a gameplan when she was startled by the voice of someone exiting the tavern in a hurry and ducked behind a parked car, waiting with bated breath for the figure to depart.

"Sending me to run an errand. I'll send *you* to run an errand. Of all the..."

The voice belonged to the busty redhead that always seemed to be dressed in a shade of red. This day was no exception as she was dressed in red from head to toe: red sunglasses, red heels, and a chic red designer dress as the dazzling highlight of her lavish ensemble.

"'*Meh meh meh—my name is Ada and my name's McAllister and we're so interesting.* Pssh. Please."

"Mistress Agatha—"

"Not now, Sanchez. Can't you see I'm in the middle of something?"

As Mary Sue observed the argument between the redhead and the tavern's handyman, she continued waiting anxiously, searching for the perfect moment to make her move. Both parties appeared to be upset about something, but soon the glamorous seductress was off in a taxi, and Sanchez was glaring at the departing vehicle. This presented Mary Sue the perfect opportunity to hurry her bike past the side of the tavern before anyone had a chance to notice her.

After stowing her bike and locating the back door, she snuck through the rear entrance and up the stairs. She knew that Izzy must be on one of the upper levels and assumed the top uppermost floor would be her best bet, tip-toeing up the staircase with her heart-rate accelerating every time she heard one of the ancient wooden floorboards make a loud and agonizing creak.

In no time at all, she made it to the top floor and found herself mesmerized by the haunting mood and bohemian ambiance of the old space. She never explored any of the upper levels when the establishment was just a restaurant, and the place felt much different in the residential areas of the building. A lot more old-fashioned and suggestive of the decadent brothel it had once been.

Before she had time to take in her surroundings, she received another startling shock to the system: McAllister, emerging into the hallway from one of the bedrooms, shuffling restlessly with a half-finished beer in his grip.

"Tom Thumb, Godfrey, Masters, Crowley..."

In a panic, Mary Sue ducked down and huddled herself close to the railing. The night McAllister visited her parents and burned a pentagram into their front lawn was still fresh in her memory. It was fortunate he appeared distracted—and the nagging frustration he was feeling was apparent. His devious mind was working overtime on whatever nefarious project was consuming him.

As McAllister finished his beer with a bitter scowl pasted on his face, Mary Sue held her breath and watched him cross slowly down the hall, trying the knob to the bathroom only to find it locked.

"Just a second!"

"Rudy? Are you jerking off again?"

"I, uh... Just trying to finish what I started."

"Unbelievable."

For a moment, it looked like McAllister was going to peer over in her direction—a proposition that made all the nerves inside her body start to scream. But Mary Sue firmly stood her ground, even as her whole body began shaking, watching McAllister blankly observe the empty bottle he was holding before exhaling a weary breath and kicking the bathroom door in.

"Holy—what the—"

"I'm not looking, I'm not looking. I'm pissing in the sink."

"How could you—when I—aw no, I made a mess!"

"I'm not looking! Damn you, Rudy!"

Not wasting a second, Mary Sue saw this as her lucky chance to hurry down the hallway with her heartbeat racing nonstop, trying to be as light on her feet as possible as she proceeded to search all of the rooms close by.

"Hell's bells, man! You have your own room to screw around in!"

"Oh, well excuse the hell out of me for wanting to do my private business in the one room that has a lock!"

"Not anymore it doesn't."

While listening to McAllister's scornful snarling tone, Mary Sue silently prayed to herself that the boys would continue to argue and remain distracted—at least until she found her beloved gypsy. The first room she poked her head into was empty: a messy room with two single beds that she could easily imagine as the room where Rudy was staying. Across the hall was a room just like it, but, sure enough, in one of the beds was the sacred object of her affection: Izzy, dressed in her PJ's, her skin looking more colorless than usual, her body damp and feverish.

Seeing Izzy in the flesh instantly set Mary Sue's heart aflutter, no matter the state she was languishing in, and the infatuated teenager nervously entered the room and kneeled by her side. Taking into account the seriousness of Izzy's condition, Mary Sue's turbulent emotions went into overdrive. She couldn't think of anything to say or do for the poor invalid, so she took Izzy's hand and gazed at her with tears welling up behind her eyes.

Izzy stirred and smiled brightly at the sullen guardian angel beside her. "Mary Sue, what are you doing here?"

Even in her present state, the smile was enough to set Mary Sue's passions dancing, her body trembling from all the butterflies she was experiencing.

"I heard you weren't feeling well. I wanted to see you."

Izzy's smile widened at this admission. "Wow. Your aura is so bright right now. It's like a pinkish-blue or a blue-violet? Far out."

Izzy suddenly fell quiet, shivering uncontrollably.

"Izzy? What's wrong with you?"

The poor gypsy forced a grin but still couldn't mask the fear and concern in her eyes. "Ada says I've been hexed. Someone in town put a curse on me, and now this freaky supernatural entity is trying to possess me."

"That's crazy. You said somebody in town did this?"

"Think of us as the Away Team."

This last statement came from Ada, positioned by the doorway, her haunting eyes gazing at her companion while wearing a sad, heartfelt smile upon her face.

"Not a lot of fans cheering us on," Ada remarked regrettably. She entered the room and crossed over to stroke her friend's silky hair. "Poor Izzy. Guilt by association I'm afraid."

At the time, Mary Sue never imagined she would ever get this close to the notorious witch. Under normal conditions, she would have been at a loss for words, but she was so wrapped up in worry that nothing else mattered. She simply smiled and sniffed as she wiped at her tear-stained face.

"You're Ada," she said. "Izzy told me about you."

"This is McAllister and Rudy. And you are?"

Mary Sue glanced to the doorway where the two young men were now standing, both of them gazing at her cynically.

"Mary Sue," she answered.

The gloomy teenager noticed Ada's eyes were studying her, and her next move was unexpected. Without warning, Ada reached out, taking Mary Sue's face in her hands and furrowing her brow in sudden realization of something.

"Mary Sue... You're Wilbur and Nancy's child. Oh, you poor thing..."

Ada's words startled her. She wasn't quite certain whether this acknowledgment was the result of an abrupt recognition or if something preternatural had happened when she touched her. But before Mary Sue could question the witch, Ada had turned her back and was crossing to the doorway.

"You should get going," Ada said. "No offense, but right now we want to avoid bringing any extra added attention to ourselves. I think Sister Nancy's still a bit sore about our little dance-off in the street last night. *Cuz somebody got ser-erved.*"

Mary Sue laughed weakly at Ada's joke before turning her gaze back to Izzy. "Please," she pleaded. "Just a little while longer."

Ada smiled fondly at the girl. "Sure. Just a little while longer." She flashed a knowing smirk at her stepbrother, and they took off down the hallway while Rudy remained.

Mary Sue stayed at the tavern for the rest of the day, and the moon was high in the sky by the time that she left. Rudy wasn't being very talkative, and she got very little out of him in terms of conversation until the end of the night. She still felt confused as to how Izzy became hexed in the first place and wanted to ask him more about this since Ada and McAllister had already left to deal with their own pressing engagements.

Rudy was smoking a spliff out back while talking on his cell phone as she began her timid approach. She hadn't a clue who he could be talking to and found herself holding back before making herself seen, allowing for her to eavesdrop on the conversation before heading out for the evening.

"Can you believe it? I'm stuck babysitting again... Yeah, I know. Lately, Ada's been letting her punk-ass brother call all the shots. Things were so much more chill-a-licious when it was just Ada around, you know?"

Mary Sue found Rudy's comments intriguing. She was largely unaware of the ongoing conflict within the group, but now that he had mentioned it, it did appear that both he and Agatha weren't looking too happy with the existing state of affairs. Still, she had no idea who he was speaking to and continued to listen intently as he suddenly looked taken aback by something.

"He's having you search for the Seventh Scholar? I thought McAllister murdered the Seventh Scholar. In the Czech Republic or something."

The conversation ceased once he spied his observer, and his mood instantly soured at the sight of her.

"Yo. Hang in there, Miles. I gotta peace out."

Rudy ended the call, and he glanced at Mary Sue suspiciously.

"Leaving for the night?"

"I should be getting back."

Before heading out, she had one final question to ask him.

"Do you know who did it? The one who put the hex on Izzy."

Rudy stifled a humorless laugh and answered bitterly after taking a long drag off of the spliff.

"Why don't you ask your mom?"

While juvenile in its delivery, Rudy's suggestion actually had a lot of merit. Mary Sue knew that Ada and her mother were essentially mortal enemies, but would her mother really go so far as to seek harm on others merely to remove someone she didn't like from her community? And how far would she be willing to go to achieve this?

Rudy's words were still echoing in her mind, accompanied by the distressing visual of her sickly-looking girl crush, as she parked her bike next to the garden shed. Then it hit her: the rainy night when she saw her mother departing the shed.

The answers were in the shed! They'd been there this whole time!

Mary Sue forced a determined expression onto her face before padding over to the entrance. In retrospect, she could have guessed what she would find when she entered, but the full extent of the horrors that awaited her was another matter entirely.

The door creaked loudly as she pulled it open, and her face lost all color at what she saw before her. The shed was filled with ritualistic items hanging on the walls and positioned on every available flat surface. Burnt black candles were everywhere, along with the skulls of animals covered with runes and other obscure occult markings, and the air smelled of scorched herbs and unfamiliar fragrances. Most disturbing of all was the altar sitting at the rear of the small enclosure. Hanging above a small cauldron were a collection of photographs: Ada, Agatha, McAllister, Miles, Rudy, and Izzy; pictures of the members of the maligned coven with their eyes scratched black.

It was true: It was her own mother who had hexed the girl she'd developed such intense feelings for—although, ironically, it was never Nancy's intention to do such a thing.

When Nancy retrieved the hairs from the shower drain and used them in her ritual to curse Ada and bring harm to her specifically, she was unaware that the hairs belonged to Izzy. Ada had only been bathing in the creek as part of her secluded nightly outings to the woods, making the only other dark-haired girl at the tavern the unexpected target of her malefic spell. That was the funny thing about magic: when wielded by an amateur—and Nancy was definitely an amateur, despite her undeservedly high opinion of herself—magic often had a "monkey's paw" effect on the object of the witch's desire. And this effect carried over to spirit contact as well—something that was much more dangerous and potentially disastrous than a simple hexing spell.

In light of this fact, Nancy's relationship with Mary Sue being ruined forever on account of her daughter's discovery with the angry teenager confronting her mother and then running off right after to witness the Sheriff's raid of the tavern—this was only just one of the many side effects to her desperate actions. And it amounted to only the tip of the iceberg in terms of what she had unleashed upon her once-perfect life and existence.

32

MESSAGES FROM THE OTHER SIDE

For those who dealt with matters of the occult, it was no secret that many of the residents in the spirit world held one desire above all others: the desire to communicate with the living. A spirit could go about this in many different ways, but possessing the body of a mystic and using it as a second skin was one such method where this desire could not only be made manifest but allow the spirit the opportunity to attend to whatever fancy or unfinished business might be drawing them to the material world. Typically, this experience didn't have to be a uniformly unpleasant endeavor. When being possessed by beings such as the Loa or by a lost soul looking to pass on a message to a loved one, the experience could often be quite positive and transcendent. But when being possessed by a deranged murderer or a frightening composite of dark spiritual energies summoned into our world through malefic practices, it could only be one thing: absolutely devastating.

It was safe to say that Izzy's wraith, whatever it was—the ghost of the mad butler, Tom Thumb, or something else entirely—definitely fit the latter category. Izzy remained convinced that at least some of Tom Thumb's consciousness was attached to the entity, often only sensing the spirit as a shadow, barely perceivable. The wraith still occasionally appeared to her as the same pale and ghoulish monstrosity that first showed itself back at the madhouse, and it was during these times that it seemed most desperate to possess her; always interrupting the fleeting moments of peace and tranquility when its cagey victim's flighty, absent mind would wander for an instant. Izzy now had multiple scratches and claw marks across her body as proof of these visitations, the vast majority of which had occurred when she was alone. This was why it was so important to have someone by her side while she was undergoing this ordeal, but, unfortunately, these preparations were never entirely successful. Even when someone was with her, Izzy could feel the pull of the spirit feeding off of her life force in an attempt to sustain itself, having already formed a strong physic attachment to her back at the asylum.

Despite her normally cheerful outlook, Izzy was doubtful she would be able to shake the phantom. She already knew it would only be satisfied once it had possessed her body completely, and, in doing so, finally be granted the capacity to express the desires that had been repressed following a distressingly agonizing death. Interestingly enough, contrary to whatever Izzy might have believed, Ada remained unconvinced that any human-like quality attached to the wraith was genuine. She thought it more likely the hex had formulated a creature out of the dark spiritual refuse attached to the broader environment of the town itself; the result of painful historical wounds that had yet to fully heal. Such was the case when dealing with magic and the world of the spirits: sometimes definitive answers for these types of anomalies were hard to come by. But that didn't change the fact that things weren't looking optimistic.

The one saving grace for Izzy was that throughout her trials and tribulations, she was surrounded by so much love and affection. Everyone in Ada's coven was trying to be as supportive as humanly possible and passionately rooting for her to pull through. Every time she caught herself drifting in and out of consciousness, she usually found herself awakening in the company of a loving soul watching over her to help her make it through her perilous difficulties. The hours following the witches' escape from the Sheriff's mangy backwoods murder brigade were no exception, and shortly after being tucked into bed in the safety of Tyler's hotel room, she found herself being greeted by one such loving individual after forcing herself out of yet another restless sleep that was filled to the brim with all the opposite ingredients of what pleasant dreams were made.

Izzy had been down for the count for quite some time, but when she opened her eyes, the first thing she saw was Mary Sue. The shy, introverted teenager was sitting by her bedside and smiling affectionately in a cute and bashful sort of way that could only inspire Izzy to smile back, even while in her sorry, weakened state.

"You again," Izzy observed. "Are you here to take care of me?"

Mary Sue nodded, her eyes sparkling.

"How are you feeling?"

"Much better seeing you here."

Izzy surveyed her surroundings as she shivered under the covers.

"Where am I? It's so cold. I don't know why I'm so cold..."

"I'll draw you a warm bath," Mary Sue offered. "Would you like that?"

Such kindness and affection she was receiving from someone she'd known only briefly. Izzy didn't know why so many people in her life were so nice to her, but the gesture was much appreciated.

Izzy flashed a feeble smile to express her eternal gratitude. "You're so kind, Mary Sue," she mused. "I don't know why this is happening to me, but maybe you'll be the one to save me."

Mary Sue lit up like a firework display and quickly rose to her feet, smiling brightly at her heart's obsession before ducking into the bathroom to fill the tub for her.

For Izzy, what inspired her to utter this last remark was a mystery—probably the knowledge it was precisely what Mary Sue longed to hear. For a moment, she debated if obliging the girl's starry affections despite her own feelings made her a bad person. But really, trying to think about things was hopeless. In her current condition, she was too tired to think straight and found her mind drifting to Miles, whose remarkable gift with words outmatched everyone.

Oh, Miles. What good times they shared.

This wistful reflection brought bitter sadness, reminding her that the only night they'd been intimate together would likely be the last. Izzy knew the wraith was getting closer to consuming her soul completely and wouldn't be giving up before it had achieved its desperate task. Something must have been driving it furiously to possess her. All she knew was she had to remain vigilant if she had any hopes of warding off the specter's violent attacks.

Alas, despite the impassioned pleas of her restless mind screaming at her to remain attentive, she had such little fight left in her. The sound of the bath being drawn in the other room was so comforting and soothing that the running water was like a silvery siren call urging her to dreamland.

However, it was another noise coming from close by that steadily summoned her attention: the sound of scratching and listless movement directly above her head. By the time she discovered what it was, it was too late. Izzy had only enough time to release a helpless gasp as she spied the dark apparition of the wraith in its fearsome charcoal-colored shadow form clawing its way across the ceiling before dropping on top of her.

* * *

Steam filled the room as Mary Sue turned off the taps and tested the water, making sure like Goldilocks it was just right. She smiled to herself at the thought of how much more at ease Izzy would feel once she had settled into the soothing waters. She might even flash another smile in her direction, and the anticipation of this moment was enough to give her goosebumps.

Much to her surprise, when Mary Sue reentered the main room, she discovered it empty. She frantically scanned her surroundings as a wave of horrible premonitions started to consume her.

Had the Sheriff's goons gotten to her? Or the locals?

The disturbing options were endless.

Mary Sue didn't have time to let her imagination run away with her as she suddenly heard the crash of breaking glass. Her eyes darted to the doorway with Crowley's magical motto etched right above it, and she noticed that the door was wide open.

"Izzy?"

She knew that announcing herself was risky, but her desire to discover the cause for Izzy's absence outmatched her need for caution. She had no idea that when she exited the hotel room, nothing would prepare her for the gruesome sight that awaited her.

The sound had come from Izzy punching her arm through a window at the end of the dark hallway before pulling it back through, her pale and colorless flesh becoming scratched and shredded twice over with her arm now bleeding all over the carpeting. Strangely, Izzy didn't appear distracted by the injury, wholly consumed with the frantic task she was engaged in as her unnaturally stiffened body began to paint a message in blood onto the wallpaper, all while keeping her back turned to her terror-stricken audience.

The unnatural sight before her took Mary Sue's breath away. Izzy appeared to be locked in a trance and was mumbling incoherently. Her head was twitching like a metronome and her hair was looking wilder than she had ever seen it. Mary Sue knew this could only mean that something unthinkable had happened. But all she could do was stand frozen in fear, unable to move or speak.

Tyler and Rudy showed up next, having heard the crash of the window from downstairs. When they arrived and spied the ghoulish figure at the end of the hallway, they were just as stunned by what they were seeing as the wide-eyed teenager standing paralyzed several feet in front of them.

"Izzy!"

"Dude. What is she...?"

Rudy placed a hand on Tyler to silence him, taking charge to address the situation, which seemed to have landed them beyond the border to the Uncanny Valley and into another world entirely.

"Izzy," Rudy muttered hesitantly. "Izzy... What are you doing?"

The unsightly figure froze, her back still turned.

"Izzy, you aren't well. You should be in bed."

While crossing over to her, something unexpected happened—something as startling as it was sudden. Izzy dropped to her knees, her belabored body turned to face them, and she released a loud, blood-curdling scream.

The tortured sound of Izzy's harsh and scarring cry was enough to wake the dead, and the harrowing face she made while the piercing sound poured out of her was so shocking Mary Sue instantly covered her eyes with her hands.

Rudy was startled by the sight as well, too nervous to take another step. But the heart-rending moment was surprisingly brief.

As soon as Izzy emptied her lungs, she lost all consciousness and dropped like a broken doll onto the carpet.

Tyler took this as his signal to spring into action. He rushed to the limp and bloody body while trembling uncontrollably, assisting Rudy with turning Izzy over and holding her steady as the savage gash on her arm continued hemorrhaging blood all over.

Rudy ripped up Izzy's shirt to form a makeshift tourniquet, struggling to whisper some consoling words to her.

"It's OK," Rudy said—his voice was shaking. "Everything's OK."

Mary Sue didn't move, staring in glassy-eyed horror at Izzy's fragile shell of a body. Tears were streaming down her face, still too mortified to think straight. She felt ashamed that during Izzy's darkest moment, she found the sight of her so abominable and repellent she could barely stand to look at her. Racked with guilt, she swallowed her discomfort and focused on the wall right next to her to discover something that was equally as shocking and even more bewildering.

As Mary Sue's eyes went wide and her breathing picked up, Tyler took notice of the intense reaction and glanced at where her eyes were glued.

On the wall was a message written in blood:

THE MYSTERIOUS ONES WAIT IN THE WOODS

What these words meant was anyone's guess. There was no reference one could turn to or any rhyme or reason that could be decoded from the phrase. Just one thing felt certain: the spirit that fought so hard to possess Izzy had done so to deliver this message.

33

THE HOUSE AT THE TOP OF THE HILL

When it came to heroics, Tyler was far from a white knight or an illustrious do-gooder, but when he set his mind to something, he liked to see a task through to the end. Being someone who wasn't accustomed to accepting failure lightly was one of his most admirable qualities—a quality that helped him to excel at things, despite his modest upbringing and a relatively mediocre intellect.

However, Tyler's habit of jumping into a situation while flagrantly displaying more guts than sense was something that had already backfired more than once in his life. And since getting into trouble was something that came quite naturally, this made suffering severe consequences from sticking his nose too far into something practically inevitable during his short time of visiting Little Salem.

When Tyler awoke the morning after escaping the Sheriff's thugs, he returned to the hallway to view the bloody scrawl that had been left there the night before. The message said something called "Mysterious Ones" was "waiting in the woods" apparently. He hadn't a clue as to the words' meaning, but by the time he returned to his hotel room, he was already devising a strategy for investigating all of the pressing mysteries that were quickly stacking up.

Before diving into another one of his impulsive and hastily prepared schemes, he felt obligated to check on Izzy. She wasn't looking any better, but she didn't appear to be getting any worse. As a suspected witch, it wasn't safe to bring her to the hospital, so it was a good thing Mary Sue was willing to watch over her while she got some badly needed rest.

With Izzy all sorted—at least, to the best of their abilities—Tyler recruited Rudy to accompany him on his mission to, in his words, "get to the bottom of what the hell is going on in this weirdo town." The plan was to talk to as many people as possible in the broader Little Salem community until they finally received some answers regarding the daunting web of mysteries attached to so many recent experiences. After grabbing some nourishment, the boys took off to the main drag, questioning every person they came across. While Tyler was carrying out his interrogations, Rudy filmed the tense exchanges, using a camera from the collection the Ghost Bros brought on vacation to chronicle their prospective ghost hunts.

"Excuse me. Are you familiar with the Salem witch trials? Ever heard of the Mysterious Ones? No?"

"Excuse me. Ever heard of Aleister Crowley? What about the Scarlet Council? Anyone ever mention that name to you?"

Unfortunately, the humble residents were largely uncommunicative. This could have been expected as the town held a long tradition of being wary of outsiders, which included random tourists.

For Tyler, failure was not an option, and the cold shoulder only motivated him to be more persistent. He continued to confront the locals while consistently being ignored by every tight-lipped citizen he came across, the lack of participation eventually wearing down his resolve and leaving him in low spirits. Several hours later, he was running short on ideas, and Rudy was looking ready to throw in the towel altogether. No helpful answers had been provided, and no new light had been shed whatsoever.

"We are getting nowhere," Rudy groaned.

To help harden his resolve, Tyler searched one of his camera bags for a protein bar to give him a quick energy boost. As luck would have it, the search provided something unexpected.

Inside the bag was the map Ada had scribbled on—an item Tyler had yet to take a proper look at. When he did, the excessive amount of detail Ada placed into highlighting all the haunted hotspots and notable locations of witchy history blew him away.

"Haunted Asylum #1," "Nightmare Alley," "The Slipknot Hotel"—there were dozens of names and labels just like these, with lengthy descriptions attached to each of them. There was even a selection of drawings and symbols linked to the locations to give them a unique, slightly creepy visual flourish.

"What you got there, playa?" Rudy inquired.

"It's a map Ada drew up. All the spooky places in Little Salem."

Tyler's eyes narrowed while studying one place in particular.

"Yo. What's this place marked with a skull and crossbones?"

Rudy glanced over to have a look-see, frowning while observing Tyler's finger pointing to a location on the north side of town.

"That's Sir Godfrey's mansion. Ada told us he's bad news."

Bingo. Now they were getting somewhere.

Upon receiving this information, Tyler gave Rudy a thumbs-up as he set off to where Ashton's silver Prius was parked on the street.

"Aw hell no," Rudy moaned. "Tell me you're not thinking what I think you are."

For Tyler, his mind was made up. He was convinced they'd found the place where all of his questions would be answered.

"No guts, no glory, homie," Tyler grinned. "Time to visit the dragon's den."

The boys arrived at the old mansion in less than ten minutes, which, in every practical sense, was a unique sight to behold and not something one would suspect to find in a town as small and humble as Little Salem.

Located near the New Albion Country Club, the Godfrey Mansion was an absolute marvel in comparison to its closest neighbors—a huge palatial residence with grounds that stretched off into the nearby woods and architecture suggesting it had been positioned at the site for several centuries. While ostensibly posh and lavish, there was also a distinctly spooky ambiance about the place. The wrought-iron gates gave the setting a chilling and disinviting air, and the house at the top of the drive looked equally stark and gloomy. It was the type of setting that reflected a strong sense of history but also of putrid deterioration and felt more like a home to the dead than to anyone that was still living.

"Place looks like something out of a Tim Burton movie," Tyler dryly observed. He stood outside the gates admiring the intimidating structure while Rudy frowned uneasily beside him. Rudy clearly knew more about the residence than he was letting on, which only provided him all the more reason to find a way to hustle his way inside to get a closer look. With this intention in mind, and without displaying any signs of hesitation whatsoever, Tyler rang the buzzer, and a moment later, a voice responded on the intercom.

"Yes?"

"Candygram."

"Excuse me?"

"Yes, I have a Candygram here for Sir Godfrey."

Rudy did a facepalm in reaction to the sheer brazenness of the charade. The gesture didn't discourage Tyler in the slightest.

"Hello? Anyone home?" Tyler barked. "Chop chop, Jeeves. I'm sure Godfrey's not a fan of melted chocolate, and I have other deliveries to make."

A moment of silence followed this statement and was broken by the buzz of the thick iron gates slowly opening.

Tyler smiled proudly at his reluctant associate.

"You coming?"

Rudy remained motionless, staring uncomfortably at the ground. The secret knowledge he possessed seemed to be advising him not to go any closer. Tyler already expected this and continued to stride confidently up the drive to the dark, sprawling fortress in the distance as his edgy accomplice chose to remain at the main gates.

The walk up the drive seemed to take ages, and the mansion appeared more looming and bewildering the closer he got. There was definitely some bad juju attached to the setting, but this only intensified Tyler's suspicions he had come to the right place. Besides, it was already too late to turn back, and before he knew it, he found himself at the front door where a stuffy old butler stood waiting.

"You don't look like a delivery man," the butler glibly noted.

"Gilles, it's fine."

The new voice alerted Tyler to turn his head to the side of the building. There, he observed a ghoulish silver-haired gentleman in brown tweed hunting attire crossing toward him. Instantly, the man left the impression as one of the oddest figures he had met in Little Salem. He spoke with a distinct upper-class British accent and carried an antique rifle in one hand and two dead rabbits in the other, swinging them from side to side as if barely acknowledging they were present. Without having to announce himself, Tyler knew he could only be one person.

"I'm sure our visitor means us no trouble," Sir Godfrey said.

He tossed the dead rabbits on the porch, and after scraping his boots on the mat and offering an icy grin, he gestured to his visitor to accompany him.

After emerging into a large foyer, Tyler was led into an opulent trophy room that contained dozens of dead animal heads lining the walls, mostly of the horned and antlered variety. The floor was tiled in a black and white checkerboard pattern and covered in exotic skins with expensive antique furniture cushioned with red velvet sitting on top. The whole room stunk of old money and aristocratic prestige, and was quite lavish and impressive, to say the least. But at the very same time, Tyler found himself hopelessly distracted by the dreary atmosphere permeating throughout the room, as well as the explicitly potent variety of death that was on display—something that gave some eerie additional context to the chosen marker Ada drew to be associated with the place.

"You're one of those two college students. The paranormal...?"

Tyler nodded politely as he continued to survey the room.

"We hunt ghosts and stuff. People around town have been talking about us?"

"Well, you know. Small town, lots of gossip. Drink?"

"Uh, no thanks."

"So what can I do for you?"

At least the conversation was getting off to a quick start. So far Godfrey was acting quite casually toward him, almost as if he'd been expected. This caused Tyler to view his host's behavior as highly suspect, inspiring him to state his intentions rather bluntly to observe how the man would react.

"Oh, I've just been inquiring around town about things. Reports of strange things happening around town."

"Oh? Strange things like what?"

Godfrey expressed this last comment rather flippantly while he busied himself with fixing his beverage. To Tyler, it seemed almost certain that the refined and overly personable old fellow was testing him and was completely unconcerned with whether his guest knew this or not. This unpleasant observation inspired him to notice that, in reality, he was the one who was being interrogated as he watched his calm and levelheaded host settle into an easy chair, smiling at him with scotch in hand like a predator examining his prey.

"Are you familiar with the Salem witch trials?" Tyler asked.

"Are they still going on? I thought the books were closed on all that."

Godfrey smiled slyly at his personal attempt at humor, but his predacious grin only made Tyler feel even more unsettled.

"People have been reporting strange things happening in the woods," Tyler said. "Maybe secret rituals or—"

The honorable Sir Godfrey cut in, brushing this matter off rather quickly. "Yes, I'm afraid that's just local superstition. You see, there are certain individuals in our community who like to fantasize that this town is a lot more interesting than it actually is."

"Right. A lot more interesting."

Tyler glanced once again at the exorbitant exhibition of wealth surrounding him; the dozens of dead creatures staring back, their hollow, lifeless eyes now appearing to be watching him intently.

"But there must be a reason for someone like you to be living here," Tyler said. "In this boring old—you know, there are a lot of dead things in this room."

"The house has been in the family for generations," Godfrey swiftly rebutted. "My great-grandfather was quite the sportsman. World traveler. I don't recall the precise reasons why my family first set down roots here, but after a while, you discover the town does have its...charms."

Yeah, likely story, Tyler thought. But his eyes were suddenly drawn to something peculiar.

Hanging on the wall amid an eclectic assortment of curiosities was a framed piece of aged canvas showing a scarlet circle that was broken on the left side. It appeared the drawing had originally been hanged while still wet, allowing the pigment to drip down the canvas in a way that only intensified the disquieting quality the image possessed. There was something primitive and ritualistic about the artifact, and it projected a sinister sense of power and eminence.

"What's that?" Tyler asked. "Hanging on the wall."

Godfrey glanced over to where his guest was looking.

"That? Hmm, I don't really know."

Tyler felt himself growing pale as he continued to stare transfixed at the unusual relic, suddenly feeling very panicked and regretting ever coming there.

"It looks like... Like it was painted with blood."

He expected Godfrey to mock him for jumping to conclusions, but this didn't happen at all. His host didn't dispute the observation in the slightest, and, instead, turned to smile in intense admiration at the framed symbol.

"If I remember correctly," Godfrey casually recalled, "the symbol is the seal of a powerful group of individuals who at various times in history possessed the power to build and destroy entire civilizations. The shapers of the modern world you might say. Most knowledge of their ways and customs has unfortunately been lost to antiquity."

Tyler gazed at the man with burgeoning unease.

"You actually seem to know a lot about that thing."

"Just bits and pieces I've picked up over the years."

Godfrey leaned forward, flashing his wolfish grin at his visitor.

"How is *Ashton* by the way? Why don't the two of you swing by some time for a drink and a jaw? It's so rare for us to receive visitors of your nature. It would be quite droll."

This statement quickly brought Tyler back to his senses, and he began searching his pockets in earnest. The situation with Izzy had led him to forget about Ashton entirely. The last time they'd spoken was before his fellow ghost hunter had taken off with Ada to explore the AM Chemical Plant.

"Ashton. I need to call Ashton—"

"You can use the phone over here if you wish."

"No—I should get going. Thanks for your...hospitality."

Tyler jumped up from his seat as Godfrey continued beaming.

"My pleasure. Say hello to Ashton for me."

Tyler nodded, looking more pale and distressed by the minute.

How the devil did the man know Ashton?

He was about to leave but suddenly stopped himself. He came all this way to find answers and wasn't about to abandon his mission and come back empty-handed. Before exiting the room, he redoubled back inside and took a quick cell phone picture of the strange symbol before nodding at his host and exiting in a hurry, while Godfrey, showing no concern at all for the gesture, remained seated; maintaining the same relaxed state of composure he'd upheld throughout their entire conversation.

Godfrey's quizzical behavior and unflappable demeanor were still on Tyler's mind while he marched down the long driveway and found Rudy standing at the bottom, waiting expectantly.

"Something is not right about that place," Tyler asserted.

"See? I told you!"

Tyler's chief concern was reconnecting with Ashton to inform him of the chilling discovery he made. It was later that night at the local Chili's that he showed his friend the cell phone picture from the mansion and shared his opinion that the symbol could only be one thing: the seal of the dark cabal known as the Scarlet Council.

"So the Scarlet Council's real?" Ashton asked.

Tyler shrugged immodestly while finishing his third margarita of the evening. "That's what the evidence suggests."

Ashton gazed at the picture in fascination.

"Ada said if I wanted to know more about the Scarlet Council, I should talk to McAllister. There seems to be a connection there."

"You know, I think I'm starting to like this Ada chick," Tyler drunkenly acknowledged. "Seems like she has all the bright ideas."

However, when the boys returned to the reservation, they found only a dark oily stain left at the meetinghouse, and to their surprise, they discovered that Ada had mysteriously vanished as well.

34

AT DEATH'S DOOR

McAllister frowned grimly at the reflection staring back at him. He'd seen better days.

As a result of his devastating injuries from the shootout, combined with his strange, debilitating affliction, his face was now a dark tapestry of blackened capillaries. He'd slept on the floor of the meetinghouse for most of the night and much of the day that followed, but he was still feeling rough and ragged, and it was difficult for him to remember when he had looked or felt any worse.

McAllister's shattered composure wasn't even the worst of it. He knew if a crisis were to happen, the timing couldn't be more inconvenient. As long as he was stuck in this regrettable condition, he would be far from physically able to fight any battles for anyone—and the chances he would survive such an ordeal were slim.

Such was the luck he was experiencing: horrible and unpleasant, and only continuing its steady decline as a disembodied voice rang out, filling him on in on some pressing information that had yet to come to his attention.

"Your side chick's in trouble, baby."

At the sound of the familiar interloper, McAllister thought he saw a flash of violet in the bathroom mirror. When he turned to address it, there was no one there.

"Dakota?"

"Tick-tock, lover."

As quickly as it appeared, the voice faded into the ether, and McAllister's eyes narrowed, his anger rising to an irrepressible degree. Despite his wretched condition, his mind was already working itself into a fury to determine his next course of action. He knew that his torrid love affair with Agatha had been on the ropes lately, but he still cared deeply for her and knew he would never forgive himself if he allowed their relationship to end under such poor and regrettable circumstances.

Regardless of whatever was going between him and Ada, Agatha was always destined to hold a special place in his cursed and blackened heart. To save her, he knew he might have to risk everything. The pain and suffering he was bound to endure would be devastating, but he was more than willing to make that sacrifice.

Before McAllister left the reservation, he stopped in on Ada to say goodbye, nearly startling a Native American woman to death when she spied a dark hooded figure bent over the young maiden before vanishing into the shadows. If he had stuck around for a moment longer, he might have witnessed the single tear gliding down Ada's cheek in response to the kiss he left her, but he was now in a race against time. Speeding toward town in the dusty Cadillac with red and black bloodstains still coloring the backseats and pummeling industrial beats and rhythms blaring on the car's stereo—war music for the lonely battle to come.

While McAllister was en route, he received a call from Rudy, hanging up after learning the coven's location. He pressed the pedal to the metal, pushing the belabored behemoth as he sped past the border to town, braking hard when he pulled up outside the hotel and hopping out of the driver's seat.

While staggering to his destination, he clutched his aching side. The pain shooting through him was excruciating, but he was determined to tough it out like a soldier until all of his allies were out of harm's way.

When the door to the hotel room flew open, Rudy and Mary Sue were just as startled as everyone else McAllister had come across when they saw his new appearance. They found themselves gawking at what could easily have been mistaken for a walking cadaver wearing dark sunglasses and a face that was more spiderweb than skin.

"*Santa Muerte*. McAllister—"

McAllister had no time for explanations, ignoring the panicked expressions as he pocketed his sunglasses and gestured to Mary Sue.

"Get her out of here."

Rudy dutifully followed the request. Before Mary Sue could argue, he started pulling her out the door, causing her to struggle back with all the strength that she possessed.

"No! What's he going to do to her? Stop! Let me go!"

Once the two youths made it into the hallway, McAllister locked the door. He needed answers and didn't know how much longer he had until his body gave out on him—a situation he didn't take lightly as he crossed to the feeble gypsy and shook her by the shoulders.

"Izzy. Izzy, wake up."

As Izzy groaned weakly, McAllister could hear the voice of his ailing comrade's lovesick teenage admirer shrieking in the hallway and banging on the door repeatedly. Despite the interruption, all of his focus continued to stay on the sallow, sweaty invalid lying in bed beside him, his voice remaining remarkably steady in light of the stubborn and obstinate behavior that was delaying him.

"Izzy, I know you're there. I need you to do something. I need you to tell me where to find Agatha. Izzy, do you understand me?"

Izzy winced painfully, tears welling up.

"I...can't."

McAllister took a testy breath.

There was no time for this. The interrogation wasn't going well, and negotiations weren't his strong suit. He needed to convince her to help him before he lost control and all hell broke loose.

"Izzy, Ada told me you're the most powerful clairvoyant she ever met—you just don't know it. Now I need you to stop doubting yourself, OK? I need you to suck it up like a champ and tell me—"

"I...can't. Too...weak."

McAllister felt his blood pressure rise on cue in response to the refusal. He shook Izzy violently, ready to snap.

"*Izzy! I'm not playing around! Where is she?*"

"*I don't know!*"

"*You know! You know! Just let go and tell me!*"

Tears were streaming down her cheeks, but these words appeared to awaken an unexpected realization. Her eyes widened, and her mouth dropped open—like all the air had been knocked out of her.

The sight of Izzy's reaction was alarming, but what was going on inside of her was even more astonishing. McAllister's invocation seemed to inspire an internal valve to be released, and a series of evocative visions started flooding into her like a tidal wave.

Outside the hotel room, the sudden silence sent Mary Sue into a panic, desperate to know what was going on while Rudy continued his efforts to restrain her. She wasn't aware that a powerful oracular state of being had taken hold of the young gypsy. Once Izzy's breathing returned to normal, her head fell onto the pillow, and an unsettling calmness came over her.

"Izzy?" McAllister muttered. "Izzy, are you—?"

"She's being held at the Reverend's," Izzy said. "A house on the edge of the woods. Save her, McAllister. Hurry."

McAllister was something of an expert on all things strange and supernatural, and even he was utterly baffled by the change in the girl's composure. But time was of the essence. After receiving his destination, he took a tense breath and squeezed Izzy's hand with gratitude before staggering to the doorway.

While McAllister was leaving, Rudy and Mary Sue appeared just as confounded that he had acquired the information he needed. As he shoved past the odd pair, Mary Sue peered inside the room and was horrified to find Izzy lying stiffly on the bed and looking paler than ever with her eyes staring up at the ceiling. Seeing Izzy now trapped in a brand new state of discomfort was almost too much to bear, and she immediately held their hostile visitor accountable.

"*What did you do to her? What did you do?*"

Despite Mary Sue's relentless badgering, McAllister steadily limped forward, refusing to acknowledge her. He knew he had to force himself to keep it together until the battle was won without wasting a precious ounce of strength in the process.

As he returned to the convertible with Mary Sue and Rudy licking at his heels, he felt the urge to voice one last declaration before speeding off to the bloody confrontation that awaited him.

"Get Izzy back to the tavern," McAllister said. "The witch-hunt ends tonight."

McAllister's words were still echoing in Izzy's head as she stared at the ceiling: "*You know! You know! Just let go and tell me!*"

The words had awakened something deep inside of her, and she now knew that everything that had happened since her encounter at the asylum had a special significance she was only just beginning to understand. Whether the wraith was the ghost of Tom Thumb or something else was inconsequential. What was important was it carried a message. A message that amounted to a bewildering accumulation of vital secret knowledge that the spirit world wished to impart.

While acknowledging this realization, Izzy turned her head and gazed across the room to where the wraith sat in the corner. The maligned specter was now only barely visible due to the overexertion of life force it had taken during its prolonged attempt to communicate its unearthly mission.

Izzy could see the ghostly apparition leering back at her with its hands upon its knees, but she now appeared utterly fearless.

"I understand now," she muttered. "You want to show me something." With her eyes toward the ceiling, she threw back the covers. "I'm ready. Show me."

With these words, Izzy openly invited the wraith to illuminate her. After closing her eyes, awaiting a revelation of some kind, the first thing she felt was a sudden change in her surroundings. Her body felt an electric shock, like a strange energy was now coursing throughout her system, and she experienced the feeling that she was light as a feather and that she was levitating in mid-air. Something instructed her to open her eyes to what awaited her, but nothing could have prepared her for what she was about to witness.

When Izzy opened her eyelids, she found her body hovering over the bed, staring upward at a mirror image of herself. But the image she saw wasn't like her at all. This other Izzy was monochromatic in appearance with hollow, sunken cheeks and dark rings around her eyes—a pale imitation of the young gypsy with a body that was as frail as a skeleton and hair that was falling out.

The shocking image seemed to reflect what Izzy would look like if she were dead, but something even more distressing was still to come. She observed that as soon as she released a gasp in response to the grisly manifestation, she was treated to the sight of her deathly-looking double mirroring the gesture. Its milky eyes widened, and its gaping mouth dropped open, letting out a short terror-stricken gasp that scared the living daylights out of her.

Rudy and Mary Sue were walking back to the hotel room, arguing about McAllister's shady dealings with no clue regarding what awaited them.

"You need to chill, Mary Sue," Rudy grumbled. "McAllister was trying to help."

A loud thud coming from inside the room quickly ended their dispute—what they could have no way of knowing was the sound of Izzy's levitating body dropping onto the bed beneath her.

The two youths raced back into the hotel room and went stiff at what they saw before them: Izzy, lying on the bed with her eyes facing the ceiling, her face now frozen in a state of paralyzing fear. Her jaw was locked open with eyes wider than one would think was humanly possible, showing no signs of awareness or that she would ever return to normal following the terrible encounter she just experienced.

35

A DEMON TO LEAN ON

Several consequences came attached to the transformation McAllister had undergone back in Europe. Greater sensitivity to sunlight was one, as well as the aversion to regular everyday food. But the harshest and most excruciating of these punishments was something that would serve as a constant reminder of all the dark and dishonorable deeds he had committed.

The hunger. The unrelenting hunger that came to him in waves, ebbing and flowing with a restless desire for bloodlust; urging him toward the most savage acts of cruelty imaginable. The hunger was like a bird of prey persistently poking at his brain and nervous system, now so deeply ingrained into every fiber of his being he could no longer remember what life was like before he absorbed this terrible affliction into his daily regimen. And at the moment, it was more difficult than ever to ignore the twisted urges screaming throughout his system. It had been days since he last fed, and the cries for blood were so hellish, they were like an all-out assault on his senses.

The injuries he had sustained at the chemical plant, along with the blood loss, only made this sick and damnable craving more unbearable. His body was crying out louder than ever, thirsting for a massacre to smother the yearning that was tormenting him. Ignoring these calls for nourishment was even more difficult than ignoring the sting left over from the innumerable bullet wounds that littered his battered frame, and it took every shred of focus and concentration not to become consumed by this predicament as he raced like the devil to the secluded backwoods location where Agatha was being held prisoner.

The night was quiet and peaceful when McAllister zeroed in on the Reverend's cozy vacation home where all that could typically be heard were the sounds of the forest; the hypnotic din of the crickets interrupted only by an occasional birdcall as the cold wind blew through the tall and wizened trees shivering around the perimeter like ships lost at sea. McAllister had to hand it to the madman: it was the perfect location to execute the perfect crime since there was no one around for miles to see or hear it. However, this peaceful silence was rent asunder once the cherry-red convertible pulled up like a rocket and screamed to a halt out front, blocking the driveway while loud pummeling music blared out of the stereo.

After putting the crimson behemoth in park, McAllister killed the engine and jumped out, immediately falling to the ground in agony. His eagerness to rush to his companion's aid neglected to take into account all of his numerous unhealed injuries. Cursing under his breath, he pulled himself to his feet and limped to the front door while clutching his aching side, still fighting against the pain from the bullet wounds and the brain-splitting hunger howling through his limbs. He may not have been in top condition—hell, he may have been half-dead—but the deep-seated inner rage that drove him was as sharp as ever and pressing him forward, and he refused to be slowed down by anything.

Once he reached the front porch, not one to waste time with being subtle, McAllister used his heavy black boot to kick in the front door.

Bam!

He paused to listen for any sign of where Agatha might be held captive and was struck by the heavy atmosphere that could be felt in what was an otherwise exceedingly normal upscale type of home. There were no immediate signs of crime or violence, but his eyes were eventually drawn to a light coming from the top of the staircase where he heard the soft padding of footsteps.

Staggering forward, McAllister used the banister to support him as he pulled his injured body up the steps. He felt strangely relieved when he reached the second-floor landing and spied his target milling about at the end of the hallway, the Reverend exiting a room and entering another before closing the door behind him. It was curious that the maniac appeared oblivious to his presence, cheerfully humming a church hymn while going about his business, and the relaxed casualness of these actions only proceeded to infuriate McAllister even further.

Observing a man acting so calmly after abducting a young woman and doing who knows what to her?

How dare he. How fucking dare he.

Of all the things McAllister hated, frauds and hypocrites were at the top of the list. McAllister wasn't a fan of most people, but liars and pretenders were in their own select category altogether. It was patently obvious the Reverend was both of these; a completely different person when he was away from the pulpit and locked away in his sadistic fortress of solitude on the edge of the forest.

Once again, McAllister felt no need to apply the art of subtlety when confronting such a lowlife. After making it to the hallway and reaching the room the man disappeared into, he kicked the door in with his boot.

Bam!

The Reverend was waiting for him, sitting in a chair a few feet from the doorway and aiming a shotgun in McAllister's direction.

Boom!

Once the man pulled the trigger, McAllister's body was instantly propelled backward due to the agonizing force of the blast, slamming into the wall behind him before sliding motionless to the floor.

How foolish, McAllister thought, almost laughing at his own recklessness while gritting his teeth at the new injury.

Way to go, you dummy. A real job for the record books.

And now several of his wounds had reopened, and oily black blood was hemorrhaging all over the carpeting.

As McAllister lay bleeding in the hallway, the Reverend was relaxed and calm as could be, swelling with pride as he rose to his feet and pulled two fresh shells from his pocket.

"Thought you could get the drop on me, did you?" the man smugly remarked. "You shouldn't have come here. You and those deranged sluts. Little Salem was a righteous and holy place before your wicked little sideshow showed up."

McAllister spit up a hefty glob of black blood before issuing his deadpan reply.

"Was it?"

"People were happy!" the Reverend railed. "They were faithful and did not doubt their faith because it was accepted that *I* was the mouthpiece for their salvation! *I* was their Messiah! *I* was their Savior! It was *I* who told them they didn't need to go about performing good works in the world to prove their goodness! I told them that

God wanted them to be prosperous and grow fat off of what privilege had given them! And then *you*..."

The Reverend waved his shotgun, his lips curling into a scowl. "You and that pack of heathens showed up with your nihilistic arrogance and your debauchery. You distract them! From hearing *my* words! My authority! No! Your presence in this town will not go unchallenged. The servants of Beelzebub will be punished, just like the Good Book tells us. With God's glory favoring the virtuous, and all of his Crusaders and holy men."

With that, the raving madman turned his back on his victim, his energy momentarily spent. He was still far from finished, more than content to let his adversary bleed out a bit longer before delivering the final blow and ridding the earth of him forever. But despite the odds, McAllister was deriding his own special brand of amusement, grinning with fiendish delight in response to the fiery sermon.

"You probably won't believe me, but I met a lot of holy men throughout my travels. Men who I respected." McAllister paused, coughing up blood and wiping his face with his hand. "You're no holy man, man."

The Reverend snorted with derision. "What would you know? The devil controls your tongue." He wandered to the far end of the dimly lit study and tossed his shotgun onto the desk. "Any last words, demon? Before you greet your infernal master?"

Upon this invitation, McAllister struggled to rise to his feet but lacked the ability to carry this through. He knew he was in no condition to fight or fend for himself. Every strained and desperate movement sent a sharp jolt of agonizing pain throughout his system. To make matters even worse, the hunger was overwhelming him and blinding all of his senses. Screaming at him so loudly, it was like a war was going inside his head. But despite the endless torment, he continued to engage with the madman and couldn't help but chuckle at the man's laughable self-aggrandizement, along with his stubborn commitment to his own tragic and lamentable hubris.

"All this chatter about Old Scratch," McAllister said. "Personally? I've always been partial to the argument that the devil was invented as a scapegoat for man's more...dishonorable qualities. What do you think of that?"

The Reverend snorted once more, taking a seat at the desk.

McAllister wasn't finished.

He still had more he wanted to say.

"For how could a man created in God's image to be kind and merciful and just—how could he be all these things and also the opposite? Quite the existential dilemma, don't you think?"

"Blasphemy. Pure blasphemy." The Reverend's anger steadily shifted to surprise as he noticed his victim had somehow mustered enough energy to pull himself to a standing position and was slowly but surely crossing into the room. Alas, the heavy exertion quickly proved too much for him, and McAllister's bloody, mangled body fell against the doorway and toppled to the floor.

The sight of his quarry struggling so mightily before his inevitable send-off provided the Reverend with a satisfying rush of adrenaline. It also offered quite a bit of comfort to observe that his opponent posed so little of a threat to him. The young man had been shot at point-blank range after all, which should have been enough to kill anybody. But McAllister wasn't just any ordinary monster, as the Reverend would soon discover. In the very next moment, he was struggling to get back on his feet, steadily propping himself up, his entire body straining, muscles shaking, as he continued his lengthy diatribe, ignoring all interruptions.

"I think it's a laugh riot," McAllister hissed. "How all this 'logic' breaks down in the face of someone who may not suffer... Oh, let's call it a crisis of conscience, yes? Someone who doesn't aspire to be kind or merciful, and holds no confidence in this... Whatever this two-faced illusion of justice is that men like you always cling to."

With that, McAllister was standing once again on his own two legs, hands balled into fists and breathing air like fire into his shabby shredded lungs. He may have been half-dead—even more than half depending on the definition—but he wasn't about to let something as insignificant as death get in the way of his aims. That just wasn't McAllister's style. Especially not with the opportunity to save a friend and murder a repulsive kidnapper all in one go. The very thought of the man's imminent demise excited him; it aroused him and thrilled him, and the hunger raging inside of him was now edging him forward. Cheering him on and propelling him toward unthinkable acts of violence and wholesale slaughter to bring the hostile confrontation to its inevitable show-stopping conclusion.

"Such arrogance," McAllister snarled, fighting back a ruthless bout of laughter. "Against a villain of my pedigree."

The Reverend could see the glint of murder shining in McAllister's eyes. He grabbed his shotgun, aiming both barrels at the creature. Unfortunately, while rushing to defend himself, he knocked over a desk lamp, with the brief distraction causing him to take his eyes away from his assailant. When he looked back, McAllister was no longer there.

The man turned pale, noting how impossible it was that his enemy could just vanish. He started becoming overwhelmed with a sense of crippling dread. He noticed McAllister grinning right beside him with oily black blood dripping down his hungry leering mouth. Cruelly observing the trembling collection of skin and body parts on display along with a palpable stench of fear that only caused his brutal smile to widen even further.

"Call me a demon?" McAllister sneered. "What a comforting fantasy."

Outside the Palmers' vacation home, the night was quiet and peaceful. The serene woodsy environment was casting forth its intoxicating air when a body came crashing out the window and landed in the garden below.

The human form that had taken flight belonged to the Reverend, but the body that landed no longer resembled the man's appearance. Contrary to how the man had looked only a few moments earlier, all life had been drained out of him. His face was now trapped in a look of pure horror, his eyes wide and bulging, and his jaw locked open in response to what could only have been the most terrifying thing he had ever witnessed.

By far, the most disturbing aspect of the deceased clergyman's formerly polished veneer was that his whole body was now a dark tapestry of blackened blood vessels—as if McAllister's horrible affliction had been transferred over in exchange for every bit of life and health he once possessed.

The lifeless hollow shell lay motionless for several minutes before the front door finally opened. Lucy staggered outside with Agatha propped up against her, helping the dizzy hostage to the beastly red convertible and far away from the horrifying atrocities she suffered back in the basement.

As the two girls approached the vehicle, a dark figure slowly exited the home behind them, pausing briefly to light a cigarette as his black boots froze on the front porch and a cloud of smoke was issued from his smirking lips. The figure was McAllister, his body now free of any wound or disfigurement whatsoever. Remarkably, other than the bloodstains and bullet holes in his tattered clothing, any sign of violence or injury he suffered had disappeared, and he was now looking stronger and healthier than ever.

The changes McAllister had experienced while dabbling in some of the darkest magic imaginable were truly extraordinary. Aside from the burdensome side effects, the transformation also had its share of benefits, including advanced healing and a return to a clean bill of health once a precious sacrifice of life was made.

McAllister had made a solemn pledge to avoid mindless killing once he was reunited with his darling stepsister, but if there was anything to be learned from the past twenty-four hours, it was that exceptions would have to be made.

Killing his way out of a predicament.

Yes, this was terribly well-worn territory.

And it felt bloody good to be back on familiar ground.

36

BEYOND GOOD AND EVIL

When Lucy arrived at the tavern, she didn't know what to make of things. After assisting McAllister in helping Agatha to bed, he disappeared. She had no one to call and nowhere to go, and it seemed that she'd been left to fend for herself in unfamiliar territory.

Despite the unsettling atmosphere of the timeless Victorian residence, she found the change of scenery refreshing. How very strange, she thought, that she would be finding safety with a coven of witches. With things as they were and all she had lived through, she could think of no safer place.

The dispassionate welcome aside, the tavern was a uniquely curious oddity, from the tasteful old-fashioned furnishings and the decadent style of the décor to the colorful collection of characters within the seductive confines that lay beyond the building's menacing pitch-black exterior. In addition to Agatha, there was a skinny, hyperactive young man darting about, and in one of the upper rooms, Lucy spied her fellow schoolmate, Mary Sue, sobbing over the bed of a dark-haired beauty who appeared to be comatose.

At the time, Lucy had no way of knowing how the poor girl had gotten this way. Regardless of what had caused the condition, she felt a great deal of sympathy for her—and also for Mary Sue. Her sullen schoolmate seemed to care a great deal for the stranger whose face now appeared locked in a state of distress. It was a state she was familiar with, her burden of seeing demons being a constant source of agitation in her life—ever since spying one of those creatures attached to her own father several years earlier.

It was true: she truly felt for these poor souls. The town thought that Ada and her group were monsters, but the real monsters were already lurking among them like wolves in sheep's clothing. And in the past twenty-four hours, no one had suffered more at the hands of the community than Agatha, who almost lost her life due to Lucy's father's loathsome fanaticism. Lucy couldn't help but feel guilty for being related to the man that performed so many cruel and sadistic punishments on her. She was still severely shaken by the experience, and it was easy to imagine that what Agatha was going through was much worse, due to the horrific variety of tortures she suffered in addition to a lifetime of abuse.

All of these excitable thoughts and emotions continued cycling throughout Lucy's restless mind and nervous system as she turned away from the room she was peering into and crept down the hall to peek into Agatha's bedchamber. There, she found the fiery redhead tucked into bed, now dressed in a provocative red dressing gown. It was no surprise finding Agatha looking exhausted and emotionally spent, but Lucy also noticed she remained uncommonly majestic and radiant, proving that recent events may have bruised her body in places but could not break her indomitable spirit.

Agatha was gazing at the emerald-colored bracelet slung around her wrist when she finally took notice of her shy observer. Lucy averted her eyes from her before summoning the courage to speak.

"Can I come in?"

"Sure, darling. Have a seat."

After sitting next to her, Lucy recalled this wasn't the first time they'd been in close proximity in the same bed together—only this time her father wouldn't be interrupting the intimate session. Whether it was the sudden sense of freedom brought about by this realization or the intense trauma she was struggling to come to terms with, Lucy found herself on the brink of tears, finding it impossible to look her charming hostess in the eye while tensely sitting beside her with her hands grasping her knees.

"Is something wrong?" Agatha asked sweetly.

Lucy wiped at her face before answering. "It's just... I'm so sorry for all those horrible things you had to go through. And I wanted you to know that—"

Tears started streaming down Lucy's cheeks, unable to hold back the waterworks any longer.

Shame. The feeling of shame was what had her acting so emotional, knowing it was catching his daughter in bed with her that likely drove her father to torture Agatha so severely. Whatever happened between the girls could have easily been written off as a harmless moment of youthful experimentation or a cheap trick. The fact that Lucy had shown no regrets for the experience surely increased her father's hatred toward his daughter's seducer.

As Lucy continued to battle her turgid emotions, she started at the touch of a hand pressing lightly on her skin.

"Shh. It's OK," Agatha whispered.

Upon the heat of her touch, Lucy found herself feeling many of the same emotions from when she first caught sight of the ravishing enchantress, these heady feelings all swirling together to form an intoxicating mixture of intense wants and needs when combined with everything else she was experiencing.

But Lucy's knowledge of Agatha had changed a great deal since the tavern's grand opening. She now knew all about her troubled history and of her relationship with McAllister, who braved total annihilation to rush to his lady's rescue. Agatha was no longer just an irresistible object of lust for her to pine for. She now felt more like a beloved sister, and Lucy longed for any relationship at all with her, given that their shared experiences of mutual suffering had her feeling so much closer to her than anyone.

"Is it OK if I stay here with you for a few days?" Lucy asked bashfully, and she was over the moon when Agatha smiled warmly and issued her response.

"Stay as long as you like," Agatha replied. She pulled the bedsheets aside, and Lucy laughed with relief before climbing under the covers and hugging her like a sibling, the nightmarish situation they suffered having brought the two girls closer than anyone could have imagined.

Regrettably, the tender moment was cut short when Rudy appeared in the doorway, smiling rakishly at the warm embrace.

"Hey, ladies. Room for one more?"

"Oh boy," Agatha groaned.

Rudy wasted no time waiting for an invitation, leaping onto the mattress and curling up against his cherished comrade.

"Agatha, you beautiful creature. I'm so happy you're OK."

"Get your hand off my tit, Rudy."

"Whoops. Sorry."

There were no hard feelings. Agatha was used to this behavior from him, and she knew his conduct was innocent. Everyone in Ada's coven liked to tease the skinny hooligan because he was so impressionable and easy to rile up. But at the end of the day, Rudy was one of the gang and a loyal friend—and Agatha knew McAllister would tear his head off if he ever tried any funny stuff.

As Agatha's mind started drifting to her lover who had saved her life for the second time since knowing him, it was Lucy who would shyly turn to Rudy and express what she was thinking.

"Rudy? Have you seen McAllister? Where is he?"

Rudy had all but dozed off at this point, still nestled close to his tantalizing beauty queen while becoming blackout drunk off of her lusty presence. "He left here a while ago," he mumbled. "Said he had to take out the trash."

* * *

The Desperado Roadhouse was a low-key roadside dive to the north of Little Salem on the border between Topsfield and Wenham. The once-popular establishment had originally been constructed as a rest stop for truckers and travelers but eventually became a venue for the local youth to meet up for cheap drinks and a dance or two to the sounds of the dusty jukebox in the corner. Those days were now only a distant memory, as the place had become the favorite hangout for the disreputable rednecks living on the fringes of civilization, and the bar had gotten a lot rougher, a lot meaner, and a lot more violent as a result.

Nowadays, the residents would no longer go anywhere near the Desperado because once the dangerous outlaws moved in, it was a rare occasion for anyone to leave without getting dragged into a scuffle that resulted in mortal injury. The treacherous atmosphere made this the perfect location for the Sheriff to recruit the murderous posse that accompanied him on his recent string of misadventures. And, likewise, it was the perfect place for McAllister to go hunting for vengeance in response.

The moon was high in the sky when McAllister pulled up to the venue, parking on the shoulder of the lonesome highway across from where the roadhouse stood. A song by Alien Sex Fiend played on the stereo as McAllister lit a cigarette and calmly breathed in the chemicals, looking much more focused and relaxed than he had for quite some time. When it came to murder and mayhem, this was when he was in his element and life was uncomplicated and simple. There were times in the past when killing had come as naturally for him as getting out of bed in the morning, and with so much rotten anger and fiery indignation raging inside of him, the idea of ridding the world of a few worthless lowlifes was about as controversial as removing a pebble from the side of the road.

McAllister had matured a lot over the past few months, so he did feel at least a tiny sliver of remorse for some of the more savage and brutal actions he'd taken in recent memory. But, as for right now, in just a few moments, he would be putting a hurting on the detestable crew of scumbags that tried to murder his stepsister, and that was unforgivable.

As he placed his unfinished smoke in the ashtray, he thought about how much he was going to enjoy the next few moments.

Dakota would be proud of him, allowing the beast out of the cage for a bit.

Yes, indeedy—it would be just like old times.

McAllister kept the engine running as he stepped out of the convertible and crossed toward the glowing red sign that was beckoning to him like an old friend. Inside, Sheriff Bucky Gates was present with a dozen drunk and disorderly members of his freakish meth-mouthed nightmare factory; the entire wrecking crew who had participated in the attempted massacre at the AM Chemical Plant. Everyone was heavily armed and having a blast, throwing back drinks and also throwing a few punches now and then while chattering like a mob of cranked up jackals. But all good times must come to an end, and for these boys, that time was moments away. Outside, McAllister, with the silver ouroboros branded on the back of his black leather jacket shimmering in the moonlight, pulled the hood of his hooded sweatshirt over his head and entered the sleazy dive.

Upon McAllister's entrance, the Sheriff and the others looked to the door, faces morphing into masks of stunned, wide-eyed astonishment. Everyone was no doubt shocked to the core to see the immortal assassin standing before them looking good as new and all in one piece. Time seemed to slow down as some of the men instinctually reached for their weapons. Little did they know, it was already too late for their precious souls. McAllister had only been inside for a matter of seconds but still hadn't broken his stride, punching the lights out with one quick gesture and hitting the switches that stood affixed to the wall so hard his tightly clenched fist went straight through. With that, the lively atmosphere changed completely as darkness enveloped the room.

Of all of the powers that McAllister gained while living in exile, his ability to disappear into the shadows was probably the strangest and most mystifying of them all. The shadows were like a supernatural transportation system, allowing him to sneak up on an unsuspecting victim or escape from a situation when things were getting too out of control. Fights against multiple attackers were a breeze with this ability, as it granted him a unique advantage. And the advancement in odds felt all too fitting given that all the powers he inherited were geared exclusively toward maximum carnage and bloodshed. Darkness was a necessity with this ability, making it somewhat limiting, but with the overhead fluorescents out of commission and the only light coming from the colorful Christmas tree lights decked around the bar, shadows were everywhere, and he was ready to get to work.

To any onlooker, the massacre that occurred would have appeared almost entirely like a blur and was over in a matter of seconds. But if a savvy spectator possessed the capacity to keep up with McAllister's movements, this is what they would have seen as he made quick lightning-fast work of his targets:

First, McAllister disappeared and reappeared behind the man in front of him, using one hand to drain the man's life force, while with the other, he directed the man's gun arm to shoot the man standing across from him. As both men breathed their dying breaths in unison, McAllister disappeared into the shadows and reappeared behind the man he just shot, only a few mere moments after the fatal bullet passed through him. He grabbed the sawed-off shotgun cradled in the man's arms and used it to fire at the bartender, who was aiming a rifle at the highly proficient killer but wouldn't be for long.

As the body of the bartender went crashing into the mirror behind the bar with his pulse no longer beating and his guts now filled with buckshot, McAllister tossed the shotgun across the room and disappeared, reappearing to catch it and use it as a club to smash the head in of his next victim; splitting it open like a watermelon before the man could guess what was happening. McAllister kicked his latest victim into the man sitting next to him, grabbing the gun in the back of the man's waistband and placing two shots into each of them before disappearing and reappearing behind two unsightly bruisers that were rushing right for him at one moment and trying to figure out where their slippery target just went the next. Their wily attacker grabbed a wooden chair and decked both of the overgrown psychopaths with one swing before disappearing into the shadows to reappear behind two slack-jawed rednecks watching in stunned amazement from the back of the room, slamming their skulls together and killing them instantly before using one of the men's pieces to execute the two enemies he decked with the chair.

Next, McAllister switched his aim and fired at a man entering from the hallway to the lavatories with guns blazing, killing him with one shot before tossing the spent weapon aside as a particularly savage-looking outlaw took a swing at him and started throwing wild punches in his direction. Before the man could land a single blow on his spry opponent, McAllister disappeared and reappeared behind him, tossing him toward the wall and impaling him on the mounted head of a deer. As another man approached him with white knuckles also raised, McAllister disappeared and reappeared behind this man as well, pulling the razor-sharp Bowie knife from the man's belt and using it to stab him repeatedly, sending another poor soul to the afterlife before setting his eyes on the last man standing.

Sheriff Bucky Gates was gazing at McAllister with his gun aimed right at him, but his hands were shaking so fiercely, it was already dead certain he'd never pull off the shot. Eager to live to fight another day, he tossed his weapon aside and turned to the exit, only to find himself face to face with his adversary whose fearsome presence showed no signs of letting the cowardly lawman leave the place alive. The Sheriff barely knew what was happening and wasn't even granted the mercy to plead for his wretched existence as McAllister grabbed him by the back of the head and, with one swift motion, smashed the man's startled features through the rock-solid surface of the bar, caving his entire face in before his lifeless, useless body dropped to the ground, twitching like a dead chicken.

With the massacre concluded, McAllister stared vacantly at his lethal doings. The roadhouse was a bloodbath, but his work still wasn't finished.

While confident that word of the deaths would spread quickly, McAllister was smart enough to know to avoid leaving any evidence that would lead back to him or Ada. He splashed alcohol on all of the corpses, built a makeshift Molotov cocktail out of the healthy supply of materials available, and pitched it into the row of liquor sitting behind the bar.

And with that, the deed was done: the bottle smashed, the room shot up in flames, and McAllister exited the once cheerful and popular venue that was now burning wildly behind him and returned to the convertible. He climbed inside and placed the smoldering cigarette still burning in the ashtray to his impassive and expressionless lips before casually driving off into the distance.

The whole ordeal was over in less than three minutes. This wasn't a record for him, but still a notable success. The New Lords had gotten their retribution against the Sheriff, and the witch-hunt had been rendered null and void.

While driving back to the tavern, McAllister reflected on how troubling it was that taking peoples' lives remained like second nature to him, all thanks to the burdensome sickness he was cursed with. Deep in the depths of his jet black heart, he knew that even though he'd sworn to turn over a new leaf and be a better person once he was reunited with his beloved stepsibling, the unnatural bloodlust flowing through him had different plans entirely.

The showdown with the Reverend and the endless buffet of pain freshly dished out at the roadhouse had helped to satiate the hunger for now. But McAllister knew that, eventually, it would be coming back with a vengeance, like it always did.

When you were a bloodthirsty, immortal vampire like he was, that sort of thing came with the territory. Which meant he would have to be ready.

37

OLD KILLERS DIE HARD

Word was slow to spread about the series of attacks against Ada's coven or the counter-attacks that followed, but during this time, Nancy and Wilbur were arguing more than in all their time spent together. Mary Sue was primarily at the center of these arguments, with Nancy accusing Wilbur of not doing enough to protect their daughter from the dangerous and seductive influence that resided at the all-black Victorian sitting directly across the street from their formerly flourishing family-oriented business.

"You know, it would be nice to know you were on my side for a change," Nancy lamented at one point. "I don't know if you've taken a good look in the mirror lately, but it feels like I'm the one who's been doing all the work! While I've been doing my best to keep our daughter out of danger and protect her from Ada and McAllister and those witchy creeps, you've just been standing in the background! Just futzing around while I'm being humiliated!"

"Honey," Wilbur offered sheepishly, "I'm sorry about last night, but what more do you want me to do? We called the police, we got the neighbors involved—"

"No, it's not just last—Wilbur, tell me. Why? Why do I have to be the bad guy all of the time? All the time! The one who's setting all the rules and boundaries with her while you get to sit back and be Mr. Nice!"

This accusation hit Wilbur hard.

It was true: Wilbur did put forth a great deal of effort to come across as nice these days. To his neighbors and various members of their community and also to their adopted daughter. He knew that some people even mocked him for the overly upbeat and congenial attitude he was always projecting. But for Wilbur, this behavior was more than just a shallow performance. It was part of a longstanding effort to wash away the lengthy list of sins he had participated in throughout his distressingly violent and woefully misguided life.

After spending so much time in a world that was brimming over with endless bloodshed and cruelty, Wilbur wanted to bask in an environment that was quiet and peaceful. He wanted to contribute to this gentle way of existence as someone who was as affable and outgoing as humanly possible. And Nancy knew all about his checkered past, so it should have come as no surprise that he felt highly unsettled by these accusations.

"What is it, hon?" Wilbur asked morosely. "Do you want me to go back to being the bad guy?"

He never received an answer. Nancy just changed the subject, ending with one final jab at her husband, stating that sometimes she wondered how much he even wanted to be a dad.

The damage was already done. Wilbur could read her like a book and knew that while she didn't say it, it was easy to gather what she wanted from him: to transform into the man he once was and deal with Ada and McAllister personally. Then, and only then, would she feel that he deserved to go back to his usual peppy self—only after their daughter was safe.

For Wilbur, this transformation was becoming more and more difficult to avoid. He'd already heard his neighbors buzzing about how Sir Godfrey wanted to see him and received a personal summons from Godfrey's butler, which meant that the Council had some business they wanted to present to him. So far, he'd been avoiding the meeting because of his reluctance to return to his former profession—the mere idea of this made him feel queasy and sent his body into a sweat. This reaction was understandable because, despite his dark history, he was someone with all the qualities of a genuinely kind and decent person who had no business in pursuing that kind of life in the first place. As silly as it may have sounded, it was just something that had presented itself at one point; a golden opportunity he was far too weak to turn down. And while he took pride in being a hard worker who always got the job done with a positive attitude and a "can-do" spirit, he was grateful when he was allowed to finally put those days behind him and swore he would never return to his former profession, no matter what the cost.

Once Mary Sue went missing, Wilbur seemed to experience a change of heart in these matters. Seeing all the pain and anguish that his loving partner was going through had a strong effect on him that was almost too much to bear. His wife was convinced their daughter hated them. She was starting to doubt the love of her own child—something she would never have considered before Ada and McAllister returned to Little Salem.

"Honey, our daughter doesn't hate us," Wilbur told Nancy during an unusually uneventful day at the yogurt shop. He was doing his best to console her, but his words only fell on deaf ears.

"I know she's just a teenager," Nancy lamented, "and she had a hard life back where she's from. But we do our best, don't we? We try to be good parents and to create a positive environment for her, which is why we have the store and why you no longer do business for Godfrey and those..."

Nancy stopped herself, still perhaps hoping to avoid addressing the path that now lay wide open in front of them. But Wilbur could already tell that as long as conditions remained as they were, his wife would continue to be despondent.

"Maybe I was too harsh with her," Nancy mumbled as a gloomy afterthought. "And Ada. Little Miss Perfect."

"You were doing what you thought was best, like any good parent," Wilbur reasoned. "You sensed danger, and you reacted. And you were right to get on my case about not being helpful because what I've been putting in hasn't been enough."

Wilbur started toward the door after suggesting for Nancy to put some more calls out to see if Mary Sue was staying with a friend.

"Where are you going?" she asked him.

"Relax. I'll be back soon."

As Wilbur slouched to the family station wagon, a look of intense worry spread across Nancy's face.

She had every right to be worried.

She knew exactly where he was headed.

It had been years since Wilbur had visited the Godfrey Mansion. The last time he could remember being summoned to the intimidating palatial residence was the time all that business went down five years earlier. And here he was, being called in once again for something to do with the Council's favorite treacherous *enfant terrible*. Only this time, Ada was also part of the package.

Even when he was doing regular jobs for his employers, Wilbur rarely visited the place. The mansion was more of a location reserved for the Council's upper echelon and hardly an appropriate setting for low-level grunts like him. It was a place for high society, not the common workingman. That's all he was at the end of the day: just a simple man trying to earn a living and put a little food on the table for his family. After so much time had passed, he found it crazy to think about what this "living" of his actually consisted of. That's just how his life had turned out, and there was no way he'd ever be able to abandon it fully.

After being shown to the massive dining hall, Wilbur found himself wrestling with how he got himself into this predicament. Feeling restless and uneasy, he scanned the familiar atmosphere: the large bay windows, the finely crafted antique furniture. The flagrant display of opulence made him feel dreadfully uncomfortable and out of place, serving as a stark reminder that despite his many other privileges, he still didn't belong in this world and had somehow broken through and ended up on the lowest rung.

It was a sad fact that there was no room for advancement when it came to his former position. It was just a job you did and went home straight after, like most occupations. While some Council members were destined to rise in the ranks, like a "certain someone" before he went native, for Wilbur this was never meant to be. He was always destined to serve power and never wield it, and he was feeling mighty anxious, dreading what the orders from up top would prove to be for him and how he would be asked to serve power next.

Wilbur found himself waiting in the vast and empty room for quite some time. After hearing noises, he peeked into the front hallway and spied Tyler, one of the two tourist boys, shuffling to the door and exiting in a hurry. Shortly after this, he spied Godfrey himself crossing to the entranceway, watching the young man hoof it down the long and winding front drive before turning away and casting a wolfish grin in his direction.

"Wilbur, sorry to keep you waiting. How's the family?"

"I was told you wanted to see me?"

Wilbur was still trying to remind himself he was there of his own volition. He was as concerned about sorting out the Ada and McAllister situation as everyone else in the community. It was like he told Nancy: he felt ashamed he'd been so ineffective up to this point and now felt obligated to do something to prove his own self-worth. But being back in the company of Godfrey made him want to shrink back inside himself and take off in a manner similar to the ghoulish silver-haired titan's previous company.

"Straight to the point, I see." Godfrey crossed into the hall and opened the curtains, allowing what little daylight that remained to soak through the lavish environment. "I won't waste your time. I'm sure there's no question regarding the pertinent business of the day."

"Witches."

Godfrey nodded, maintaining a stern expression.

"If McAllister finds that book, the world will be in great danger."

That's right. There was also the whole matter of the book. So much had happened Wilbur had almost forgotten all about it.

"Which is why we're calling you back from retirement. Find the Witchfinder General and bring him here."

And there it was: Wilbur's mission.

A task that was so unexpected, it made him turn pale instantly.

"Find the Witchfinder G—? But I don't know where he—"

"We both know that's a lie. The two of you were thick as thieves back in your day. I want you to bring him here to clean up this mess. And need I remind you, the life that you enjoy is all thanks to your loyalty to the Council, and we can take it all back whenever we wish. That's all I have to say."

And that was it: In just a handful of phrases, Godfrey had illustrated the vast wealth of power and influence he still held over Wilbur's puny existence.

It was true: Wilbur owed the Council everything. They paid for his house and his transportation and part of the frozen yogurt shop that provided his current livelihood and that of his family's. They even agreed to look the other way when he, a Council witch hunter, decided to marry a witch of all the crazy things. When he announced to his employers that he wanted to retire, he knew he would only be allowed to do so under a list of conditions; one of which was that he could be called back at a moment's notice whenever his superiors wished it. After all, no one ever really left the Council. Once you had worked for them, they owned you, body and soul.

"Now don't be a stranger," Godfrey added while making his exit. "And do make haste. I find these delinquents...tiresome."

Perhaps McAllister had the right idea all along, Wilbur thought to himself. When McAllister desired to sever his alliances to the Council, he immediately fled to Europe. Maybe it still wasn't too late for him to do something similar; escape with his family to a far-off destination away from the Council's reach. But Wilbur also knew that while McAllister was on the lam, the Council had pursued him incessantly. It was a bloody miracle he was still ticking—especially after whatever it was that had turned him into the creature he was currently. No, it was a nice fantasy, but this problem would only resolve itself by doing what he had done in the past: keeping a stiff upper lip, obeying orders, and doing exactly what the Council demanded.

It had been approximately five years since the town was paid a visit by Ada and McAllister, which was precisely how long since Wilbur abandoned his position as the hired killer known throughout the underworld as the man that specialized in exterminating witches.

Godfrey's suspicions turned out to be right on the money. Wilbur and his former associate had grown especially close during their time working together, and he knew precisely where he had disappeared. There was a catch, however. Wilbur wasn't confident he could convince the killer to come out of retirement for one final illustrious encore, even if the assignment involved the notorious Van Dreyer child and her troublesome stepsibling.

Wilbur had a lot to lose should he choose to disobey the Council's orders, but the man he was being asked to find had run out of things to lose a long time ago. This is why he knew he would be instrumental in convincing him to return to Little Salem to go hunting for witches once again. And he could also count on being personally called in for this assignment. If he was going to convince his ex-colleague to agree to the task, he knew he would be expected to participate alongside him.

That was unavoidable.

The Witchfinder General was being called back into action, and the Wheel of Fortune had already determined that someone in Little Salem was destined to be meeting their end. Only time would tell if that person would be one of the slayers or a witch.

38

INTO THE WOODS

Sunlight bled through the curtains as Ashton sat at his laptop. The phrase, "Mysterious Ones," had been inputted into his browser's search bar, but all the hits turned up nothing but nonsense.

Witches, secret societies, Mysterious Ones. Little Salem was shaping up to really be something—definitely a whole lot more than the sleepy old town he anticipated. Ashton still had no idea of where to go or what to do next when he joined Tyler for breakfast, scouring the map Ada had doodled on as his friend and fellow ghost hunter rambled on in the background.

"We need to check the woods," Tyler said. "That's what the blood on the wall told us."

"Oh, so you think we should do whatever the blood on the wall tells us?"

Ashton knew that Ada had left them a clue somewhere. The bloody message on the wall may have been pointing them to the woods, but the patches of forest that surrounded Little Salem stretched for miles and miles. Even if they did decide to search it, they wouldn't know where to start.

This made Ada's guidance in this matter even more valuable. Unfortunately, she was nowhere to be found, leaving Ashton more frustrated than ever with the lack of progress he was making. The last thing he expected was for Tyler to call his attention to a feature on the map that had evaded him completely.

"Hey, what's this? Right here."

Ashton glanced to where Tyler was pointing: a place next to the forest with two question marks drawn over it.

$$[??]$$

Ashton furrowed his brow at the discovery. "Ada scribbled drawings and information all over this thing. Those just look like two question marks."

Tyler raised an eyebrow. "So it doesn't mean anything."

No, the item would only be there if she was trying to call his attention to something. After taking a closer look, Ashton noticed the site of the Old Little Salem Parsonage sat on the edge of the forest right next to the curious markings.

Could this mean what he thought it did?

"Maybe, maybe not..."

On their way to the tavern, Ashton revealed to Tyler what Ada had told him at the Little Salem Witch Museum.

"Ada said the events of the Salem witch trials started after two girls had an experience in the woods of some kind. Two girls who happened to be related to the town reverend."

Tyler could easily do the rest of the math on his own. "So maybe the girls entered the woods from next to where the Old Little Salem Parsonage once stood. But what does any of this have to do with the Mysterious Ones?"

Ashton wasn't entirely sure himself at this point, hoping to verify some of his suspicions with Ada or McAllister if he could locate them. When the boys arrived at the tavern, it appeared empty and deserted. The only signs that anyone had been there since the raid was the tattered police tape flapping in the breeze and a vandalized shutdown notice that read, "Closed For Innovation."

Not being able to locate the two most knowledgeable occult sources in their immediate circle was disappointing, but Ashton's mind was already racing. After returning to their hotel room, he revealed to Tyler his latest hypothesis.

"Maybe that's who those young girls ran into," Ashton mused. "Maybe that's what started all the hysteria surrounding the Salem witch trials."

Tyler remained skeptical about this assumption. "So you think we should just go along with whatever that Ada chick tells us?"

No, the time for hesitation was over. Ashton was convinced that the two question marks were the most significant clue Ada had left them. It was time to do the one thing she'd been telling him to do since he arrived: to take a walk in the woods one night if he wanted to learn the truth about witchcraft, and what the strain of witchcraft in Little Salem was all about.

Once the boys had determined their destination, everything was off to the races. They quickly packed their camera gear and camping supplies and were ready to rock. Before they took off, Ashton decided to check in with the giant regarding their prospective game plan, finding him sitting in his usual place at the hotel's front desk, eyes reliably buried in a newspaper.

When questioned, the giant remained curiously uncommunicative. The boys were on their way and exiting out the front door when he called after them.

"Have you ever heard of something called a witch's ladder?"

The giant laid the newspaper flat on the desk and drew a picture. "It's a charm used by witches. A knotted rope braided with bones, feathers, and dead leaves. If you look up into the trees and you start seeing any of these things...you should be on the right track."

Several minutes later, Ashton and Tyler arrived at the old parsonage and were scoping out the area. Right before this, Tyler had spotted Lucy ducking into the tavern and managed to question her about how she'd been, what she was up to, and, most significantly, what she was doing at Ada's coven's HQ.

"Everything's fine," Lucy insisted. "Why wouldn't it be?"

Lucy remained adamant that no one else was currently staying at the tavern except for herself, no matter how ridiculous it sounded. Tyler was able to brush the matter aside quite easily (he obviously still had lustful feelings for the pretty young thing). As for Ashton, he could have cared less about Lucy's blatant posturing, having already lost interest in what could be going on with Ada and her weird friends. What really had him concerned were the last words the giant said to them:

"*Be careful. There are more dangerous things out there than witches.*"

"This is it," Tyler stated, surveying the aging wooden structure in front of them.

Ashton glanced at the map and pointed to the historic building.

"Old Little Salem Personage."

He pointed into the woods.

"Question marks. This is it."

The camera gear and camping packs were retrieved from the car, and after a couple of deep breaths, the boys began their march deep into the shadowy and uninviting stretch of woods that awaited them.

"Ashton?"

"Yeah, Tyler?"

"If this trip ends up like the end of *The Blair Witch Project*, I'm totally going to kill you."

Hours later, daylight was quickly disappearing, but the boys were making great progress. As they walked through the forest, they filmed the trees with their portable video cameras, and every now and then they would spy a witch's ladder hanging from the branches. Proof they were on the right track.

At first, the conversation between them was tense and awkward, what with their routine bickering of late and Ada creating a huge wedge between them. Their recent discoveries while surviving some rather hairy ordeals in each other's absence had helped them immensely in their investigation, but neither of them felt like reviewing these incredible findings. It felt more essential to use their time getting their friendship like it was before changing their plans to spend spring break in Cabo and setting off for Little Salem instead.

Tyler was the most active in trying to bury the hatchet between them. To keep things interesting, he quizzed Ashton on his greatest fear. Ashton laughed this off, claiming he wasn't afraid of anything. Tyler didn't believe his friend's assertion but didn't press him. When the question was turned back on him, he tried to provide an honest answer, admitting that his greatest fear was to find a friend in danger and not be able to do anything.

The back-and-forth continued to loosen up significantly, and as the sun disappeared and the boys carved a steady path through the vast and intimidating landscape, they left the spooky conversations behind them and fell into regular guy talk. They both became so consumed in their discussions that they started paying little attention to where they were going or looking at the branches above them. Strangely, even though they'd been walking in the forest for hours, they hadn't seemed to cover much ground. The forest didn't appear as deep as when they had entered it, and they may have started to wonder if they'd been going around in circles if they hadn't been enjoying their conversations so immensely.

By the time it had gotten completely dark out and the boys were using the night-vision settings on their cameras to guide them, they were so absorbed in their casual banter they neglected to notice that nearly every tree they were passing contained a witch's ladder swinging from the branches. Or that carved at the base of one of these trees were the letters, "RIP XG."

"You had sex with Sarah Fogelman?" Ashton remarked. "Oof. That walk of shame must've felt like a marathon."

"I was drunk, and she was present," Tyler said. "Don't understand how that makes me Hitler."

Ashton punched Tyler in the shoulder.

"Ow! *Dude, what was that for?*"

"Godwin's Law. You lose, dude."

"Oh, whatever," Tyler moaned. "I mean, you're the lunatic. We're only in college for four years, and in our final year, Mercy is the only chick you've taken to Pound Town?"

"You see? That's where you don't get it. You find the right girl, you don't need anyone else."

"Right. Which is why you've been thirsting after that Ada chick like a parched fish."

Ashton was about to open his mouth to argue with this, but while they were talking, the boys had inadvertently stumbled onto something of much greater significance. They observed they were now standing in an open clearing in the shape of a circle with thirteen stones dotting the perimeter and a pair of rotting fallen logs just beyond this.

"Dude! You see this?" Tyler was becoming more excited and creeped out by the second. "Do you see what I'm looking at?"

"The clearing looks like it's in the shape of a circle," Ashton noted.

Tyler aimed his camera all around him and filmed the forest floor. Sensing something distinctly unusual about where they were standing, he got on his knees and touched the soil beneath their feet.

"The dirt. It's ash."

Ashton scanned the ground and noted this was no exaggeration. All of the earth encompassing the circle and slightly beyond it was entirely composed of fine gray ash. And this wasn't from the remnants of a campfire; it was from something else entirely.

Curious that there might be even more to the bizarre location, Ashton began to film the trees that surrounded them.

"You see these trees?"

He approached one and knocked on the trunk.

"They've been petrified."

However, this chilling discovery wouldn't be the last as Ashton noticed Tyler staring at the trees lining the perimeter of the clearing.

"Tyler? What is it?"

Ashton may have asked this question, but he could already guess what had his friend so unsettled: witch's ladders everywhere, covering the branches. The discovery made him feel both uneasy and thrilled—excited that it appeared they were on track to uncovering something genuinely astonishing, but still dreadfully uncertain of what that would be.

Tyler seemed to be harboring the same emotions as he turned to his loyal amigo after the color had returned to his face.

"Looks like we found our place to camp."

In no time at all, the boys had a fire going at the center of the clearing and were chowing down on hot stew. Once again, the expedition appeared to be bringing them closer together as they sat on the fallen logs on the outer edge of the site, chatting with each other like old times.

"I can't believe I'm sitting next to you at a campfire instead of bird-dogging babes in Cabo."

"And yet here you are."

Tyler snorted, and Ashton smiled with wry amusement.

"Been a few days since I heard you bitch about this trip," Ashton said. "For a second, I was worried that maybe the body snatchers might have gotten ahold of you."

Tyler whistled an eerie melody, and the boys laughed in unison, ahead of a brief lull in the conversation with the crackling of the fire filling in for the duration.

The two companions still had no idea what they would discover that night, and Tyler was the one who finally broke the silence, his face taking on a thoughtful and somewhat haunted expression.

"So what got you into all this?"

"Hunting ghosts and stuff? I thought I told you."

"Nah."

"Really?"

"Well, I mean—you never *really* told me."

Ashton frowned, reflecting on the question.

"I dunno. I've just always been into that stuff. Spooky stuff. Scary stuff. I always wanted to see how close I could get to all of it. Like, real up close and face to face without even flinching, you know?"

"Ha. You're the Terminator. '*Your clothes. Give them to me now.*'"

Ashton smiled at Tyler's cheesy Schwarzenegger impression and nodded in his direction.

"What about you? How did you get into this?"

Tyler took a moment before answering and let out a dramatic breath, his eyes turning pensive as he stared off into the darkness.

"I used to live in this old house. A really old house. This was before my dad left and... Actually, it was right after he walked out on us. On me and my mom. My mom—she started feeling the presence of malevolent spirits I guess you could call them. I was only, like, a child at the time, but even I could... You know, I could see it was driving her crazy.

"So between that and all the late nights and double shifts, trying to raise a spoiled brat like me on her own... Anyway, eventually, I decided it was up to me. I was going to capture the presence of these spooks and scare them off. All for my mom, you know? So I got really into watching all of the classic ghost shows and reading up on that stuff. I was ten years old at the time, watching those shows late at night under the covers. So, yeah—long story short, I started doing ghost hunts in my own home."

"Whoa ha ha."

"I shit you not, bro. But I never found anything. Like, there were a few times where I thought I was close but... And then one day this doctor—this family friend of my mom's—she came over to see us and told me some people were going to be looking after my mom for a bit. It turned out my mom had suffered a nervous breakdown, so they took her somewhere and put her on some pills.

"We moved into this new apartment shortly afterward. One that was a—oh, what's it called? Whatever. After that, we were on government assistance, and my mom was working fewer hours, and she had her pills so... So she wasn't bothered by spooks no more. But it always bothered me. It always bothered me that I couldn't be the one to fix it. To fix the ghost problem for her, you know? It's like, if I could've found those ghosts and really scared them—scared them away for good... Then we would've been all right on our own."

Ashton stared at his friend in silence, not knowing how to respond. Tyler was a total joker most of the time; a typical bro who was obsessed with getting drunk and getting laid. It was a rare moment for him to open up emotionally like this, but Ashton was glad he did and felt a lot closer to him as a result.

The bonding experience was harshly interrupted when the boys suddenly heard the snap of a twig from somewhere in the depths of the forest. Startled, they both glanced to the perimeter of the clearing in unison, and Ashton aimed his video camera at a dense cluster of trees and switched the camera to night-vision.

Everything appeared to have gone quiet without even the sound of an insect stirring. Tyler was about to call attention to this, but before he could speak, Ashton put a finger to his lips and gestured with his eyes to follow him.

Clouds had engulfed the sky, cutting off any light from the moon and the stars, leaving the two investigators with only the night-vision settings on their cameras to guide them. The noise could have come from anywhere, but Ashton was confident it came from a tightly packed cluster of trees and overgrown brush where they were searching, his eyes glued to the grainy green footage on the viewscreen.

"See anything?"

"Just dark, dark, and more—"

Ashton's reply was suddenly interrupted by a crackle of leaves. He quickly spun around and aimed his camera into the dense foliage.

"Did you hear that?"

"Probably just a deer, right?"

At the time, Tyler may have wanted to believe this, but the noise was from more than just a deer—something Ashton confirmed while observing the pixelated image of a dark figure moving across the landscape.

"That was no deer."

Receiving a rush of adrenaline, Ashton took chase with Tyler at his heels. "Hey! Who goes there! Hey!"

After reaching the place where he spied the shadowy figure, there were no signs of anyone.

"Dude, where did it go?"

Ashton craned his ears, listening intently. As luck would have it, he heard the sound of movement coming from some bushes. He puffed out his chest and let out a nervous breath, aiming his camera into the overgrowth.

"Hey! Who's there?"

"Dude. That better not be a hunter hiding in there. If I get my ass shot off... I've grown very attached to my own ass, ya feel me?"

Tyler fell silent as the bushes started shaking, and Ashton, persevering until his last breath, took a defiant step forward in response.

"We know somebody's in there! Come out and reveal yourself!"

Silence followed—a silence that was interrupted by the last thing they expected to hear: a haggard female voice answering back.

"Stop pointing those infernal cameras at me!"

Ashton and Tyler exchanged blank expressions. To discover they'd come across a live human being wasn't the least surprising, but that it was someone who was a complete stranger was disorienting. They were still feeling increasingly uncertain as to the explicit purpose of the unusual clearing they stumbled on, what with the strange ashen ground and the abundance of witch's ladders, so they weren't about to throw away a chance at clarity just to obtain some dubious camera footage.

"OK. We're turning off the cameras."

Ashton clicked off his camera and Tyler hesitantly did the same.

"There. They're off."

"Good. Isn't polite to shoot a woman's likeness without asking."

Gradually, the woman revealed herself, rising from the bushes and looking unlike any other person they'd come across.

The stranger was small and portly with a grime-stained face that was heavily lined. She wore a tattered scarf over her stringy graying hair, and the rest of her ensemble was equally disheveled. It was easy to see she'd been living rough for a while, but this hadn't weakened her sense of humor. She winked a cloudy eye at her observers while issuing a disarming gap-toothed grin.

"Just so happens I didn't get much beauty sleep last night," the woman said. Throwing her head back, she let loose a long, delirious cackle and began marching into the depths of the forest.

Ashton and Tyler were bewildered by this behavior, but it didn't steer them away from wanting to find out more. After exchanging dumbfounded expressions, they both raced after the peculiar figure.

"Hey! Wait up! Where are you going?" Ashton called.

"Me? I'm going home! What does it look like I'm doing?"

The woman turned back to face them while flashing her distinctive grin. "It's not far if you care to follow. I'll put the cauldron on."

Amused beyond words, the woman erupted into another riotous cackle and disappeared with the boys taking after her. Struggling to keep their wits about them, they pushed past the withered branches and vegetation until they found themselves in another clearing. But this setting, like the other one they discovered, wasn't just any clearing, and they stared with jaws agape at what they saw before them.

There, in the middle of the wilderness was a decrepit hut with smoke billowing out of a small chimney. The dwelling was about the size of a small shed and appeared to have been assembled out of discarded materials from the forest, with the dim glow of firelight illuminating the interior from within.

Ashton and Tyler had hiked for hours to get to the burnt-out setting nearby, so what this hut was doing so deep in the forest was anybody's guess. If either of them had stopped to think about it, they would have concluded that the perceptions of their surroundings were being toyed with and that the forest possessed its own special plans in terms of what it intended to reveal to them and when.

The burning questions were piling up, but they would have to be saved for later. Before entering the strange and unsightly home, the woman turned to face them, her appearance looking much filthier and unkempt when viewed in the flickering firelight.

"Well, c'mon," the woman beckoned.

After flashing another smile, she disappeared inside, and the boys exchanged cautious expressions before crossing to the entrance. Deep down, they knew their harrowing journey was at their backs, and they had reached their destination. It was the middle of the night, and the moon was high above them: the perfect time to hear a captivating ghost story...

39

DEVILS AND DUST

_____

Mary Sue sat on her bike wearing a stony expression as she stared into the dark stretch of forest in front of her. It was still morning, and the skies were crystal clear. But you wouldn't necessarily know this from inside the woods that surrounded Little Salem. The voluminous canopy of needles and leaves stole most of the sunlight before it ever reached the ground, turning the area into a dark, hazardous maze that was difficult to navigate and easy to become lost in.

The Mysterious Ones Wait In The Woods.

Mary Sue could still see the look of tortured horror on Izzy's face as she released a piercing scream. Tragically, during the lead-up to this incident, she and the others were starting to believe the poor girl was getting better. But after cutting her arm open to assist the spirit with delivering the cryptic riddle, it was nothing but a speedy descent to the disturbing catatonic state she was now trapped in.

The Mysterious Ones Wait In The Woods.

Was this really a message from Tom Thumb or something else entirely? A cry for help or a cold statement of fact issued by cruelly ambivalent forces from the other side of the material realm?

Mary Sue felt like she had no choice but to investigate further. Izzy had suffered so much pain and torment just to relay the bizarre communication, and if the Mysterious Ones were out there, waiting in the woods as the message said, she was determined to find them.

But what were they?

As Mary Sue pondered this question, three neighborhood kids rode up on bikes and stopped beside her. They were all middle schoolers who were a year or two younger than her, but she'd gotten to know them before transitioning over to high school. The trio all held Mary Sue in high regard for being every bit as much of a wiseass as they were, but were also the type of kids who could be depended on to give her a hard time before ever showing any veneration to an older kid. Peter, in particular; the de facto leader of the group who also had a bit of a schoolboy crush on the moody teenager.

"How's it going, reject?" Peter said, making him the first of the three little hobgoblins to address the object of their admiration.

"How's it going, Limp Dog?" Mary Sue coolly replied.

"Ugh! I've told you a million times! It's *Pimp Dog!* God!"

It's true: Peter had taken on the nickname as part of a phase he was going through. But no one ever called him that—especially not his wiseass friends.

"What are you doing staring off into the woods, Mary Sue?" Jordan asked this; the fat and fluffy sidekick to Peter.

"Have any of you losers heard of the Mysterious Ones?"

Becky, the token girl in the group, scrunched up her face before issuing her candid reply. "Mysterious Ones? Is that like a creepy campfire story to keep kids out of the woods or something?"

"You know what my dad says?" Peter remarked with a grin. "My dad says there's a bunch of frickin' *devil-worshippers* living in town. And they come to the frickin' *woods* to sacrifice frickin' *babies,* and they drink the babies' *blood,* and my dad says they have these frickin' *orgies* where everybody's just going at it and doing *drugs* and listening to *loud music* and just—frickin' just—"

"You don't frickin' say," Mary Sue dryly stated.

Jordan was equally skeptical of Peter's claims.

"C'mon, Limp Dog. That doesn't happen."

"Ugh! I frickin' told you already! My name is *Pimp Dog!* God!"

"All the stories I've heard about the woods involve witches," Becky offered matter-of-factly. "The woods are supposed to be a big deal for them. I heard they leave signs or tribute in the trees."

For Mary Sue, that cinched it: If there was witchcraft going on, she felt obligated to go exploring and see what she could find. She had no idea what these Mysterious Ones were connected to, but any talk about witches immediately brought up thoughts of her mother and the evil hex she cast. If the Mysterious Ones had to do with witches, she was going to find out what. She might just give them a piece of her mind in the process.

With her mind made up and no point in dawdling any longer, Mary Sue hopped off her bike and tossed it to the side of the road. She started marching to the forest's edge, carving a path into the heart of the setting that supposedly held the key to all of her pressing inquiries.

"Mary Sue, where are you going?"

"Be careful, Mary Sue!"

"Yeah! Don't get frickin' butt-raped by those devil-kids!"

"I'll do my best, Limpy!"

Mary Sue disappeared from view, and it was about time for the neighborhood kids to disappear as well. A cold wind was moving in from the east, and the air was growing thick with unease. This would be the last they would think about their chummy former school-mate—at least until a few hours later when Nancy would pay Peter a visit, revealing to him that Mary Sue had run away from home and she was desperate to locate her.

The last thing Mary Sue would have characterized herself as would have been a nature person. She enjoyed being outdoors and loved horseback riding, but only explored the woods that sur-rounded Little Salem a couple of times, and only briefly. She always found the atmosphere of the place to be slightly off—and not in a spooky fairy tale kind of way. The eerie ambiance consuming the natural environment had more to do with the energy the forest emit-ted that made a person feel strange after roaming the bewildering landscape for too lengthy a visit. And it always felt like something was watching you and waiting, drawing you deeper within.

The damn place felt haunted was the easiest way to put it. And the general lack of sunlight and suffocating mood of the place didn't make it any less unsettling. The oddest thing was that despite these disturbing and unpleasant attributes, the forest was also quite beau-tiful once it had opened itself up to you. On that particular day, the sun was shining, and the weather was fairly agreeable. After covering a short distance, Mary Sue reached a place where the daylight cast its rays about more freely and from somewhere close by she could hear the peaceful and soothing sounds of a running stream.

However, despite the occasional reminder of the dazzling beauty that surrounded her, after finding herself becoming lost in this sight, Mary Sue would glance upward to see an occasional witch's ladder shivering in the breeze—something that would turn the forest back into a godforsaken wilderness that one should only wander through at their own peril and not spend too much time lingering about.

Nevertheless, on that day, Mary Sue was determined to wander as far as it would take to receive the answers that she desired. At least with the sight of the weird paraphernalia hanging from the branches, it felt like she was heading in the right direction. After a significant amount of time had passed, she eventually found herself listening to the rhythm of her sneakers marching through the wild. She found herself becoming hypnotized by the sounds of the birds, the insects, the wind moving through the branches, all coming together to form a harmonious symphony overlapping the steady staccato beat of her footsteps. But after a few moments, she started to hear something else—what sounded like a person sobbing.

It felt unusual for someone besides herself to be so deep inside the woods as she was, and Mary Sue was even more surprised by what she would discover once she weaved her way through the densely packed cluster of trees and down an overgrown path to the slippery bank of a small creek.

There, kneeling at the edge of the water and weeping into his hands was a hefty mountain of a man in muddy overalls. The man had his back turned so she couldn't see his face, but based on his immense size and familiar wardrobe, he could only be one person.

"Sanchez?"

The bulky colossus tensed up at the voice and quickly reached for a burlap sack sitting on the ground next to him, pulling it over his head before slowly turning to face her. His face may have been hidden, but she could still see the signs of deep scarring on the outer edges of the shoddy, misshapen eyeholes cut into the fabric, in addition to the bulging, bloodshot eyes staring back at her with a dreary combination of sadness, terror, and troubling loss.

It was true: There was no mistaking the man was the former proprietor of the restaurant that Ada and her cohorts had transformed into the tavern. But something terrible had happened that had left him severely shaken.

For a while, the two acquaintances stared at each other without speaking, with the masked man finally turning to face the stream once he no longer had the stomach to address his youthful observer. The two sat in silence until Mary Sue summoned up the courage to cross to where the sullen Goliath was seated.

While startled by his appearance, she knew that, like her, Sanchez was one of the few "others" in the community and understood how difficult this was in a town as homogenous and culturally uniform as Little Salem. With his face now horribly scarred, finding acceptance would be harder than ever. The least she could do was offer him some moral support—a gesture he must have sensed at some point. Once he confirmed that she was an ally and not a threat, he started spinning his tale for her.

"I betrayed myself. Betrayed everything that was good. I set out to punish others who never wished to do me harm. I made my soul monstrous, so I fled to where the devils can no longer use me. To a place where I can reflect on my past crimes."

Mary Sue found her eyes gazing into the flowing water and turned to her companion with sorrow and understanding.

He said he sought to punish others, but who these others were was still a mystery. She hadn't seen him among the gang of killers the corrupt town sheriff had assembled. As for his claim that "devils" were using him—even if this was only a clever euphemism, it meant it was a group that was to blame for his tragedy but failed to make it any clearer who this group could actually be.

Sanchez didn't go into any more detail and eventually left his spot by the water, and Mary Sue followed him to a small cave. As she approached the entrance and gazed into the gaping darkness in front of her, Sanchez remained cautiously behind, continuing to stare outward into the wilderness while crouching low to the ground with his back to her.

What Mary Sue saw inside was heartbreaking: a pile of dead leaves that were gathered into a crude bed in one corner and the remnants of a small campfire sitting nearby. There was a dark cloud hanging about the setting, and she felt immensely saddened that he found it necessary to resign himself to such an existence.

"You must get lonely out here. All on your own."

Mary Sue turned back to face her edgy acquaintance and was startled to notice he was now rocking back and forth; holding his head in his hands with his thick stubby fingers, looking ready to claw his brains out.

"So much pain. So much pain, I can't..."

Mary Sue cautiously crossed toward him, hand outstretched.

"Here, let me—"

She reached for his mask, but Sanchez swatted her hand away from him.

"*No!*"

For a moment, it looked like he was about to turn on her and tear her limb from limb. But when he noticed the fear in her eyes, he once again shrank inside himself and backed away.

"No, not pain here."

Sanchez pointed to his masked face.

"Pain..."

He pointed to his heart.

Mary Sue gazed at him with sympathy. What he was doing out there was not entirely clear, but she knew all about the pains of a broken heart. It pained her to think about everything that had happened to Izzy, and also of her mother's betrayal. With so much violence and treachery revealing itself within the dull and lifeless town she felt so reluctant to call home, she was curious to know the identity of those who deceived him. Maybe there was a connection to those that wronged the one she harbored so much affection for.

"Who hurt you, Sanchez?" Mary Sue asked him. "Tell me."

The question felt very cut and dry, but when she asked this, his breathing started to escalate. Whoever had wounded him and led to his horrifying disfigurement still had him so high-strung that alone in the woods and miles from anyone, he dared not speak their name. Mary Sue could tell by his eyes there was a part of him that desperately wanted to reveal this information. She watched him twitch his fingers and start searching the forest floor before darting to the ground and picking up a discarded stick.

The message he was trying to communicate was simple, but it took a tremendous amount of effort to summon up enough courage to spell it out, his hand shaking uncontrollably while he attempted to complete the task.

What Sanchez drew in the mud were the initials, "SC."

Mary Sue stared at the letters in confusion. To her, the letters didn't mean a thing. There was no "W" for "witch" or an "M" and an "O" for "Mysterious Ones" or any letters identifying Ada's coven, "The New Lords" or "Lords of Light."

"I don't understand. What does it mean?"

Unfortunately, she never received an answer. A short distance away from them, a murder of crows scattered into the sky, cawing loudly. Sanchez stared up in horror at the noisy harbingers, and his whole body went rigid.

"They found me! Stay away from me!"

"Sanchez! Sanchez! *Wait!*"

As he ran off, Mary Sue searched all around her for what had gotten him so spooked. She was unable to receive a clear answer, although if she'd taken a closer look, she might have noticed a small figure wearing a dark cloak watching her from a hilltop.

Sadly, this vision evaded her, leaving her with only the observation of the extent of how frightened Sanchez was of those that had led him to his present complications. This was something Mary Sue reflected upon for quite some time. Sanchez wasn't just hiding his face from the townspeople out of fear for how they might react to him. He was hiding from those that influenced him to commit his miserable sins.

Mary Sue eventually left the cave and spent the rest of the day engaged in her search for the Mysterious Ones, but she never found them. During her search, her mind often wandered back to her recent interaction, feeling pity for the fallen leviathan and trying to guess the identity of "SC." In all honesty, she was totally stumped. She had absolutely no idea what the letters could mean.

It was only just a small town, but Little Salem was a town filled with mysteries. As much as Mary Sue thought she knew the place, along with its excessively ordinary inhabitants, it was slowly beginning to dawn on her that she didn't know them at all. This proved to be a very discomforting realization for the girl who could often be found moping about, thinking about how no one seemed to understand her. While looking at the lights of the town from the top of a hill once the sun had disappeared, she found herself growing to accept the fact that she didn't understand anyone all that well either.

Perhaps everyone was all alone in the world, and that's just how it was, and there was no one you could depend on or turn to for answers. The Mysterious Ones were mysterious because no one knew what they were, and witches were to be scorned and feared because they were so different from everyone.

But people all over the world could be difficult to understand at times and still needed someone to turn to—that was something that Mary Sue found true for everyone. And she would eventually end up seeking out Sanchez for a warm shoulder to cry on after receiving a text from Rudy, confirming they had dropped Izzy off at a mental hospital after determining her situation was hopeless and there was nothing more they could do for her.

By the time Mary Sue returned to the cave, she was already beside herself and in tears, spying Sanchez roasting a dead squirrel over a campfire before throwing on his mask at the sound of footsteps.

"Sanchez?" Mary Sue sniffed. "Is it OK if I crash here for the night? I thought that maybe we could both use a friend."

40

THE LEGEND OF THE MYSTERIOUS ONES

Ashton and Tyler cautiously approached the hut, the glimmering firelight allowing them to take a more thoughtful examination of the unsightly dwelling. While drawing closer, Tyler slapped Ashton on the shoulder, pointing out a long, intricate witch's ladder hanging from one of the four corners of the shoddy, slanted roof.

The two amateur ghost hunters had definitely entered witches territory. Recognizing this, Ashton nodded determinedly; acknowledging they were on dangerous ground and should be cautious, but also that they had come too far on their journey and there was no turning back.

After hunching their bodies over to cross through the low shallow doorway, the boys quickly scanned their surroundings, noticing a bed of straw in one corner and a small iron stove sitting across from it. The grate to the stove was left open to allow the fire to light the tiny ramshackle room, and a small black cauldron was boiling on the stovetop with the grimy middle-aged woman scratching her head while tending to the bubbling concoction.

Due to the cramped and restricted nature of their surroundings, the boys proceeded to sit on the floor, which consisted of packed dirt. They observed the shadows dancing in the firelight and noticed several more witch's ladders in different stages of completion, hanging on the wall across from them.

"Do you have a name?" Ashton asked the woman.

The woman stopped her itching and sniffed the air dismissively. "Names don't hold much meaning in these parts," she said and fell quiet, poking at the fire in the stove with a sharp stick.

A long silence followed, which Ashton broke again with another question, trying to ease his reticent hostess into a more open and conversational mindset.

"If you don't mind me asking, why are you living out here in the woods?"

"Little Salem doesn't have much sympathy for undesirables," the woman said. "Long history of that, I'm afraid."

"Some say that the forces behind the Salem witch trials are continuing to persecute witches to this day. Ever heard anything of that nature?"

The woman seemed to find great amusement in this, cackling uproariously while poking the fire. "You've been talking to the young skinny one. Likes to dress in all black like a lovesick widow."

She returned to stirring her concoction as Ashton glanced over to Tyler, who mouthed the word, "Ada."

"Aye, she has a good heart, that one," the woman added. "Most powerful witch to ever venture into these here woods. Even more powerful after she crossed paths with..."

The woman stopped herself and tensed up as if she heard a noise from outside. For a moment, it appeared that Ashton had softened her to such an extent she might actually reveal something useful. She now looked unsettled and too apprehensive to continue.

Fearful that their conversation might end prematurely, Tyler abruptly joined in. "Crossed paths with...?"

"Shh! Don't say their names, you fool!"

After listening for a few more moments, the woman appeared to relax a little and returned to tending to the fire inside the stove.

"Aye, that's how all the Salem Witches attained their knowledge. Ever since Day One."

She set aside the stick and began to pack a dirty corncob pipe and light it with a match, the toxic fumes collecting with the steam from the boiling cauldron and the silvery exhaust from the stove.

"Tell us about them," Ashton requested, his eyes gleaming. "The early witches of Salem."

The woman smiled wryly at the request like she was expecting they'd be getting around to this topic. As she crouched in the firelight, Tyler reached inside his pocket and pressed Record on a small digital recorder.

"It all started in these very woods," the woman said. "Various women in Little Salem of all ages and backgrounds. They all came to the woods for what-have-you, had their encounter, and suddenly...these women were different."

The woman cast a hard look at the boys before continuing.

"*They were witches,*" she said. "And not in the vulgar sense of the word, mind you. In these women, the experience had awakened parts of the body and the mind that are inaccessible to normal people. Some of them were even granted special powers or bizarre supernatural gifts. Others, a thorough knowledge of 'the craft' and all of its hidden secrets. They were transformed completely. *Changed and transformed completely.*"

Ashton and Tyler didn't know what to make of these claims. It was startling enough to hear the woman declare that Ada was the most powerful witch to visit the woods that surrounded them, but what was even more unsettling was to hear that witches in the past had only become witches after enduring some type of experience in this setting. All of this flew in the face of what little the two of them knew about witchcraft, the Salem Witches, or the trials themselves. It certainly provided a much different account than what Ashton had heard at the Little Salem Witch Museum. But Ashton also remembered what Ada had told him about the two young girls who were afflicted; about how they became this way after having an encounter in the woods. To understand what this encounter was, he would have to continue to listen to the woman's story.

"Now, the early Salem Witches eventually learned to identify each other on sight," the woman said. "They began to hold regular meetings in the forest to discuss what they should do with their newly found gifts and talents. This brought about a great deal of debate among the women. There was talk of how they could use their powers to become a positive force in the community and to exert a powerful influence over the draconian politics of the period. But there was also a great fear of persecution. And extermination."

The woman's glassy dirt-encrusted eyes softened after this, and she took several puffs on her pipe before resuming her tale.

"Eventually," she continued, "it was agreed that the witches would remain silent about their gifts and only initiate young girls. Ones who already displayed strong intuitive knowledge in the craft and all of what that entailed. For only they could ever hope to understand the true nature of what they had been given.

"And it was also decided that from there on out, the Salem Witches would call their secret order the Sisterhood of Circe after the fabled witch from Greek myths. The one that transformed

Ulysses' sailors into swine. This was all unanimously agreed upon, but there was one woman who did not wish to obey these rules."

At this point, Ashton could see all the events slowly connecting and could already guess the identity of the woman their fascinating hostess was discussing.

"Tituba," the woman confirmed while glancing in his direction. "A servant in the home of the Reverend Parris and one of the first of the Salem Witches. She saw an opportunity for bringing about great change by initiating the reverend's daughter and niece into their ranks. She led those girls into the woods one day, and, well... It was a disaster. Those young girls were not ready for such an encounter, and the whole ordeal traumatized them. Nearly shattered their fragile adolescent minds.

"After this event, the Sisterhood got together and prayed for the healing of those girls, and within days they seemed to be right as rain. But the damage had been done. It just so happened that the girls came from a truly merciless family. One with ties to perhaps the most diabolical secret organization in all of human history."

"The Scarlet Council," Ashton muttered.

The woman nodded soberly in reply.

"It was only a matter of time before the girls were used as instruments to weed out and convict all of the witches of Little Salem, along with any other undesirable the Council wished to get rid of, thus further entrenching their growing power and influence all across the New World. Most of the Sisterhood was put to death or jailed 'till death." The woman's cloudy eyes began to fill with tears upon this confession. "My very own daughter was accused. She was only four years old."

Tyler's jaw dropped in response to the revelation, but Ashton immediately touched his friend's arm to silence him. In addition to suspecting Tituba's special significance in the woman's tale early on, he also already recognized the resemblance of their hostess to the subject of one of the portraits at the museum: the portrait of Sarah Good, one of the first of three women to be accused of witchcraft that paved the way for the later trials.

Similar to the experience at the Rebecca Nurse Homestead, it appeared that manifestations of figures from the past were showing up to assist the two investigators, helping them to uncover a dark and daunting mystery that certain powers in the spirit world sought to bring to light. Not knowing how long the visitation would last, Ashton was keeping as quiet as humanly possible. He wanted the woman to be allowed to complete her explanation before anything unexpected happened to cut her story short.

"But some of the witches survived or hid," the woman said, after wiping her nose and drying her eyes with her hand, "and the Sisterhood of Circe enjoys a continued presence in Little Salem up to this very day. And the Scarlet Council is aware of their activities and tolerates the witches because they know their founders' dreams of becoming a positive force in history will never come to pass. The Council has become too powerful and most of the members of today's Sisterhood are concerned with much more pedestrian affairs. Like property values and Happy Hour at the local Chili's."

The woman's story appeared to be wrapping up. Tyler and Ashton continued to listen solemnly as her eyes stared emotionally into the firelight.

"So many women killed or tortured on account of those strange encounters," the woman sighed. "So many lives changed, all because..."

"The Mysterious Ones," Tyler said, making the connection.

Just then, a noise was heard coming from outside. The woman's eyes darted to the doorway before glaring at the two young men sitting across from her, her body now tense with fear.

"They followed you! You must leave!"

"Who followed us?" Tyler asked. "What are you talking about?"

By the time he opened his mouth, the woman was on her feet and shoving her guests out the door.

"Out! Get out! Why would you do this to me?"

"Do what?" Ashton argued. "We don't understand!" But the woman looked too panicked to reason with, ready to turn violent if her two visitors didn't vanish at that very instant.

"Out!" the women shrieked, and with one last shove, the boys were pushed outside, watching in total bafflement as the small wooden door was slammed in their faces.

"What was that about?" Tyler asked.

Before Ashton could respond, the forest answered back with a noise from the bushes. Now on high alert, they aimed their cameras into the darkness with the recording set to night-vision.

At first, nothing seemed amiss, but when viewing the scenery through the green-tinted images on their devices, they both noticed something curious. Both of their cameras were now blinking Low Battery—as if something had drained them to almost nothing.

"Yo, Ashton. My camera's saying low battery. What about you?"

Suddenly, a deer jumped out from the bushes and ran straight past them. The deer's unexpected appearance delivered quite a jolt, but this was nothing compared to the shock that they received when they turned around and noticed the hut had vanished, along with all signs it had ever existed.

"Whoa! Dude! Did you—"

"But that's—Wasn't there—?"

"Dude, this is impossible! This can't be happening!"

As Ashton aimed his camera at the empty clearing, he racked his brain, trying to come up with a logical explanation for what was going on. Soon he would have to deal with another untimely obstacle: the battery icon on his camera blinked a few times before the screen went to black.

"Dammit. Dead."

Fortunately, the clouds overhead were intermittent, and there was still enough moonlight, so he wasn't trapped in total darkness. This, in itself, provided great relief to Ashton, and he assumed Tyler's camera would be more than enough to help guide them back to camp. But when he looked up, he discovered Tyler had disappeared, and there was no sign of him anywhere.

"Tyler?"

At the time, Ashton had no way of knowing that, without thinking, Tyler took off in the direction of where the deer had emerged. He thought if it was running away from something, he had a good chance of capturing this on video before his battery ran out of juice.

Tyler had raced into the overgrowth with his adrenaline pumping, but he was now creeping forward nervously. His surroundings seemed to have gone completely still, and as his eyes scanned the forest, he noticed his breathing sounded much louder because all the other sounds had ceased.

At the realization that something strange was occurring, his hands started shaking. He aimed his camera in every direction, and at the sound of a crunch of leaves mere inches from him, he spun around to record the most frightening thing he'd ever seen.

Standing in front of him was a giant skeletal creature with a glowering deer skull for a face. The being had dark hollow sockets in the place of eyes and carried the rotting stench of a thousand graveyards. Its towering humanoid body placed it at about ten feet tall in stature, and it was shrouded in the black cloak of a Grim Reaper.

As the creature emitted a low guttural groan, it reached forward to grab its startled observer. This was the moment where Tyler lost his composure, crying out in sheer terror.

"Holy shit! HOLY SHIT!"

Tyler fell to the ground, yelling several additional panicked expletives while the ghastly skeletal monstrosity swiped the air in front of him.

"Fuck this! No, fuck this! FUCK!"

Fortunate to avoid the monster's bony fingers, Tyler pushed himself to his feet and started running into the woods like a man possessed, taking his camera with him and recording an incomprehensible blur of trees and bushes as he ran at top speed.

After running for several moments, he spun around to glance behind him, reflexively aiming his camera at the cold, expressionless features of the massive figure. Before he had time to question what this dark and twisted incarnation even was, he felt something brush against him and swung his camera around to find himself now face to face with another towering skeletal entity, hungrily reaching toward him as well.

Just like the first one he encountered, the unsightly abomination was ten feet tall and just as nightmarish in appearance, dressed in a black cloak with a deer skull right on top. For this one, the skull looked more like a grotesque carnival mask with a long crack down the middle to separate the darker half from the half that was lighter in color. The hand reaching out for him was also not skeletal in nature and appeared withered and ancient. But this was hardly a consolation, and Tyler, finding himself surrounded by these hellish things, began to freak out with even greater intensity.

"HOLY SHIT! HOLY SHIT!"

After the second encounter, Tyler started running and running and running, paying no attention to where he was headed and only occasionally glancing behind him while screaming out to Ashton in a blind panic. Eventually, he noticed the forest was thinning, and a crossroads was up ahead. There, the shadowy form of a human-sized figure was standing, and the terror-stricken ghost hunter quickly rushed over, thinking his friend had somehow gotten ahead of him and they must be close to camp.

"Ashton! Fuck, is that—?"

Tyler was about to receive another rude awakening. The figure wasn't Ashton at all—something he wouldn't discover until the very last second. A nagging feeling of crawling unease steadily spread through him, and when he was just inches away, the figure slowly turned to face him, revealing a man in tattered black clothing with a partially decomposed face that contained swollen, bulging eyeballs and a lopsided slit for a grin.

The encounter with yet another unexplainable and gruesome spectacle caused Tyler to stumble to the dirt. He suddenly felt paralyzed in the face of this endless waking nightmare, cowering helplessly while his camera filmed the unearthly creature studying his observer with wide, maniacal eyes as it presented an object to him.

"Wanna buy a book?"

As the figure moved closer, Tyler sat frozen, with his camera still capturing every moment until the images started turning to static. He released a piercing scream right as everything cut to black.

Tyler was still screaming when Ashton finally arrived after an unknown amount of time has passed. When he appeared, he knelt on the ground and shook his friend by the shoulders, hoping that he showed up in the nick of time to help pull his fellow investigator from the brink of total madness.

"Tyler! Tyler, snap out of it! Talk to me!"

"Who was that?"

"Did you see them?"

"*Ashton! What the fuck was that?*"

"Those were the Mysterious Ones."

Recognizing the voice, the boys spun around to spy Nancy

emerging from the forest. She was dressed in a long white cloak over a long white gown—what they would learn was the standard uniform for members of the Sisterhood of Circe.

"They are the entities that haunt these woods. They only reveal themselves to certain people."

Following Nancy's explanation, Ashton and Tyler glanced to the forest that lay behind them, noticing two shadowy silhouettes fading into nothingness.

"It seems that fortune smiles on you," Nancy said. "Or perhaps the opposite."

With the boys now safe and out of harm's way, Nancy slowly retreated, not saying another word but leaving an open invitation for them to follow her if they had any more questions she could answer. This was something they took her up upon immediately, though they didn't know why she was being so forthright in explaining the dark secrets of Little Salem to them.

Perhaps she was just tired. Yes, that was it. Tired of having to hide her true nature from people and of supporting the elaborate illusion obscuring the truth of what happened centuries earlier.

"Then those things—those were the—"

"Is there only two of them or—?"

Nancy nodded as she continued her stroll. "Yes, just the pair. Nobody knows exactly what they are, but there are those who say if they let you get close enough, they will show you the nature of your very soul. This is what awakens 'the craft' in certain people. In others, it drives them completely mad."

"There was something else I saw," Tyler confessed nervously. "It was a man in black, and he was carrying a book."

"The ghost of Sebastien Jedediah Bishop," Nancy said. "Legend tells us he was a black magician who accidentally summoned the Mysterious Ones during a botched alchemical ritual. One he performed out here in the woods several months ahead of the Salem witch trials. He was one of those who was driven mad, of course. Staggered to the crossroads right afterward and dropped dead right on the spot. No one ever found his body. Or the strange book that assisted him in the summoning."

Eventually, the group arrived back at the burnt-out clearing and Nancy joined the boys by the campfire.

"So the Mysterious Ones taught you the craft," Ashton confirmed, with Tyler quickly chiming in as well.

"Does that mean you can control the weather? Or shoot lightning from your fingers like a Sith Lord?"

Nancy cracked a smile at the question.

"No, no. Nothing like that. The gift the Mysterious Ones gave me was pretty simple. Just an enhanced perception of what's going on in the world. Or, at least, a different understanding of it.

"They say illumination is often gained from an encounter with the incredible. With something unusual and often monstrous. If that's the case, these strange creatures lurking in the woods... Well, I'd be a fool to claim that I understand them, but I'd like to believe they can't be bad entirely."

Ashton studied Nancy's face in the firelight.

"What other powers do they give people?"

"The power to read a person's thoughts, the power to control objects with a person's mind. Precognition, clairvoyance, other psychic gifts. These are all very uncommon, mind you. Then there are powers such as healing and resurrection, which are one in a million. There was one person who seemed to be granted every supernatural gift imaginable, save for the truly rare ones. Do you know who that person is?"

Ashton's face turned pale at the realization. "Ada."

Nancy nodded and flashed a sad, defeated smile at the two boys.

"I'll tell you her story if you like. I was out here looking for my daughter, but it appears she doesn't want to be found. I have a feeling this is my punishment for being a bad mother. And a bad witch."

"I'm sure she's fine," Tyler said. "She probably just needs to cool off for a bit."

Nancy once again nodded and forced a hopeful smile.

"I hope you're right, Tyler."

"Of course I'm right."

She glanced to the heavens and proceeded to get comfortable.

"So, you wish to know the story of the notorious Ada van Dreyer and how she first came to Little Salem..."

The boys both smiled and started to get settled as well, listening eagerly to their second story session of the night; a story Ada herself would be hearing, clothed in only a Navaho blanket as she listened from her place of hiding behind an old tree, her otherworldly eyes narrowing suspiciously once her reviled nemesis started weaving the tale exploring all the gory details of her personal history.

"Now...where do I begin?"

Part V

Ashton: So you, Agatha, the others...

Ada: Witches, more or less.

Ashton: Do you guys worship the devil?

Ada: Don't be silly.

Ashton: What do you believe in?

Ada: We believe in ourselves. Like John Lennon.

41

THE GIRL WHO COULD TALK TO
SPIRITS I

_____

"There are certain moments in a person's life where something happens and everything changes. You often don't even realize the true impact of these moments until much later. But every once in awhile, you get a feeling that tells that after this moment, your life will never be the same. That is how I felt when I first met Ada van Dreyer.

"Ada had always been a very special girl. She was an indigo child, which means she was born with unnaturally high intelligence, intuition, a sense of purpose... In addition to this, Ada possessed other much more unusual abilities that began manifesting at an early age. Word of these abilities attracted the attention of the Sisterhood of Circe, the order of white witches that reside in Little Salem, and they—well, we—took a special interest in Ada. Yes, quite an interest.

"When Ada finally turned fifteen, she reached the age where she was ready to be taught how to unlock her full potential. It was that summer, *approximately five years ago, and several years after her first encounter with the Sisterhood, that Ada's mother packed their bags for a short trip that would prove to be a life-changing experience for both of them. That was the summer she brought her daughter to Little Salem to be initiated into the path of a full-blown witch."*

Nancy wasn't prepared at all on the day when she met Ada. She may have been pushing forty at the time but was still very much young in spirit. A steady career was absent from her life, she had no plans to have children, and she could barely keep on top of her daily tasks and chores due to her constant daydreaming and planning exotic getaways in her head. When the doorbell rang, she was still busy getting the house ready for the young witch she agreed to house for the summer. She only knew her guest by name and knew she was apparently a fifteen-year-old girl named Ada. Ada...something-something.

As Nancy hurried down the stairs to answer the door, she inspected the foyer for dust and clutter and searched her clothes for stains. She wanted to look presentable after all. Her mind would instantly forget about these things the moment she opened the door, and she and Ada were face to face.

The Ada of five years earlier was unsurprisingly similar in many respects to the distinctive young woman she was today. The slender form, the long dark hair, the huge dazzling eyes filled with limitless intrigue and mystery. However, Ada was much quieter and more introverted at this point in her life. She rarely said a word and mainly interacted with the world by observing her environment with wonder; with a twinkle in her eyes and a curious smile upon her lips. And yet, despite the quiet nature of the young girl, Nancy was immediately struck by her magnetic presence and felt instantly enamored and spellbound.

Ada's mother, Ursula, left a strong first impression as well. She had long black hair and dressed in all black like a modern-day incarnation of Morticia Addams from "The Addams Family." But it would have been a mistake to characterize her as some dopey caricature since she was someone who dressed quite classy and was a remarkably intimidating beauty.

To her surprise, Nancy found Ursula to be an exceptionally pleasant and likable woman during their brief time chatting together. She obviously doted heavily on her daughter while giving her a long lead to interact with the world on her own terms and be her own person. In retrospect, it was likely she was advised to raise Ada this way after learning her daughter was a child prodigy.

"I'll be staying at that old hotel in the center of town," Ursula explained. They were at the top of the stairs, with Nancy watching Ada out of the corner of her eye as she went about exploring the second floor. "If you need anything, feel free to—"

Ursula paused as she watched Ada wander into the guest room with her suitcase and cast a warm smile at her daughter's hostess, beaming at her young ward's uninhibited inquisitive nature.

The guest room where Ada was staying would one day belong to Mary Sue. For now, the room was quite plain and contained only the bare essentials: a bed, a dresser, and little else.

Upon entering, Ada took an immediate interest in something left on the bed for her: a hardback copy of *Aradia – the Gospel of the Witches*. After finding and observing the book, Ada turned to the wall and noticed something else that aroused her curiosity: what looked like a cross-stitched Bible verse that read, "Blessed Are The Pure In Heart For They Will See The Truth." The object caused her eyes sparkle and an impish smile to form on her lips.

As Ursula was saying her goodbyes, she told Nancy one last

thing: "Um, incidentally, Ada can be very quiet at times when she's adjusting to unfamiliar people. Don't mind her. It's just her way."

Once Ursula had left, Nancy returned to check on Ada and was surprised to discover how anxious she was feeling. It was true she didn't have much experience with kids at this point, but this was different. For some reason, she found herself praying that Ada would like her and approve of the happy home she was providing.

When Nancy peeked inside the room, she was startled to discover Ada lying on the bed, already flipping through the book she found before glancing to the doorway and spying her timid hostess.

"I see you discovered the book I left for you," Nancy said. "Make yourself at home and holler if you need anything, OK?"

Nancy was trying her best to follow Ursula's instructions to the letter by giving Ada lots of room to do things at her own pace. What Ada did next was something she would never have expected. Ada closed the book to approach her and gave her a warm hug.

It was as if the young girl had sensed how hungry Nancy was to impress her and was offering a small gesture to illustrate how all this fuss was unnecessary, leaving her genuinely shocked by her young guest's apparent sensitivity and by the open display of daughterly affection she used to console her.

"But Ada wasn't the only stranger that arrived in town that month. It was during that fateful summer that Little Salem would be visited by another distinctive outsider. Ada's future stepbrother, McAllister."

While Nancy was slowly succumbing to total fascination in getting to know young Ada, miles away from Little Salem a familiar red convertible was parked outside a decaying two-story home in a not so idyllic and pleasant neighborhood. Inside, McAllister sat half-dressed in a dimly lit bedroom, lazily tracing the tattoo of the Sigil of Lucifer on his left forearm as The Cure's "Pornography" album played on the dusty hi-fi in the corner.

Like Ada, McAllister was also a very different person at this point in his life, with a heart of stone and a lifetime filled with cruel and callous behavior that he was only just beginning to question. The hedonistic lifestyle he spent the last decade drowning in had nearly swallowed up his soul completely. He wasn't caught up in a full-blown existential crisis just yet, but life was growing tiresome, and the cracks were starting to show.

Regardless, whatever McAllister was thinking or feeling, he kept it locked behind a cold mask of indifference that even the pretty young woman lying next to him lacked the ability to see through. She was a charming art school dropout named Claire—a semi-goth girl with a notable witchy appeal. She had a morbid sense of humor, whimsical tattoos, and long, raven-colored hair with an undercut shaved on one side. Despite both of them being in various states of undress, McAllister was all but ignoring her at present. But in her eyes, his utter detachment made him more appealing as she lay on her side, watching him dreamily and with longing.

"I can't believe I ran into you," Claire sighed deliriously. She exhaled a cloud of smoke from the spliff wedged between her fingers. "It's too bad you can't stay a little longer."

Claire passed the spliff in his direction, and McAllister took a drag before retrieving a crumpled black tank top from the cluttered bedroom floor. "I'd love to but I have a business trip to attend to," he answered mechanically.

"No rest for the wicked," Claire slyly grinned.

"Ever think about moving to the city?" he asked her, sounding relatively uninterested.

"I was actually thinking about traveling out west. I hear the desert calling my name."

Claire pulled a postcard from the wall and passed it to over to him. The item featured a picture of a dazzling desert landscape interrupted by the presence of a yellow road sign that had been vandalized with a strange occult symbol.

"You could always come with me," she purred, eyes sparkling. McAllister remained distant, scanning the cracked wall beside him while pulling on a burgundy sports coat—a piece of his current uniform to match the posh upper-crust lifestyle he'd grown up in.

The wall was covered with colorful posters and photographs, and he focused on one photo in particular. The photo showed Claire when she was younger, wearing white ceremonial robes and smiling next to two women who were dressed exactly like her. Two women that he knew as Ruth and Nancy, but he never revealed this to her.

Without reacting at all to the photograph, McAllister turned to Claire and planted a lusty kiss on her lips before pulling away and directing a cold and emotionless smile in her direction.

"It was good seeing you, Claire."

"It was good seeing you too. McAllister."

McAllister left the house and climbed into the beastly red convertible. After starting the car, he retrieved a smartphone from his pocket and texted a contact listed as "Bozo Clownshoes."

"*Cat's in the bag,*" the text read.

Swallowing his weariness and self-loathing, he pressed Send and tossed the phone onto the seat next to him. Once a lit cigarette rested between his fingertips, he turned up the heavy metal on the stereo and drove off.

For McAllister, Claire was just a pit stop before taking off to deal with his main assignment. He had to pick up a snotty trust fund brat named Xander—a disreputable young chap he'd be spending the next couple weeks mentoring as instructed by his superiors. McAllister was already dreading the experience, knowing that the time he would be spending with this kid was going to be unbearable. These assignments had him feeling like little more than a glorified errand boy than someone who held a fairly high rank in his organization, but playing this role had essentially been all he had ever done with his life—and for more years than he could remember. At the time, he had no reason to imagine he would ever amount to anything else or that anything else even existed for him.

His cynical assessment regarding the insufferable cretin he would be stuck babysitting was almost perfectly accurate in every way. As Xander crossed from his outlandishly expensive apartment building toward the vintage Cadillac DeVille parked on the street, what McAllister saw was just another cocksure prep school nightmare wearing a two hundred dollar haircut and a stupid plastic grin. The very worst of it was that despite the fact that McAllister already had almost a decade on this kid, Xander was dressed in a burgundy blazer just like his and traveling with a large black duffle over his shoulder. Tools of the trade for the circle they both ran in.

They'd barely even met and they were practically brothers already—a prospect that made him feel like he was going to be sick.

The situation worsened when Xander opened his big fat mouth to reveal he spoke in a British accent that was affected to sound much tougher and lower class than he was—a quality McAllister could have easily predicted and made his eyes want to roll back into his head and stay there for all of eternity.

"You must be McAllister. I've heard a lot about you."

"Xander, right? Get in."

Once they were on their way, Xander made quick work proving to be even more of an irritating prick than McAllister could have imagined as he skimmed the stack of black metal and stoner metal CDs on the floor of the passenger seat.

"I've been looking forward to this trip like you wouldn't believe, yeah? Got anything else to listen to besides this devil rubbish?"

"You don't like Uncle Acid and Electric Wizard, you can shut the fuck up."

"Bloody hell! What's this?"

McAllister glanced over to see what the fuss was about. Xander had pulled a gun from the glove box and was now cavalierly waving it around while grinning like a world-class dope.

"Hey! Are you an idiot? What's wrong with you? Put it back, you dumb idiot."

Xander laughed gleefully. "Like Natural Born Killers, yeah? You don't expect we're going to need guns on this trip?"

"Reconnaissance only. We do as we're told, then we go back to living the good life."

To McAllister's relief, the idiot slammed the handgun back into the glove box before scoffing with annoyance. "If they're not bringing us out here to have a little fun, what's the point?"

"Loyalty. They're testing our loyalty."

McAllister knew all about that kind of thing: loyalty. Pass the test, and you were in, and you were in for life. A devil's bargain if there ever was one. But the life he'd been given did have its perks, and the Godfrey Mansion stood as a testament to what one could achieve by staying committed to this specific brand of obedience. "Work hard, and all this could be yours someday." Not that McAllister believed in any of that inspirational crap to begin with.

The Godfrey Mansion was, in fact, their precise destination. They arrived around sundown with Xander still running his stupid mouth non-stop and McAllister feeling extra thankful he smoked that joint back at Claire's, which helped take some of the edge off. Still, it had been a long drive, and his buzz was wearing thin. Once they reached their journey's end, he could feel his body revolting, the tension steadily building up inside of him.

Sir Godfrey and his butler were the first to show themselves as McAllister parked the red convertible out front. Godfrey appeared much more interested in greeting his flesh and blood than the testy black sheep of the organization, which was an unexpected blessing and saved him an additional headache.

"Nephew! And McAllister—good to see you. Your usual room is ready, ol' boy. Your father arrived earlier this morning."

Right, his father. McAllister didn't get along with his father and only saw him on work trips, which was perfectly fine in his opinion. Less interaction with the old man meant a lot less tension he would have to deal with. Unfortunately, he knew he was expected to at least acknowledge the bastard before entering the sprawling fortress and couldn't disguise his outright disdain for the man as he did.

"Son."

"Dad."

After the brief exchange on the front porch, McAllister followed Godfrey's butler to a guest room on the second floor, eager to be left alone to get nice and stoned and allow his spiteful emotions for the world to go numb.

Growing up with a life of privilege hadn't had a positive effect at all on McAllister. If anything, it had allowed him to sharpen his intellect to the point of total disillusionment, and decadence and self-annihilation had been his two closest allies for quite some time. Privilege and the esteemed company he ran with provided him the knowledge of exactly how the world really operated, so he was intimately aware of the fact that the world was nothing more than a black iron prison where everyone was an inmate for life, and it was pointless to even think about trying to escape.

"So McAllister—that's how he knows—?"

"Shut up, Tyler."

"Yes, how he knows Sir Godfrey and the rest of them. And while McAllister and Godfrey's nephew were in town on their assignment, the Sisterhood's annual Young Witch's Retreat was about to begin."

Nancy could remember clear as yesterday all the effort she put into making the first day of the retreat as special as possible for her young visitor. Despite Ada's assurance that everything she was doing was appreciated, she woke up at the crack of dawn to prepare a breakfast fit for a princess. She was still in the midst of cooking this up when Ada crossed into the kitchen, dressed in a white cotton nightdress and lazily wiping the sleep from her eyelids.

"Ada! Good morning! I made you some pancakes. There should be some non-burnt ones somewhere on the bottom. Oh! And I also have some tea for you, and juice..."

Nancy couldn't hide her excitement to be showing off her cooking skills, or lack thereof. But her voice trailed off as she noticed her visitor staring silently at the decorative wooden cross hanging on the wall before her lips curled up into one of her token smirks.

Ada truly was an object of fascination for Nancy, and she treasured the idea of being her teacher and mentor for the summer. But at the same time, she still didn't know why she was bending over backward trying so hard to please the girl, who up to this point still hadn't said a single word to her.

Fortunately, while it was inevitable that Ada was bound to draw attention and turn some heads in Little Salem, later that day it was Nancy's time to shine; playing a starring role while instructing thirteen bright and inquisitive girls in the core principles of witchcraft.

"Each year, during the middle of the summer, the Sisterhood of Circe

holds a secret retreat for aspiring young witches. The first week is filled with education, trials, and games. As for the second week... Well, we'll get to that."

The first day of the retreat was held near Gallows Hill, the historic setting serving as a solemn reminder of how the witches in Little Salem were treated in the past. But the day was far from a dreary and moribund affair, as Nancy, dressed in her white witch's robes welcomed the thirteen girls, all dressed similarly in all white.

To start with, Nancy called the girls' attention to a dry erase board with terms such as "Esbat," "Book of Shadows," and "Wheel of the Year" written on it. It was Nancy's assignment to teach the girls the basics, and for this, she was more than capable—although she found herself unusually distracted with her eyes constantly checking in on how Ada was responding to her teaching.

Nancy noticed that a stringy North Carolina girl named Morgan seemed to be keeping a watchful eye on Ada, sizing her up as competition. The reaction was unsurprising as the retreat did contain a competitive aspect to it, and the first competition would be later that day—a challenging evaluation of the girls' special abilities known as "The Trial of the Blind Witch."

The trial's main purpose was to test the girls' psychic reflexes and involved a race through the forest with their eyes blindfolded and their hands tied behind their backs. Not all witches were gifted with the abilities needed to master this trial, which could prove to be a rather painful and humiliating experience for any girl expecting to succeed just because she'd "drawn down the moon" one time or performed a little spell or two. But this particular trial served more than one distinct purpose and was an essential step for the young witches on their path to initiation. The girls were instructed to give it their best, even if they were confident they wouldn't cut it, and reminded that if they failed, all would be fine because it was only the small group that would witness it.

Unfortunately, this assurance was somewhat empty. Little did the witches know, they were being watched by McAllister and Xander. Spying on them with binoculars as they observed the girls from a distance, and watching the vast majority of them tripping over themselves and smacking into tree trunks.

"Oi! Did you see that?" Xander laughed. "That bird will be pulling splinters out of her lip for weeks!"

McAllister remained unresponsive, his eyes fixed on Ada and Morgan, running neck and neck at the front of the pack. He noticed that Ada was looking cool and collected while Morgan was visibly struggling to stay focused. This was something that could have been predicted as The Sisterhood had already tested Ada's psychic potential with Zener cards, and she passed this test with flawless accuracy. Morgan's special abilities were a little more suspect, and it appeared she was getting through the race by sheer will alone. Alas, when a flock of birds scattered into the sky, she lost her concentration and slammed into a tree. This left Ada the undisputed champion.

"Do we have a winner?" Xander announced exuberantly. "*I said, 'Do we have a winner?' Are you not entertained?*"

Through his binoculars, McAllister watched Ada and Morgan cross back to the opening of the woods together, with Ada presenting her hand to her fierce competitor and Nancy smiling approvingly. For McAllister, it was unlikely he thought much of either of them. To him, they were just another pair of witches who would have to be dealt with eventually—although it was still a bit surprising that the girl who won was so young.

For Xander, the fact that Ada had only just turned fifteen didn't put him off one bit. The fresh and innocent looks of his prey were already beginning to stimulate his warped and deviant inclinations.

"Shag me senseless and call me Shirley. I call dibs, mate."

"She's too young."

"Too young for what? Besides, she's the Ace."

"Whatever. Don't push it though."

"Oh, I'm gonna push it. Push it real good."

To McAllister's annoyance, Xander pretended to hump him from behind.

"The hell off me, you idiot!"

With the first day of the retreat wrapping up, the boys gathered their gear and returned to the convertible. It may not have been apparent what they were up to, but McAllister later confronted Morgan in person while she and two friends were exploring Little Salem's main drag. There, he demonstrated to Xander how to make contact and leave a good impression with these witches while assuming the role of a "charming lost tourist," with his conversation with Morgan proving quite productive and quickly turning flirtatious.

"So McAllister was a member of the Scarlet Council."

"At the time, yes. Just like his father and also my husband, Wilbur."

Nancy was pacing with the phone cradled to her ear. "There's something special about her. She might be the most gifted witch the Sisterhood's ever seen."

Her loving husband was out of town on business, but she couldn't wait until he got home to gush about Ada. She was still marveling over Ada's earlier performance, and how much farther ahead she seemed of all the other girls at the retreat.

Wilbur was only half-listening as his darling wife rambled away on the other end of his mobile; planted in the driver's seat of a parked rental car miles away from Little Salem.

"That's great, honey," Wilbur said. "Uh, can't wait to meet her."

"Wilbur?" Nancy's hand was fidgeting by her side. "Have you ever thought about...?"

"Thought about what, honey? Listen, I gotta run. I love you."

Without letting her finish her thought, Wilbur ended the call and focused his attention across the street. He was staring at the second-story window of a dreary, derelict home where a pretty young woman was dancing in her bedroom. The pretty young woman was Claire, and it was the same house McAllister visited to engage in a brief but passionate affair with her before taking off for Little Salem.

"Cat's in the bag, all right," Wilbur said. "Should we do it now?"

The question was addressed to the man sitting in the passenger seat: a towering snowy-haired gentleman dressed in a boxy black suit. The man's heavy rheumy eyes carried a far-off expression as he caressed an antique rosary held between his fingers.

"Not yet," the man answered. "Drive."

Wilbur didn't have to receive the instruction twice. He had known his associate long enough not to question him as the man's legendary reputation preceded him. After all, the large and imposing figure was Dr. Franklin Baker, known infamously in his profession as "The Witchfinder General." Finding witches and nullifying this threat was his prerogative, and Wilbur had his own special role in this business. So did McAllister.

At the time, Ada was still unaware that there were people that existed in the modern-day who made a profession of this. Persons whose sole purpose seemed to be hunting down witches and sending them off to meet their maker. As the most talented witch of her generation, she was bound to meet up with these types sooner or later. And, as luck would have it, her fateful meeting with McAllister would tragically speed up this process.

42

THE GIRL WHO COULD TALK TO SPIRITS II

Nancy never received the full story from Ada regarding all of the events from five years earlier, so a lot of the details she was describing to Ashton and Tyler were based on hearsay or came from other sources like Wilbur and Ada's mother. But word spread fast in Little Salem, and some incidents took on legendary status quite quickly.

One of the events that would live in infamy was the scuffle at the Desperado Roadhouse, which was still a booming social venue and a place where physical altercations were an extremely rare occurrence. It was quite an unsettling shock to the community that all accounts suggested McAllister had beaten the living daylights out of someone for no reason—although if they'd known the full story, they would have been presented with a different picture altogether.

On that evening, McAllister and Xander had been at the road-house for quite some time, and it was starting to get packed and lively. Xander was grating heavily on McAllister, to the extent that he'd concluded that all the booze and loud music in the world wasn't going to make a lick of difference and he was counting down the days until he could ditch the insufferable clown.

McAllister would have liked nothing more than to watch Little Salem fade into a dot in his rearview mirror. Still, he wasn't just free to do what he wanted. He was part of a rank and file that received orders straight on down from the top. Since Xander was the nephew of a high-ranking member of the Council, this meant if the bosses wanted him to suffer the company of a walking dumpster fire for two weeks, he would just have to grin and bear it.

Xander was smiling with abandon while eying all of the attractive cuties present. "This is mental. I feel like a wolf in a henhouse. Oi. Did you invite that bird you chatted up earlier?"

"The Council just wants us to make contact with them. I got her digits, so my job is finished."

In McAllister's mind, he already accomplished all he needed to with Morgan when they exchanged information during their run-in on the street. The prospect of meeting up had been discussed, but this was merely a formality. Chasing random flings with teenagers held no allure to him; all that was important was to express just enough interest so the witch would invite him into her confidence. Usually, he accomplished this from a brief physical encounter followed by ongoing interaction over social media, always with the insinuation that a passionate romance lay somewhere in the near future. Then, if the witch ever started to be perceived as a threat, that was when he'd come knocking, inspiring his target to let her guard down with the Council's slayers taking care of the rest.

A lengthy operation like this was often years in the making, so McAllister wasn't expecting to have much of anything to do with his latest quarry for a long and indeterminate amount of time. But Morgan knew nothing of his sinister intentions—something Xander got a kick out of as he directed his companion's cold, disinterested gaze to spy the young witch while she entered the dive with two friends, all of them dressed casually but with just enough skin on display to suggest they were on the prowl and looking to party.

"Three of a kind, am I right?" Xander sleazily observed.

McAlister watched as his dark-haired target made eyes at him before grabbing a seat where she and her friends could hold court while waiting to be approached by the local gentry. To say he wasn't thrilled would have been an understatement. On top of already feeling restless and irritable, he was now dreading the prospect of having to put on another exhausting performance.

Xander, on the other hand, remained in high spirits.

"Listen, because I'm your mate, yeah? I'm gonna do you a little favor." He revealed a pill from a medicine bottle tucked inside his pocket. "Mother's little helper, yeah?"

Xander dropped the pill into an untouched beer sitting on the bar and passed it in McAllister's direction.

"Go on. Give it to her. Have fun canoodling."

This was the point where McAllister felt like he was going to lose it. As loathsome as he may have been, date-raping witches was beyond the pale to him. Without any hesitation, he splashed the drink to his left, carelessly soaking a preppy college kid, and slammed the empty glass on the bar.

"Bloody hell!" Xander giggled. "Are you mental?"

Clean out of patience, McAllister glared at Xander, his eyes burning with rage. "You're a goddamn savage," he said and headed for the exit. Xander called after him, reminding him they were untouchable and could do whatever they want, but McAllister was already making a beeline to his convertible, feeling ready to explode.

If a person was judged by the company they kept, McAllister

wondered what that really said about him. It was one thing to be a killer, but a loudmouth rapist was about as low as a person could get. The previous interaction left him so wound up he barely noticed the beer-soaked college kid rushing after him.

"Hey, dog! You spilled booze all over my Izod!"

This minor complaint is what did it. As soon as the bratty student opened his big mouth, McAllister snapped and released all of his anger, punching the kid's lights out. He left the roadhouse quickly afterward, feeling just as wound up as before the confrontation. When he arrived back at the Godfrey mansion, his bloody knuckles were gripping the wheel, and he felt like a total wreck.

McAllister was sick to death of this life. He didn't want to be doing any of this—palling around with human garbage and spying on teenage girls for old buzzards. He was so sick of all of it and wanted so badly to be headed in a different direction. But this was the only life he'd ever known up to this point, and he knew that to fight the empire was to become infected by its derangement.

After entering the mansion, McAllister crossed to the staircase, trying to avoid any interaction that would push him any further over the edge.

"McAllister? Is that you? Why don't you join us?"

Damn it. The voice belonged to his father. Not wishing for the situation to become any more awkward than it had to be, he balled his fists and crossed stiffly to the dining hall.

What he found was unexpected. His father was smiling, and sitting next to him was an attractive woman in dark clothing. Both parties seemed to be enjoying each other's company immensely, but what was most unusual was the identity of the guest accompanying them. It was one of the young witches—the one who won the competition in the forest—and seeing her up close for the very first time was an experience he would never forget.

For McAllister, the budding young witch was still only a child, but she appeared to possess the most unusual quality; a strange charisma that was as beguiling as it was effortless, along with the biggest pair of unearthly-looking eyes he'd ever seen outside of a Japanese anime. Surprisingly, these enchanting blue-violet eyes appeared to light up once they took notice of the intense young man staring back at them, and as McAllister continued watching her from the doorway, a playful and mysterious smile spread across her lips.

"McAllister, this is Ursula and her daughter, Ada," Emmanuel explained. "I met Ursula in town. They're from—where was it?"

"It's a small town just a few hours from here," Ursula answered good-naturedly. "Pleasure to meet you, McAllister."

A glance and a handful of comments were all McAllister needed to see that his father and this woman had developed mutual feelings for each other. It made sense: two single parents enjoying a fortuitous encounter while on vacation, then arranging for an occasion to get both of their children sitting in the same room together. Clearly, they wanted to see if their families were compatible with one another. Ursula had been all alone in Little Salem while Ada was attending to her activities, so meeting Emmanuel at the hotel's humble ground floor café had been an unexpected treat. McAllister could easily do the rest of the math all on his own, but at the moment, he was finding himself distracted by Ada's stirring and bewitching gaze.

Pleased to see his normally volatile and hot-tempered son remained following the introductions, Emmanuel invited him to have a seat. McAllister didn't oppose this and sat at the dining table, resigning himself to join them in the hopes of avoiding a scene.

"Ada's in town for a special retreat," Ursula explained. "She just completed the first week. Next week they have something very special planned. Right, Ada? She says it's something very special—"

"Ay-tha ay-sa iles-smay sugacon-tay-tay."

McAllister glanced up in confusion. Ada was the one who exclaimed this, and her eyes remained fixed on him.

"What?" McAllister asked warily.

"Ay-tha ay-sa iles-smay sugacon-tay-tay," Ada replied, inspiring her mother to shift in her seat as Emmanuel stared dumbly at his strange company.

"Oh, Ada," Ursula groaned. "I'm sorry—she does this sometimes. Talks in this made-up language of hers. You can just ignore her or, um—Tell me more about your teaching job, Emmanuel—"

"Ea-a own ooza anhk undstunder emma." Ada uttered this slowly, her bright eyes staring at McAllister intently.

It was peculiar. He knew the language was made up but found that he could understand what she was saying quite easily. Which was precisely what she just articulated:

"I know you can understand me."

McAllister blinked his eyes as he deciphered these words, and Ada's smile widened, observing she'd been correct in her assessment.

"Ea-a edsa, oo-yoo oh-na, ay-tha ay-sa iles-smay sugacon-tay-tay," Ada commented.

To his surprise, McAllister understood this statement as well.

"I said: you know, they say smiles are contagious."

McAllister cleared his throat, answering apprehensively.
"O-ha oda ay-tha?"

"Oh, do they?"

Ursula was beside herself with embarrassment, shaking her head in disbelief. "Oh, Ada. This is ridiculous."

But Ada wasn't quite finished.

"Netra too-lad versaconshaws ginrob?"

"Aren't adult conversations boring?"

McAllister continued staring back at her, feeling mystified. "Eyah. Eyah ay-tha ray."

"Yeah. Yeah, they are."

Upon this confirmation, Ada leaped to her feet.

"Excuse us, mother. McAllister's going to show me his room."

"What?"

Before he could argue, Ada was pulling him to the doorway.

"Darling, I don't think—" Ursula was considering rising to her feet to stop her when she felt Emmanuel's hand upon hers. "It's fine. It's fine," he said.

She started blushing, knowing he was eager to enjoy a conversation on his own with her and she felt exactly as he did. She had no idea she was allowing her daughter to go off on her own with a stone-cold killer. But Ada was a clever girl who actively sought out various types of experiences that interested her, and she had already developed a unique interest in McAllister in particular.

When they reached his room, Ada stood in the doorway, admiring the lavish surroundings before her eyes steadily returned to her newest obsession, pouring himself a drink at the far end of the bedchamber.

"Pour one for me, OK?"

"Yeah, nice try."

McAllister noted his guest remained beaming as she crossed further into the room to a small table containing a modest stack of books on magic and the occult.

"Fascinating choice of reading material. Bit of a dabbler in the dark arts, are we?"

"If you say so."

He watched her scan the selection.

"What about...this one? Who was he?"

McAllister noticed the book she was holding: *The Book of Pleasure* by A.O. Spare. It was his personal favorite out of all the books he brought with him.

"Austin Osman Spare. Artist, painter, magician. Probably one of the most influential minds of the twentieth century and most people have never heard of him."

"What was so special about him?"

"He could draw a picture. Like, the most detailed picture in total darkness using a single line. He said that the spirits talked to him. Guided his pen."

Unable to hide his enthusiasm, McAllister approached the table, and Ada held her breath as he reached around her to flip through an art book. The book contained an impressive collection of Spare's work—a hypnotizing phantasmagoria of surreal pagan images demonstrating a remarkable level of draughtsmanship and precision.

The material captivated Ada instantly, but as her host flipped through the pages, she found herself becoming even more fascinated by the bloody bruises still visible on McAllister's knuckles.

"Impressive," Ada said, smiling up at him.

McAllister nodded, glancing somberly at the pictures. He greatly admired Spare but rarely had the opportunity to sing his praises. Especially to anyone with an open mind who would listen.

"He lived on his own terms according to his own mythology, his own beliefs... He was free."

"You don't think you and I are free?" Ada asked him.

"No, I don't think we're free," McAllister answered bitterly.

In response, Ada's bright, otherworldly eyes narrowed to observe her companion more carefully. As if she was finally beginning to understand what so greatly fascinated her about him.

"But you want to be," she said quietly. "You're like me."

"Ada! Time to go!" a voice called.

"Coming!" Before taking her leave, Ada glanced back at *The Book of Pleasure* and gazed at McAllister fondly. "Maybe I'll read this someday. Then you and I can have a more in-depth conversation."

McAllister nodded weakly, startled by his disappointment to see her heading off so soon. After receiving another warm smile from her, she was on her way.

"Pleasure meeting you."

Without expression, McAllister watched her exit the room, his face masking a lingering confusion as to why they seemed to share such a keen mutual interest in one another. After she left, he watched from the top of the stairs as Ada joined her mother at the door and flashed one final impish smile at him before taking off, her bright, oversized eyes burning with intensity.

"Bloody hell, mate."

Startled by the voice, McAllister turned to spy Xander standing in the hallway. As usual, he was grinning like he just won the prize for "Top Idiot" in the "World Championship for Idiots."

"Looks like you've racked up another admirer! Mr. Goddamn Ladykiller!"

"Piss off."

Xander grabbed McAllister by the shoulder and pinned him

against the wall. "I thought we agreed I would handle this one. Are you trying to make me look foolish? *Bloody useless?*"

"Let go of me, Xander, or I'll—"

"Or you'll what, Mr. Big Balls?" Xander had a gun pressed against McAllister's forehead. His gun from the glove box evidently.

"I tried to play nice with you," Xander snarled. "I tried to be a good sport, but now you're getting in my way, yeah? What was that saying we have back at Council Chapter Nine? Ah yes—'*The only good witch is a dead witch.*' And I am going to bury that one right here in Little Salem. Right after I have a little fun with her first."

Xander finally released him and backed away.

"Don't try to stop me or I'll bury you with her," he warned and stumbled off toward his bedroom while McAllister remained in the hallway, feeling more disgusted with his life than ever.

"Ada's mother mentioned something special the following week..."

"Yes, the following week was the solitary portion of the retreat. Where the three most gifted candidates are offered the chance to undergo the same initiation the original Salem Witches experienced."

If Nancy had known that Ada would be invited to visit the mansion at the top of the hill, she probably would have warned against it. At the time, she and the other members of the Sisterhood were too distracted by their excitement for how the young witches had performed during the first part of the retreat. Three girls had stood a full head above the rest with Ada as the most gifted of all of them, and Nancy had high hopes for her with what she would experience when she was sent into the woods after enjoying a restful weekend.

Once the weekend had ended and Monday morning finally came, Ada joined up with two others: Morgan, and a Native American girl named Wendy, all three of them standing at the edge of the forest with camping packs strapped to their backs as Ruth and Nancy explained what was expected of them.

"As the three most promising witches at our yearly retreat, each of you will be spending a full week in the forest all on your own," Nancy said. "Think of it as a spirit quest. Keep your eyes and your minds open."

After this, the three girls headed into the woods. Each of them split off in a different direction and wouldn't cross paths for the remainder of the retreat.

The Sisterhood's honor roll weren't the only ones exploring the forest that week. As Ada was journeying down a grassy path and gazing at her surroundings in wonder, she steadily began to slow her stride at the sound of footsteps coming up from behind.

Sensing something disagreeable, she balled her fists and spun around to face her pursuer, discovering a cocky young man dressed in shorts, a colorful Hawaiian shirt, and hiking boots, leaning against a tree and smiling devilishly.

"Hey there, sunshine," the young man said in his affected Cockney accent. "Aren't you a little young to be out on your own?"

Ada's eyes narrowed.

"Who are you?"

"Just an admirer," Xander said. "I spotted you doing your little blindfold thing through the trees last week. You probably think you're hot stuff, but you wouldn't want to play around here after dark. Place gets pretty dangerous."

"Does it?" Ada sneered. "You think the Big Bad Wolf is going to eat me?"

"Maybe. But don't worry, love. You'll be safe as long as you have me around to protect ya."

What Xander expected to happen would have been anyone's guess. He may have been trying to charm Ada in the way that McAllister had so expertly charmed Morgan during the early days of their trip. If so, his clumsy schoolyard tactics were exceptionally off-putting and left a lot to be desired. Ada wasn't the type of girl who would be charmed by this behavior in any situation—something she made clear to him as she smiled at Xander dismissively.

"Thanks but no thanks," Ada said. "You see, I'm deathly allergic to creeps, and I feel a bad break-out coming on. Toodle-loo, sailor."

Ada turned on her heels and took off, but Xander wasn't put off at all by this. The rejection only made the chase more thrilling, inspiring him to chuckle, his eyes glued to Ada's posterior as she stomped down the overgrown path. Once she was out of sight, he unfolded a map of the forest and marked it with a pen before howling like a wolf and exiting in the opposite direction.

Ada may not have known it, but Xander had big plans for her and their brief interaction that day wouldn't be the last. But by the time that day turned to night and the moon was shining high above her, she had already forgotten the incident. While searching for a place to camp, her mind drifted to McAllister, wondering what he was up to, blissfully unaware of the crushing existential crisis he was facing that had finally reached its peak.

McAllister was sitting on the bed in Godfrey's guest room, tracing the outline of the Sigil of Lucifer tattoo on his left forearm. His conversation with Ada had awakened something deep inside of him he was still struggling to come to terms with: the realization that his whole life was nothing but an elaborate lie and that he could be so much more than the detestable person that life in the Council had shaped him into if he only started living up to his personal principles.

The prospect of this transformation terrified McAllister. While glancing at *The Book of Pleasure*, still sitting on the table untouched since Ada's visit, he decided there was only one thing left to do. He had to make a run for it.

McAllister packed his possessions in a heartbeat, but he wouldn't get far. His body tensed up as a familiar voice called out to him after he reached the convertible and tossed his luggage in the trunk.

"Running away, are we?"

McAllister spun around to spy the intimidating presence of Sir Godfrey, watching him like a predator from the front steps.

"My work is done here," McAllister muttered.

"So you thought you'd just pack up and leave without telling anyone?" The ghoulish silver-haired gentleman approached the would-be fugitive and presented a cell phone to him. "Somebody wants to speak to you."

McAllister felt the muscles in his throat tighten, not looking forward to where this situation was headed. After a moment of hesitation, he accepted the phone and answered the call.

"Hello?"

"Hey, McAllister. Wilbur here. How's it going, ol' buddy?"

McAllister turned pale, too shaken to answer.

"Is something troubling you over there, ol' buddy?"

"No. No trouble."

"Yeah? Godfrey told me you might be having some issues."

"I'm fine. I just—"

"*McAllister*. The Council doesn't have room for *losers*. You play your role and do as you're told, or it's game over. *We. Own. You.*"

That was it. It was all that had to be said.

After affirming the grim reality of the situation, Wilbur ended the conversation. "OK! Good talk, buddy. Give Godfrey back his fricking phone."

The call went dead, and McAllister stared helplessly at the sterile device in his hand. For a moment, he wanted to toss the phone to the ground and shatter it into a million pieces, but he knew this wouldn't accomplish anything.

McAllister was stuck. There was nothing he could do. Nowhere to go, nowhere to run.

Overcome with emotion, he snarled desperately at Godfrey, tears welling up and running down his cheeks.

"*I can't do this anymore! You turned me into a monster!*"

"My boy, you turned yourself into a monster."

Godfrey slowly approached the broken assassin, standing just inches away as he peered into his crazed bloodshot eyes.

"My spy tells me the Sisterhood has some strong candidates this year," the man oozed. "These so-called white witches have been thinking rather highly of themselves. Why don't you go take care of one or two of them."

Godfrey retrieved his phone and slapped a gruesome ceremonial dagger sheathed in black leather into McAllister's grip. It was an athame; a blade used by witches that would be the perfect instrument of death for him to administer in a sick and sadistic maneuverer to use the witches' tools against them.

"That should bring those troublemakers down a few pegs."

Godfrey smiled sinisterly and headed off, now that things were about to come to a violent head: the Scarlet Council's resident rebel angel versus the new golden child of Circe's Sisterhood.

43

THE GIRL WHO COULD TALK TO SPIRITS III

The first week of the Young Witch's Retreat had been a breeze for Ada. Soaking in all of the vast knowledge being passed down to her while surpassing all of the other girls had been no problem, and she found the whole experience to be rather amusing.

Before coming to Little Salem, Ada had never done much in the way of studying what it meant to be a witch; it was just something she was. Her relationship with the world that surrounded her, along with her special talents, sharp cunning, and intuition, was all that she needed to hone in on the magic flowing inside of her and strengthen her connection to the craft and to her neighbors in the spirit world.

These so-called "rules" and "traditions" the Sisterhood spoke of were very entertaining but felt mostly dull and inconsequential—at least in terms of how they related to her own practice. As fascinating as all the trials and lessons were, she would have much rather spent the week learning more about the trove of esoteric literature possessed by McAllister. All those dark and forbidden books that felt exciting and dangerous and sexy—a bit like McAllister himself.

Ada could imagine that most of the books were items the Sisterhood found shocking or heretical, which made her more eager to peruse their scandalous contents. She also wouldn't have minded having McAllister personally school her in the material. Despite being a witch, she was still a teenage girl after all.

While the first week of the retreat focused on a lot of things Ada found somewhat tedious, the second week was much more up to her particular speed. When Nancy explained that the week amounted to something similar to a "spirit quest," she could already sense that something special was about to happen. Learning about the craft while being alone and amongst nature was where Ada felt like she was in her element, and this is how the full retreat would have been if she was the one in charge of planning the daily proceedings.

Ada began the week doing exactly as Nancy instructed: keeping her eyes and her mind open while taking account of all the fearsome and inspiring beauty of her surroundings. On her second day, she awoke at the first rays of daylight and emerged from her tent dressed in a simple T-shirt, shorts, and sneakers. She was pleased to notice that despite the presence of a dark storm gathering on the horizon, the sun was still shining, and it looked like she could expect fair weather for the most part. It was going to be a beautiful day.

The fresh morning air felt galvanizing, and after stretching her limbs, Ada took a quick account of where she set up camp: a strange burnt-out clearing that had intrigued her instantly due to the gray, ashen ground and the petrified trees around the perimeter. She wandered west on her first day so, on her second day, she decided she would head east. After having a quick nosh and hanging a witch's ladder on the path where she would begin her journey, she resumed her trek through the untamed magical wonderland that awaited her with her arms stretched out like she was offering a warm embrace to Mother Nature, her fingers lightly brushing against the abundance of foliage and tall, spindly trees.

Ada's imagination ran absolutely wild every time she tried to picture the magical experience that she was promised. To her, it sounded like a secret initiation of some kind or a close encounter with something out of this world. Ada had seen several videos that showed witches enduring various types of initiation, which usually involved a lot of gratuitous nudity sprinkled with touches of stilted ceremony and pseudo-Masonic claptrap. She found the videos very educational, but also a bit passé. For Ada, the craft was more of an experience than a tradition; it was a way of seeing the world and understanding the way of things where traditional lore and rit-ual were only just a small part of the larger picture. She often felt this was something that was being lost within the spectacle of prac-tices that most modern-day covens seemed to order themselves around—although she was still leaving herself open to being con-vinced otherwise.

This is why she was so appreciative that at least she would be undergoing her initiation while out amongst nature. Growing up in suburbia had given her very little opportunity to explore this world freely, and she was enjoying her present experience a great deal. For Ada, the forest that surrounded Little Salem was like a blooming par-adise that was hidden in plain sight; a veritable Garden of Eden for her to become lost in. Connecting with the web of life was much eas-ier in such a place, and throughout her blissful wandering, she could feel all of life whispering to her in a manner that suggested she was in a location that was very special and in the presence of transforma-tive wisdom and mystery. However, this wondrous and glowing per-spective of hers would suffer a drastic change when she felt her eyes being drawn to a crow flying overhead. Her ears picked up a riotous cacophony of cawing and squawking, filling her with apprehension and drawing her deeper into the woods to investigate.

With her ears perked, Ada followed the noises to a small grassy area, and her whole body tightened up at what she saw.

Just a few yards away, lying on the dew-kissed grass, was the body of an injured fawn. Its dark eyes were blinking helplessly at the gathering of crows a short distance away from it, and the sight of the scavengers swarming together filled her with intense emotions. She immediately rushed the black feathery mob, aggressively shooing them away. But while the crows scattered into the air, they did not flee entirely, simply moving to the branches and cawing loudly. When she grabbed a rock and made a gesture, the birds finally disappeared—although she knew they had no plans of leaving the area entirely and wouldn't be flying far.

Once the crows had left, Ada knelt beside the fawn and stroked its neck as the animal's soulful almond eyes blinked back at her, its body too weak to move. She observed the fawn's side, noticing its coat already matted with dried blood, and she suddenly became very panicked, searching all around her in desperation, looking for any assistance available.

Ada was distressingly unsure of what to do for the poor creature. She'd heard tales about witches who could heal with the touch of their hands, but this wasn't a power she possessed herself. Maybe, just maybe, if the forest did house something magical, then it could possibly lend its power to her for just an instant. After all, that's why she was there, wasn't it? She was there to have a magical experience, which was the reason why Nancy and the other witches were having the girls exploring the forest on their own to begin with.

Wasn't it?

Ada could no longer tell if she was thinking rationally or just fooling herself. She knew she had to do something. Anything. She took a deep breath and closed her eyes, trying her hardest to focus.

Once her mind was clear, Ada laid her hands upon the wound, concentrating intently. She visualized the injured fawn getting better with all of her energy pouring out of her and into the dying animal. She imagined the wound disappearing and the animal rising up and trotting off into the forest to join up with its family, who was probably worried sick. All of her intentions were focused on making this a reality for the creature, but unfortunately, nothing was happening.

As Ada felt the animal's breathing begin to slow, her eyes started to fill with tears, driving her to redouble her efforts, face straining, muscles shaking as she continued projecting all of her energy at the fatal wound. It was no good. Her thoughts only proved to be wishful thinking, and moments later, after a final shudder, the poor fawn released its dying breath.

As Ada opened her eyes and observed her hands covered in blood, she felt her throat tighten up, and she immediately broke down in tears. Ada quickly fled the area after this experience, despairing at the fact that she couldn't do anything to change things. It made her feel like all her gifts and talents weren't worth a thing at the end of the day, and she was still drying her eyes and feeling extremely shaken when she heard a familiar voice call out to her.

"The beauty of nature. Am I right?"

Ada froze in place and turned in tense recognition to spy Xander, smiling with the tiresome cocksure arrogance he was known for as he pretended to be occupied with cleaning his nails.

A deep inner rage began to overtake her. While hearing the voice of another human being this far into the woods had initially caught her off-guard, she was already determined not to let this happen again—especially when there were creeps like Xander out and about. She was practically boiling over that he could say something so callous while also feeling incredibly irritated that she would let him catch her unaware while undergoing such an emotional moment.

"You can stop following me," Ada said, disgusted by her stalker's mere presence. "I really find you less than interesting."

With that, Ada headed on her way—but Xander wasn't through with her. "Oh, I'm no McAllister, that's for sure. I know you find *him* pretty interesting. For whatever reason."

Ada stopped dead in her tracks. Her mind was working overtime to place how Xander would know anything about her feelings for someone she only just met. Had he gotten this information from McAllister? Or perhaps he obtained it through much more sinister methods. Either way, she didn't trust the cocky loudmouth for one instant and knew she would have to be extra careful with all of the reactions she gave him from there on out.

"What's it to you?" Ada asked dryly, turning back to face him.

"Ah, you see, that's what I'm here about. McAllister told me if I should run into you, there was a book he wanted to loan you. Said it might help with the whole... Whatever you have going on out here."

Ada's eyes dilated, remembering a specific book in McAllister's collection—*The Book of Pleasure* by Austin Osman Spare. She had indeed professed a genuine fascination with the text, but the idea that he would send one of his buffoonish buddies to give it to her was a prospect that felt so laughable it was surely too good to be true.

"So?" Ada answered with caution. "Hand it over."

"Slow down, angel," Xander replied, chuckling obnoxiously. "I thought it would be a cold day in hell the next time I saw your pretty face. I left it in the glove box, but I'll bring it to you. How about we meet on that hillside? First moonlight."

Ada followed Xander's eyes to a rocky mountain slope in the distance before glancing back at him, trying to figure out his motives. The situation felt like a set-up, but on the off chance he was actually telling the truth, she didn't want to disappoint her recent object of admiration by rejecting a gift he specially arranged to pass on to her. In her heart of hearts, Ada was a hopeless romantic, so of course she would want to rationalize the situation to see it this way. After all, how heavenly would it be if the swaggering windbag's dubious claims turned out to be true?

"Don't forget it," Ada said after making her decision. "I won't be showing up for the conversation."

She turned away and headed fearlessly down the forest path as Xander grinned sinisterly after her.

"Neither will I, angel. Neither will I."

There was no way for Ada to know it at the time, but at that very moment, McAllister was not so far away from her but in another part of the woods altogether. Thoughts of his recent conversation with Sir Godfrey were still gnawing away at him, his hopes of quitting the Scarlet Council and riding off into the sunset dashed completely with Wilbur's discomforting phone, followed by Godfrey's order to slaughter a pair of witches like a good little monster.

McAllister knew that three witches were out on their own exploring the wilderness but wasn't sure if he'd come to there to fulfill the Council's demands or if he was drawn there for a different purpose. The reluctant assassin had a very shallow grasp on his own sanity at this point, and his outward physicality suggested this. His eyes were searching skittishly all around him as he walked stiffly down the path, dressed from head to toe in nightmare black.

With the tension in his body practically killing him and his skull feeling like it was ready to split open, McAllister turned his head at the sound of footsteps. As luck would have it, it was Morgan who was the first to spot him, emerging onto the trail with her eyes lighting up and a flirtatious smile forming once her vibrant gaze met his.

"Hiya," Morgan said in her perky Southern dialect. "Fancy seeing you again."

McAllister felt his body tighten up even further, and a cold sweat started to form upon his skin. He knew there was a good chance of running into her, so her mere presence wasn't what had him so on edge. It was the harsh reminder of the strict orders he'd been given, along with the weight of the dagger burning a hole in the pocket of his funerary black trench coat.

"I was thinking the same," McAllister replied, slowly backing away from her. He knew he was in trouble; the look in Morgan's eyes said it all as she sensually sashayed toward him in her trendy designer athletic gear. She looked like someone who'd been hoping for a playful run-in in the woods like this one and had a lot more on her mind than an innocent walk in the forest to help bring her closer to nature.

"You didn't come all the way out here looking for little old me, did you?" Morgan asked mischievously.

"No. Not you," McAllister said, finding himself removing the dagger behind his back and drawing the gruesome blade.

"Really? That's too bad." Morgan struck a seductive pose while letting her long dark hair drop to her shoulders. "I was thinking we might be able to have a little fun."

Before she could say another word, McAllister lunged forward, grabbing her by the throat and shoving her against the nearest tree.

"Easy, tiger," Morgan said, startled by the aggressive gesture. But her eyes widened once she realized this was far from an intimate moment. "Oh my God—what are you—?"

Her voice turned into a whimper after spying the blade against her throat. Sadly, this was all she could manage; so stricken with terror, her body had frozen up. Morgan had lived a fairly sheltered and carefree life up to this point. To have her life threatened by someone she'd developed a special fondness for was the most traumatizing thing she ever experienced; a living nightmare where the most unthinkable thing imaginable was happening.

There he was: the one she had fantasized about and captivated her wanton desires, glaring right at her and drinking up the paralyzing horror that was shining in her eyes like blood diamonds. Towering over her and gritting his pearly white teeth, struggling internally.

It would be so easy, McAllister contemplated. *So easy to do what the Council commanded.* Deep down, he knew that was no longer an option. Thanks to his short interaction with Ada, a new path now lay wide open.

All he had to do was take the first step.

"Listen to me and listen good," McAllister growled, gripping the dagger tight as Morgan cowered before him. "I want you to do yourself a favor and forget you ever met me."

As Morgan continued to blanch at the sight of him, McAllister pushed himself away from her and hurried along on his decisive journey. He was several steps away when her trembling body crumbled to the ground, her mind now shattered.

"Psycho," Morgan managed to exclaim. "You goddamn psycho!"

McAllister kept on walking, his eyes fixed in front of him.

What a defiant and ardent fool he was. He had disobeyed a direct order and allowed a young witch to live; in the eyes of the Council, he committed the ultimate heresy. Now that he was a free agent, there was no going back—a prospect that was as terrifying as it was thrilling. With freedom in his sights and a new destiny on the horizon, he hoped that luck would be on his side as he scoured the vast expanse of forest that surrounded him, hoping to find the witch that roused his thirst for liberation and save her before it was too late.

Storm clouds had engulfed the sky by the time all daylight had disappeared, with the soft, luminous glow of the moon just barely visible overhead. As thunder rumbled in the distance, Ada hiked up the treacherous mountain path, the rain suddenly emptying from the heavens without a moment's notice and coming down in sheets.

Xander was standing on the mountainside, waiting for her. He was quickly becoming drenched in the heavy downpour as he spied the soggy rain-soaked enchantress approaching from below. With her modest clothes and long, tangled hair now soaked, Ada felt like a drowned cat; the sudden change in weather signifying a bad omen that was impossible to ignore. Her wariness only intensified as she grew closer, distressingly unable to shake the feeling this had been a horrible idea from the start.

Ada stopped in her tracks with several feet still left to climb, apprehensive about approaching any further.

"I think this was a bad idea."

"Don't worry, doll." Xander reached into his jacket and gestured for her to come closer. "McAllister wrapped it up for ya. Come here, my darling."

This is where Ada's curiosity got the better of her. She remained eager to possess the knowledge that would help bring her and McAllister closer, which made her feel that whatever her shady messenger's intentions, it was worth the risk. Ada had a big heart that yearned for deeper connections to people, but unlike Morgan, she was also aware that even the most innocent person was capable of the worst atrocities imaginable, given the circumstances. If only love had lost its ability to blind her typically sharp and insightful senses, then that stormy evening would have turned out much different.

"Don't be shy." Xander's smile widened as Ada made her cautious approach. "Hurry—I'm getting soaked."

Once they were standing on level ground, he made his move, grabbing her and holding her tight with Ada letting out a high-pitched shriek as she felt the touch of cold metal—the barrel of a gun now pressed firmly against her cheek.

"Like the little surprise I had wrapped up for you? I'm going to have a ball unwrapping you."

Xander swiped at her shirt, tearing it to shreds as Ada squirmed helplessly, exposing the white bra she was wearing as well as the distinct flower-shaped birthmark underneath her left breast.

"Young birds think they're so smart." Xander prodded the gun into her rain-soaked flesh. "Don't feel so smart now, do ya? *Do ya?*"

Ada never felt so terrified in all her life. Flashes of everything horrible that could happen to her began to besiege her normally overactive thought process. As she squeezed her eyes tightly shut, she prayed for a miracle, thinking this might be the end, when suddenly, she heard a commotion and felt Xander spinning her around to find McAllister barreling down the mountain straight for them.

Before Xander had time to react, Ada's golden-haired rescuer had shoved the gun away from her and knocked her craven captor to the muddy earth. The weapon went off with a loud *bang* that instantly initiated a brutal no-holds-barred competition to retain possession of the firearm. Her despised would-be killer versus her daring dark horse protector with Ada caught right in the middle.

Ada toppled to the muddy ground during the scuffle. As she picked herself up, breathing hard and shivering with fright, she watched the two young men tumble in the mud while thunder boomed overhead. When a sharp blow was delivered to Xander's face, leaving him temporarily stunned, this gave McAllister just enough time to deliver a brief instruction as he glared at her with a fierce and ironclad resolve, bellowing with intensity.

"RUN!"

In Ada's case, she didn't have to be told twice. Ada was a clever girl and knew that as much as she would have loved to stick around and help, it would only increase the likelihood of someone getting shot. So Ada ran and ran; running down the mountain and into the forest as the rain continued to pour down in buckets and thunder rumbled overhead. A flash of lightning illuminated the woods every so often, casting frightening shadows all around her as she sprinted onward like all the forces of hell were at her heels.

While initially a blooming paradise for Ada, the stormy darkness transformed the forest into a black and treacherous maze. As she ran, her body shivering with terror and startling at everything, her mind went completely blank; her desperate, impetuous actions being driven only by her will to survive and primal instinct as she struggled to plow her way through the disorienting environment, still barely able to see what was in front of her with the rain pouring so hard the ground had turned to sludge.

Deeper and deeper into the woods she went, paying little attention to anything but what she could see that was directly in front of her when suddenly, she ran into a dark massive shape.

A flash of lightning briefly illuminated her surroundings as her saucer-sized eyes stared wildly at the two towering figures before her, both of them dressed in stark black robes with monstrous deer skulls for faces. These were the beings known as the Mysterious Ones, though Ada had never even heard about such creatures.

As she attempted to back away, one of the figures lunged forward and grabbed her by the neck. Unable to move and with no veritable means for escape, Ada struggled for breath as the being plunged its cold, bony fingers into its guts before pulling them out to reveal a ruddy claw now covered in blood.

The figure drew a pagan cross on Ada's forehead and released her. Or, at least, that's what she thought, as, with a shaky hand, she reached up to touch the bloody marking before being shoved over to the second figure who took her frightened features in its damp and withered hands and pulled her body closer to offer a terrifying glimpse at the two hollow pits in the place of eyes staring into her.

Ada felt her breathing start to escalate, pangs of suffocating dread overwhelming her shivering body with painful jolts of sheer horror vibrating throughout her nervous system. Despite these intense emotions, she couldn't look away. Her face was fixed on the cracked black and white carnival mask that formed the monster's impassive skeletal face.

While becoming lost in the being's dark stygian gaze, Ada found herself reciting an impulsive impromptu mantra in between short panicky breaths:

"Blessed are the pure in heart. Blessed are the pure in heart, for they shall see—they shall see—"

With no clue as to why she would do such a thing or what would inspire her to do it, she found herself grabbing the creature's head and caressing the textures of the skull with her fingertips as cracks began to appear along the surface and blinding rays of luminescence burst forth from underneath.

Once the blinding light was all she could see, Ada watched as the morbid vision positioned before her morphed into an exact copy of her own girlish wild-eyed visage molded entirely of white light. Her own face was looking straight at her, waiting expectantly. Once again, Ada couldn't explain her actions, but she fought the urge to look away and leaned in and kissed the image of herself fully on the lips as the white light she was embracing started glowing even brighter and enveloped her completely.

The next thing Ada could remember was hearing a familiar voice calling out her name. When she opened her eyes, she discovered McAllister cradling her in his arms, and the two fearsome creatures had disappeared. Her bruised and muddied associate looked relieved to see her conscious and helped her to her feet—although he also appeared mildly distracted by the strange flower-shaped birthmark on her side that was now glowing bright red.

Ada felt wobbly and disoriented, her head now throbbing like it was filled with live bees. She wondered what on earth had just happened to her, and yet, the battle still wasn't over—something that became startlingly clear as a sudden blast of lightning cast its light on Xander, standing just a few short feet from them.

Xander was a muddy wreck, his head still bleeding from where McAllister had clocked him with a rock. But the villain refused to go softly into the night, switching the aim of his gun from McAllister to the sopping young witch standing next to him.

"Ladies first," Xander said.

McAllister's body went stiff while Ada, still dizzy and barely conscious, closed her eyes and raised her hand.

Bang!

The gun went off, but Ada remained uninjured, opening her eyes to discover the bullet frozen in the air just inches from her forehead. McAllister was just as stunned as she was, gazing at the bullet and then all around him to notice the falling rain that had been pouring nonstop was now frozen in place as well.

"Bloody hell," Xander softly uttered.

Ada had stopped the bullet with her mind—something even the most gifted of witches shouldn't have been capable of. It would prove to be the last thing her rotten foe ever saw. She issued a simple thought, and the bullet fired back and pierced his forehead.

It was more than a fitting end for such a fiend—something that wasn't lost at all on the duo as McAllister stared silently at Ada and a wave of riotous laughter erupted from her lips. With her chilling laughter echoing through the woods, she capped off the performance with her body jerking high off the ground and into the air, freezing alongside the frozen falling rain as she issued an ecstatic smile and two tears of blood washed down her seraphic face.

Ada received a gift that night. Or more accurately, she received many gifts. Even more accurately, one could say she didn't receive anything at all that she didn't possess already, but her encounter with the Mysterious Ones awakened the true nature of the powers inside her and switched the setting to beast mode.

Nancy had always known there was something special about Ada. She even guessed early on that the tiny bright-eyed thing was the most gifted witch of her generation. But she had no clue as to the heights Ada's powers would reach once her special abilities had been released; abilities that were not only well beyond the reaches of average humans but also truly alarming in their potential. And the most frightening aspect of these powers was that they appeared to be without limit, with Ada herself the only one who knew all that she could do and all she had gained from the experience.

Even more terrifying was that Ada was still relatively young and innocent. She had yet to encounter all the sorrow and misery that life had yet to deal to her. Once she'd gotten a taste of this, it would only be a matter of time for the world to learn the true unbridled nature of her unearthly powers and bear the full brunt of her fierce and inescapable wrath.

44

THE GIRL WHO COULD TALK TO SPIRITS IV

The rain was coming down in sheets when Ada and McAllister arrived back at the mansion. After parking the beastly red convertible out front, McAllister hurried Ada inside, now draped in his black trench coat.

"McAllister! Ada! Could you come here for a moment?"

The drenched and disheveled pair froze and tensely turned around, surprised to see their respected parents exiting the trophy room, their bright shining smiles disappearing once they caught a glimpse of their bloody rain-soaked progeny.

"What happened to you two?" Ursula gasped. "You look like you were in a war!"

"Mother, what's going on?" Ada was growing visibly more nervous at the sight of her mother in the company of McAllister's father. The tension in the room was palpable.

"Ada, your mother and I—"

"Emmanuel asked me to marry him...and I said yes."

"We're getting married," Emmanuel joyfully confirmed.

The announcement stunned both children. After exchanging bewildered slack-jawed looks with one another, Ada left McAllister's side, rushing up the stairs on the brink of tears.

"Ada..." Ursula stopped herself once she realized it was best to give her daughter some space to process things. Emmanuel was much more apathetic, and McAllister cast a cold hard glance his way before stomping up the stairs in the wake of his future stepsibling.

"This can't be real," Ada exclaimed. McAllister made a beeline to the bar as she continued to pace the room. "So that makes us...?"

"'Fraid so." He peeled off his wet T-shirt and tossed it to the floor.

"But I don't want that. I won't put up with it."

Ada was clearly distressed by the news, but McAllister had already adopted a much more cynical attitude, speaking calmly and dispassionately as he helped himself to a glass of scotch.

"Ada, listen closely because I'm going to let you in on a little secret." He offered one of the glasses to her, wearing a hardened expression. "Live a little. The bad guys won a long time ago."

After this, McAllister explained to Ada all the disturbing machinations for how the world really operated, revealing to her the type of secret knowledge that would only be possessed by a high-ranking insider belonging to a powerful secret society—and an avid reader of heretical occult books. Ada found herself both horrified and spellbound by all she was hearing, with the timing of the conversation being especially fitting given that while they were engaged in their discussion, miles away from Little Salem, a witch was being forcibly removed from the roles of the living.

Death came slow for Claire. In the middle of the night, she awoke to find two men wearing dark suits and featureless white masks standing over her. After her screams had been stifled by the two intruders, she was tied to a chair and "put to the question"—a process that involved a lot of pain, torture, and downright nastiness that left the downstairs kitchen covered in blood by the time she was finally put out of her misery. The witch's executioners were Dr. Franklin Baker and Wilbur Truegood. When they were finished, Franklin hummed a church hymn as he cleaned the blood off of his collection of gruesome medieval torture instruments while Wilbur frowned at the body sitting motionless in the middle of the room.

"This witch killing is some dirty business," Wilbur sighed.

"Which is why this will be the last for me," Franklin said.

Wilbur gawked in wide-eyed disbelief at the confession. "Franklin, you're kidding. You're the Witchfinder General. The Council's never going to let you go."

His imposing snowy-haired colleague nodded somberly. "Which is why I'm going to have to disappear. You should consider doing the same." Franklin's rheumy gaze fell on the formerly lovely young woman who was now dead and bloody, reflecting on who knows how many he had killed in his lifetime. "Life is for living, my friend. No one knows exactly when it's their time to go, but whenever that is, it's always much too soon."

The burnt-out executioner passed a photograph to his rattled associate. It was the picture from Claire's bedroom showing her smiling next to Nancy and Ruth; a sight that inspired Wilbur to reflect thoughtfully on the picture, letting Franklin's words wash over him as the gruff, battle-hardened warrior made his exit, this short conversation proving to be the last meaningful interaction he would have with the Council's infamous Witchfinder General.

During this reflective moment, while Franklin's final remarks were floating around in Wilbur's brain, back in Little Salem, Ada's mind was buzzing in more ways than one. While equally disturbed and fascinated by everything McAllister had told her, her mind eventually switched gears to thinking about all the things that she and her new stepbrother could do to change the world for the better and disrupt the intricate plans of their enemies that were drowning the world in misery.

Ada was quite tipsy off of the scotch at this point, talking excitedly while refreshing both of their drinks. McAllister was proving to be the worst role model in the world during this scenario, but Ada had just survived a murder attempt, in addition to snuffing her would-be killer and learning everything she'd been taught about how the world really operated was a total con. If she wanted to indulge in a couple of drinks after all this, he wasn't going to stop her—and Ada was such a lightweight, he doubted she would even finish the second one she just poured.

"You know what we should do?" Ada cheerfully chirped. "We should start our own Scarlet Council. Or Sisterhood of...whatever."

Smiling widely, she passed McAllister a freshened glass and nestled up close to him at his place on the floor next to the fireplace. Probably a bit too close for comfort for McAllister's liking, but despite the difficult circumstances, he found himself enjoying her company immensely.

Ada was like a breath of fresh air to McAllister, considering the cruel, mercenary world he was used to, and she found a unique and special comfort in him as well. McAllister was exciting and cool and dangerous—and so much more cultured and sophisticated than anyone she knew back home. He was also pretty easy on the eyes, and she found herself routinely distracted by the firelight dancing on his lean bare torso and becoming lost in his dark, intense gaze whenever he peered in her direction.

Given their pronounced difference in age, McAllister may not have shared the same level of attraction as she did. But Ada already knew since the first time she saw him there was something special about their relationship and was convinced they were destined to be much more than casual acquaintances.

"You think there are others out there like us?" McAllister asked.

"There has to be!" Ada exclaimed, pawing at him playfully. "And they don't have to be witches or dark magicians. They can be total normies! Like, totally normal people! So long as they're willing to fight like we are against the oppressive mediocrity in this world."

McAllister cracked a smile, taking great amusement in Ada's choice of words for their prospective mission statement.

"What will we call ourselves?" he asked her.

Ada furrowed her brow as she leaned into him, staring at the crackling fire in the fireplace. That's when it came to her: the name they would unite under, drawing all their future allies together.

"*The Lords of Light.*"

The two talked straight into the night. Ada asked McAllister to tell her everything about himself, and she shared various details about herself in turn. They talked about everything under the sun and the moon that night, sharing different ideas and experiences, along with selected tidbits they never revealed to anyone. Both of them were surprised to discover how much they shared in common, but rather than being completely identical, they were more like two different sides of the same coin. McAllister had a much more studied and cynical take on various matters that complemented Ada's more intuitive and emotionally intelligent opinion on things. Both probably wished they could continue talking straight into the following evening, but once it was getting close to sunrise, their words began to falter, and their eyes started feeling too heavy to stay awake.

Just a little bit longer, Ada thought dreamily as she lay next to the fire with her head positioned on McAllister's chest. *Just a few more moments and then whatever is meant to come, it will all have been worth it.*

"McAllister? Tell me more about what our group will be like."

"We'll create a system like Spare did. No dogma, no stuffy old ideas. Just whatever works. Chaos magic."

"And then we'll finally free ourselves from all the cold-hearted villains of the world. The ones smothering the joy out of everyday existence."

McAllister snickered at the poetic nature that Ada's words took on whenever she was ranting about the things that gave her displeasure. It was a trait he'd grown rather fond of during their extended conversation.

"When do we start?"

Ada's eyes lit up, and she bolted upright.

"Right now. We'll make a pact."

"Like a blood oath? Cuz I've already lost a lot of blood."

"No! An oath binding us together forever! Our bond will be stronger than blood!"

After searching the room and finding a black ribbon from who knows where, Ada knelt by the fireplace, facing McAllister. With her body shaking, she clasped her hand in his and bound them both together with the ribbon.

"I, Ada van Dreyer, commit myself to McAllister Kinneary."

"And I, the same."

"I commit myself in wholeness and brokenness, joy and adversity, peace and turmoil. 'Till the end of my days, so help me."

Ada grasped McAllister's hand, and he returned the gesture, innocently unaware of the intense feelings that amounted to a whole lot more than a "schoolgirl crush" that she had for him. Or the truly solemn nature of the ceremony they just performed. The sacred rite felt like a fitting way to end such a night, and with the ritual concluded, Ada smiled at him with tears welling up behind her eyes.

"There. It's done. Brother."

"Sister."

Ada laughed and sniffed, holding her arms out to embrace him like a family member. When McAllister took her into his arms, the reality of their situation hit her like a hurricane: She began sobbing into his shoulder, laughing and crying intermittently as she squeezed his body tight.

McAllister wasn't a fan of this reality either, but as he caught sight of the first rays of daylight, his mind began drifting to much more disconcerting matters.

Hours later, when Ada awoke on the floor and clutched her aching head, she became alarmed to discover her reluctant step-brother was nowhere to be found and a letter addressed to her was sitting on the pillow beside her:

Dearest Ada,

By the time you read this, I will be miles away. The Council will no doubt blame me for the death of Xander and be out for my blood. I'll be leaving for somewhere far away from here where I don't think they'll ever find me. The brief time I spent with you has meant the world to me.

Yours In Light,

McAllister

Ada read the note at lightning speed, her hands shaking as she struggled to fight back tears. As if on cue, she heard the sound of the doorbell and crept into the hallway. She observed Ruth having a grave discussion with Godfrey's butler, no doubt related to the recent discovery of his master's dearly departed nephew.

The clever young witch didn't stick around to witness what happened next, only frowning defiantly at Ruth when their eyes briefly met before returning to McAllister's bedchamber, throwing open the window and shimmying down the drainpipe. Once her feet hit the ground, she took off running with the letter clutched tightly in her grip. She knew that McAllister had just sacrificed himself on her behalf, leaving town to make it look like he was the guilty party in question when she was the one that sent that irritating boy to the afterlife. She knew he was trying to protect her since, as a witch, she would have been an easy target for the Council to make an example of. That's what the Scarlet Council did after all.

With only one person to turn to, Ada ran like hell to the quaint suburban home that first welcomed her upon her arrival. When she finally reached it, she banged her fists on the front door.

"Ada! What's wrong?" Nancy asked, gawking at the girl standing panicked and out of breath on her doorstep.

"Nancy, you have to help me."

Ada had been on Nancy's mind for the past several days, but this wasn't at all how she expected to reunite with her young protégé. For the past two nights, she'd been waiting anxiously for the week to end to learn if Ada had undergone a successful encounter with the Mysterious Ones. She knew if the talented witch had the chance to cross paths with these curious entities, the gift she was likely to receive would be tremendous. But there was also the possibility she'd be driven mad from the experience. Nancy felt this was highly unlikely given how remarkable Ada was, but the prospect did cause her to worry. And she was surprised to discover that her maternal instincts were closer to the surface than ever in Ada's absence, finding herself visiting the guest room in the middle of the night, laying her head on the pillow and caressing the empty space on the mattress.

Nancy had never shown any interest in motherhood up to this point, but after meeting Ada and getting to know her, it felt like her life was missing something when the tiny bright-eyed thing wasn't around. Her first concern may have been related to whether contact with the Mysterious Ones had driven Ada totally batty, but after inviting her inside, she learned the situation was more complicated. She stared at Ada in total bewilderment as she paced back and forth in the kitchen, explaining all that had befallen her, with most of the conversation centering around a newly adopted loyalty that bordered on obsession toward a notoriously troublesome young man that Nancy was passingly familiar with.

"McAllister explained everything," Ada said—her words were pouring out of her like water from a broken spigot. "He and this guy Xander are *Sires* in this thing called the *Scarlet Council*. Basically, it's this *ancient secret society* that's secretly in control of the *world!* And McAllister and Xander were sent to Little Salem to take out the most powerful young witches at the retreat—*can you believe it?* Because the Council sees all magic-users as a *threat!* To the extent that they even employ *witch hunters!*"

"Honey, I'm home!"

Dear Lord, why? Nancy thought. Of all the times for Wilbur to be arriving home from a "business trip," here he was, with the worst timing imaginable.

"I received a call just now," Wilbur hollered, completely oblivious to his wife's present company. "Apparently that McAllister fellow shot Godfrey's nephew. The Council is going to fry that kid."

Nancy closed her eyes and cringed at her husband's distressing lack of tact in this situation. When she reopened them, she saw Ada standing like a stunned animal before turning to face her, her jaw gaping and her oversized blue-violet eyes as wide as could be.

"You're in on it! You!"

"Honey, please. You have the wrong idea!"

Wilbur entered the kitchen, still blissfully unaware of the crisis he created. "Is this Ada? Nancy's told me a lot about you."

Ada didn't stick around for introductions. She bolted for the front door and dashed into the street.

"Ada van Dreyer, listen to me!"

Ada stopped and turned, spying Nancy and Wilbur standing at the front door.

"I can't help you," Nancy said, somewhat regrettably. "The Council will do what they will with McAllister. The Sisterhood is an order of peaceful white witches. We remain neutral. It's...just our way."

With this revelation, Ada felt like something had snapped deep inside of her. Her lips curled into a snarl, and she angrily balled her fists.

"Then it's all the same thing!" Ada shrieked. "Scarlet Council, Sisterhood of Circe. IT'S ALL THE SAME SHIT!"

"Whoa there," Wilbur interjected. "Language, young lady—"

But Ada was far from finished as she stared with harsh intensity at the couple, her bright and captivating eyes filled with fiery rage.

"You'll regret your actions here today," Ada said. "Today I lay a curse on you and all the other two-faced lying hypocrites in this town. Mark my words, someday my stepbrother and I will return and burn your artificial paradise to the ground! *That* is a promise!"

Despite the ferocity of her delivery, Ada's threatening words only fell on deaf ears. Wilbur struggled not to laugh as he gazed at the frail and emotional little girl standing in the center of the street.

"Uh, don't forget your suitcase," Wilbur said.

Strangely, Ada remained eerily calm after the insult as she already felt it was no longer necessary to indulge in any further conversation. Without breaking eye contact, she extended her arm, and there was a loud crash as her suitcase flew out the second-story window on a sailing comet of broken glass before landing in her outstretched hand.

This was something Wilbur took much more seriously, the True-goods staring in slack-jawed awe at the enraged teenager.

Nancy experienced a sinking feeling, confident she was being given a taste of the terrible powers the Mysterious Ones had awakened. And the grand performance was far from over. For the finale, Ada gritted her teeth and pumped her arm, and all of the windows in the neighborhood shattered at once with explosions of broken glass raining onto the asphalt while car alarms and home security systems rang out from all directions.

If the Truegoods had been in awe before this, they were now well and truly stunned. Wearing looks of dumbstruck amazement, they watched Ada turn her nose up, stomping aggressively down the middle of the glass-ridden street with her fingers tightly clutching the handle of her suitcase.

Wilbur stuttered over the alarm calls filling the air.

"She... She... I've never..."

Nancy's reaction was slightly different.

"Wilbur, I want a kid."

The next few days were a total blur for Ada. After leaving the Truegoods', she returned to the Godfrey mansion and planted herself on the stairs, reading McAllister's letter over and over as her mother and McAllister's father discussed their upcoming marriage plans. By the following week, Little Salem was only a memory and Emmanuel was part of the family, living in the small suburban home Ada shared with her mother.

Ada didn't take at all to the new arrangement but mostly stayed quiet. With her whole world turned upside down, she adapted once again to her standard tight-lipped approach to things: saying nothing, observing everything. On the inside, she felt like she was dying a little more each day, and her bright, enchanting eyes were getting darker and duller, a look of pained irritation now plastered permanently onto her face.

Ada was wearing this gloomy scowl at the breakfast table one morning, stabbing at her cereal with her spoon while her mother fluttered around the kitchen. Singing a happy song, she kissed her husband on the cheek and gave him a warm squeeze on the shoulder, beaming with devotion as she served his morning meal to him.

The embarrassing display was enough to make Ada want to puke blood. The man was changing her, and Ada knew in her soul it wouldn't be long until her mother was lost to her forever; a poor and shallow substitute for what could have been if only her mother and that detestable fellow never met and her relationship with McAllister had been left to evolve on its own.

Ada still thought of McAllister often, wondering what became of him and if he ever made it to the place the Scarlet Council would never find him. The time they spent together was brief, but the world felt like a much less interesting place with him absent. And with her mother now too busy playing Sally Homemaker to give her much affection, she felt lonelier than ever.

In the meantime, these turbulent feelings weren't helped by the fact that everything Emmanuel did, from the way he sipped his coffee to the way he shifted in his chair, drove the young witch crazy—to the point that she wanted to scream her head off until her ears bled or everything exploded. However, that morning was going to be different. Ada didn't know it, but once again, an unexpected meeting was about to change her life forever.

"Ada? Can you answer that, honey?" Her mother was referring to the doorbell. Ada was so caught up in her personal hell that she didn't even hear it.

Not wishing to get into an argument, Ada silently left the table, looking like a stormy day at the cemetery. She had no idea as to the surprise that awaited her, finding at her doorstep a gorgeous redhead dressed decadently in all red and classy designer labels, with the newness of the clothes creating the appearance that she was trying her hardest to impress on the occasion. Ada couldn't think of a reason for why anyone would feel obligated to do this for her sake, but it quickly became apparent that the charming ginger beauty was there to see her specifically.

The redhead cast her a nervous smile, her emerald eyes lighting up like a showroom window after first making contact with the young witch.

"You must be Ada," she said. "McAllister told me about you."

She reached into her handbag and passed a note to her startled observer.

Heart racing, Ada unfolded the offering to discover a drawing of an Algiz rune with the initials, "lol," placed over it, along with four words written directly underneath the evocative image:

THE LORDS OF LIGHT

As soon as she saw the message, the shroud of melancholy that engulfed her evaporated like a fine mist.

The letter was like a fallen gift from heaven. She knew exactly what it meant and precisely what McAllister was challenging her to do next.

Her mind was spinning like a whirlwind when her mother called out from the kitchen: "Darling? Who is it?"

With her bright, otherworldly eyes gleaming, Ada directed her token impish smirk to the young woman she would learn was named Agatha and gestured for her to follow her inside.

"Please. Come in."

* * *

This concluded Nancy's tale to the two boys, leaving Ashton more fascinated by Ada than ever while Tyler was feeling a bit more frustrated.

"So let me get this straight," Tyler grumbled. "Ada's some kind of super-witch and McAllister used to be in the Scarlet Council, along with your husband who was also a witch hunter."

"Sounds about right," Nancy begrudgingly acknowledged.

"A witch married a witch hunter. And the Council just let him leave because..."

"Well, that's another story," Nancy said. "Boys, Little Salem is a town that is full of stories. Stories that aren't always easy to understand and don't always have a happy ending."

No one could have resonated with this enlightened sentiment more than Ada herself, who had overheard everything; growing misty-eyed after indulging in the dramatic recollection of the events that helped shape her into who she was.

As for McAllister, he was sitting alone in the tavern's attic, staring in grim contemplation at an unsettling illustration of a demon adorned in a jester's hat in the pages of the old red leather book in his collection.

Buzz. Buzz.

McAllister checked the caller ID on his smartphone before answering.

"Yeah."

"Nancy told them everything."

Silence followed.

"Do you think this changes anything? Ada?"

The voice on the other end of the call appeared to be fighting back sobs.

"Ea uv-la oo-ya. R-ruth-bra."

...

"I love you too."

45

A DATE ON THE ASTRAL PLANE

Empty bottles, obscure occult books, and loose scraps of files and papers lay scattered across the floor. McAllister had locked himself away in the Black Death Tavern's attic for the past twenty-four hours, examining each of the items relating to the missing diary in painstaking detail. He reviewed all the facts and explored several different theories and possibilities countless times over, but, unfortunately, despite his obsessive efforts, he was getting nowhere. The moon was high in the sky, another day had passed, and to make matters even more precarious, he was drinking excessively, placing him in an increasingly excitable and unpredictable state.

"*Where is it?*" McAllister roared, sweeping away the items at his feet. He was desperate. With nowhere else to turn, he was left with one person to call out to.

"Dakota! *Dakota!*"

It was an act of lunacy to reach out to a villain of her nature, and there was no telling if she would respond. But surprisingly, in no time at all, the familiar disembodied voice rang out to answer him.

"Hello, McAllister. Something I can do for you, baby?"

"We're running out of time. The diary is out there and none of this—none of this is making any sense!"

In a rage, he picked up his trunk and hurled it across the room.

"Temper temper, baby," Dakota cooed. "Tell me...what do we know so far?"

Strangely, her voice seemed to have a calming effect on him. He managed to swallow his frustration and started pacing.

"What do we know? What do we—right, the clues..."

McAllister knelt down and picked through various items; notably, Tom Thumb's file from the asylum, Alfonse Masters' reading list from Boston, and the copy of *Tannhauser* by Aleister Crowley.

"We can assume," McAllister grumbled, "that Masters stole the diary from the library in Boston and brought it to Little Salem. Then he used the book to gain the knowledge for all of his miraculous scientific breakthroughs."

"Mm-hm. Good so far."

"We know that Masters had a meeting with Crowley, which is how he gained his copy of *Tannhauser*—a book of poetry Crowley often presented as a gift to new friends. And we know that Crowley most likely possessed the diary at some point but lost it, which would explain the evocation circle for Vassago in the hotel attic. Remnants of a ritual for summoning a demon to locate lost things.

"We also know that Tom Thumb, Fonzi's trustworthy servant, most likely murdered his master on orders from the Scarlet Council. The name of Godfrey's ancestor on the burial certificate suggests this connection. And while the book was in Tom Thumb's possession, he was apparently driven madder than a box of spiders."

"Mm-hm. Getting closer."

"So if Masters had it, and Crowley had it, and Tom Thumb had it, *where is it?* There has to be another person!"

"I'd wager someone in the Council probably knows," Dakota playfully sang.

McAllister had already thought of this and slumped to the floor in defeat. "Forget it. I sent Miles to question the Seventh Scholar in Boston, and here I am, holding my dick in my hand."

This comment inspired a delightful cackle from Dakota, receiving a great deal of pleasure from watching her brooding companion withstand so much torment. With McAllister looking close to broken down completely, it was time to get down to the business of offering a solution to his depressing predicament—a solution where she also might get something out of the bargain.

"Mmm, you know," Dakota purred mischievously, "the two of us used to have quite the reputation for coercing sensitive information out of people. If you're willing to put your mind to it, I believe we could take your little Nostradamus routine much further."

Nostradamus routine. She was referring to the scrying ritual that led his former partner in crime straight to him. That was it then? McAllister was tired and frustrated, ready to dismiss whatever was on her mind at this juncture as he gloomily fired up a smoke and rested his head against the wall.

"Dakota, what are you...?"

His face changed after realizing what she was suggesting.

"Wait a second."

"The solution is simple," Dakota said. "To get to the Seventh Scholar, we would simply have to communicate with him in the same manner that's allowing me to communicate with you right now."

"Astral projection," McAllister bluntly acknowledged.

"Only instead of projecting to the real world, we'll stalk him in his dream state. I recall rendezvousing with you more than once in this fashion. Ah, memories."

The suggestion had definite merit, but McAllister remained hesitant, brushing off the plan with a heavy sigh and grabbing his face with his hands.

"Dakota, you know I was never any good at that whole astral business."

"Such a shame too. So well-read but when it comes to doing the real work—"

"Ah, you see? *You see?*" McAllister leaped to his feet. "That's what used to drive me crazy about you! Always riding me about my innumerable 'flaws.' That and, oh yeah—you're fucking crazy."

Dakota cackled with girlish glee at the dramatic display of indignation. Her tone shifted once she'd gotten this out of her system. "This is your chance, baby. To find the missing diary, to discover all the answers you've been searching for. And besides, wouldn't it be nice to spend a little more quality time together? If only for a few fleeting moments..."

A strange wind rustled through McAllister's hair as he considered the proposition. His eyes narrowed, and his face became determined. To execute a successful attempt at astral projection, he would need some assistance. Astral projection was a tricky devil. The key to it was a strong focus and unbreakable concentration; two things he was mostly shit at (as Dakota was so quick to verify). To prepare himself, he needed something that would help improve his focus and get him into the right headspace. So McAllister turned once again to his black steamer trunk, unlocked the snaps, and rustled through the modest selection of books and black clothing until he found what he was looking for: a full bottle of French absinthe.

McAllister next went about preparing the absinthe using a selection of items from the trunk. He poured the green liquor into a glass with the liquid running over a spoon holding a sugar cube. Then, with his gold cigarette lighter, he heated the sugar cube, dumped it into the drink, and chugged it all down in one gulp. With the heady liquid now coursing through his system, he returned to the circle in the center of the room and sat in the lotus position. He pinched his eyelids closed and held his back stiff, focusing on his breathing while chanting a special mantra inside his head.

"Do you have a lock on him?" McAllister asked, gradually entering the meditative state he was aiming for.

"Ugh—for ages," Dakota groaned. "His name is Barry Starlite. Second-rate horror novelist, first-rate prick. Fancies himself a regular Stephen King. Would you hurry up already?"

"Cool your jets, honeycakes. Now I'm warning you, the longest I've been able to hold my concentration in this state is two minutes."

"Then I'll remind myself not to get you too worked up. Lover."

With his body sliding into a state of total relaxation, McAllister took a deep breath as he pictured the material world fading all around him. He began to visualize the world of the empty room he was sitting in, the picture slowly getting clearer from behind his heavy eyelids until he opened his eyes and rose to his feet.

The world around him now looked different.

McAllister's surroundings possessed a strange hazy glow to them, the colors getting darker or brighter depending on his specific frame of perception—like he was standing inside of a finely crafted painting that was constantly changing. Turning around, he noticed he was still sitting in the lotus position and meditating on the floor behind him. It appeared he had done it: his astral form had been temporarily detached from his physical body, and he was now ready to explore the astral plane. It also meant someone was with him.

"Hey, baby."

With a slow turn, McAllister found himself face to face with

Dakota, looking exactly the same as the last time he saw her: red lips, pale skin, a long flowing mane of wavy chestnut-colored hair, her slender hourglass figure squeezed into a highly flattering yet uncommonly old-fashioned violet dress. Most of all, he noticed her wicked smile and mad eyes, her tantalizing constrained chest heaving deliriously while staring at him with feverish intensity. It was a sight one could easily become lost in—something he had been guilty of many times in the past. But with time running out and little to spare, he refused to let temptation get the best of him, his mind solely focused on the job at hand.

"Dakota," McAllister answered vacantly while wearing a detached expression. He watched her raise her arm and offer her hand to him. After taking it, they both turned and faced the window and were spirited into the heavens at a dizzying speed, the attic falling quiet with McAllister's physical body still sitting in the lotus position, deep in concentration.

In McAllister's experience, the astral plane was something that took on many different forms for many different people. For him, it always looked like a dark parallel dimension where everything was covered with black oil and sludge; where there was a notable lack of permanence to the material quality of things and every crevice and contour was constantly morphing and changing.

At that precise moment, he was traveling rapidly with Dakota through a dark and murky void with distorted dream images and visions of nightmares briefly flashing and disappearing in the oily amorphous twilight that surrounded them, their chalky white fingers firmly grasped around one another's as they voyaged further and further into the endless milky black abyss.

Eventually, after journeying for who knows how far or for how long, McAllister felt Dakota give his hand a squeeze. They suddenly descended at great speed, landing in a large formless space. The background all around them shifted like a lava lamp, morphing and flickering intermittently as McAllister blankly observed the pale translucency of his and Dakota's bodies, also glowing and flickering; the two of them both there and not there at the very same time.

"Oh yeah. Oh yeah."

"Oh! Give it to me, Barry!"

While temporarily disoriented, the unfamiliar voices brought McAllister back to his senses. Along with Dakota, he explored the disorienting landscape and discovered a brass bed sitting a few yards away from where they first arrived.

The bed contained a pudgy, middle-aged, balding man having a three-way with two busty alien humanoids wearing Princess Leia slave outfits—a sight McAllister observed with stony indifference. He wasn't shocked to discover their target engaged in something lurid. They had just hacked into Barry's dream-space; if anything, McAllister felt embarrassed by the man's lack of originality.

"Mmm, looks like we walked in on 'Middle School Fantasy Night,'" Dakota blithely commented.

McAllister cracked a wry smirk before offering his own assessment, taking extra care to project his voice loud enough to grab his target's attention.

"What kind of LARP nonsense is this?"

"Holy—what are you doing here?"

Barry started at the intrusion, his face souring instantly as he watched his alien princesses flee into the void's dark outer recesses.

"Oh, nice one. You scared away my Twi'lek love slaves."

"And we're just so broken up about that," Dakota replied facetiously.

In an instant, Barry's crabby disposition changed on a dime as he took a closer look at the two intruders.

"Wait a tick. I know you! You're Emmanuel's spawn! McAllister! Still disappointing your family on a daily basis?"

Barry laughed uproariously at his witty barb. But the moment was short-lived. Wearing an icy scowl, McAllister lunged forward and violently grabbed his throat.

"Enough small talk, Starlite. Where's the diary, shithead?"

McAllister wasn't playing around, but Barry remained unfazed, vanishing into a wave of oily static only to reappear directly behind his two visitors, dressed in a tacky Hugh Heffner-style smoking jacket. This was the astral plane after all, so it wasn't like McAllister could really do anything to harm him, giving Barry all the more reason to act obnoxiously over-confident while making conversation.

"Diary?" Barry mused playfully. "Oh, how splendid. I had a feeling you killed our European counterpart for a reason. What makes you think I'll tell you jack?"

"Tom Thumb, Alfonse Masters, Sir Godfrey's family. What's the connection? Why was Aleister Crowley in Little Salem? *He went there for the diary, didn't he?*"

To McAllister's dismay, Barry didn't bat an eyelash.

"The book's only a legend, my boy. Give it a rest. Uncle Al was probably just vacationing. And between you and me, I wager he enjoyed the place a lot more than Boleskine. Wink wink."

"McAllister."

McAllister turned his attention back to Dakota and noticed her observing him with a solitary eyebrow raised. He looked down and saw that his body was flickering wildly, which meant that back in the real world, his physical incarnation was losing focus and his journey was coming to an end.

"Ho-ho! What's this?" Barry observed, his voice taking on an air of mocking superiority. "Having a little trouble with your concentration there, young magus? I think it's time to say bye-bye. Of course, your charming high-end escort is free to stay."

"In your dreams, baby," Dakota replied dismissively.

The man was insufferable, but his observation was correct. Realizing he was out of time and wouldn't be getting any further in his cross-examination, McAllister took Dakota by the hand and flashed a disdainful sneer at his enemy.

"Nice chat, Barry," McAllister said. "I'll be seeing you soon in the real world. When I fucking kill you."

The astral bodies of the two interlopers were suddenly ripped away and sucked back into the void, leaving Barry all alone in the shapeless emptiness as an unsettled expression crept upon his face.

"Well, there goes my erection."

Back in Little Salem, McAllister's physical incarnation remained sitting in the lotus position, his eyes snapping open and his body violently falling backward from the force of his astral form returning to the material realm.

Lying on his back, McAllister panted for breath, feeling dazed and disoriented; struggling to direct all of his energies to the task of processing all Barry had said to him. This would have to wait as his fevered thoughts and musings were interrupted by an eerie silence that seemed to blanket the room before a familiar voice cut through the stillness and began echoing all around him.

"You remember now, don't you?" the sultry voice cooed. "All the fun times we had in Europe?"

Slowly returning to his senses, McAllister sat up and glanced at the Tibetan singing bowl now sitting at his feet. In the water, Dakota's reflection was gazing back at him, looking sinfully seductive and beautiful as ever and yet also sad and lonesome, with a strong, heartfelt longing behind her tempting bughouse stare.

"Life's not as much fun when it's not you and me."

Whether this was true or not was something McAllister declined to give any further thought. Part of him still felt bound to his former paramour, but he knew his heart was irrefutably bound to another and that, ultimately, their relationship was ancient history.

Dakota was someone who brought out the worst in McAllister, and the world was probably a much better place to live in with the two of them miles apart. This is why, along with several other significant factors, despite the lingering nostalgia and a nagging fondness for this beguiling creature once so deliriously beloved by him; the witty and playful yet also dangerous and irredeemably unhinged Dakota Crawford who had seen so much of herself in McAllister just as he'd seen so much of himself in her during their monstrously degenerate affair for the ages—this is why it was easy for him to turn his back on her forever, staggering to the trap door and making his exit as Dakota's lovely reflection rippled in the water of the singing bowl and slowly faded away.

Perhaps they would see each other in another lifetime and resume their torrid relationship. Or perhaps McAllister would surprise himself by showing he had enough strength to walk away from such a catastrophe.

46

HEY, MR. CROWLEY

After leaving the attic and his adventure on the astral plane, McAllister slumped downstairs, feeling worn-out and on edge.

If only Ada were there. She may not have been as deep into this whole diary business as he was, but her exceptional cleverness and natural gift of intuition would have been a great help. McAllister assumed she was still recuperating. After the fiasco at the chemical plant, she likely needed rest more than anything, and he was so consumed with his own misery at this point, he was convinced he was all on his own when it came to his special project.

At this point, McAllister had all but forgotten there were others at the tavern beside him, not expecting to find Agatha and Lucy huddled in a booth together. Something was no doubt causing them to be restless and wide awake at this wretched hour. For Lucy, she was still deeply disturbed by the actions of her father, the traumatic past few days filling her head with nightmares. For Agatha, on top of feeling run down and physically sore, she was a ball of scattered mixed emotions, the girls intimately engaged in discussing their present anxieties when McAllister entered the room, looking tense and agitated.

"Are you OK, baby?" Agatha asked him.

The affectionate term of endearment caused McAllister to twitch reflexively. He quickly pushed Dakota out of his head as he crossed behind the bar and grabbed a bottle of beer from the fridge.

"This diary thing is driving me crazy," McAllister said.

"What's bothering you about it?" Agatha responded warmly.

Agatha appeared deeply engaged in this discussion, but Lucy was looking doe-eyed and confused. Lucy didn't know the first thing about the search for the diary and knew very little when it came to deeply polarizing subjects like magic and the occult. With the exception of her haunting demonic visions, she'd grown up living a very sheltered existence, and in her family, magic and witchcraft had always been viewed as wicked and tools of the devil.

Naturally, the past twenty-four hours had changed everything: Lucy was now in deep with the coven that had graciously opened its arms to her. And McAllister was running out of time, so it wasn't like he really cared if some dotty high school cheerleader was present to observe his internal thought process.

"Crowley had it. *He had it.*" McAllister struggled to open the beer bottle in his overly excited state. "That's why he came to Little Salem. But he never mentions it. Not in his diaries or his private confessions? The man recorded everything. *He recorded everything!*"

McAllister threw the bottle against the wall, causing the object to shatter and Lucy to practically jump out of her skin.

It was true: Crowley's vanity and infamous sense of self-importance had compelled him to keep detailed personal records throughout his wildly fascinating life. He'd written an autobiography (what he called an "autohagiography") and kept comprehensive confessions and private journals—not to mention there were scores of biographies written about him, many of which McAllister had read. McAllister knew the dates Crowley had visited the United States and the date the diary went missing appeared to match up in theory, but there were no written records of Crowley ever visiting Little Salem. This matter deeply perplexed him. Without the presence of the copy of *Tannhauser* and Barry's confirmation of Uncle Al's dubious whereabouts, he would have thought the rumors of his visit were a fabrication and he was on the wrong track altogether.

Lucy lacked any detailed knowledge on the man, and upon mention of the notorious figure, she turned to Agatha, keeping her voice to a hushed whisper.

"Is this Aleister Crowley, the devil worshipper?"

Agatha gave Lucy a dismissive gesture, knowing that now wasn't the time for a lengthy lesson on controversial historical mages. Swallowing her emotions, she directed her attention to the man who continued to perplex her regarding whether he was still her lover and continued to share any affection for her.

"Any other reason he would come here?"

"Yeah. A man told me he liked the area more than Boleskine."

"Crowley's place next to Loch Ness. What was so bad about Boleskine?"

"Crowley said the town around it had a prostitute problem. Because there wasn't any."

McAllister cracked open a fresh bottle of beer and had a sip as Agatha smiled with amusement.

"Probably visited his fair share of brothels then."

McAllister nodded ambivalently, knowing there was no doubt to be found in this observation. If there were any brothels around, then Crowley most likely would have... Wait a second.

He felt his body burning up as he realized what a fool he'd been, glancing around the room at the historically preserved brothel they were conversing in.

Moments later, the search was back on, and McAllister was racing up the stairs with Agatha and Lucy close behind him. He was talking a mile a minute, offering a quick summation of everything Crowley was up to before moving to America at the beginning of the First World War.

"Crowley was deep into the occult at this point," McAllister explained. "He'd dropped out of the Golden Dawn, channeled *The Book of the Law*, revolutionized the ritual applications of Enochian magic while he was in Mexico and Algeria. *The Vision and the Voice*, all those crazy things he saw in the desert—"

"Sorry, hold on," Lucy interrupted. "Enochian what?"

McAllister didn't have time to go into the details. There was just no use trying to explain to her how two Elizabethan magicians held a series of magical evocations where they spoke to beings calling themselves "angels," and, in turn, received powerful occult knowledge from these so-called "angels." No, it would have been a waste of time trying to discuss all this with a normal.

Lucy was still a novice when it came to this world, and she had a lot to learn. In response to her question, McAllister explained that "Enochian" was the system of magic received by John Dee and Edward Kelley and left it at that. There was no use overwhelming the poor thing at such an early stage in her education. If she showed any interest in learning more at a more appropriate occasion, he would be more than happy to oblige.

In the meantime, McAllister was on a mission to learn as much as possible about the origins of the brothel prior to its recent series of transformations. As he searched through the drawers in Agatha's bedchamber, Agatha, who had originally been assigned by Ada to prepare the property for the coven's eventual takeover, reviewed a collection of files she used to secure the tavern's purchase and approval for preservation from the city—something that was gained in no small part through her uniquely irresistible charms.

McAllister was pouring over a folder of documents with Agatha and Lucy positioned nearby, doing the same. "When did your ancestor originally come into possession of this place?"

"The property passed over to her in an inheritance," Agatha answered, right before locating a document that had a black and white picture of a pretty blonde turn of the century woman clipped to the page. The name on the document read "Eleanor Malone," and Agatha got more than a little sentimental when viewing the old photograph due to the striking physical similarities they shared.

"Inherited from...Alfonse Masters," Agatha muttered.

McAllister snatched up the document and scanned the contents. "She was his mistress. Where did she live before?"

"I visited there as a kid. An old bordello hidden in the woods."

"Take me there."

In no time at all, Agatha was dressed in a killer red designer dress, coat, and heels, ready to take off on an exciting adventure. The thrill of the chase had picked up her spirits immensely, and Lucy watched starry-eyed from the doorway as she joined McAllister outside next to the convertible, now wearing his tattered black military overcoat and tossing a heavy black duffle into the trunk.

"McAllister, tell me, 'cause I'm a bit lost," Agatha said, picking at her hair absentmindedly. "What does all of this have to do with the Engelander Diary?"

McAllister slammed the trunk and pitched her the car keys.

"Drive fast, and I'll explain everything."

Feeling wholly revived and powered by adrenaline, the dashing and fetching pair climbed into the dusty Cadillac DeVille and took off like a bat out of hell—a sight that Ada herself would witness with a puzzled expression while walking down the main drag, her slender frame draped in a Navaho blanket.

While racing through the empty dimly lit streets, McAllister explained why Aleister Crowley would be so eager to get his grimy paws on the diary. The key to this was Edward Kelley. Agatha already had some idea of the diary's contents. She knew it was rumored to possess information having to do with Enochian magic and held a tentative association with the two Elizabethan mages that were presented with this magical system.

"Crowley always had a special fondness for Kelley," McAllister explained. "He even thought he was Kelley in a past life. Any work of Kelley's would have been of great importance to him."

"To find and add to his own trunk of books," Agatha noted.

"While he was in America," McAllister continued, "Crowley was experimenting with a lot of hard drugs and sex magic."

"Kinky."

"If Crowley was in town at the time that I think he was," he started to say, and Agatha finished the sentence for him, "—then the bordello would have ranked pretty high on his sight-seeing list."

Agatha stepped on the gas and turned the wheel hard to the left, merging onto a secluded dirt road and propelling them deep into the heart of the forest where their destination awaited them.

In addition to what he had told her, McAllister also harbored other suspicions about Crowley for the handful of years he was living in the United States. In 1916, Crowley took a "magical retirement" at an isolated cabin in New Hampshire, and after performing a particular ritual under heavy use of drugs, he proclaimed himself "*Master Therion*," a strange vision convincing him he had reached a higher state of consciousness and initiation. McAllister always suspected that something unrecorded in Crowley's diaries must have assisted him in achieving this state and entertained the possibility that the forbidden knowledge he gained when the diary was in his possession could have accounted for this.

At the same time, losing such a priceless and significant magical text would have been a huge embarrassment. He assumed this was the reason why Crowley never mentioned coming into possession of the item, as opposed to the possibility of wanting to keep the diary's existence a secret (the man definitely wasn't immune to vanity).

While McAllister stared with intensity at the dark and desolate road in front of him, he pondered all that had led him to the current moment, from the faint whispers hinting at the diary's existence to Crowley's rumored possession of the text to the tales about the Man In Black and the testimony of Tom Thumb and others. He recalled the bloody interrogation that revealed to him the diary's location and how this initiated his return to Little Salem, his renewed relationship with Agatha, and most significantly, his long-awaited reunion with Ada. Miles had been instrumental in obtaining the clues confirming the diary's last known whereabouts, and so had Dakota, Rudy, Agatha, and also Izzy, tragically enough.

Contrary to his earlier examination, the investigation hadn't been a lonely endeavor at all. So many people had contributed, and now, with only one place left to search before running out of steam completely, he felt confident he was so close to attaining his coveted prize he could already feel it in his grasp.

When Agatha braked hard outside the tumbledown Edwardian home, they encountered a strange feeling. A powerful strain of magic was in the air, and they were at a place of great significance.

"It's here," McAllister muttered while staring at the ruins in front of them. The comment inspired Agatha's lips to quiver, knowing that the object at the heart of their search was somewhere inside.

47

MISSING KITTENS

It was late at night, and the streets were quiet and empty when Nancy's trusty Volvo parked outside the frozen yogurt shop. She had scoured the woods from dusk to almost dawn, but her search for her daughter had ended in failure. And to top it all off, thanks to her earlier conversation, her mind was now reminiscing and was once again fixated on the notorious teenage witch, Ada van Dreyer.

Back when Nancy first met Ada, her short time spent with the charming bright-eyed young thing had inspired her to question everything. The craft was so strong with Ada that their initial interactions allowed her to see the world in a dazzling new light, granting her a more thoughtful examination of various personal choices in her life and in her magical practice. But when Ada had urged Nancy to become a powerful force of change by challenging those who were upholding the illusory sense of peace and order in Little Salem, she had resisted. Nancy was someone who greatly benefited from things staying the same in her community and didn't want to rock the boat out of fear that she might risk losing everything.

Ada had no reluctance when it came to upsetting the established order of things, and this is what led to their falling out. Nancy initially suffered a fair amount of regret for her decisions, given how much she cherished her time spent with Ada, but over time, these feelings started to evolve and take on a new life altogether. While she at first felt a strong sense of doubt and insecurity over this lost relationship, her feelings eventually transformed into a toxic mixture of defensive self-righteousness and a fervent unwavering advocacy for the preeminent powers that be in Little Salem, turning her into the head cheerleader for all that Ada found so disagreeable and necessary to rebel against in the first place.

This behavior on her part was, of course, all the more bewildering given that Nancy did hold some major qualms with those that held powerful sway over the town. But to protect her bruised ego, she steadily moved closer to the side of her adversaries and routinely turned a blind eye to her own grievances if they had anything to do with the offenses that Ada so openly opposed. This made it no surprise that Nancy would often feel at odds with herself and had a severe impact on her identity as a witch. For centuries, witches had always been categorized as "the other"—the opposition to the established order that man built so clumsily around the wild and unruly world of Mother Nature. It remained highly questionable how Nancy was providing a healthy opposition to these forces by trying to fit in like a good little changeling and siding with the enemy. The unfortunate answer to this was she wasn't, and Nancy knew this, transforming all of her witchy abilities into little more than a game of holiday dress-up—a shallow female power fantasy for bored and privileged suburbanites. As a witch, this made her weak and feckless and distanced herself from the wisdom and natural energies that gave her kind power to begin with. And at the end of the day, she only had herself to blame for this.

In retaliation to this regrettable state of affairs, Nancy continued to hate Ada more and more each day, doubling down repeatedly on the prideful defense of her own weakness and scorning the one who made her question herself—even if the ultimate question staring right back at her was whether she even deserved to call herself a witch in the first place. Most days, Nancy tried to avoid entertaining these painful evaluations, but now, given all that had happened, she was feeling overwhelmed. Her mind was wrought with uncertainty. She wondered if perhaps the answer for why Ada was so skilled at seducing others and was perceived as such a marvel to people was because her personal perception of the world happened to hold the most enlightened truth to it, while imposters and pretenders like herself were out there selfishly chasing pure fantasy.

All these thoughts about the past were weighing Nancy down and lowering her spirits when she unlocked the door to the yogurt shop and flicked on the blinding fluorescents. She was searching for something to distract herself from the plague of regret and self-criticism, setting her purse on the front counter before going through all of her usual preparations for tidying up the shop.

For a while, a little hard work and elbow grease seemed to do just the trick. While scrubbing the tile, she found herself imagining she was using the brush to scrub Little Miss Ada out of her life forever. But while tending to Baby Blue out back, her mind returned to Mary Sue. When the pony nuzzled her neck, seeming to sense her inner turmoil, her lips started to quiver, and her eyes filled with tears. She knew her daughter's disappearance was just the beginning of the punishing repercussions she would suffer for casting her malefic spell. If anything happened to her on account of her persistent arrogance in the war with her former protégé, she knew she would never forgive herself.

With her perfect life in tatters, what happened next would take her totally by surprise. When Nancy re-entered the shop, she was distracted with drying her eyes and thinking about her missing child. She glanced toward the front, and her body froze.

There, sitting at a table in the corner was Ada (speak of the devil), clothed only in a Navaho blanket and gazing at her reflection in the front window. As she sat there motionless with her wild dark hair and uncanny eyes, Nancy couldn't help feeling that Ada looked like a fallen angel that was plucked from the sky and planted amid the bright and immaculate scenery. She found herself just as startled by Ada's appearance as when she saw her in the church, still blown away by how much she had grown and the strange alien beauty she'd taken on as her body matured into a young woman.

While Nancy silently debated how she should react to her deadly rival's sudden appearance, Ada lazily took notice of her reflection in the glass and smiled sleepily in her direction.

"Have you seen my cat? She keeps disappearing."

The question startled Nancy. It definitely wasn't what she was expecting. "No. No, I haven't."

An awkward silence followed as both women continued to stare at each other, waiting for the other one to speak. Eventually, Ada smiled coyly, her playful words severing the tension between them.

"Little late to be serving snow cones, don't you think?"

"I was in the area. Work helps keep my mind off of things."

Nancy's response was sharp and brusque. She immediately looked away to return to busying herself behind the counter. She didn't want Ada to see all of the turbulent emotions she was experiencing; the toxic mixture of fear, anger, and pride that was driving all of her actions of late. But Nancy could feel Ada's eyes studying her intently and knew she could read her like a book. It was useless trying to hide anything from her—the damn prodigy.

After coming to accept this, Nancy decided to employ an entirely different strategy by telling the nauseating wonder-child exactly what was on her mind for a change, albeit in a manner that was decisively passive-aggressive and petty.

"Actually," Nancy declared bitterly, "I've been looking for something too. My daughter. Have you seen her?"

In all honesty, she was desperately seeking Ada's help at this moment. Ada seemed to ignore Nancy's concerns, offering her reply while smiling impishly.

"Have you checked her bed?"

"Funny."

Nancy regretted she even bothered to ask, but Ada wasn't finished. She stretched out her neck and cocked her head while studying the meticulous hand-drawn menu above the front counter.

"I used to disappear for days when I was her age," Ada said. "Always threatening my parents I was going to run away to Europe. Back then, my mother did something I could never forgive her for. But I always came back home afterward. Until one day, I didn't. The day I turned eighteen, I left home forever and never looked back."

Ada turned her head and directed her huge, dazzling eyes to Nancy, a sad, detached seriousness sparkling within them.

"Some people are beyond forgiveness," Ada said.

Nancy stared back at her former pupil, mystified but not wanting to show it. "Really? Is that what you believe?"

She returned to scrubbing the counter, and Ada gave a sad smile and turned away from her. "Keep looking, and you'll find her," Ada said. "But don't be surprised if the one you find isn't the same as the one you seek."

After this, Ada rose to her feet to take leave of her company.

But Nancy wasn't going to let her off that easily.

"You know, you always were too smart for your own good."

Ada didn't seem thrown off at all by this comment and merely paused at the door before flashing her impish grin at her former would-be teacher and mentor.

"I think I've been too hard on you, Nancy," Ada said. "All this time you've been trying to protect the ones you love, and I've been doing the same. I suppose we're more alike than one might think."

"That I'm not so sure," Nancy dryly asserted.

"No, maybe not," Ada conceded. "And love is a battlefield. Or so they say. Goodnight, Nancy."

After saying all she cared to say, Ada left the cozy warm glow of the frozen yogurt store and exited into the moody moonlit darkness outside. It was at that moment that Nancy suddenly realized this was the longest conversation they'd shared in five years and were unlikely to have another interaction like this ever again. This realization made her feel consumed by a profound sense of loss and sadness. As she watched the young witch make her departure, she secretly longed for a more prolonged conversation between them.

Ada had meant so much to her back then. To the point that she gave her the desire to have a daughter just like her. Now they were mortal enemies, and there was nothing that would change this. Past was prologue, and the events that damaged things were already set in stone. Nancy just hoped she hadn't also ruined her relationship with Mary Sue in a similar fashion.

Later, when Nancy returned to her once happy suburban home with the remnants of the burnt pentagram still scarred into the front lawn, the quiet streets were becoming flooded with a welcome early morning haze; sure signs that the sun was about to rise and another day was about to begin. The warm and blissful sight was truly a marvel to behold and so perfectly serene that if she had been feeling more like her usual self, she would have felt overwhelmed by the moment; a special reminder of why she felt so fortunate to have a home to call her own in Little Salem of all places. But for the time being, the world was absent of beauty for Nancy. After parking her car in the driveway and entering the front door, she headed for the stairs toward the restless sleep that awaited her.

Her daughter hated her, Nancy reasoned. That was the real reason why she hadn't returned home. She had permanently blown it as a loving parent, and now she'd have to live with the consequences.

While slumping down the hallway, Nancy remembered Ada's words and decided to peek into her daughter's bedroom, not expecting to find anything unusual or anything that was out of place. She was absolutely certain there was nothing to anything Ada had told her, but as soon as she glanced inside, her body froze, and her heartbeat started racing.

Her daughter had returned to her bed, just as Ada predicted.

How did Ada know? And everything else she had told her...

How did Ada know?

After begging the question, Nancy pushed Ada out of her mind so she could place all of her focus on Mary Sue, who was lying huddled in the fetal position, quietly sobbing in the darkened room.

Nancy was still feeling unsure about how to face her, remembering what her daughter said to her during the heated fight between them and the way she stormed off in a rage after having the final word. And yet, all this would be inconsequential in a few short moments. While her thoughts were racing, they were interrupted by the soft, tearful voice of her loved one, having already sensed her mother's presence in the doorway at some point.

"The Izzy we knew is no longer with us," Mary Sue quietly said. "All of the wonderful things she had to give to the world and the shining brightness inside of her have gone away."

Not knowing how to react, Nancy's eyes were drawn to Mary Sue's drawing of Izzy, which had been removed from the wall and was lying on the bed beside her. She still lacked the confidence regarding what she should do in this situation and hesitantly approached the bed, taking a seat as her melancholy daughter kept her face hidden.

"It's not fair," Mary Sue said. "She was my friend. I was in love with her."

Following this admission, Mary Sue began bawling, and Nancy held her in her arms with her daughter hugging her back as she sobbed into her mother's chest.

Nancy was in a state of shock.

Her daughter was in love with another girl? And a witch to boot?

Had she been attracted to other girls this whole time while her own mother, *white witch extraordinaire*, hadn't even happened to notice this?

Nancy was now seeing her daughter in a whole new light. And what was it that Ada said? Something about how not to be surprised if her child was someone completely different than what she thought she was?

God damn it.

Ada had made a fool of her again.

* * *

When Ada left the frozen yogurt shop, she walked across the street to the sublime warmth of the magnificently morbid Black Death Tavern, smiling dreamily. For Ada, the night made her feel alive and was like a close friend that loved her dearly. When the stars were shining above her, she felt captivated by their presence and always felt right at home.

Still, Ada was feeling a bit worn to the bone on account of her recent adventures and was looking forward to catching some Z's in her own bed for a change. With thoughts of dreamland on her mind, she was about to walk up the front steps when her ears perked up at a faint "*mew*" coming from close by.

Ada's bright, otherworldly eyes began searching around her until her gaze eventually landed on her little black kitten sitting next to an open grate that led to underneath the historic Victorian residence.

"There you are," Ada remarked. She picked up the tiny purring feline and nuzzled her close to her face. "You weren't lost. You were waiting for me all along."

With her precious familiar back in her arms, Ada looked up to the heavens, smiling at the starry cosmic canopy above her.

Nancy couldn't help feeling more disillusioned with life and her current place in the universe, but Ada continued to approach her existence with wonder; marveling at the dazzling majesty of a world she felt so privileged to have a place in. And Ada knew that the following evening the moon would be full and the time would arrive to finish what she had come to Little Salem to accomplish. For on that evening, the spirits would be out and there would be great mischief, and the streets would be red with blood before the night was through. At least, all this would be true if the notorious teenage witch, Ada van Dreyer, had anything to do with it.

48

DANGEROUS EVOCATIONS

———————

When Agatha reached the bordello, she had no idea what McAllister figured they'd do next. They suspected the diary was somewhere in the decaying two-story structure in front of them, but in a building that large, something that was hidden was likely to remain hidden unless a person knew exactly where to look. This is where the second part of McAllister's plan came into the equation, which involved finding the book with the assistance of magic—and also recreational chemicals since they were in a hurry.

A rock song crooning about leather and licentious behavior played on the stereo as McAllister used a stolen bank card to cut a series of lines of white powder on a small hand mirror. He'd already explained to Agatha his heavy expectations should they choose to execute his plan to the letter and could likely sense her hesitation as she watched him snort a line and pass the mirror her way.

"You don't have to do this if you don't want to," McAllister reminded her. Agatha's turbulent history was well known to him. The abuse she had suffered, her problems with drugs and addiction—the whole nine yards. The last thing he wanted was for her to suffer a relapse or find herself drawn back to dangerous habits just to get his hands on a silly priceless artifact, no matter how much possessing the diary meant to him.

But Agatha could see how eager McAllister was to obtain his coveted prize. Plus, she was feeling closer to him than she had felt in days. Their relationship had been on such tumultuous ground lately, and the look in her lover's eyes told her he wanted her and needed her more than ever, the combination of these factors eventually inspiring her to lower her head and take the plunge.

"Woo! God damn!" Agatha exclaimed after a long sniff. "We have lift-off."

McAllister smiled devilishly at the spirited exclamation, and they each filled both nostrils and exited the vehicle. After grabbing his black duffle from the trunk, he wrapped a loving arm around Agatha's waist, and they entered the abandoned setting. Inside was like another world. Since the brothel's closure, it had been fully taken over by the forest, with thick vines and knotted roots springing out of the cracks in the walls and ceiling. Any sign of a seductive past had vanished, but the natural world outside seemed to be giving the former den of iniquity new life as it slowly swallowed it whole.

Agatha was in awe of the way the forest had transformed the building. She cautiously wandered into the main room, using the flashlight setting on her smartphone to guide her as she stepped over the endless clutter of debris and decaying matter. When McAllister set the black duffle on the floor, they quickly went to work, setting up four white candles and drawing a large circle on a part of the floor that had been cleared of obstructions. Once the stage was set, the pair stood inside the circle, and McAllister performed a banishing rit-ual with both of them mirroring each other's gestures.

"*Kaos. Babalon. Eros. Psyche. IO Pan.*"

With the initial preparations out of the way, they took each other's hands and sat on the floor. Now it was time for Agatha to per-form her role in the ceremony. The black and white photo of Eleanor Malone was placed in front of her, along with several of Eleanor's possessions; the deed to the brothel, an old hairbrush, a scatter of personal letters. Agatha focused on each of these, and after taking them into her hands and offering a lengthy petition to the Goddess, she closed her eyes and began to rock her body back and forth, mut-tering a powerful incantation as she steadily slipped into a trance.

"*By earth and fire and water and smoke, Eleanor Malone do I evoke. By earth and fire and water and smoke, Eleanor Malone do I evoke. By earth and fire and water and smoke, Eleanor Malone do I evoke. By earth and fire and water and smoke, Eleanor Malone do I evoke—*"

McAllister watched stone-faced as Agatha bent her body for-ward and backward, again and again, her chanting starting soft and low but getting louder and faster with each impassioned appeal; her movements becoming sharper and more rapturously erratic as the magic started to take hold.

After carrying on with this behavior for quite some time, Agatha abruptly fell silent, and her body dropped to the floor. McAllister remained without expression, waiting with anticipation as her body suddenly sprung back up with her eyes pressed shut and her mouth breathing short, heaving breaths.

Agatha's head started turning from left to right, taking in the sur-roundings as if she were somehow able to experience them without seeing anything at all. What she was seeing was a different setting altogether: what the bordello once looked like during its glory days, viewing it painted in front of her plain as day.

The tiled floor was polished and free of clutter, and the paper on the walls looked vibrant and elegant, now totally free of mold and the suffocating vegetation from the forest. As she blinked her eyes open, the images of the past only became brighter and in sharper focus. But what was most startling was she could now see a blonde-haired "lady of the evening" in stylish turn of the century fashions as she entered the room and crossed past the place of their ritual.

"I see her!" Agatha gasped. "My great-great-grandmother."

The revelation was extraordinary, but before McAllister could react to their stunning achievement, Agatha leaped to her feet and left the boundaries of the protective circle to follow her departed ancestor further into the room. More pieces of the past came into focus the closer she was to Eleanor's ghostly presence and faded in an instant or appeared more muddled the farther she was from her.

As Agatha continued to observe the unusual occurrences, she discovered Eleanor approaching a tall, handsomely dressed man on a plush velvet-cushioned couch, quickly rising to his feet to greet her.

"She's with another man. I think it's Crowley."

Agatha watched the man kiss Eleanor's hand, taking into account his thinning hairline and hawkish features. Crowley was still a relatively young man at this point and not the balding steely-eyed magus that would later characterize how he'd be remembered by history. And yet the features were unmistakable.

"Yes, it's him!" Agatha exclaimed, her chest rising and falling, becoming more and more thrilled by the remarkable events she was witnessing. "They're going upstairs. I'm going to follow them."

Agatha rushed up the staircase and McAllister rose to his feet, retrieving the black duffle and throwing it over his shoulder, his eyes filled with intrigue.

The stairs were falling apart and being steadily consumed by the forest like everything else in the building, with the upper floor in very much the same condition but in a much more hazardous state. Parts of the floorboards had rotted away, and the roof in several rooms had collapsed. But for Agatha, the brothel still appeared in its prime as she followed her ancestor to a room at the far end of the hallway with McAllister trailing behind her.

"This was her room."

When McAllister peered inside, he saw nothing that was unexpected: It was a bare room stripped of furniture with a dirty wooden floor and large rectangular windows in heavy disrepair. Agatha was witnessing something else entirely: She saw a lavish bedchamber decorated with exotic trinkets and gifts from the Far East. A pair of fleshy bodies were lying half-naked in bed together post-coitus, both parties looking sleepy and a little bit stoned.

"They're asleep now," Agatha explained. "Or—no, there's some opium on the nightstand. They're... Wait!"

That's when she saw it—an old leather-bound book sitting next to the opium pipe.

"The book. It's here!"

Agatha was panting with disbelief when she began to witness a series of events that were even more surprising, struggling to describe in detail all she was seeing.

"I see another man."

"There's a struggle."

"It's Tom Thumb. He wants the book!"

"Crowley's been knocked out."

"Tom. He has it now."

"He's leaving."

"Eleanor's going after him. I'm going to follow them."

With the brief melodrama concluded, Agatha fled the room with McAllister slowly following after her, so far pleased and somewhat amazed by the impressively potent results of their ritual.

When Agatha reached the bottom of the stairs, she spied her ancestor's apparition adjusting her robe and exiting the bordello.

"They're going outside. They're heading for the woods."

McAllister remained calm and aloof while trailing several steps behind her. But for Agatha, the situation seemed to be getting more bizarre by the second. It was one thing to observe a residual event involving her ancestor in a place that had a strong connection to her body and spirit, but the event was now stretching itself out to the point that it involved a chase on foot through the forest—like a bad acid trip that had started off much stronger than anticipated and had already gone on for much longer than desired.

However, Agatha chose to hang in there, now more wrapped up in this daunting mystery than ever as she trudged across the uneven ground, the gnarled branches of the trees casting nightmarish shadows all around her while in pursuit of the flickering phantoms drawing her deeper into the heart of the forest.

"Tom entered this clearing," Agatha explained. Her eyes glanced back at McAllister, but a sudden noise drew them back forward. "*What was that?*"

Like at the bordello, McAllister couldn't see any of the visions Agatha was experiencing, only able to follow what was going on by listening to her breathlessly delivered running commentary. When she let loose a piercing scream, he had no idea of the cause for this, trying to piece the picture of past events together from the fragments of panicked observations.

"He—he saw them. Those things that drove him crazy."

"*Eleanor, don't!*"

"They... They didn't harm her."

"They gave her a gift. She understands now."

"Eleanor has the book. She needs to hide it."

"She's heading back to the bordello."

Agatha turned on her heels, hurrying after the apparition, and McAllister, wearing a crooked smile, followed in her wake. Based on her descriptions, it sounded like she witnessed Mr. Thumb's lamentable encounter with the Mysterious Ones—the event that had driven him barking mad. It was a bit surprising to learn that Miss Malone experienced her own encounter and managed to retain her sanity. Still, this was Agatha's ancestor, so the outcome wasn't too shocking.

Regrettably, this strange spiritual connection did have its limits, and McAllister was unaware that the visions Agatha was seeing were starting to flicker like a candle in the wind. She feared that her playtime with the spirit world was coming to a close—a suspicion that was confirmed once her ancestor re-entered the bordello.

"No! Don't leave me!" Agatha begged. "Not yet!"

The somber plea was genuine and was followed by something astonishing: Eleanor's apparition turned and smiled at her future descendant before vanishing.

"She's gone. I can't see her anymore."

Agatha was startled to discover that tears were forming behind her eyelids, the brief moment of contact with her family history proving a much more moving and emotional ordeal than she expected. But Agatha knew that now wasn't the time for getting sentimental. She could feel McAllister watching her, waiting patiently for her to reveal where Eleanor had placed the book. They were so close, and McAllister needed her—needed her and was relying on her.

Receiving a second wind, Agatha clenched her jaw and rushed back inside, no longer bestowed with the decadent visions of the past but feeling the lingering presence of her ancestor. She knew if she trusted her instincts, her rapidly beating heart would guide her.

Moments later, Agatha stood panting for breath in Eleanor's old bedroom with McAllister standing beside her.

"I think it's in here. I'm not sure."

McAllister set down the heavy duffle and observed the room.

"I know it's here," Agatha insisted, her eyes darting all around her before being drawn to a spot on the floorboards beneath their feet. "Where we're standing. Right here."

With that, McAllister smiled devilishly, and it was time to get down to business. He removed a sledgehammer from his hefty carryall and placed a hand on Agatha's hip, helping her to the side before directing his focus to the floorboards. He raised the heavy instrument and smashed the floor to pieces.

In no time at all, a gaping black hole had been hammered into the floor, and he tossed the sledgehammer to the side. He dropped to his knees as Agatha stood close by, waiting with bated breath.

His arm disappeared into the hole and felt around...

Nothing.

Nothing.

So far, he felt nothing, and his frustration was building when suddenly... Something—something brushing against his fingertips. He stretched out his arm as far as he could and pulled out a small rectangular object wrapped with an oilcloth.

Agatha placed her back against the wall, chest heaving, as McAllister unwrapped their discovery, revealing an old leather-bound book that exuded a powerful aura of unparalleled proportions. An audible gasp escaped her lips as she watched his eyes light up at the sight.

They found it. The Lost Diary of Engelander.

McAllister had been right all along about its existence, and the confirmation made his thought process turn feverish. He bristled with excitement, and a twisted grin swarmed elegantly across his pallid face.

Moments later, McAllister and Agatha were rushing down the stairs hand in hand, laughing like a pair of naughty teenagers. Agatha's wishes had been fulfilled: helping McAllister locate the book had strengthened the bond between them, and this inspired her to smile brightly as they hustled out the front door.

However, Agatha's smile would disappear once they made it outside and were confronted by an adversary they never expected.

"Hold it right there."

Several yards away stood Ruth, one of the senior members of the Sisterhood of Circe. Instead of the coven's white witch's robes, she wore a long black cloak and held a .44 Magnum.

"The book. Hand it over."

Not intimidated in the slightest, McAllister took a defiant step forward.

"I wouldn't make another move if I were you," Ruth warned. "You and your sister might be bulletproof, but I know for a fact your redheaded slut is not. Now hand the book over, and she may have a few more years of whoring left."

"Geez. All the slut-shaming in this town," Agatha groaned. "I thought New England was supposed to be progressive."

"Silence! Enough chatter! Hand it over!"

Agatha glanced at McAllister, feeling guilty that her presence was putting his plans in jeopardy. Her spirits falling, she watched him toss the book to the dirt, inches from Ruth's feet.

"Smart move," the woman said. "Now, she's coming with me."

"As if!" Agatha objected, hugging her lover beside her.

"Insurance policy," Ruth icily stated, her eyes fixed on the scornful vision in black staring her down. "So you don't sneak up and slaughter me before I return to Godfrey's. I know your games."

"But what if I don't want to take a ride with you?" Agatha whined. "Hateful old hags make me carsick."

"Shut it! If I wasn't going to get such pleasure out of killing you later, I'd shoot you dead right now. Hurry up!"

Agatha felt McAllister's body grow increasingly tense as he continued to glower at his opponent. She clutched onto him even tighter, not wishing to be separated when their stormy relationship felt like it was finally back on solid ground.

"If you touch her..." McAllister said.

"You'll what?" Ruth boldly scoffed. "I am a Dark Mother of the Scarlet Council, and the Scarlet Council owns this town! You, your cursed stepsister, the Lords or Light or whatever you call yourselves—you'll never win! And we will watch you *die* and do so with *pleasure* because no matter how hard you try or how close you get, you will *never ever* defeat us! Not in a million years! *Do you hear me? Your kind will never*—"

Crunch.

The sound of dead leaves underfoot startled Ruth. But by the time she spun around, it was already too late. She was so wrapped up in her impressive speech she neglected to notice her hostages briefly glance over at the shadowy figure slowly sneaking up behind her—a figure wearing dirt-stained overalls with a clumsy makeshift mask covering his face.

Before she had time to react, the man's massive hands lunged forward, snapping Ruth's neck in an instant and twisting her head so hard her skull practically spun around her body twice before following the bag of bones it sat upon to the dusty ground.

The gruesome murder was over in an instant, and with their reviled opposition finally out of the picture, McAllister rolled his eyes with annoyance.

"Finally." McAllister nodded to their mysterious ally on his way to reclaim his precious plunder. "Thanks, masked stranger. If you don't mind—"

"Mistress Agatha..."

Agatha's eyes narrowed in recognition of the voice. "Sanchez?"

Her savior knelt on the forest floor in front of her with his head humbly bowed in consolation. "I'm sorry," he confessed nervously. "I was led astray by others. I never meant to bring you harm. Please accept my apology."

In all honesty, Agatha was caught off-guard by the request. The frightening ordeal at the slaughterhouse was still fresh in her mind, and it would take her a few moments to realize that Ruth was most likely the one to influence the gentle handyman into letting his fiery passions get the best of him. If Sanchez's betrayal had been the product of witchcraft—well, that would put the whole matter in an entirely different light. Ruth may have been responsible for manipulating the lustful feelings of the man, but the whole affair was the result of blowback from Agatha's enchantment, his love for her being switched on a dime and turned from desire and restless infatuation to unbridled jealousy and hate. That was what she got for recklessly toying with people's hearts and emotions at the end of the day, all thanks to the crazy stupid gift she was cursed with.

Agatha may have been guilty of being a tad unscrupulous, but it was never her intention to harm Sanchez. He was merely a necessary pawn they needed while setting up shop at the tavern. Now that he had saved her as a way of repenting for his earlier actions, it was time for her to atone for her sins as well.

Determined to acknowledge her responsibilities and forgive the brute, Agatha slowly stepped forward and removed the burlap sack to reveal the scarred and mangled face of her champion. She kissed him on the cheek before leaving him where he sat, his heart melting like butter as Agatha returned with McAllister to the tavern with the diary in their possession.

When they entered, Agatha was surprised and overjoyed to find Ada sitting in the main room. Now that she and McAllister had made amends, the charming waif was no longer a threat to her, and they could return to being best friends. Still, Agatha couldn't help but notice Ada's gaze lingering on her darling stepbrother, who was taking special care to keep his eyes forward and not look back at his stepsister as he steadily climbed the stairs.

"I'm glad you're OK," Ada told Agatha later outside her bedroom. Noticing they were being watched, Ada cast a warm smile at Lucy, observing the witches while tucked under the covers in Agatha's luxurious queen-size bed.

"Rest up, my beauties," Ada said. "Tomorrow's a special day."

"What's so special about tomorrow?" Lucy asked.

"Tomorrow's one of the special witch holidays," Agatha said. "The holiday, Walpurgisnacht. It should be quite...interesting."

As soon as her head hit the pillow, Agatha knew she would be asleep in an instant, glowing with satisfaction while listening to the sound of footsteps in the attic above her head. As she felt herself dipping into slumber with Lucy nuzzled against her, she thought she heard the strangest thing—what sounded like a playful female voice singing "The End of the World" by Skeeter Davis. But she ultimately chose to ignore this, dismissing it as only her imagination.

49

MAGIC BOOKS AND HUNGRY GHOSTS

A week that had started strange for Mercy had somehow gotten even stranger. It had been two days since her last conversation with the ghost that was haunting her boyfriend's apartment, and the spirit hadn't shown herself since. Under normal circumstances, the change of pace would have been welcoming, but despite the supposed inactivity, whenever she stopped by to visit, she felt like something was watching her and observing her—waiting for her to make her decision on whether to travel to Little Salem to confront Ada or to allow the witch to lead her boyfriend on a path to total ruin.

Ever since the little girl had spirited her away to observe her significant other interacting with the peculiar young woman with the wild dark hair and piercing blue-violet stare, Mercy started avoiding the apartment, spending the majority of her time back at her dorm and only stopping by to feed Ashton's cat and leaving quickly right after. Even then, during these brief outings, she felt a disquieting presence all around her—the darkness inside the apartment pressing her to make her final decision. Initially, she thought she would sleep much better back in her own room away from the ghost and haunted closet, but it was no use. Her mind was still reeling from all the information the little girl revealed to her, and she really truly wondered if she would ever enjoy a good night's sleep ever again.

On the second evening after receiving the spirit's commands, Mercy found herself in a state of procrastination, putting off her trip to the apartment and searching for a distraction. Eventually, she decided to stop by a pep rally being thrown by an African-American frat house that was taking place in the college quad. The event was very lively and already popping off when she arrived, with loud Southern rap echoing throughout the campus and multiple dance teams and drill teams competing to see who had the most spirit, as well as the freshest style and the best moves.

Unfortunately, despite the infectious energy that surrounded her, Mercy discovered she couldn't relax. She always felt incredibly awkward at these types of events, being someone who never truly felt at home in a crowd. At a certain point, she settled on viewing the entertainment from afar, sitting on a cafeteria table. There, she quickly drew the attention of a group of brothers who approached her to tease her for being a wallflower and also to hit on her, with one action quickly transitioning into the other. It was all part of the same tedious game to her, and she was looking forward to the brothers growing tired and leaving her on her lonesome. However, the alpha of the group remained persistent, his tactics switching over to giving her grief for having a white boyfriend when a young sharply dressed African-American man approached them.

"These guys bothering you?"

"Well, look at this smartly dressed brotha," the alpha grinned. He approached the stranger and got up close to his face. "You got a problem, young brotha?"

"No problem," the young man said. "You were just leaving."

The alpha snapped his fingers. "That's what I thought, son! Cuz we was just leaving!" He then turned on his heels and took off with his confused posse rushing after him.

Mercy shook her head in disbelief, impressed that the new arrival apparently possessed the talent to shoo away a mob of thirsty jackals with only a few simple words. But when he asked if he could join her, she started to regret the encounter and anxiously shrugged her shoulders with indifference.

"Free country," Mercy answered, but found herself tensing up once he sat down next to her.

"Go to a lot of these things?" the young man asked her.

"No. Is it obvious? My boyfriend's out of town, and I had to get out of the house." Before he could respond, she added, "Don't get any ideas."

The young man appeared genuinely taken aback.

"No, I—I'm sorry. I wasn't trying to pick you up. I was just going to say I know how it feels sometimes. Feeling like an outcast because you're...different."

The comment was unexpected, but Mercy didn't take it seriously. She thought this was just another slick line being fed to her.

"You think you're different, huh?"

Her reply was facetious, but her expression changed as she caught him gazing enviously at the raucous crowd of partyers in the distance. Like someone who had a hard time feeling like he belonged anywhere.

Maybe he's telling the truth, Mercy thought. Maybe he was the type of guy who had difficulty getting along with the rest of the herd like she did and this was something they shared in common.

After reflecting on this, she hesitantly extended her hand to him. "I'm Mercy."

"Miles," he replied.

After this, they both returned to watching the pep rally; two social outcasts that seemed to cross paths merely by coincidence. Like two ships passing in the night.

Mercy actually felt a moment of peace with the stranger sitting next to her, but the moment was ruined when, after acknowledging she had a boyfriend, he asked if she wanted to join him for coffee. Mercy sighed wearily at the invitation, feeling like her initial estimations may have been correct. She declined the offer, but when he insisted he sincerely thought she'd love some coffee, the strangest thing occurred: she suddenly felt a desire to enjoy such a treat.

The next thing she knew, she was at an all-night diner grabbing a cup of Joe with this handsome and mysterious young man—and if there was one thing that Miles possessed, it was a genuine air of mystery, along with a prominent sense of style and sophistication. While studying him, Mercy felt he must be someone who was full of secrets. She found herself entertaining the idea that it might be amusing to try to get him to open up to her about one or two of them to see what made a fascinating character like him really tick.

"You're not from around here, are you?"

"No. Just in town on some business."

"What sort of business is that exactly?"

"Some guy I know sent me to look up a rare book."

"My, how fascinating. What's so special about this book?"

After releasing a soft chuckle, her companion settled in and went on to tell her a tale that was about as wild and extraordinary as anything she'd ever heard. Mercy definitely wasn't expecting to hear a story like that one that evening—one that was chock full of magic and intrigue. But this was precisely what Miles was revealing to her, and at the core of his tale was a man named John Dee.

"So you have this guy, John Dee," Miles explained. "One of the brightest minds of the sixteenth century. Scholar, mathematician, naval strategist. He was even the personal astrologer to Her Royal Majesty, Queen Elizabeth."

"Quite the lengthy resume," Mercy observed.

Miles was only getting started. He had yet to reveal to her anything about the mysterious book he was searching for or what made the story so astonishing.

"Dee was also obsessed with magic," Miles said. "He spent years trying to communicate with the supernatural, but he never had much success. Until one day, he met a man named Edward Kelley."

Miles went on to explain that this Edward Kelley fellow, contrary to his esteemed colleague, was a bit of a rogue and a shady character that had had his ears cut off for forgery. One day, Kelley showed up on Dee's doorstep with a selection of alchemical artifacts and an old book stolen from the tomb of a saint. The book was an obscure text called *The Book of Dunstan*, and Kelley had high aspirations that Dee would help him translate it in hopes of discovering all the hidden secrets of alchemy. However, Dee was convinced that if it was secret knowledge Kelley desired, they should seek it by asking the angels, and thus began a series of magical experiments: the summoning of and conversation with mysterious supernatural beings that were dubbed "The Angelic Conversations."

At this point in the story, Mercy had no idea where their casual chat was headed. She'd heard stories about people who used magic to try to contact angels or demons or something in between. She was also familiar with the concept of channeled material, where someone would contact an entity and receive information through bodily possession or with the utilization of special crystals or something akin to a crystal ball. Mercy wasn't sure she believed any of this spooky business, but her recent experiences left her a lot more open to the possibility. And what a positively enchanting name for the whole ordeal: "The Angelic Conversations." Truth really was stranger than fiction. She may have looked only half-interested, but under the surface, she was well and truly captivated.

"The Angelic Conversations lasted for five years," Miles said, "with Kelley acting as medium and seer and Dee acting as scribe and recorder. During this time, Dee and Kelley traveled all across Europe from England to Poland and then over to Prague. And during their experiments, the so-called 'angels' transmitted to them a number of documents in a language later dubbed 'Enochian'—supposedly humanity's original language before the Fall of Man.

"Unfortunately, the angels didn't offer much in terms of how to decipher this language. Sometimes they provided a translation, sometimes they didn't—they could be very difficult at times. And many of the documents from these exchanges remain impossible to translate up to this very day.

"But regardless of these limitations, it is a firmly held belief in the magical community that the Enochian system contains some of the strongest and most dangerous magic to have ever existed. And some believe that within this information—the information that was transmitted to Dee and Kelley—is a secret key to jump-starting the Apocalypse."

Mercy released a low chuckle, her imagination running wild.

An ancient secret language from before the Fall of Man? One that could literally jump-start the end of the world as they knew it?

"Holy cow," Mercy said. "But why would angels do that?"

The plot was thickening, but Miles only shrugged. "No one knows. Dee's private journals list some clues. Kelley's diary was never found. At least, not officially."

Mercy had definitely opened up a huge can of worms with her inquiry, but she found she was enjoying the discussion a great deal. "So what ended up happening to them? Dr. Dee and Mr. Kelley?"

"They eventually suffered a break in their relationship, and that supposedly marked the end of the Angelic Conversations. Dee returned to England while Kelley remained in Prague. No one knows if they ever tried to obtain more knowledge from the angels or if it was all one big con from the beginning."

Mercy smiled knowingly at this comment. She knew that when it came to matters of the occult, it was always helpful to approach such tales with a healthy dose of skepticism.

"Still, one thing remains certain," Miles said. "All the angels and Enochian magic in the world couldn't save Kelley in the end. He died following a failed jailbreak after the Holy Roman Emperor condemned him to prison for fraud."

Mercy's eyes widened at this revelation. Later, after they finished their coffee, she was still processing all of the fascinating things he told her: apocalyptic magic, "angels," Elizabethan mages. She found herself observing Miles in quiet contemplation as he paid the bill for them. There was so much more to this interesting young man than met the eye, and she actually felt glad she agreed to have coffee with him. It turned out to be the perfect distraction for the evening, and by taking a chance on someone, she now felt more knowledgeable about some of the more remarkable mysteries of the world.

"So, the book you were sent here to look for. It originally belonged to...?"

Miles smiled slyly before answering.

"The people in Prague have many stories about him. Edward Kelley, a stranger in a strange land. The locals called him Engelander."

Miles had given Mercy a lot to think about in terms of how his story related to her current predicament. She may not have sought out contact with the spirit world like Dee and Kelley did, but the story showed how receiving communication from strange spiritual entities perhaps wasn't such a strange ordeal after all. She also found herself enjoying the company of her new friend immensely as they traded jokes while he walked her to her boyfriend's apartment. However, once they reached the doors to the lobby, she felt a wave of anxiety rush over her, with images of the pale black-eyed little girl and the darkness inside the closet filling her with mounting dread.

"So this is me," Mercy weakly muttered.

"Something wrong?" Miles asked her.

Mercy shook her head as she searched her purse for her keys. "It's nothing."

"Want me to come up? Check under the bed for monsters?"

She cracked a smile. "You really shouldn't."

"Please. I just want to make sure you're OK."

Moments later, Miles was exploring her boyfriend's apartment, gazing at a Magic 8 Ball while his edgy hostess tended to a kettle on the stove. Mercy didn't know why she allowed him to accompany her—safety maybe? No, that was a lie. She knew it was because she yearned to have someone to talk to, feeling incredibly alone as of late and desperate to get something off her chest.

Miles accepted a mug of tea from her. "Thanks. Nice place."

"It belongs to my boyfriend. I'm looking after his cat while he's vacationing in Little Salem." Mercy glanced nervously at the shadows around the room. "He hunts ghosts and stuff."

"Ghost hunting?"

"Yeah. You believe in ghosts, right?"

"Yeah," Miles answered with a hint of uncertainty. This was all the validation she needed—at least for the time being.

"Then you won't think I'm too weird because of what I'm about to tell you."

Mercy told him everything: about the first time she made contact with the spirit and how it all felt like a dream at first, and about the dark void inside of the closet and the places the darkness had taken her. She told him about the pale young couple in the attic and being spirited away to the reservation and why the little girl seemed to be haunting her in the first place and about the bloody deed she wanted her to execute. The conversation had moved to the bedroom where all of these disturbing experiences were taking place. Miles sat on the bed with Mercy huddled close beside him, listening to her mind-boggling fury of troubles with rapt interest.

"Murdered by witches," Miles thoughtfully mused. "And this little ghost girl wants you to travel to Little Salem to...?"

"She wants me to kill some hotshot teenage witch my boyfriend has been hanging out with." Mercy had to stop herself from laughing at the absurdity of it. "I know! It sounds crazy! I sound crazy!"

"So...you're not going to do it."

Mercy firmly shook her head, her eyes gazing at the carpeting. She hadn't made a final decision because she still struggled with the notion that all of these crazy things might actually be real. With Miles sitting beside her like the supportive friend she needed, she felt that it was time to declare her answer.

"No. No, I'm no killer," Mercy said. "I feel sorry for that little girl and for her family, but if all of this is really real, and I've been talking to ghosts that want me to right certain wrongs and avenge the past... Well, they're dead, and nothing's going to change that. I have to live with my actions. Oh God—the thought of me killing someone because a spirit asked me to! Can you believe that?"

"So you're...not going to do it," Miles checked again.

"No. God no—the thought of it."

Miles chuckled lightheartedly, and Mercy gladly joined in. She felt so grateful to have him there and that he'd been so patient while listening to her mad ramblings.

"Good. Good." Miles gave her a warm hug with Mercy returning the gesture, pressing her head into his shoulder when he leaned toward her with his lips pressed close. "The only thing is... Now we have no use for you."

At that moment, Mercy felt like she had been shoved off of a tall building. Her eyes widened, her heart sank, and her breath felt stuck inside her chest. She knew she was in immediate danger—and not from something supernatural that may or may not be real, but from something much more harsh and definitive.

Before she could react to the emergency, Miles swung the Magic 8 Ball in her direction, smashing it across the side of her head and leaving her stunned. As she lay on the floor in shock, her vision having gone all spotty, she listened to the sound of footsteps slowly crossing over to the kitchen, followed by the sound of a drawer being opened—the one that kept the knives. Out of the corner of her eye, she thought she saw a pale little girl watching from the shadows, her dark eyes coldly observing the morbid scene.

* * *

After stabbing Mercy to death, Miles stared vacantly at the striking young woman's bloody remains. His face was a quiet mask of indifference, but his eyes held the faintest glimmer of a man not quite sure what he was doing and had plunged too far into the darkness to turn back.

Sensing an uninvited presence, he glanced to the corner of the bed where an eerie blonde-haired child was sitting.

"Is it finished?" the little girl asked him.

Miles nodded.

"Good. Open the door for the others and meet me outside."

The image of the girl started to flicker like a broken streetlamp and disappeared from the room.

After she was gone, Miles took one final glance at Mercy's broken, lifeless body before taking a moment to collect himself and heading for the exit. When he opened the door, he discovered three serious-looking men dressed in black business suits standing in the hallway, carrying heavy stainless steel suitcases. Without acknowledging Miles in the slightest, the men muscled their way into the apartment as he continued on his way, no reason for him to stick around while they started to clean the grisly scene.

Once he was outside, Miles crossed calmly to a black Town Car parked across the street. After climbing into the backseat and shutting the door behind him, he stared forward while a woman wearing dark clothing sat motionless beside him.

"You have proven yourself quite useful," the woman said. "Your powers of suggestion are already quite advanced."

Another voice suddenly joined the woman as the image of the little blonde girl materialized beside her.

"Once you have joined the Council, I will teach you how to project illusions from great distances, just as I have been doing," the two voices said. "Under my instruction, you will become a *master.*"

The little girl vanished into thin air as Miles continued to stare blankly in front of him, listening to the woman's instructions without emotion.

"You must return to Little Salem and finish this. For the future of the Council."

With his orders laid out, he opened the door.

"Miles."

He paused.

"Ada and McAllister..."

He glanced back at the woman as she leaned into the light, giving him a full glimpse of Ada's mother, Ursula, wearing a harsh and bitter expression.

"Show them no mercy," Ursula said.

Miles nodded and closed the door after him, taking off into the quiet moonlit night as the black Town Car drove off in the opposite direction.

50

A TEENAGE GIRL'S INITIATION

———

While it's safe to say that Ada's supernatural powers made her a force to be reckoned with, it was her gift for creating lasting impressions that intimidated mothers like Nancy most of all. Mary Sue was the first to develop a soft spot for Ada (rivaled only by her infatuation for Izzy), while Lucy had been in awe of the witch since viewing her in her gothic masquerade incarnation at her father's church.

Lucy didn't get to enjoy a proper chat with Ada until several days later—after surviving her harrowing experience while locked in her father's basement. She'd been having trouble sleeping ever since. Staying at the tavern with Agatha had done wonders in helping to calm her frazzled nerves, but her mind was still reeling from the horror of it all, her father's deranged transformation remaining on endless playback inside her head.

On Lucy's second night with the witches, Agatha discovered her milling about downstairs. The look of sick pleasure on her father's face, along with his twisted sense of self-righteousness that went against everything she felt her religion stood for—she couldn't get this out of her head. But most disturbing of all was that *thing*. The thing clawing into her father's back that laughed at her with that jarring, jabbering cackle every time she glanced in its direction.

As usual, Agatha tried her best to comfort Lucy, suggesting that, in order to heal, she would have to accept that her father became a lost cause once he surrendered himself to madness. Being in the presence of someone to talk matters over with helped to lift her sagging spirits, but Agatha soon became caught up in McAllister's treasure hunt and Lucy was left all alone while another distressing personal matter continued nagging away at her. These were the circumstances when she had her first private exchange with Ada, and the discussion that followed would change her life forever.

After Agatha left the tavern, Lucy prayed to herself that the search would be eventful and she would return to her soon. In the meantime, her nightmare-addled brain was searching for distractions. She found herself pondering the bizarre names of all the unfamiliar bands and artists on the jukebox—mostly deathrock, punk, and various types of metal that would have given her father a coronary if he ever caught his perfect daughter listening to such a thing. It seemed she couldn't help reminiscing about her father no matter what she thought about, which instantly brought back memories of... No, she'd have to try harder not to think about it.

Lucy was fidgeting absentmindedly with the sterling silver cross around her neck when all of a sudden, she felt the presence of someone watching her—a feeling that wasn't so welcome considering the state of her nerves at present. The tavern may have been the safest place for her to be staying, but it was hardly an ironclad sanctuary. There was still just no telling who you could trust, and looking to quell her suspicions as quickly as possible, she spun around to discover Ada standing at the front entrance, wearing nothing but a thick woolen blanket and stroking a tiny black kitten cradled in her arms.

"Hello," Ada said, cracking an impish smile. "And you are?"

Ada had no idea how relieved Lucy was that it was only one of the witches present—or how pleased, albeit still a bit rattled, that she was now in the company of the coven's star queen bee herself.

In the presence of Ada, Lucy felt awestruck; like she was in the company of a rock star. What Agatha had told her about Ada and McAllister made them sound superhuman. Lucy had already met McAllister, who was certainly intriguing...but Ada?

For Lucy, McAllister was like a close friend's cool older boyfriend, but Ada was absolutely mystifying—and it was more than just the wild dark hair and bewitching, unearthly stare. When Ada marched into the church to face Lucy's father, she appeared to be completely unafraid of anything. She seemed to possess an almost preternatural ability to read the crowd, not just seducing them with her striking looks and scandalous attire but with the knowledge she appeared to glean from simply observing them.

Lucy felt that Ada must have already had her all figured out after taking one look at her, but she didn't feel intimidated by this. She genuinely wanted Ada to get to know her and open up to her, in hopes she might begin to understand where this astonishing level of confidence and charisma came from. Perhaps she might even learn to possess a tiny sliver of it herself at some point, to help her deal with all of the troubles that weighed so heavily on her daily life.

"Lucy," the flustered teenager finally answered to Ada's question. "Agatha told me a lot about you."

"Did she?" Ada smiled warmly as she crossed further into the room. "Now's my chance to hear all about you."

Their conversation started slow, but soon Lucy was revealing all her most pressing thoughts and anxieties to the young witch while the two of them were sitting across from one another in one of the tavern's black vinyl booths. While petting Ada's tiny black kitten and running her mouth non-stop, Lucy eventually worked up the courage to open up about the thing that had been consistently picking away at her. But she still felt a cold shiver when discussing the topic aloud.

"Shortly after I...became a woman," Lucy recounted, "I started seeing people around town with... It's like this horrible red demon clawing into their backs.

"When I first saw one attached to my dad, I was terrified. I couldn't tell if it was just some silly mental projection or if this was actually some kind of evil...parasite? I—I still have no idea. I don't have a clue.

"After seeing that thing attached to my dad, I thought—I mean, I've always had strong feelings that demons existed, but why me? Why is it only me seeing these hellish things? I don't understand why this is happening to me. It's...too much."

The whole time Lucy was talking she had found herself focusing on the sleepy purring furball curled up in her lap, hoping that the comfort derived from petting the precious feline would help her from becoming too emotional—and also so she wouldn't become distracted by Ada's piercing blue-violet gaze.

After revealing her dark secret, Lucy was on the verge of tears, all of her anxiety now bubbling to the surface. Ever since these experiences started, she felt like she was slowly going insane. Having to hide this from the world to avoid becoming a social outcast or, worse yet, a mental patient, had shot her nerves straight to hell.

And who would have guessed it? All of these awful feelings bottled up in the daughter of the town preacher who never got into any trouble and was popular at school. Things may have been picture-perfect on the outside for Lucy, but internally she was a total wreck.

Even after revealing all of this aloud, she still couldn't stop the nagging feeling that maybe she really *was* crazy, which was when she suddenly felt the soft touch of Ada's hand resting on top of hers.

"Lucy, your father was part of a sinister collective known as the Scarlet Council," Ada said, "and they are the living embodiment of evil incarnate. But you should never fear them because their kind preys on fear, and without this, they are powerless.

"When your father sold his soul to the Council, he exchanged his humanity for mental illness. This is what the Council does. They find good people and turn them utterly insane. As for these visions of yours—it doesn't matter if demons exist or not. You might see it as a curse but when *I* look at you, what I see...is a gift."

Ada squeezed Lucy's hand and flashed one of her token mysterious smiles at her. "This gift serves a greater purpose. You should treasure it and use it."

Throughout the rest of the night and the following day, Lucy thought a great deal about what Ada told her, with the witch's observations effectively silencing her heavy mixed emotions about things.

Lucy could barely believe it. These visions were a gift? And they served a greater purpose? She had no idea what this purpose could be, but for the first time in her life, she felt like someone understood her, and this drove her to want to get closer to Ada.

This desire was completely separate from her yearning to get closer to Agatha. While initially attracted to Agatha physically, this had been replaced by something resembling a strong bond between sisters. With Ada, her interest was much different; a fervent longing sparked by a powerful fascination that bordered on hero worship.

Lucy's longing intensified when Agatha returned to the tavern and told her about how the witches would be celebrating Walpurgisnacht and that Ada had special plans for them. With the event fast approaching, she was determined to go all out for the festivities, taking part in whatever was on the menu and doing so with gusto.

Little did Lucy know that before she'd even come to this conclusion, Agatha had already done the same. On the day leading up to the night in question, the first order of business involved choosing Lucy a new wardrobe—something that would replace her boring Sunday School style of dressing in favor of something more daring and provocative. Lucy found herself more than a little nervous about making this change, but she knew the transformation would be liberating, acting as a powerful exclamation to the world that the life she suffered under the cold hard thumb of her father was behind her and she was looking ahead to better and more exciting times while living amongst a coven of witches.

With Agatha as her personal stylist, the two girls searched through the selection of options at their disposable, borrowing most of the final selection from Ada, Izzy, and Rudy since they were all much closer to Lucy's proportions than her curvaceous cohort. Hours later, right as the sun was setting, the girls were finally dressed and ready to party, and Agatha struck a pose in the doorway at the rear of the main room.

"Listen up, boys and ghouls! May I have your attention, please?"

Rudy and McAllister were the only ones present, occupied with popping magnums of champagne and spraying each other with the foam. Both of them appeared to be dolled up as well for the occasion. McAllister was rocking a black cowboy shirt and leather jacket, a black bandanna slung around his neck, while Rudy was dressed in his usual pinstripes, bright Day-Glo war paint transforming his face into a skull. Agatha was also looking especially striking in an absolutely mouth-watering red strapless gown, but she was less concerned with attracting attention to herself for a change and more interested in directing her admirers to someone else.

"I'd like to present the newest member of our merry band of misfits," Agatha heartily declared. "Miss Lucy Palmer."

With her showy introduction wrapped up, the shapely redhead stepped aside as Lucy entered the room, looking like a completely different person than the modest teenager who showed up at the tavern a few days earlier. The look Agatha designed for her was something she lovingly referred to as "Catholic Schoolgirl From Hell," which was quite the fitting persona for Lucy to play with as she celebrated finally breaking free of her father's influence and the pressures of trying to cater to the stuffy Little Salem community.

Lucy did feel somewhat awkward in her new ensemble. The dark lipstick and raccoon-eyed makeup were something she definitely wasn't used to seeing. The outfit was also a lot more revealing than anything her father would have let her wear, but that was part of the point. And regardless of her initial discomfort, everyone appeared notably impressed by the transformation—especially Rudy, who was already hopelessly smitten.

"*Santa Muerte*," Rudy gasped, his jaw practically on the floor.

Lucy let out an amused giggle, tickled pink by the reaction.

"Welcome to the family," Agatha said.

"Yes, welcome, Lucy."

Lucy turned her head to address who had spoken. She'd felt like the belle of the ball up to this point, but upon Ada's entrance, it became clear who the real star of the party was and why everyone was so devoted to her.

For the celebration, Ada had gone all-out and was dressed in a black lace party dress, cobweb patterned stockings, and black heels—something she wasn't used to wearing, but it was a special occasion, so she was determined to treat it as such. On top of the stunning outfit, Ada's hair and makeup were picture-perfect, and her eyes seemed to be shining much brighter than usual as she lovingly addressed the others while donning an impish grin.

"Gather round everyone," Ada said. "I have some special words I'd like to share on this most sacred day."

Lucy expected everyone to gather in a circle, but instead, Agatha, McAllister, and Rudy went and stood at a different corner of the room, and Lucy hesitantly did the same. She watched Ada drop five small white capsules into five glasses of champagne, waiting for the drugs to dissolve before delicately raising a glass and addressing her cherished companions.

"Friends," Ada said. "Tonight is Walpurgisnacht. And rather than celebrate by offering tribute to the gods in the stuffy, old-fashioned way, I'd like to begin this evening by proposing a toast to a very special deity. To the goddess, Eris—goddess of Chaos and Discord."

Ada slowly crossed to Rudy and presented the champagne to him before returning to the bar to collect another.

"Eris," Ada said, "who one day, while walking past a party attended by the most celebrated goddesses of the day—goddesses such as Hera, Aphrodite, Athena... Eris, disappointed she'd been snubbed and neglected to receive an invitation, rolled a golden apple into the room inscribed as belonging to the most beautiful of all who were gathered."

Ada smiled at Agatha as she presented a glass of champagne to her and crossed back to the bar after receiving a smile in return.

"As you might know, the argument that followed over the true ownership of the apple was what sparked the Trojan War, the first great war among men. So let us drink to Eris, who reminds us that all order is illusory and that lurking in the background behind every hollow and delusive example of order is chaos and discord, waiting to tear back the curtain and shatter the known universe."

Ada passed the next glass to McAllister, struggling not to blush as their smiles met one another's, before turning to face the others.

"This is the cosmic dance to which we all belong."

McAllister raised his glass in response.

"*To chaos*," he said, and everyone raised their glasses in turn.

The whole scene fascinated Lucy and left her utterly speechless—and also a bit confused by Ada's elegant anecdote. She felt her entire body tense up as the young witch steadily approached her, daintily holding two glasses and offering one her way as she gazed at her with her bewitching eyes and flashed her impish smirk.

"You're one of us now, Lucy. Do you accept the sacrament?"

Lucy stared hesitantly at the offering, but she already knew her answer. She wanted to be one of them—to belong to the group and learn all the secrets that Ada and the others could teach her.

What she wanted...*was to become a witch.*

If the celebration marked the first step on her path to initiation, she was up for whatever they had in store; no matter how improper or defiant or outlandish or how nervous and excited she felt. She took the glass and downed it in one consistent motion as Ada mirrored her actions, with the others following in quick succession.

After this, Ada set the glass aside and held out her arms, smiling warmly as Lucy embraced her, with the others quickly joining in for a loving group hug. At that moment, Lucy knew in her heart she had made the right decision, feeling like she finally found the group where she truly belonged.

Ada also seemed to get caught up in the moment, soaking in all of the affection before eventually breaking free and wiping a stray tear from her eyelid. "Come, there's work to be done," she announced, likely feeling that anything else was better left unsaid.

Rudy slammed his fists on a table.

"Damn straight!" he yelled. "*No rest for the wicked witches!*"

The group all broke out into savage howls and cheers with Lucy joining in, excited to discover what was on the evening's agenda and where the night would take them. She had no knowledge of the dark path that awaited them, and that it wasn't only a night for celebration but also for settling final scores and more bloody retribution.

Part VI

Rudy: You know the saying. What's lost doesn't stay lost forever.

51

A NIGHTMARE TO REMEMBER

The sun was rising above the horizon and bathing the town of Little Salem with a soothing orange glow when Ashton's silver Prius parked outside the hotel. Before going to sleep, Tyler made sure to review his camera footage to relive his personal run-in with the supernatural. He could still barely believe the experience had been real, and yet there was the evidence right in front of him: definitive proof that ghosts and monsters existed.

The paranormal video of the century.

Capturing something so significant should have made Tyler feel elated, but he managed to maintain an even-mannered demeanor while backing up the recording and uploading it to the internet. He figured that once he'd gotten some rest, only then would he know if it had all really happened and if there was any cause to celebrate.

Ashton was in a rather somber mood as well, barely even registering what Tyler was doing as he monotonously unloaded their camping packs and went through his pre-bed routine. So much had been revealed to them over the span of a few hours from the secret history of the Salem Witches and their connection to the creatures known as the Mysterious Ones to the story about Ada and McAllister and why they harbored so much ill will toward Little Salem.

Despite the uncanny nature of the revelations from the supposed apparition of Sarah Good, it was the latter tale told by Nancy that kept cycling through Ashton's restless headspace. This wasn't too shocking given his fascination with Ada and her personal history. Thanks to Nancy's story, he now knew a great deal more about the remarkable young woman and the experiences that made her who she was today. The story also answered some of his questions about McAllister, a truly fascinating character in his own right, though it didn't explain how he had gained any of the supernatural abilities Ashton had witnessed during the ambush at the chemical plant and their time spent at the reservation. There was something else about Nancy's story that was bothering him—something he couldn't put his finger on. And he wouldn't know what this was until he'd fallen asleep and began to experience the same dark and disturbing dream he'd been having since arriving in Little Salem.

In the dream, a young Ashton was once again sitting on the floor in his family's living room as sunshine filtered through the curtains, obscuring the identity of the dark figure in front of him.

"Hello again, Ashton," the figure said. "Your mother tells me you'll be going off to college soon. You have some very exciting days up ahead."

Ashton was confused by this remark. He thought he was only a young boy in these dreams, but perhaps he'd been growing progressively older in each of them. If that was the case, what was the significance? A reflection on his life at different ages? Or maybe they were more than just dreams and were actually...

"Ashton, I believe you remember my friend, Mr. Frau."

The other man was now present.

With that grating soft chuckle.

That chilling reptilian smirk.

And then it hit him—a flash of the city of flesh and bone.

Back in his hotel room, Ashton was tossing and turning, but in the dream world, he was still sitting on the floor, watching as the shadowy figure on the couch, the one who wasn't his father, revealed the worn yellow book he carried and started flipping through its tattered contents. As usual, what the man read to him was confusing and disorienting, stirring up dark visions; the sights and smells gut-wrenching in their intensity and sickening to both body and soul. When the man finished—this strange and baffling figure known as Mr. Frau—Ashton's father once again joined him on the couch.

"Well, Ashton. That should be all for now," his father said. "But before we go, Mr. Frau and I would like to give you a gift to take away to college with you." A large wrapped package was revealed, and his father presented it to him. "When you look at it," he added, "I hope you will think of us and all the special moments we've shared."

In the real world, Ashton's breathing started picking up as he watched the hands belonging to him as a teenager tear off the wrapping to admire what was underneath. And his heart started beating like a jackhammer once he realized what he was holding.

The gift...was a framed piece of canvas displaying a red circle broken on the left side, with the color dripping down the surface in a manner that resembled dried blood. It was the same image as the scarlet circle that Tyler had taken a picture of at Sir Godfrey's. But this one belonged to Ashton., and the visions came fast and furious as he stared at the unsettling artifact.

It was at that instant that Ashton forced himself awake, his body shaking and covered in sweat. This whole time he'd been assuming the nightmares he was having were just stupid fanciful dreams. He now knew he'd been horribly mistaken.

He was finally awake at last.

Several minutes later, Ashton emerged from taking a shower while a distracting bevy of questions danced inside his head—questions Tyler remained oblivious to as he sat blissfully at his laptop.

"Dude, so I uploaded our encounter with the Mysterious Ones to our YouTube channel. Posted that shizz to Facebook, Instagram, Twitter. I emailed everyone in my list of contacts. Bloggers, reporters, different people in the paranormal community. I also posted the link to various blogs, message boards, supernatural websites, web forums, online zines..."

Tyler flashed a euphoric smile at Ashton, getting more and more excited as his companion dressed mechanically in the background.

"This is it," Tyler said. "This is gonna put us over the top. And it's all thanks to you. You were the one that wanted us to come out here, and you made it happen. Best spring break ever."

Ashton wasn't smiling at all at this concession and suddenly slumped over on the bed with his face pressed into his hands.

"Ashton? You all right, bro? Do you need a coffee or something? A Fresca?"

Ashton glared in anguish at his clueless friend.

"Why are we here, Tyler? Why did we come out here really? You think this is it? Some creepy B.S. that happened in the woods?"

The series of questions confused Tyler.

"Well, yeah, isn't it? I mean... You tell me. Isn't that why we came out here? For us? For the web channel?"

Ashton looked away from him, drowning in inner torment.

"Professor Emmanuel was the one who told me to go to Little Salem. *McAllister's father. Ada's stepdad. And who do we run into as soon as we arrive?*"

It was true: For the past few months, Ashton had been attending American History classes being taught by one Professor Emmanuel Kinneary, and mere days before spring break started, he attempted to flatter his professor after the mid-term. During their conversation, he mentioned his ghost-hunting hobby and received the suggestion to forget spending the break in Mexico and visit a much more haunted locale instead—like Little Salem. The class was discussing the Salem witch trials, so he didn't think much of this. At the time, he had no reason to suspect his professor had any ulterior motives. Now he wasn't so sure. Now it felt like he had been encouraged to visit Little Salem for a highly specific purpose. The fact that the man's wayward children were there to greet him shortly after his arrival only helped to confirm this suspicion.

"You think this was all a coincidence?" Ashton roared. He had no doubts there was a lot more going on, but Tyler remained skeptical.

"Dude, you gotta help me out here," Tyler said. "You told me you wanted to come to this place because it was a spooky place. And it took some convincing, but I came along. But you knew I was gonna follow you because I'm your bro, homeslice. We're the Ghost Bros! You and me are homies! Ada, McAllister, and the rest of their Creepshow buddies—they have their own reasons for being here. 'Season of the Witch' and all that. And it has nothing to do with us. Nada. Nothing at all."

Unfortunately, Tyler's explanation failed to calm his shaken friend. "There's something else," Ashton muttered. But he was much too disturbed to continue, balling his fists before rising to his feet and heading for the doorway.

"Where are you going?"

"Out."

"Well hang on—"

"Alone."

Ada and McAllister—what were they doing in Little Salem for real? Nancy assumed it was for revenge and Tyler had mentioned something about some crazy magical artifact McAllister was after. Ashton had a nagging feeling there was a lot more going on with them than what was assumed.

Ada had fallen quiet when he initially mentioned the Scarlet Council to her. She suggested he should ask McAllister about this. She knew about McAllister's connections to the Council; the question was, did she know that Ashton... No, he didn't want to think about it, let alone consider it.

And yet, he never got the chance to discuss the Council with him—a detail that didn't change when he worked up the courage to visit the tavern later that day but decided against it. His patience with Ada and her so-called "stepbrother" had run thin, and he doubted another conversation with them would resolve anything.

Ada knew all along about the Council's ties to Little Salem, and in every conversation with her about the town's history or legends about the trials, she never mentioned the Council once to him. It almost felt like ever since he arrived in Little Salem, she'd been steering him away from learning about the shadowy collective and pushing him toward much more benign activities instead: the museum, the graveyard, possibly even the chance of a romantic fling. Was that the real reason she suddenly popped into his life? To prevent him from becoming closer to... To go seeking answers from...?

Ashton no longer knew what to think. His doubt and uncertainty were poisoning all the activity inside his head. But he knew there was one place he could go to sort things out once and for all.

The Scarlet Council. There were plenty of stories about how significant secret societies were to the country's founding, and not all of these organizations were sinister and diabolical. The question was:

What type of secret society was the Council really? And what was his connection to it?

When Ashton reached the Godfrey mansion, he walked cautiously up the front drive, passing about twenty men wearing black business suits, all of them armed with semi-automatic weapons. Several expensive foreign cars were parked out front, and Sir Godfrey was standing in the doorway, dressed in a burgundy blazer, his lips curling up with wolfish delight.

"Ashton Rose. Good to see you."

Ashton stopped dead in his tracks. It felt unnerving to discover his strangely offputting host waiting for him and that he already seemed to know his full name. He still felt distressingly unsure about what he was doing, but, just like Tyler during his earlier visit, he'd come to the mansion seeking answers, and it was too late to turn back after having gotten so far already.

Once inside, Godfrey's butler closed the door behind him, and Ashton listened to the sound of several locks and deadbolts being drawn. In addition to Godfrey, there were four middle-aged party guests gathered to greet him, all of them brandishing cocktails and smiling eerie saurian smiles in his direction. The men were wearing matching burgundy blazers and were uniformly Caucasian, something in the way they carried themselves reflecting an air of privilege and high society. And just like their host, they were all as welcoming in their conduct and demeanor to the point of discomfort—as if they were eager to make Ashton feel like he was in good company.

"Make yourself at home, Mr. Rose," Godfrey said. "We were wondering when you'd finally pay us a visit. This is Gerald Chase and his wife, Renee."

"Ashton."

One of the men stepped forward and shook Ashton's hand. The fashionably dressed woman standing next to him did the same.

"Hello there."

"Hello," Ashton answered tentatively.

"And Headmaster Fine."

Another man tipped an imaginary hat at their guest.

"And the honorable General Joseph Stephens."

"Pleasure to meet you, son," the General said, giving a hearty handshake.

"Some others were going to make it but canceled last minute," Godfrey said. "Care to join us for dinner?"

"How—how did you know my name?"

Several of the guests chuckled under their breath as Godfrey stepped forward, his wolfish grin growing in intensity.

"We've heard a great deal about you, Mr. Rose," Godfrey said. "I'm sure you have plenty of questions."

Questions, yes.

Ashton's purpose for being there suddenly came back to him. His hands fumbled in his pockets, finding his phone and scrolling through the contents.

"This. This right here," Ashton mumbled. He referred to the picture of the scarlet circle in the trophy room.

After stepping closer to observe the image, Godfrey gazed briefly at his guest and gestured emphatically for him to follow him.

"Right this way."

Ashton trailed his host down a nearby hallway, and there, in the trophy room, surrounded by dead animals and decaying tokens of upper-class prestige that included several priceless paintings and framed antique playing cards he couldn't have cared any less about, his eyes were drawn to the blood-red circle hanging on the wall in all of its monstrous and terrifying glory.

"There she is," Godfrey said, smiling proudly. "Take your time and come join us whenever you like. It's been an honor to finally meet you, Mr. Rose."

The silver-headed titan exited the room and closed the door behind him, leaving Ashton all alone. For the past several hours he'd been anticipating this very moment, thinking that all the answers would suddenly become clear to him. And yet, with the bizarre item now in front of him, it remained a total mystery. The stormy chaos of contents inside his head did not change, and the idea that a personal audience with the obscure symbol would somehow brush aside the cobwebs or provide any illumination now seemed utterly absurd.

Ashton questioned what he really expected to accomplish by seeking the object. Perhaps it went back to his desire to prove he could stare down any frightening situation placed before him or to satisfy his undying curiosity involving Ada and her turbulent past. Despite the lack of answers, there was something curiously unpleasant about the framed symbol—malevolent even.

Was it true he received one just like it? And from his father, of all people? Ashton couldn't understand for the life of him how something so innocuous could also be so terrible and frightening, or what this image from his dreams—no, from his life and his experiences—had to do with *him*.

"The seal of the Scarlet Council."

Startled, Ashton turned to search for the voice that had spoken, his eyes landing on a young bearded man in an easy chair who was probably on his third or fourth glass of scotch. The man was dressed in a black business suit, and Ashton recognized him as the sniper at the AM Chemical Plant.

"A red circle, drawn in blood," the man said. "Blood, because it is sacred. Scarlet or crimson, because it is the color of royalty and kings. And a circle?" The man drew a circle in the air with his finger, swallowing a sizable gulp of scotch before continuing. "In the time of the ancients, the circle was seen as having magical properties. It was viewed as a portal. *A doorway between two worlds.*"

After receiving this explanation, Ashton turned to stare at the framed image for quite some time. Regardless of whether he learned anything conclusive or even remotely satisfying, he now knew beyond a shadow of a doubt he had somehow been led to this moment. To a stirring reunion with a piece of his cloudy memories that had been buried and forgotten. For some strange and indefinable reason, he sensed that a brand new path was opening up to him—although he still had no idea for what purpose or where this path might lead.

Could this all have something to do with his father and the strange man that accompanied him? And what about the grinning group of posh middle-aged party guests waiting for him to join them in the dining hall? Ashton was now feeling more uncertain about everything and wouldn't be receiving any answers anytime soon. While he continued to stare at the blood-red seal hanging before him, the benign image seeming to be sending a disturbing cacophony of indecipherable whispers into his head, he heard a series of explosions—what at first sounded like children's firecrackers.

"Did you hear something?" Ashton asked.

The man in the easy chair, whose name he would have learned was Dave if he ever got the chance to ask him, only gave an ambivalent shrug. It wasn't long before they recognized the sounds were a far cry from anything safe and harmless.

It was the sound of gunshots.

Gunfire from outside.

Upon this realization, Ashton put on a brave face and raced out of the room with the young man calling after him, no doubt having already concluded the identity of the dangerous trespasser he was rushing into the thick of battle to greet.

52

REVENGE OF THE LORDS

When the New Lords left the tavern on the night of Walpurgisnacht, their appearances attracted more than a healthy amount of attention from the locals. Many felt compelled to stop dead in their tracks and stare at what was roaming the streets in front of them: five steely-eyed youths parading down the boulevard like a Technicolor street gang, walking silently and fearlessly across town to the wrought iron gates of the Godfrey mansion.

In comparison to the more conservative townspeople, the group looked distinctly provocative and intimidating, with the girls all dressed to the nines, Rudy in his skull paint, and McAllister wearing his leather biker jacket with the silver ouroboros shining on the back. Clearly, they were up to something, and mischief was hanging in the air. But what their intentions were and the full nature of their devious shenanigans wouldn't be revealed until they reached their destination. There, with a wave of Ada's arm, the heavy gates ground

open, and while making their way past the twenty armed guards firing away at them, with a wave of Ada's arm, each and every man they
came across aimed their weapon at their own head and pulled the
trigger, blowing their brains out.

With the New Lords on the warpath, Godfrey's honorable sen-
tinels would only be the first in a string of casualties that night.
When Rudy called Ada's attention to an armed chauffeur exiting a
vehicle, all she had to do was make a simple gesture and this man shot
himself as well, blood splattering the windshield.

Due to the mansion's isolated location, the only ones aware of
the coven's activities were those within a close earshot. To the inhabitants, the sounds of gunfire were incessant, but Ashton had little
awareness as to the full extent of the shocking carnage that was
occurring when he chose to leave the trophy room to investigate.

As he crossed down the hallway, his body jumped at the sound
of a loud blast echoing through the front hall. He pressed himself
against the wall to stay out of sight, trying his best to blend in with
the shadows. It was distressingly clear that intruders were trying to
enter the home, and he received the shock of his life as the unknown
gatecrashers' identities were revealed to him, watching as Ada in her
black lace party dress and heels followed McAllister toward the dining hall with Agatha and Lucy trailing close behind them.

Too startled to move, Ashton remained in this state of height-
ened surprise and agitation as McAllister shoved the doors open
to the lavish setting. "Salutations, ladies and gentlemen!" he
announced; "Please! Don't get up!" with the request made compul-
sory as Ada waved her hand and the high-backed chairs shoved the
guests against the table, locking them firmly into place.

Ashton found the whole affair utterly mystifying, and his inquisitive nature drove him to abandon his place of safety, his eyes zeroing

in on the enchanting waif standing at the back of the dining hall with a mischievous sparkle in her eye and an impish smile on her lips.

"Ada," Ashton found himself muttering, the full gravity of what was happening crashing down on him when he glanced to the front door and spied the body of Godfrey's butler lying in a pool of blood. Apparently, the man had blown his own head off with a shotgun—at the time, he had no idea why the man would do such a thing.

As Ashton struggled to process what all the violent and bloody signs were suggesting, he suddenly felt his body being pulled away from the bizarre scene.

"C'mon. We need to stay out of sight," Dave whispered.

It was impossible to see everything going on from where they were standing. Ashton's view from the doorway was limited, but this meant that as long as he didn't call any added attention to himself, he could observe how the dinner party responded to all the monstrous events that were about to occur.

Ignoring Dave's pleading for a quick getaway, Ashton pressed his body against the doorframe. From this position, he watched McAllister climb onto the dining table and strut menacingly toward the trembling dinner guests, his heavy boots carelessly crushing all of the fine antique china and foodstuff standing in his path.

"A shame we weren't invited to the party," McAllister coolly grinned. "So many familiar faces." He flashed a chilling glance at each of the guests, all squirming helplessly as he paraded across the table. "How's the law office, Jerry? And the Missus? New haircut, General? Headmaster."

McAllister crouched down and playfully slapped the face of the bookish middle-aged man he just addressed—a man staring at the tabletop, trying his damnedest to avoid making eye contact.

"Hey. Wake up, Sunshine," McAllister dryly quipped. "How's

everything at Council Chapter Nine? Is everything under control? That's a little motto of theirs, Lucy. *'Everything is under control.'*"

Lucy started in surprise when McAllister called out to her. Since witnessing the bloody executions outside, she was harboring serious regrets for accompanying the coven on what had proven to be a highly dubious outing. But she was also distracted by something even more unsettling, her eyes fixed on the gaggle of snarling red demons on the backs of all the guests at the dining table.

With his body hugged close to the doorway, Ashton continued to watch the scene while Dave peered over his shoulder. It appeared that McAllister was getting a huge kick out of terrorizing the bewildered gathering. They all appeared paralyzed by fear, with the exception of Godfrey, who looked more annoyed than anything.

"McAllister, Ada," Godfrey said, staring icily at his former subordinate. "I suggest you state your business and leave. Before things—"

"*Get out of control?*" McAllister yelled. "*Well, howdy fucking doody that would be a real tragedy, wouldn't it?*"

This comment elicited a warm smile out of Ada, delighted to see her beloved fake sibling in such energetic spirits. And the tension in the room continued to rise dramatically as McAllister crossed to the front of the table and crouched down to confront the silver-haired ghoul staring back at him.

"We have some unfinished business, don't we?" McAllister's black leather glove caressed Godfrey's cheek. "Some unfinished business indeed."

Reaching behind him, McAllister removed a gruesome ceremonial dagger from the waist of his jeans. He held the blade up to the chandelier, allowing it to glimmer in the lamplight.

"You see this dagger?" McAllister raised his voice to address the room. "The honorable Sir Godfrey gave me this dagger. He wanted me to use it to kill a young girl. *A young girl!* A witch."

Ashton could feel Dave shuddering behind him. He already seemed to be anticipating the horrors that were about to take place.

"That was five years ago, give or take a month. But the Council has been in the witch-killing business for much longer." The immortal assassin rose to his feet and waved the dagger at each of the guests in turn. "How much blood is on your hands? All of you. You? You?"

McAllister slowly turned and waved the dagger at the icy, humorless host at the head of the table. "What about you? Hmm?"

"Not half as much as I would wager is on yours," Godfrey replied.

Burning with rage, McAllister once again crouched in front of him, his eyes filled with fury as he held the blade to Godfrey's face. "YOU SHUT UP! You've heard the story of Frankenstein! How the monster always comes back to slay his creator! *Are you surprised?*"

McAllister's crazed demeanor suddenly changed. He started chuckling and removed a glove to stroke the face of his quarry, causing the capillaries under his skin to pulse from red to black at the brush of his fingertips.

"Well, are you?"

Ashton could now see the reason for Dave's extreme reaction. He didn't have a clear view of what was happening, but from the shock on all the guests' faces, he knew the pale golden-haired anomaly with his devilish smile and nightmare black ensemble must be doing something that was against the bounds of science and reason. This brought back memories of his time at the reservation and McAllister's haunting words about black magic. As horrible as it may have sounded, it felt painfully clear that the end was fast approaching for the proud, austere host who arranged the intimate gathering.

"I've been looking forward to this," McAllister hissed as the terrible blackness continued to spread, dagger still pressed against Godfrey's throat. "I've waited so long to return this treasure to you."

But what McAllister did next was a complete surprise. He suddenly released his captive and sheathed the ghastly blade.

"However... Tonight is Walpurgisnacht, so it's not my business to judge you."

For a brief moment, all the guests seemed relieved as McAllister backed away. But the moment quickly passed once they observed Ada leaving her place at the back of the room to approach the head of the table with an intense and vengeful fire burning behind her eyes, her token impish smile on full display.

Ashton felt a lump form in the back of his throat as he watched the young witch's fragile pixieish physique gracefully shimmy across the room, his imagination going into overdrive as she came to a halt several feet before reaching the head of the table and folded her hands in front of her.

"Sir Godfrey, members of the Scarlet Council," Ada calmly announced. "I judge you today on behalf of all the Salem Witches, defenseless young girls, and others murdered or punished by this order for the vile and shameful sake of your cowardly self-preservation. I charge you with mass murder and crimes against humanity. How do you plead?"

The accusation sent a chill down Ashton's spine. He could only imagine that those seated at the table were even more discomforted. Godfrey had turned pale as a sheet and beads of sweat were dampening his brow. But his pride wouldn't allow him to show any humility to his enemies.

"Is this a farce?" Godfrey scoffed. "*She* is the one to judge us? A *witch*? An *abomination*?"

Ignoring the pointless melodrama, Ada stared unblinkingly at the man. "Sir Godfrey. Your plea."

Godfrey gulped, sweating profusely as he felt the eyes of the other guests watching him, no doubt praying his quick and capable thinking would save them. He knew McAllister was glaring at him, likely waiting for the signal to emerge as his executioner. He knew he was behind the eight ball, and things weren't looking optimistic. If death was already a certainty, there was only one way to play this: with complete composure, and with dignity.

"Not guilty" Godfrey answered. "And to hell with all of you."

The tension in the room rose to a new level. Ashton couldn't see how Ada responded, but her physicality didn't change in the slightest. However, if he had seen her face at this moment, he would have noticed her impish smile had widened significantly, and her otherworldly blue-violet eyes were burning even brighter, her thirst for vengeance growing in intensity.

"Too bad," Ada said. "I was hoping you'd see the light."

Ada closed her eyes and bowed her head, concentrating intently as her body started to relax. Once she had settled into a state of total equilibrium, she proceeded to use her hands to make a series of bizarre movements, as if working to shape a small spherical object in front of her chest.

At first, it wasn't entirely clear what she was doing, and the guests appeared baffled by the witch's actions. But the situation soon became plain to everyone, and an audible gasp was heard after one of the guests noticed a small golden orb shining above Godfrey's head.

"What is this?" Gerald screamed. "*What's going on?*"

Gerald's wife, Renee, spoke up next.

"Gerald? What is that? *What the hell is that?*"

The guests erupted into a panic, squirming in their seats. As Ada opened her eyes and addressed the hysterical crowd, a sinister smile became fixed to her charming, angelic face.

"Friends, do you not see? *There is a light that shineth in the darkness, and the darkness...comprehends it not.*"

Pale as a specter, Godfrey stared jaw agape at the glowing golden orb above his head, and his eyes widened in terror as he was forced to watch it slowly descend into his mouth. His body started thrashing and shaking like something in his stomach was disagreeing with him, and blinding rays of light began breaking through all of his various bodily orifices, burning him alive from inside.

This special death that Ada prepared was so torturous and horrifying it was beyond compare—even for the most battle-hardened spectator to witness. So excruciating that Ashton felt nauseous, realizing with deep regret that his starry-eyed characterization of the sweet misunderstood girl he initially pinned her for couldn't have been further from the ghastly truth.

But Ada's stunning retribution against the Council was far from finished. The screams only multiplied as the guests turned their eyes to observe that they all had glowing gold-colored orbs above their heads as well, howling with desperation as the orbs descended into their bodies, scorching their insides as beams of blinding luminescence shot out of their eyes and mouths.

For Ashton, the sight was traumatizing, but there were those who were present who were cut from a different cloth altogether; unique specimens like Agatha and McAllister, who not only appeared to endorse this highly twisted brand of justice but seemed to be getting a sick thrill out of the experience.

Lucy, on the other hand, was another matter entirely, standing petrified, her hands covering her mouth. What she was seeing involved watching all of the demons clawing into the backs of the dinner guests being filled with the blistering golden light themselves, howling with agony as the shining radiance pulsed through their bodies and created cracks in their skin, burning them alive in an instant and causing them to explode.

Once the demons had been subdued, the guests all slumped forward like broken marionettes, their bodies now shrunken and frail and burnt to a savage crisp. Lucy shuddered at the sight, still not quite able to believe all she was seeing was really happening, while Ada dropped her hands to her sides and admired her devastating handiwork.

From the doorway, Ashton's eyes remained locked on the terrifying object of his misplaced fascination, noticing she was smiling—smiling widely after causing so much violence and mayhem. The naïve young ghost hunter was in a state of shock. All he could do was stare at the cruel and strikingly malicious girl standing in the dining hall—this unrepentant murderess—hoping to high heaven it was all just a dream.

But this night of crime and punishing reprisal was no fantasy, and Ashton eventually felt Dave's hand on his shoulder pulling him away. There was no telling what Ada would do to them should she catch them observing her unspeakable punishments.

Ada and the rest of the coven left the mansion shortly afterward, joining up with Rudy who was busy vandalizing all of the expensive foreign cars parked out front; smashing the windows, spray-painting the bodies, and as a final stroke of artistry, tossing flaming Molotov cocktails into the interiors.

The rowdy delinquent was howling at the full moon shining above him when the rest of the group emerged. And despite the disturbing nature of their recent actions, just about everyone appeared fully energized and in high spirits.

"Riveting performance, love," Agatha said to Ada.

"Yes," Ada agreed. "*So shines a good deed in a weary world.* Rudy?"

Rudy tossed Ada a spray can.

"An artist always signs her work," Ada said, spraying an Algiz rune on the mansion's front door in fluorescent yellow spray, the initials, "lol," placed over it.

"There. Anyone down for pizza?"

As Ada turned her back on the decaying residence, Agatha linked arms with her beloved accomplice. The two of them took off into the woods before escaping onto the grounds of the nearby country club, parading across the golf course while smiling like a pair of cartoon cats, with McAllister and Rudy trailing close behind them. Lucy was the only one that remained, hanging back as she tried to process what she just witnessed. It didn't hit her instantly, but she was soon feeling the rush of the evening's adventures along with everyone else, laughing at the exciting lawless unruliness of it.

For Lucy, her demonic visions and personal witness to her father's malice, a Council member himself, confirmed to her that Ada's resentments could be nothing less than entirely legitimate. It was true that Ada's punishments were a bit harsh and unsavory (and all too fitting for a Gemini with a completely different side to her underneath her primarily pleasant persona), but Lucy had enough faith in the witch to feel convinced that the actions were warranted or else her enemies wouldn't have had to suffer such a fate.

Ashton wasn't so easily swayed by such thinking and hovered by a window watching Ada's departure in a state of grave astonishment. He came to Little Salem looking for something that would frighten him, and so far, the actions of a wispy and ethereal teenage girl had given him more shivers than anything. When coupled with the knowledge that his nightmarish dreams could actually be memories and he might have a connection to those that were executed, he felt like his whole life was being called into question and unraveling right in front of him.

53

DELIRIUM PERHAPS

On the day leading up to Walpurgisnacht, Ada woke up close to noon, enjoying sleeping in for a change after experiencing so many long nights of late. Being back inside the cold but comforting walls of the tavern and in her own bed was much appreciated. But as she gazed at the spirit traps above her head, she thought about Izzy, and she suddenly felt terribly alone.

Ada forced herself fully awake and visited the bathroom where, after completing her daily morning rituals, she stared critically at herself in the mirror for a long time. She was always thrown off by the comical, cartoonish nature of her appearance—comical according to her, at least—but even more so than usual that day. The huge eyes of a plucky anime heroine staring back at her, the wild tangled mess of dark hair. She knew she was considered very beautiful to some but often wished her looks more closely resembled those of a full-figured woman instead of some twiggy, saucer-eyed magical creature.

She felt her life would be much more manageable if this could only be the case.

Ada splashed water on her face in an attempt to bring herself out of her tiring hypercritical funk. She reminded herself she was her own worst enemy at the end of the day, and while drying herself, she glanced toward the ceiling, having already determined her first order of business now that she was up.

The attic was cloaked in darkness when she entered, still dressed in only her sleepwear—a simple tank top and pajama pants. Candles were everywhere, and McAllister was lying fast asleep within the protection circle, dressed in his usual black jeans and tattered black sweater.

Ada smiled warmly at the sight, unable to remember a time she'd seen him looking so calm and at peace. But her nerves kicked in when she remembered the purpose of her visit.

"Hey. McAllister." His body stirred immediately before steadily wrestling itself into a sitting position as she knelt on the floor beside him. "How long have you been sleeping up here?"

"Sorry," he muttered, rubbing the sleep from his eyelids. "I must have passed out."

Ada found herself studying his appearance intently, enjoying that they were finally alone together as her hand reached out to touch his neck.

"Your rash is gone. Along with everything else."

"Yeah. What about you?"

"Look."

Ada lifted part of her tank top to show him her left side where the strange floral birthmark was visible, the bullet wounds from several days earlier fading away around it. McAllister's dark, intense eyes narrowed in quiet disbelief, genuinely astonished by the rapid progress of her healing.

"Touch it," Ada said, staring at him earnestly.

She pulled McAllister's hand to her skin to feel the place where the wounds were disappearing. He pulled his hand away when he noticed his caresses were giving her goosebumps.

"You're amazing," McAllister said, flexing his fingers.

"No, you're amazing."

They shared an awkward laugh, and she turned away from him with embarrassment.

Ada knew that her actions were just testing him; searching for signals to allow her the confidence to express what she so desperately wanted to reveal to him. They'd been reunited for almost a week, and she hated the fact that she was still too frightened to express her feelings to him. It felt like he was retreating from her, so her eyes searched the room for something to relax the mood. That's when she saw it: a worn leather-bound book she'd never seen before, sitting at the edge of the protection circle.

"Is that the diary?" Ada exclaimed. "You really found it?"

McAllister grinned mischievously while reaching for the object.

"Here, let me show you."

Ada took a seat close beside him as he flipped through the pages, and it suddenly felt like old times. The moment reminded her of the first night they spent together when she had trembled with excitement as he pressed his body close against her to flip through an art book—that moment five years earlier when he introduced her to the work of Austin Osman Spare.

"See this writing?" McAllister noted. "This is John Dee's. This is Dee and Kelley's missing alchemical journal from 1585. Kelley must have kept it after they parted ways in Prague. It's written in the language of the alchemists, full of coded language and symbols. Here, see this? Different handwriting from across the years. All the people who possessed the diary, trying to decipher it."

Ada peered at the pages as McAllister pointed to the various inscriptions; an eclectic assortment of scribbles noting different interpretations of the coded alchemical symbolism being referenced: "Net = Sulfur"; "Lion = ??"; "Nigredo = Death." McAllister could recognize a lot of the handwriting from the book's various owners, believing one to be a famous alchemist known as the Cosmopolitan, who he was convinced Kelley had passed the diary to before it was sent to an alchemist living in New England named Christian Lodowick. The whole time he was talking, he could barely contain his excitement—like a young boy showing off one of his favorite toys to a very special playmate. Ada hoped that the fact he was sharing this with her specifically provided some extra gratification to him. She always felt they were the same in a lot of ways, so sharing these details with someone who was his equal would make it more meaningful for him, wouldn't it? And yet she still wondered if...

"Here. This is the handwriting of Alfonse Masters." McAllister tapped a series of notes with his finger. "The inspiration for all of his discoveries."

There was one thing she still didn't fully understand.

"So why is the diary called...?"

"OK, I'll speed up. So the first part has to do with alchemy. The part John Dee wrote. We get to the second part—you see where the writing changes?"

McAllister flipped to the later sections of the book and pointed to a page for Ada to note the change in penmanship.

"Kelley. 'Engelander,'" he explained. "Alchemy, once again. Dee and Kelley had ceased the Angelic Conversations when they separated, but then we get to this entry..." He flipped to a section toward the end and began to read. "'1597. *Madimi visited me in a dream last night*'—Madimi was one of the spirits Kelley communicated with. '*Madimi visited me in a dream and told me our earlier work was left unfin-*

ished. The angels hath one final communication to give to me.' And now you see here, in the back..."

Ada watched as he flipped to the back cover where a piece of aged parchment was kept. McAllister unfolded it to reveal a large mathematical table; twenty-five by twenty-seven squares, with a series of intricately positioned Enochian letters forming a strange pattern at the center.

"An Enochian table that has yet to be decoded," he explained. "One that was never brought to light. I believe that hidden within this cipher is the Forty-ninth Enochian Key."

Wholly and thoroughly amazed by the discovery, Ada gently caressed the ancient piece of parchment, staring at the blot of strange letters peering up at her.

"The key to the Apocalypse," Ada muttered. "To a new future."

Her face broke into a wide grin, and she embraced her beloved stepbrother and kissed him on the cheek. Eyes closed, she rested her head upon his shoulder while pressing her slender body against him. "Oh, McAllister, I'm so happy for us. I wish this moment would last forever."

At that moment, she yearned for him to return the affection—to touch her, to place his lips against hers, to confess he shared all the same feelings for her. But the words did not come; and while she felt him momentarily run his hands through her dark unruly mane, he stopped himself and broke the embrace. Perhaps after remembering her reaction to the intimate gesture moments earlier.

McAllister glanced at the sunlight streaming into the room and smiled nervously. "We better get ready. Big day ahead."

He started to gather together the whirlwind of items scattered on the floor, busying himself with tidying up the place. For a moment, Ada felt like she couldn't move. Something was nagging at her, compelling her to force the truth from him before... Before what exactly?

It felt like the spirits were urging her on and whispering to her. But her nerves were getting the best of her.

In the end, Ada chose to remain silent. She rose to her feet, only summoning up enough courage to turn and face him once she reached the exit.

"McAllister, do you...?"

"Do I what?"

It was no good. She was just too fearful to say the words to him.

"Never mind. I'm just...so happy for us."

Ada hurried out of the room, turning away quickly so she was unable to catch the stinging look of regret on McAllister's face. Moments later, she was crossing down the hallway, kicking herself that she didn't just come out and say it. But why would he share the same feelings for someone like her anyway? To harbor love for a total oddball with her head in the clouds and one foot in the spirit world who was inflicted with a blasted curse on top of it? Why would he love her above anyone else? Especially when he was surrounded by so many gorgeous women who desired to be with him?

Ada was drowning in these emotions when she heard a voice call out to her: "Ada? Ada, can you come here pretty please? I need your help with something."

Putting on a brave face, Ada doubled back to the doorway to Agatha's bedroom, spying the feisty redhead sorting through a pile of clothes as Lucy stood pouting in the background.

"Ada, tell Lucy she has to dress up tonight," Agatha begged. "She can't celebrate the holidays wearing..." Agatha gestured to Lucy's conservative outfit with disgust. "Whatever this is. Ick."

"Am I really that hopeless?" Lucy whined.

"You're not hopeless, darling," Agatha said, hugging her from behind. "It's just tonight is going to be special, so we want to make you look flawless. Ada, tell her I'm right. Get my back, bitch."

"Oh, Agatha. You're always right," Lucy sighed.

Ada cracked a smile, finding great amusement in the girls' inter-actions. She was equally warmed by the fact that the girls had only met recently and were already interacting like close friends.

Ada remembered this was exactly how things had started off between Agatha and herself. Both of them took an extreme liking to one another right away. Of course, there was one minor difference: Ada had always been aware of the potency of Agatha's supernatural charms, and she was a lot less susceptible to her lusty influence. It was too bad they were rivals. It was hardly a situation one would desire to be in. To preserve their friendship, she would have to leave it up to McAllister to choose who he would rather be with—a deci-sion she was determined to receive a final answer for later that night.

Crashing Godfrey's dinner party may have been the highlight of the evening, but Ada had a lot on her mind during the hours before and after this event. As with everybody else, Ada put forth an enhanced effort to look her best and was taking careful note of McAllister's reactions to her ensemble and everything else she was doing. She knew there was affection there and seemed to notice a sparkle in his eye every time the two of them made eye contact. But he also appeared to be avoiding her and was being extra flirty and touchy-feely with Agatha at every possible opportunity.

This behavior became especially apparent after they returned from the mansion where, while Lucy found herself mesmerized by the tavern's set of billiard balls and Rudy busied himself with review-ing the treasure trove of ancient mysteries within the pages of the Engelander Diary, McAllister sat with Agatha in one of the tavern's cozy black vinyl booths, whispering sweet nothings into her ear as they helped themselves to more champagne. Agatha laughed like a giddy schoolgirl every time his hands playfully pawed away at her; the drugs they'd taken were now coming on strong, and the desire for lust and adventure was no accident. Ada knew in her heart if she wanted the truth from McAllister, now was the time to get it. But first, she planned to turn up the sex.

While everyone was preoccupied downstairs, lavishing in the afterglow of their creative acts of destruction, Ada returned to her room and stripped out of her fancy party dress and changed into a flattering black corset that showed off her bare shoulders and tiny waist. She accompanied this with a long flowing black skirt, and while fixing her makeup, she paid extra special attention to her large swollen lips, painting them a dark cherry-red. Ada had played this evening in her head countless times and wanted everything to be perfect—to be everything to him, to be utterly irresistible to him. And when they were finally able to show each other how much they truly loved one another, she wanted it to be a moment to remember and for both of them not to hold anything back.

But when Ada returned to the main room, McAllister was no longer present. Her eyes anxiously searched her surroundings and noticed that Agatha was also missing, leaving only Rudy and Lucy, setting up a game of pool and laughing like a pair of pie-eyed hyenas.

"Have you seen McAllister?" Ada asked breathlessly.

"Yeah, he—" Rudy was temporarily rendered speechless by Ada's sultry transformation, weakly glancing to the exit.

Before he could finish his sentence, Ada rushed past him and into the street. But it was already too late. By the time she made it outside, the red vintage convertible was speeding off, burning rubber down Little Salem's quiet main drag with Agatha's spirited laughter echoing into the wild moonlit night.

Ada stared longingly at the vehicle's blazing taillights as they disappeared, and with them, all the years of fantasizing about a moment that would tragically never come to pass.

She had failed. Her golden opportunity had fallen out of her grasp, and now it felt like... No, she didn't want to think about it. She didn't want to think at all. Her carefully-laid plans rendered worthless, and she now had nowhere else to go.

Ada knew she didn't want to follow him or return to the tavern—to try to pretend around the others that nothing was the matter, or to retreat to her room and let the pangs of endless self-loathing and regret besiege her. No, the tavern was out for sure, which left her with only one place to turn.

* * *

When Ashton returned to the hotel, he was still shellshocked. The last thing he expected was to hear a familiar voice calling out to him.

"Hello, Ashton."

Startled, he looked up from where he was standing, and there she was: Ada, sitting in the lobby, gazing back at him.

"What are you doing here?"

Ada shrugged, staring at the carpeting.

"I wanted to see you."

The sentiment didn't appear to be mutual. Ashton swallowed his emotions as he headed for the staircase.

"You should leave."

"Why? Ashton—"

Ada reached out to him, but he violently pulled away from her.

"Don't touch me!"

"Ashton, I don't—"

"*I saw you.* At the mansion. I saw you—"

Ashton fell silent as Ada placed a finger to her lips. Her eyes glanced to the giant at the front desk, watching them from behind his newspaper. Taking the hint, Ashton grabbed her by the arm and pulled her up the stairs, and the giant frowned dourly while listening to their departing footsteps.

When Ada and Ashton reached the hotel room, Tyler was already present, chatting on his smartphone with several empty beer cans on the table and his laptop propped open beside them.

"Dude, I know! Can you believe the audacity? That poser, Eddie Specter, trying to accuse me of faking that shit? And I called him out like a total boss cuz that's how a playa do, son!"

Tyler noticed Ashton was silently glaring at him.

"Ashton! Check it out! Our video has six thousand more hits!"

Ashton turned to Ada, his eyes gesturing to the bed.

"You. Sit."

He turned back to Tyler.

"You. Leave."

Once they had the room to themselves, Ada sat motionless with her eyes fixed to the carpet. She wondered if she made the right decision in going there. The drugs in her system were starting to switch into high gear, toying with her emotions and confusing her senses. She definitely wasn't in the best state of mind for the type of conversation Ashton wanted to have with her. And he wasn't in the most stable condition either; pacing the room like a caged animal, his body tense and rigid, showing great difficulty in looking at her.

"I saw you, Ada. I saw it."

"Saw what?" she answered vacantly.

"You killed them."

"And?"

Ashton made a wounded expression. "*And?* Is that your response? How can you be so nonchalant about this?"

Ada exploded. "They were members of the Scarlet Council! Human garbage that lurks in the shadows and seeks control over everything so they can destroy all that we hold dear! I feel *no* regrets for killing them and not even the *darkest corner of hell* is good enough for *any of them!*"

"Ada..."

She really didn't want to be having this conversation. But he had asked her, so now he was going to hear it. To learn about the worst type of evil that existed and feel the full raging force of her fury for the ones she had executed.

"Do you even know these people?" Ada asked him. The whole time she remained seated, but she was becoming more fired up by the minute. "This world is a zero-sum game for them! They wish to destroy everyone who opposes them! To destroy anyone who's free! If they win, everybody loses—*don't you see?*

"You want to ask me how I can live with what I've done? *In a world where people like this go unpunished?* If you knew the things that I do about all the damage these people have caused—*and I know these things!* How do you think you'd defend your nerve to question me? *How can you even dare to question me?*"

"Ada! Stop! Listen to me!"

Ada felt faint, the whole world dissolving right before her eyes.

If everything had gone as planned and she ended up alone in a room with McAllister, the experience would have felt warm and reassuring as they surrendered wholly to the intoxicating delirium, their bodies falling into one another's, bringing them closer together. The current conversation was only making matters worse. The tidal wave of atrocities that held the Council's signature was flashing before her eyes: the bodies of witches bound to burning pyres, terror-stricken soldiers bleeding on battlefields, children starving in alleyways. She was greatly relieved when Ashton's voice pulled her away from these hellish visions, unaware that her edgy associate needed to describe his own personal hell to her.

"In my dreams—no, not my dreams," Ashton muttered. "In my

memories, there's this symbol. The same symbol that was hanging up at Sir Godfrey's. I remember receiving a framed picture of that thing from my father on my eighteenth birthday. Every year, he would come to me with a stranger who would read to me. He'd be reading from a—it was a tattered yellow book. And every year it was—it was like it was all leading up to something. They were preparing me for something, and I see this *thing*. I see all these crazy things in my dreams that I can't even..."

Ada remained silent during the exchange, and Ashton eventually took a seat on the bed right next to her.

"Ada. What's happening to me?" He asked this with urgency. He sounded like he was falling apart at the seams. "McAllister. He went through it too. When he was younger. When he—"

All of the anguish he was struggling with was finally pouring out of him, and Ada took his hand and stared deep into his eyes.

"Ashton, listen to me. Before this year is through, they will be coming for you. Just like your father and his father before him. A group of men will be coming to recruit you to become a future member of the Scarlet Council.

"You'll start out with the rank of a *Sire*, just like McAllister did. And because of your strong family background, you will eventually be allowed to move on to one of the Council's highest grades. A rank known as *Prince*.

"With this, you will be given access to names. Names that my brother ... that *McAllister* and I require to take down the Council and exterminate them once and for all. This war we are fighting is only just beginning."

With that, the truth was out. And whether it was because she wasn't in her right mind or because she genuinely felt like being honest with him, the results were still the same: Ada had finally revealed the full score to him.

Ashton looked astonished by the admission, taking things much more personally than she had anticipated.

"You were using me."

He pulled his hand away from her.

"At first, yes. I was using you," Ada admitted. "To serve a higher purpose."

"I don't—"

"To seduce and get close to someone on the inside who could help us achieve our goals."

Ashton couldn't help but laugh.

"You were using me like a piece of meat."

"Oh, don't flatter yourself."

"No?"

Ada frowned at the floor. She felt lightheaded, struggling to stay tethered to reality. "No, Ashton. I like you but I..."

He leaned in closer.

"You what?"

She struggled with the words, her heart barely able to take it.

"I like you, but I love... I love..."

Ada felt him grab her by the arm, pulling away only to be drawn back as he kissed her hard on the mouth. And she found herself returning the kiss in kind, hungrily devouring all of his ravenous and impassioned desire for her.

She felt her mind go blank, seeking to lose herself in the exchange; all those years of desperately pining for one person and withholding herself from being with anyone else out of fear she would injure them with her strange powers or the abominable curse she was stuck with.

And who better to enjoy such an experience with than a strapping young heartthrob like Ashton? With his dashing dreamboat features and the chiseled body of a Greek god who desired her more than anything—lips, tongues, fingers, hands exploring and devouring each other's bodies like a carnal feast of endless delights. What she wanted was to forget. What she wanted was oblivion. And things only proceeded to escalate as they madly tore off each other's clothes and ravaged each other's bodies, giving in to the fire of pure unadulterated lust.

Hours later, Ada's haunting blue-violet eyes popped open, not quite sure where she was and wondering if she had crossed over to a different reality altogether. After glancing beside her, she discovered she was lying naked under the bed covers in a hotel room with her casual lover sleeping next to her. The real mystery was what had awoken her.

Everything in the room seemed to be cast with a hazy amber glow. Normally, this wasn't something that would feel too unusual. It could have been close to morning; she had no idea what time it was or if she was still feeling the effects of the powerful indulgences left over from the previous night. The one thing that seemed notably off was the curious sound of something scraping against the window—clearly the cause for her waking. A noise that sent an uncomfortable chill throughout her bones, drawing her to investigate.

Wearing a puzzled expression and still half-asleep, Ada searched the floor and pulled on Ashton's T-shirt to cover her bare body before climbing out of bed and staggering toward the peculiar sound. She drew aside the curtains to discover a large moth battering itself against the windowpane, appearing desperate to get into the room with her. But when she opened the window and the moth flew inside, it swiftly fell to her feet, dying in mid-flight.

Ada's breathing began picking up as her mind started processing everything she was seeing. She discovered her body was shaking as she fell to her knees and cupped the moth in her hands, pulling it to her face for a closer inspection.

On its back was a pattern resembling a human skull, helping her to place the precise species of the insect. As she recognized the creature for what it was, a wave of panic shot through her like a chorus of agonizing screams. Her eyes rolled back as she fell backward and fainted, her fragile frame crashing to the carpeting with the dead moth laying on the floor right next to it, the result of her distressing realization as to the true terrible significance of this horrible omen and that the worst thing in the world had happened.

54

PROMETHEUS, TORN BY VULTURES

After the New Lords reaped their satisfaction from crashing the Godfrey mansion, Agatha started taking notice that McAllister was acting extra affectionate toward her. On the walk back to the tavern, he seemed to be looking for any excuse imaginable to touch her and be close to her, with the conversation getting much steamier and more intimate once they were enjoying some private time alone together in one of the tavern's black vinyl booths. Whether this extra attention was motivated by the party favors Ada slipped into their drinks or the thrill of watching Godfrey and the others get their violent just desserts, it didn't matter either way to her. When McAllister suggested they should jaunt over to the beach for a quick spell, she put up no argument whatsoever. She was feeling deliriously light-headed—in the mood for whatever her twisted demon lover could think up.

Agatha remained convinced that recent experiences had brought them closer than ever. The renewal of their relationship began with her rescue from the Reverend's basement and became stronger still after she helped him find the diary. By the way he was looking at her, and all that night in particular, she knew he desired her and that the excursion to the beach was for more than an innocent picnic.

For the outing, McAllister drove them to the nearby town of Marblehead, speeding through Little Salem and past the borders of the larger proper town of Salem itself to a peninsula where the beach was a lot less rocky than others in the area and offered some additional privacy once you ventured past the protective gates. Breaking in after-hours was no problem, and upon reaching their destination, McAllister built them a small bonfire in a fire pit and proceeded to caress Agatha's body and fondle her breasts while hungrily nibbling her neck.

Things quickly heated up from there with Agatha inviting every touch, kiss, and embrace he had to give to her, the potent drugs blinding their senses to everything except their mutual passions for one another. In no time at all, their clothes were strewn about the sand and they were wrapped up in coital bliss, with her ecstatic sighs and moans overlapping the gentle crashing of the ocean.

But on that night, something felt off.

Their lustful activities started out hot and heavy, but as they continued, their naked bodies sliding against one another in a feverish and animalistic fashion, Agatha began to feel like she wasn't really there—or that he wasn't really there—and there was an unbridgeable gulf between them. Despite the dizzying intensity of everything, it felt like they were disconnected and engaged in separate experiences. This gloomy realization inspired her to drive her lover to be even more forceful with her than usual that night. She tried as hard as she could to make their intimate affair as pleasurable as possible for both of them, but couldn't help feeling that they were trying too hard to please each other and the experience that had started off so perfectly was ultimately hollow and unsatisfying and tragically spelled the end to their romantic relationship.

After both parties were spent, physically and emotionally, and their carnal activities had reached their anticipated outcome, McAllister zipped up his jeans and walked away from her. He planted himself next to the fire with his overcoat draped over his bare shoulders, perusing the fabled diary as he searched his pocket for cigarettes.

Agatha watched him sitting apart from her with a mournful expression, torn with emotion as she slipped back into her undergarments. Once the silence between them became too much to bear, she turned her body away from him, donning a stormy expression while staring at the restless waters in the distance.

"A lot has changed in five years."

"What do you mean?"

Agatha shrugged half-heartedly. "Kinda feels like we've been going through the motions lately. Something's changed. Hasn't it?"

McAllister remained silent. He placed the book aside and leaned forward, staring at the dancing flames in front of him.

It was the end of the road for them, and they both knew it. Agatha just wanted him to be honest with her and tell her the reasons for this.

"Really, it's fine," she asserted. "I've dealt with rejection before. I just...want us to be happy."

For several moments, McAllister continued to stare into the fire. His hand disappeared into his pocket and flicked open his gold lighter, drawing it to the unlit cigarette resting between his lips.

"Do you believe in fate, Agatha?"

The question threw her for a loop. The flickering glow of the firelight danced across his glazed features as she watched him take a long drag and exhale a cloud of smoke before continuing.

"The night before I went away, Ada told me a story. It was the story about how every woman in her family was destined to fall in love once and only once and that her lover was doomed to meet an unfortunate end. Over the years, I think she resisted falling in love with people because she was afraid of hurting them. But she always did everything I asked of her. And when I told her I wanted her to find a future member of the Council and make him fall in love with her... I never considered how much I might regret that decision."

Agatha stared at McAllister stunned, noticing he appeared to be growing misty-eyed, even though his face remained cold and impassive. She knew he was fond of Ada, but hearing him talk openly about this was a whole new experience. She never knew how deep his feelings ran for the young witch.

"The situation's absurd, I know it is," McAllister said, continuing solemnly and not without difficulty. "She was just a girl when I met her. But somehow I always knew she'd be my best friend. And losing a lover is one thing... No, it's more than that. It's something... It's something much more than that."

McAllister directed his eyes toward the heavens before lowering them back to the flames, seeming to resign himself to acknowledging something he knew he could no longer run away from.

"Fear is death, Agatha," McAllister said. "When you let fear into your heart, it becomes a tyrant. And then you'll never be free."

He turned his head to notice something glimmering in the distance. Maintaining a stony expression, he rose to his feet and slowly circled the fire pit.

"Did you know there's a traitor in our group?"

Agatha's lips parted in shock. But what he did next surprised her more than anything: He came to a halt and smiled mysteriously.

"Death to all tyrants," McAllister said—right before the bullet pierced his neck.

Agatha screamed in horror, rushing toward him as his body dropped to the sand with streaming torrents of black blood oozing out of his mouth and throat.

The shooter was none other than Miles, who had parked his black Range Rover a short distance away, the location of the lovers' intended tryst having been accidentally handed to him by a member of Ada's coven. After confirming his target's presence, he painted a black cross on the bullet that would inevitably incapacitate his victim before assembling his sniper rifle and setting it on the hood of the vehicle to take the deadly shot.

Miles wasn't the only one who arrived at the outing uninvited. As Agatha screamed McAllister's name, she felt a pair of hands pulling her away from him—hands belonging to Wilbur and Dave.

"Let go of me! LET ME GO!"

Agatha struggled furiously as the two black-suited men held her arms behind her. Alas, it was no use, and she felt a creeping sense of unease as she watched a large and imposing figure emerge from the shadows and cross to where McAllister lay convulsing in the sand: Dr. Franklin Baker, the Witchfinder General; one of his hands gripping a heavy object that left a long deep trail in the ground behind him as he dragged it toward the fire pit.

Once there, the man stared blankly at the exposed Sigil of Lucifer tattoo on McAllister's forearm and the desperate eyes gazing in his direction, his wounded prey struggling for breath as he continued to hemorrhage oily black sludge from his ruptured throat.

"Hello, McAllister. It's been a while."

He placed his foot on McAllister's chest, hands clenching the heavy instrument he was carrying: a medieval battle-ax with the phrase, "*Soli Deo gloria*" inscribed upon the blade.

"I'll see you in hell."

"No!" Agatha screamed.

Crack!

When the ax met its target, Wilbur turned away from the sight, and Dave watched with what appeared to be a certain degree of reverence for the departed. But the dark-suited assassin inevitably turned away as well as Agatha started sobbing, and Franklin dropped the heavy instrument and bent over, pulling the decapitated head from the sandy earth and holding it up to the moonlight.

One of the Scarlet Council's most dangerous adversaries, the rebel angel who was once a respected member of their organization and whose name struck fear into the hearts of his countless enemies, was now dead. Agatha could barely believe it, equally horrified and despondent to have witnessed her former lover forced to suffer such a misfortunate end.

Her darling McAllister. Savagely cut down in his prime. Slaughtered by the slayers in the most brutal way imaginable. As she stared into the lifeless eyes of her champion, now being displayed like a trophy for the hunters, she felt her anger rising to an impressionable degree. She gritted her teeth and squeezed Dave's groin as hard as she could, wrestling herself free from her captors before shoving them away from her and taking off running at full speed.

Miles was smiling with satisfaction, but he burst into action once the shapely redhead initiated her valiant escape plan, repositioning the rifle on the hood of the Range Rover and setting the witch in his sights. The witch hunters seemed to have underestimated her, and Miles ultimately proved to be too slow to be of any service, losing his chance to subdue his target as she disappeared into a grove of trees.

Back on the beach, Wilbur reached for his gun, but Franklin held out an arm to placate him.

"Let her run. She won't get far."

After this, Miles joined his three associates next to the bonfire, staring down at the lifeless headless corpse emptying its black stygian muck into the sand, while a short distance away from them, Agatha continued running, tears pouring down her face as she let loose a wild, heartfelt scream, cutting through the air like a rapier and shattering the strained tranquility of the somber moonlit setting.

The night was Walpurgisnacht, also known as "Witches' Night." A night where the veil between the spirit world and our own was supposedly razor thin. Casualties had been suffered on both sides, with Godfrey and several of his associates struck down by the New Lords, and McAllister murdered in an equally horrific fashion by assassins from the Scarlet Council.

Ada's coven weren't the only ones engaging in ritualistic mischief that night. Since Walpurgisnacht was one of the eight main holidays observed by witches, the Sisterhood of Circe was celebrating the occasion in their own delightful fashion. In contrast to the New Lords' more troublesome and deviant activities, the Sisterhood's holiday revelries were a lot more passive and mundane. Nancy and her coven, which included Cheryl, Priscilla, and several others, met at the burnt-out clearing in the forest to draw down the moon and perform a series of rituals before commencing with drinking and dancing until it was almost dawn.

What the Little Salem coven saw as a fun night of witchery probably would have caused someone like Ada to feel like she would die of boredom right on the spot, but no one enjoyed herself more on that night than Nancy. Nancy needed a festive experience after the trying and turbulent week she was having. The past several days were complete hell, with her daughter's sudden disappearance and the useless search that followed. There were also several other troubling events that had raised her stress level considerably, such as the way that Ada's coven had fallen quiet following the closure of the tavern and the discovery of several dead bodies in the torched remains of the Desperado Roadhouse. The morning news presented the details that the body of the Sheriff had been located, and the FBI had been called in to conduct an investigation. Surprisingly, the otherwise respectable lawman had been in the company of several well-known criminals and drug offenders—something that didn't place the Little Salem Sheriff's Department in a very flattering light.

Nancy felt very much on her own during this time since she was unable to rely on Wilbur for any comfort or assistance. He recently left town on an errand for the Council, leaving her to search for Mary Sue all on her lonesome. With that being the case, she was immensely relieved once her daughter returned home and was safe in her own bed. But things were still far from back to normal in Little Salem, and Nancy was eager to temporarily push everything aside for one night. She thought it was important to find happiness wherever you could, and if that meant turning a blind eye once in a while to various problems and unpleasantries, so be it.

The holidays were always a special time for Nancy, and once the night was through, she felt convinced she had made the right decision to participate, now feeling wholly re-energized and renewed. As she returned home right as the sun was rising, with her witch's kit under her arm carrying her white witch's robes and other assorted curiosities, she was still positively glowing from the experience of celebrating her practice and traditions with the rest of her fellow white witches. She knew she had to wake up in a few hours, but that was no trouble; she was already looking forward to spending the day with her daughter and taking her to visit the pony at the back of the shop. Nancy knew Baby Blue had been missing her, and she had likely been missing the animal as well (God, she loved that horse). To hold to her promise, she would have to leave the house shortly. What she wasn't expecting was her daughter would already be wide-awake when she returned home.

"You were with them, weren't you?"

Nancy froze in the hallway in front of Mary Sue's bedroom. She'd been trying to be quiet as possible, sneaking past the room in an effort not to wake her. But her daughter was already sitting up with her back against the pillow, staring at her mother as she stood motionless, not quite sure how to respond.

"You were with...your coven."

Mary Sue said this after failing to receive an answer, rephrasing her question in a manner that sounded slightly accusatory and placing her mother on the defensive.

"The Sisterhood of Circe," Nancy confirmed. "The order of white witches who have resided in this town for centuries."

"And the Scarlet Council?"

Nancy took a breath, tightly gripping the doorframe. How her daughter had even heard of this organization, she hadn't a clue.

"That's the name of a group your father once belonged to."

Mary Sue's eyes narrowed pensively, seeming to be processing something internally. She reached for her sketchbook and crumpled up an earlier drawing before flipping to a brand new page.

"You're supposed to be the good guys, right?"

Nancy didn't know how to answer, but she felt this was indisputable. At the time, she had no way of knowing that while her daughter was interrogating her, her husband was on the deck of a small fishing boat; bobbing quietly on the placid waters of the ocean only a short distance from shore, his restless features frowning at the interior of a coffin that held McAllister's perished remains.

"We've always had good intentions, your father and I," Nancy explained while Dave hammered the lid into place; "We've always done our best to look out for you and take care of you," as the coffin was dumped over the side into the glassy waters below; "We've always had your best interests at heart," as Franklin, back on the beach, noticed an old leather-bound book lying in the sand and tossed it into the smoldering embers of the fire pit. All this was occurring while back at the Truegoods', Mary Sue pursed her lips while listening, the whole time focused on scribbling something indecipherable on one of the blank white pages of her sketchbook.

"It's funny," Mary Sue finally said.

She observed her work with a cold look etched upon her face.

"Scarlet Council. Sisterhood of Circe."

She circled a pair of items and cast a vacant stare at her mother as she held up the sketchbook for her to contemplate.

"It's almost like it could be the same thing."

There, on Mary Sue's drawing pad, were the names of both organizations with the initials they shared both circled.

[S]carlet [C]ouncil

[S]isterhood of [C]irce

SC/SC

Nancy stared wide-eyed at the drawing, the implications of what her daughter was suggesting too painful for her to address. And as Mary Sue continued to gaze at her bewildered guardian, while her lips trembled and her eyes teared up with a burning sadness mixed with resentment and hate, back at the beach, Miles, Wilbur, and Dave rejoined Franklin by the remains of the bonfire and three men took off in a black BMW while one man remained.

Peace came at a price in Little Salem, and what Mary Sue was suggesting was it appeared that the shadowy secret society that controlled the town and the order of witches once standing in opposition to them were now intrinsically bound together and united in maintaining the status quo. This devil's bargain helped bring great prosperity to a select and privileged few over the years, but there was no question that something was rotting at the heart of this cozy relationship since it was a deal that could only be paid for with blood.

With Mary Sue having gained total awareness of the clumsy house of cards her celebrated community was made of, it would only be a matter of time before she wrote off her mother completely; leaving her with only the glitzy memories of her once-perfect artificial paradise to comfort her, the love of the daughter that she had been fighting so hard to preserve smashed to pieces. Just like the windows that Ada had shattered after delivering her warning that someday she would expose the Truegoods and all the other hypocrites just like them for what they really were.

Nancy's battle wasn't over, but in a way, despite all the tragedies her team had suffered, Ada had already won. With Nancy's soul surrendered long ago in exchange for the opportunity to live in a false utopia built on countless lies and fabrications—with all this lost and proved counterfeit in the eyes of her disaffected descendant, the only question that remained was how much further she would have to fall to avoid facing the discomforting truth of the matter: that Ada van Dreyer, the one she scorned and shunned, had been right all along.

55

BETRAYAL BLEEDS BITTER

Miles had been in contact with the Scarlet Council for quite some time, but he hadn't made the final decision to betray Ada until just recently. In fact, if he had to pinpoint the precise moment where it became crystal clear to him he intended to carry through with his duplicity, it would have been during a conversation he shared with her before being sent away to Boston.

Ada had accompanied him to the train station in the neighboring city of Salem. He remembered thinking she looked especially cute that day, dressed in a pair of stylish bell-bottom jeans, wedges, and a white satin blouse worn underneath her gray hoodie. Ada seemed to be paying extra close attention to her appearance lately—not like she was someone who needed to, in his opinion. Miles thought she looked beautiful no matter what she wore. But with her so-called "brother" back in town, it was clear she was pulling out all the stops to inspire him to start looking at her like a young woman, as opposed to the young girl he remembered when they were last face to face.

With McAllister back in the picture and the two "not-really-siblings" reunited, it didn't take long for Miles to conclude that everyone outside of this special relationship was now insignificant. For Ada, nothing could have been further from the truth, but the unrelenting pangs of jealousy and envy he was feeling were waging a vicious war inside of him. The fact that she didn't argue with McAllister's decision that, out of everyone, he should be the one to be sent away was the thing that stung most of all and made him resentful and vindictive.

"Kind of ironic, isn't it?" Miles had commented as they sat together, waiting for the train that would spirit him away from her and the rest of his close friends. "You discovered me in a library and invited me into the group. Day after I meet your brother, I'm out of the group and being sent to another library."

Ada smiled at her shoes, possibly regretting that this had to be the case. "You're not out of the group, Miles. Right now we just need you in a more...specialized capacity."

Miles smirked despite himself. There was no getting around how much he loved her and how crazy he was about her. Despite his feelings that he was being sent out into the wilderness, he felt genuine affection for her still. More than he had felt for anyone and more then she could ever know.

"The notorious 'Engelander Diary,'" Miles had mused. "Rumor has it it's somewhere hidden in Little Salem. And the rumors also suggest it was stolen from a library in Boston, and before that, it was in Little Salem and had something to do with the Salem witch trials. The book's the stuff of legends, and you believe it might really exist."

Ada smiled coyly at his summary.

"Wouldn't be the craziest thing I've believed all week."

There was a sparkle in her eye when she suggested this, and he couldn't help but smile in return. He was continuously finding himself blown away by her. But at the very same time, it pained him to know that even with all the love and attention she showed him, it was only a mere fraction of the feelings she had for her stepbrother. The words she said next would hurt him most of all.

"I'm going to miss you, Miles. You're like my brother from another mother."

Was that all he was to her? Like a brother? And not some fake brother who she was secretly in love with—she meant a brother she felt no romantic feelings toward whatsoever.

Miles smiled bitterly at the comment and directed a vacant stare in front of him, deeply wanting so much more from her than she'd ever be willing to give.

"Ada... I wish..."

Buzz. Buzz.

The statement hung in the air as Ada turned away and pulled out her phone. "Sorry, Miles. Let me—Agatha? Hold on for a sec, OK?"

She turned back to face him with eyes bright while wearing her impish smile, appearing to have all the time in the world for her treasured friend. "You were saying?"

But it was too late.

The moment she turned away, he made his harsh decision.

If he couldn't have her...

At the sound of a whistle, Miles stared into the distance.

"I think that's my train."

As the train approached them, he received a goodbye hug and watched her cross away from him with her phone pressed to her ear, knowing the next time they met they would be mortal enemies.

Miles would visit this same train station several days later, but when he returned it wasn't to reunite with Ada and the New Lords but to pick up Wilbur and the Witchfinder General. He would accompany them to the Godfrey mansion to discover all the violence and mayhem that Ada's coven had gotten up to during his absence. The senseless brutality and carnage on display was shocking, but he wasn't put off by any of this. He was actually quite impressed by the lengths that Ada had gone to show she meant business.

However, Ada's little murder party wouldn't go unpunished and only provided the Council with more ample reasons to exterminate the witch and everyone close to her. All Miles needed to complete the deed was the coven's location—something he knew he could obtain by relying on Rudy.

"Miles! Where are you at? We're gettin' wrecked in this bitch!"

Rudy was at the tavern when Miles had phoned him, engaged in a drunken game of strip poker with Lucy and also Tyler, who popped over after being kicked out of his hotel room. At the time, the boys were losing badly to Lucy, who remained dressed in all her clothes while they were already half-naked and down to their skivvies.

Despite the humiliating turn of events, Rudy remained in high spirits. As the only other guy in Ada's coven before McAllister's blustery arrival, Rudy felt a special kinship with Miles and missed having him around to horse around with. Even if he usually ended up the brunt of all the jokes shared between them.

"I'm headed your way right now," Miles had told him. "Is McAllister around? I have a big surprise for him."

"Big surprise, huh? Nah, he left here with Agatha a little while ago. They were headed to the beach in Marblehead. Looking for a little privacy, know what I mean?"

Excellent. It was just the opportunity he was looking for.

"I'll see you soon," Miles said.

"See ya soon, playboy. Hey, what's this surprise you have for—?"

Click.

"Miles, hey. How are you?"

"Ada, are you okay? You sound spooked."

"It's nothing. I'm just...having a strange morning."

Several minutes earlier, Ada had woken up from where she passed out on the floor of the hotel room with the dead death's-head hawkmoth lying on the carpet beside her. The night before had started like a dream that descended into a drug-fueled psychedelic nightmare, ultimately culminating in her shared passions with Ashton and the arrival of the moth—a truly unsettling omen signifying something horrible had happened. Too horrible to think about.

After quickly dressing and stumbling to the tavern in a daze as the sun was still rising and the early morning fog blanketed the streets, Ada found Rudy and Lucy passed out on the main floor. She questioned them about McAllister before suggesting they should go upstairs and pack since something wasn't sitting well with her.

Something wasn't sitting well with her at all.

"Sorry to hear that," Miles said. "You're at the tavern, right?"

"Yes?" Ada was looking more lost and bewildered by the second. "Where are you? Are those seagulls I'm hearing?"

Miles stifled a short chuckle. He had remained at the beach after the others had left and was now pacing up and down the shoreline.

"Rudy told me a couple of you were heading to the beach. But no one seems to be here."

He stifled another laugh, knowing this statement was deceptive. In a way, McAllister *was* there, only he was currently much farther out from shore and rotting at the bottom of the ocean.

Mistrust. Disbelief. Ada's intuition was signaling her like crazy, but she still wasn't sure what was going on. Things would become much clearer as she suddenly heard beeping on the other end of the line, informing her another call was waiting for her to pick up.

"Don't move. I'll come meet you," Miles offered.

"Miles, can you hold on? I'm receiving another—yes, hello?"

"You have a Collect Call from '*Ada, it's Agatha, oh my God pick*—' Do you agree to accept—"

Ada's eyes widened. "Yes! Yes! *Hello?*"

Agatha was making the call from a phone booth in what appeared to be the middle of nowhere with nothing but gray skies and blankets of fog surrounding her. She was still only dressed in her underwear, and her body was shaking, her normally picture-perfect makeup a disorderly smear of stale sweat and tears.

"Ada, it's Agatha," she rapidly said. "We were ambushed. McAllister—they killed him. Oh my God, they killed him. McAllister's dead, and I ran away and—I'm so sorry, Ada. Oh my God, I'm so sorry. I couldn't do anything to stop them—"

"*Who?*" Ada demanded. "Agatha! Tell me who did it!"

"It was Wilbur and a couple of others. I think it was the Council. And Miles. *Miles* was with them. He led them straight to us."

Ada's mouth dropped open in disbelief.

Of all the people who could have betrayed her—and she never saw it coming. Ada was a clever girl, but she was still young and inexperienced. She knew all about the darkness that resided in people's hearts, but for this darkness to emerge in someone so close and reliable was unthinkable.

"Ada? Are you still there? Hello? *Hello?*"

If Miles was working for the Council, then that meant... Yes, two silhouettes at the window. They were already here.

Ada terminated the call as Wilbur and Franklin entered the room, guns drawn and pointed straight at her. Fast as lightning, she raised her arm and made a gesture that sent both men's bodies flying backward into the walls. She had succeeded at disarming the slayers, but they were not alone. Sensing something threatening, she spun around to discover Dave standing behind her, armed with a Taser and firing the barbs into her ribs, sending 50,000 volts into her system and knocking her off her feet.

With Ada lying crumpled on the ground and out of commission, Wilbur saw his opportunity to end this madness. He picked himself up and approached her, aiming his gun at her heart.

"Wait."

At the sound of Franklin's objection, Wilbur watched his associate approach their victim with a syringe between his fingers. The large and imposing man leaned down and injected the contents into Ada's arm, inspiring her to squirm before easing into unconsciousness. Seeming satisfied, he pocketed the syringe and scanned the seedy environment before issuing an order to tie Ada up.

Miles never waited for Ada to return once she switched over to accept the call from Agatha. He already had a good idea of just whom the call was coming from, but it was no matter because it was already too late. He knew their conversation marked the end to their relationship and likely the mortal end to the witch as well, marking the occasion with a smile as he hurled his phone into the ocean before engaging in a peaceful stroll along the shoreline, his hands thrust deep into his pockets.

Later, Miles would return to the fire pit to observe the splatter of black blood upon the sand and notice the remnants of a badly burned book, smoldering in the ashes. He would even catch a brief glimpse of Agatha as she stealthily returned to the scene to retrieve McAllister's convertible before peeling away at top speed. He considered giving chase, but he had more important things to think about. Betraying his comrades had placed him in the Scarlet Council's good graces, and he expected to be rewarded handsomely as a result.

Miles had been looking for a place to belong for a long time, and the idea of joining up with "the bad guys" bothered him less and less the more he thought about it. As the newest member of a powerful secret society that a unique individual like himself would normally be denied a place in, he looked forward to all the colorful advantages he would gain from such an association. The removal of Ada and McAllister was for the best, and he would only shine brighter without them. This was his destiny, and now no one could hold him back.

Then again, there was always the possibility this could only turn out to be wishful thinking. Despite his doubtless intellect, there were a lot of things Miles didn't know about—especially when it came to matters of the nefarious secret society he was now serving.

56

LEAVING LITTLE SALEM

———

It was still early in the morning when one of the upper story windows of the tavern slid open, and Lucy and Rudy emerged and shimmied down the drainpipe. They overheard Ada's futile battle against the witch hunters and knew if the slayers were strong enough to defeat her, they were clearly no match for them. To survive, they needed to turn tall and find a place to hide before figuring out if there was anything they could do to help her.

Lucy's feet hit the ground first, followed by Rudy's. They were running past the side of the renovated Victorian when Lucy felt him firmly grasp her shoulder, bringing her to a halt.

While peering around the corner, Rudy observed Wilbur and Dave exiting the building with Ada in their arms, her hands and feet bound together. Following close behind them was the imposing fig-ure of Dr. Franklin Baker. This was the closest Rudy had ever gotten to an official squad of Council witch killers, which made the experience especially terrifying. But what Lucy was seeing was even more unnerving: hideous demons clawing into each of the slayers' backs, their fearsome red faces snarling at the air.

Curiously, Wilbur's demon appeared to possess an almost transparent quality to it, like it was stuck between worlds. Dave's was the same as many others she'd seen, and it was the demon attached to the back of the Witchfinder General that was most disturbing: a huge bloated monstrosity with long spindly arms that looked almost too skinny to support the weight of the infernal parasite, its giant sagging belly dragging close to the ground as it croaked and wheezed with agitation.

From their hiding place, the two youths watched the killers drop Ada's body into the trunk of a black BMW. After this, Dave returned to the tavern with his gun drawn, reappearing minutes later, holstering his weapon and shrugging his shoulders.

"I searched the place top to bottom. There's no one else here."

Wilbur wiped the sweat from his forehead, looking increasingly uneasy about what he'd gotten himself into. He glanced at his snowy-haired superior who was staring at the tavern while caressing the antique rosary in his hand.

"Burn it," Franklin said.

Dave nodded and headed back inside.

"And Ada?" Wilbur asked.

Franklin's rheumy eyes narrowed as he scanned the foggy street.

"Drive her out to Gallows Hill and string her up. Leave her as a message for the others."

Wilbur registered the order with tacit alarm. He struggled to maintain his composure, knowing the punishments he would suffer should he fail to carry out the brutal assignment.

"What about you?"

Franklin answered bluntly before turning his back on him.

"My work is finished. There's already enough blood on my hands."

It was only a short while after Wilbur left the tavern when Nancy's trusty Volvo pulled up outside the frozen yogurt store. The sun was steadily rising overhead and Nancy was feeling tired and weary from the sleepless night beforehand, toughing it out like a champ.

"I have a feeling it's going to be a good day today," Nancy said. She turned to her morose teenage daughter, sitting in the passenger seat. "Baby Blue's been missing you."

Nancy was putting forth a noble effort to be cheerful and optimistic. But while searching for her keys, she noticed Mary Sue staring longingly at the tavern across the street. Her daughter was still suffering from a broken heart due to that troublesome gypsy she'd fallen for—and also hungering for some further interaction with Ada no doubt. *Imagine that.* Her actions to protect her daughter only ended up driving her to become closer to Ada while that silly teenage crush of hers was struggling to recover from that stupid hex she cast.

Nancy deeply regretted placing herself in a position where she was now being regarded as an enemy to her daughter's happiness. Fortunately, she had high hopes that things would soon be returning to normal. She made a mental note she would have to phone Wilbur to hear about how he was getting on with that horrible business.

"Cute shop."

Nancy turned sharply, spying Franklin leaning against a nearby column. It had been years since she'd last seen him, and she noticed he continued to possess the same stoic stature and world-weary gaze.

"You open for business?"

Nancy smiled awkwardly, not knowing what to say. Seeing her

husband's former associate standing there like he never left was startling enough, but she was even more surprised when he followed her inside and had a seat.

"Back in town for work I'm assuming?" Nancy asked him, making small talk. "Did you come with Wilbur?"

"I left him a short while ago. My job is finished."

Nancy smiled nervously at this confession. She took it by his choice of words they'd made an encouraging amount of progress in dealing with the rebel witches.

"We appreciate your coming out here on such short notice." Nancy crossed to her daughter and lovingly caressing her shoulder. "We've been so worried—for the children. It will be nice for the town to get back to normal."

Despite the hopeful sentiment, Franklin's manner remained restrained as he watched Mary Sue squirm uncomfortably and pull away. This seemed to be all the information he needed to confirm how the Truegoods had been faring with their present difficulties.

"You know what they say," Franklin offered dispiritedly. "About gaining the whole world but losing your soul in the process?"

Nancy gazed curiously at the man, feeling strangely unnerved by this cloudy observation. But she ultimately decided to push it from her mind as she turned away from him to scrub the counter.

"Mary Sue, go check on the horse."

Nancy forced a smile as she watched her daughter depart for the back with her head lowered and her shoulders slumped. Eyes glued to the tabletop, Franklin listened to the sound of her footsteps, his heavy eyes growing more somber and reflective.

Nancy had no idea that Wilbur was currently on the road with Ada tied up in the trunk, deeply regretting he ever agreed to the task assigned to him. Ada was still unconscious when he started his journey, and he assumed she would still be out cold when it came time to cinch a noose around her neck and hang her from one of the tall, spindly trees overlooking the historic setting where so many witches had met their untimely end.

Witch killing was indeed a dirty business. Such was the life he ended up with. Hopefully, after completing the job, his career with the Council would come to a close, and he and Nancy could finally start sleeping more easily.

The knowledge that this gruesome endeavor would soon be over was the one reassurance that served to comfort him as he drove through the foggy urban setting, still deserted for the most part, with twisted trees dotting the landscape like giant dried-up sea anemones. But as he approached the famous execution site, his car started behaving erratically, the electrical system going haywire with random buttons blinking on and off and the engine growling abnormally, all the gears grinding and screaming for some reason.

"Aw fudge." Wilbur tightly gripped the wheel as the car started picking up speed. "Dammit. C'mon—"

Slamming on the pedals did nothing—everything he did was useless. In one final act of desperation, he tried the door only to discover he was locked inside, panic engulfing his entire body as the vehicle suddenly jerked off the side of the road, accelerating faster and faster before crashing headlong into a tree.

Wilbur's head slammed against the windshield from the force of the impact, and he was out like a light as the totaled vehicle collapsed into motionlessness. While he was unconscious, he missed the sight of something that would have set his hairs on edge: the trunk of the BMW ejecting itself several feet into the air with such a colossal amount of force it looked like it had been shot out of the mouth of a cannon or launched by powerful springs.

Buzz. Buzz.

Nancy was still puzzling over what Franklin had said to her when she heard the vibrations of her cell phone and checked the caller ID. It appeared that Wilbur was trying to reach her, but for some reason, the idea that her husband would be calling didn't feel right. As the buzzing continued, she felt a disturbing sense of unease, with the cold, vacant stare Franklin was giving her adding to all the unsettling emotions she was experiencing.

Nancy mumbled into the phone. "H-hello?"

A voice answered immediately—and it wasn't Wilbur's.

"It's over, Nancy. Do you hear me?"

The voice belonged to Ada, standing next to the smoking wreckage of the black BMW with the driver's door open, her waifish frame covered in grime, blood, and soot, body shaking with emotion.

"Tell me, '*it's over*,'" Ada demanded, drying the salty tears from her cheeks. "Say it. SAY TO ME IT'S OVER!"

Nancy remained silent as she listened to her former protégé's impassioned shriek. She had no idea where Ada was calling her from or how she'd gotten ahold of her husband's phone or what had become of him.

While struggling to reply, she discovered her hands were trembling, and her voice had become trapped inside her throat. It was as if her body was telling her that now was the time to finally back down and make peace so that no more people would be harmed or would have to suffer in this ridiculous conflict.

But Nancy had too much pride to do such a thing.

To give in to the demands of her sworn enemy?

The idea was heresy.

To agree to Ada's terms after everything she had done to protect her daughter and the town? She felt her hatred start to swell, and her face became ice-cold as she pursed her lips and answered:

"Ada, it will never be over."

Hand shaking, Nancy hung up the phone and felt immensely pleased for a shining sliver of a moment—right until she noticed her daughter standing at the back of the shop, looking stunned and astonished by the cold iron malice painted on her mother's face.

However, Mary Sue's attention was quickly directed elsewhere: The sound of a car screeching to a halt led her gaze to the red Cadillac DeVille pulling up to the tavern with Agatha sitting behind the wheel. The redhead was dressed in only her underwear for some reason and pulling on a trench coat to cover herself when Rudy and Lucy came dashing outside, their arms overloaded with luggage. After tossing the baggage into the trunk and back seat—items that included a small cat carrier and a battered black steamer trunk—the two youths hopped inside and the convertible took off like a shot, with the coven of witches now on the run.

The sight of Ada's gang appearing to be getting the hell out of town once and for all seemed to trigger a visceral response in Mary Sue, and she ran full-speed to the yard out back as her mother watched in a state of shock.

"And there it goes," Franklin dryly commented.

Nancy didn't have time to translate the veiled statement. She rushed out back, making it just in time to watch her daughter adjusting herself on the back of the pony before jerking the reins and speeding off.

"Mary Sue! Mary Sue!" Nancy yelled, but it was already too late. She was powerless to do anything but watch the pony gallop down the alleyway with her daughter sitting confidently on top.

Meanwhile, at Gallows Hill, Wilbur was slowly coming to his senses. His forehead was bleeding, and broken glass lay like a blanket of jagged snowflakes all over the front seats. Feeling lost and disoriented, he squinted his eyes in pain to observe that the driver-side door of the BMW was now open and a dark figure was looming over him amidst the cloudy haze of fog and smoke.

While addressing her wounded adversary, the menacing figure spoke to him with her jaw clenched tight, her haunting eyes boring into him, burning with rage.

"I spy with my little eye a leopard that never changed his spots."

Still in a daze, Wilbur reached into his blazer but couldn't find what he was searching for, glancing back to notice the young witch brandishing his handgun and aiming it directly at him.

"IS THIS WHAT YOU'RE LOOKING FOR?" Ada shrieked.

He raised his hands in submission, tears streaming down his face.

If this was going to be the end... Oh, God, why'd he have to do it?

Why had he allowed himself to go through with it?

Why had he agreed to do it?

"Please. Please," Wilbur whimpered, begging for mercy.

Ada's hand was shaking as she stared hard at the pathetic simpleton, fighting to keep herself under control.

"If it weren't for your daughter, I'd kill you right now."

She tossed the gun away from her, and Wilbur proceeded to blubber away with gratitude until a sharp and ferocious gesture rendered him silent.

"*Sleep!*" Ada yelled, and he immediately fell unconscious.

Ada was sitting on the side of the road with her hands around her knees when the others arrived, slowly rising to her feet as the beastly red convertible made its fast approach. Mary Sue wasn't far behind, arriving at Gallows Hill just in time to spy the dusty Cadillac pulling away, with Ada, looking numb and inconsolable, sitting next to Rudy in the backseat.

Mary Sue had driven the pony hard to get there and could go no further. As she came to a halt, she let out a desperate yell.

"Ada! Don't leave! Take me with you! Please!"

But the convertible didn't slow down, continuing onward as Ada directed a sad smile behind her, her face stained with tears.

Mary Sue's eyes remained fixed on the departing vehicle until a noise drew her gaze to the smoking wreckage nearby. She watched her father emerge from the disaster; his head bloody, clothes a mess.

While making his way to her, Wilbur found his daughter's disapproving stare chilling and disconcerting, his heart sinking even further as he noticed the tears silently streaming down her cheeks.

Wilbur was still unaware of all that had occurred between his daughter and Izzy amid the turbulent events that had been happening. But it seemed she had developed something of an attachment to Ada, and he was now being regarded as the enemy.

While gazing at her, he continued to struggle to pinpoint where everything had gone horribly wrong in his life and why Ada had allowed him to live. It was right then that he came to the discouraging realization that his daughter had watched her parents participate in something that was unforgivable and what he was witnessing was the death of the young girl's innocence.

Nancy returned to the frozen yogurt shop after her daughter's departure to discover the table where Franklin was sitting was empty. Rather than deciding to engage in a pointless and pathetic chase after the witches, she felt herself being drawn in another direction, placing the blame for her toxic emotions on one meddlesome teenage girl in particular.

The tavern appeared deserted when she entered, with the only items out of place being a pair of gas cans on top of the bar and a young bearded man wearing a black business suit tied to a chair in the center of the room. After overhearing Franklin's orders to burn the tavern to the ground, Lucy and Rudy snuck back inside and knocked Dave out with a fire extinguisher. While Rudy tied up their victim and gagged his mouth, Lucy tried to get ahold of McAllister, ultimately phoning up Agatha after being unable to reach him.

"They got the drop on me," Dave mumbled once Nancy removed his gag and loosened his ropes.

"Go. Get out of here," she said, and Dave hesitantly nodded and rushed outside as Nancy lit a match and set the bar ablaze.

Several minutes later, when the fire trucks finally arrived, Nancy was standing outside the yogurt shop, glaring coldly at the roaring inferno steadily consuming the setting that had briefly been identified as the Black Death Tavern. A small crowd had gathered, watching the firefighters struggle to battle the flames, when Ashton and Tyler appeared, rushing over to Nancy to question her.

"Where are they?" Ashton asked emotionally. "Is everything OK?"

"They're gone," Nancy said. "Left town this morning. You'll never see her again."

Nancy felt a wave of relief once she spotted Wilbur walking the family's pony down the smoky street with Mary Sue riding on top. Upon closer inspection, she was distressed to notice her husband looking bruised and beaten, and when she went to embrace him, she observed her daughter watching them with disdain as she slowly dismounted and led the pony to the corral behind the shop.

"How is she?" Nancy asked nervously.

"She'll be fine," Wilbur answered. "I think."

Experiencing a powerful rush of emotions, Wilbur gave his wife a huge bear hug, smothering her in his arms with all the love he had to give. The couple turned to watch the fire, the crowd of locals keeping their feelings hidden, but they were all no doubt relieved that the tavern would no longer be a problem for the community.

"It's over," Wilbur said, forcing a smile onto his face.

But Nancy was not so sure of this.

57

UNSOLVED MYSTERIES

———

With Walpurgisnacht drawing to a close, spring break for the Ghost Bros was drawing to a close as well, and their final day in Little Salem got off to a bit of a rocky start. The night before, after being kicked out of his hotel room, Tyler went down to the tavern to enjoy some late-night boozing with Rudy and Lucy. The boys both drank themselves stupid and had been whipped in several rounds of pool by the fiercely competitive teenybopper when a game of strip poker was suggested, and they got their clocks cleaned in this activity as well. Tyler had little recollection of what happened afterward; he assumed he must have wandered back to the hotel at some point because when he woke up, he found himself suffering a splitting headache—and in the hotel attic of all places.

The pounding hangover proved to be as hellish and painful a way to start the morning as any in recent memory, but discovering he was buck naked and his clothes were nowhere in sight was equally as painful. He reasoned that in his drunken stupor he must have left his clothes behind at the tavern following the poker game. The only bright spot to be found was the realization that at least he left his phone and wallet in the hotel room before visiting.

Getting back to his room was destined to prove to be a mission in itself. After leaving the attic, Tyler crept down the hallway like a bandit with his hands hovering over his junk. Fortunately, he was able to reach the room without incident, but once he pulled the door open and was safe, he found himself in the company of Ashton, standing frozen while pulling on a T-shirt as he stared at the bumbling naked strangeling in front of him.

"Ashton. Ashton, hey—"

"Dude, what the f—?"

"I think I lost my clothes in a poker game. Uh, long story."

Ashton rolled his eyes with annoyance.

"Get dressed," he announced humorlessly. "It's time to leave."

Feeling awkward and vulnerable, Tyler followed the order without argument, dressing quickly before getting his things together for the return trip back home. While glancing around the room, he found it curious there were no signs of Ada having stayed the night, but he could tell by his companion's hardened disposition he wouldn't be getting anywhere by asking any questions. Whatever had transpired between them was to remain secret—at least for now.

Tyler was more than willing to let this slide, his mind already turning to more prescient matters. Once he pulled himself together, the boys were ready to hit the road and he was back to being in high spirits, chattering enthusiastically on the way to pack up the car.

"Dude, so I checked the stats on our video? We've almost reached half a million clicks! We're gonna be famous!"

The discovery that the Mysterious Ones video was going viral had Tyler feeling electrified. Ashton's reaction to the news remained muted, appearing much more interested in the billowing gray and black smoke coming from up the road.

"Whoa," Tyler muttered. "Do you see that?"

It didn't take long to determine where the fire was coming from and what was the target for the ominous blaze. Ashton took off first, racing toward the tavern where a crowd had already gathered across the street, with firefighters working tirelessly at tackling the inferno that was turning the building into kindling. When the boys arrived, Nancy confirmed that Ada and the others had managed to leave before the incident, but she remained reticent to say anything further other than it was unlikely they would see Ada again.

Tyler pulled his friend away after this, knowing it wasn't going to help matters by hanging around any longer. Ada, McAllister, the tavern, the coven—everything connected to that highly divisive group had been a considerable thorn in the side of the townspeople. It remained a mystery just who could have started the fire, but it really could have been anyone.

The presence of Ada and her Lords of Light (or whatever) were too upsetting for the residents to tolerate. They were too rebellious, too unruly, and much too unpredictable. Burning down the radical coven's base of operations wasn't the most drastic thing that could have happened, but it certainly sent a very specific message about the general level of acceptance within the community—something that seemed to resonate with all who were gathered, watching the tavern burn to the ground without a shred of remorse and watching with something closer to resembling wholehearted relief.

It wasn't surprising that professional troublemakers like Ada and McAllister would be met with such uniform animosity from the locals, but just before their departure, Tyler and Ashton were startled to come up against a reasonable amount of hostility as well. It seemed that the congenial attitudes toward their visitors had changed once it was discovered that Tyler's encounter with the Mysterious Ones had been put online, and on their way back to Ashton's Prius, the True-goods' friendly neighbors confronted the two ghost hunters.

"Not so fast," Jerry warned.

"We saw that...*video* you posted," Steve grumbled.

"You can't leave," Cheryl added. "You know too much."

Tyler had suspected for quite some time that if there was already one dodgy secret cult in Little Salem, then there was plenty of room for another. The boys never discovered the identities of the witches the giant had warned them about, but things seemed to be getting much clearer as they watched the surly group of townspeople slowly advancing on them, blocking their escape.

Luckily, fortune seemed to smile on them as the giant appeared on the front porch of the hotel, aiming a rifle at the unruly mob.

"Get out of here," the giant told them. "And feel free to come back and visit anytime."

The boys were more than eager to follow his instruction, greatly relieved that in a time of crisis, it turned out they had made at least one friend during their stay. Before they left, Ashton tried to learn the name of their towering guardian angel, but the giant didn't answer, only obliging them to get the hell out of Dodge while they still had the opportunity.

"Yessir," the giant said, cracking a smile as they piled into their car and headed on their way, "if there's one thing I could never stand about Little Salem, it's these damn witches."

It was just a short journey back to Boston after this. The boys made it back during the daytime, but the world was dark as night when they arrived. The dense storm clouds that were gathering when they left Little Salem only became thicker and blacker as they made the drive back home. By the time that Tyler was dropped off at his frat house, the rain was pouring down in buckets.

Before exiting the Prius, Tyler flashed a smile at Ashton, still barely able to believe the unforgettable experiences they shared over the past week.

"Spring break, mofo," Tyler said.

Ashton smiled back, likely feeling grateful that they made it back in one piece. Tyler was the first to laugh in recognition of this, and soon Ashton was laughing as well. After giving each other a bro-hug, Tyler held out his fist, and Ashton pounded it; their week of amazing life-changing adventures had officially come to an end.

Things were fast and furious for the two Ghost Bros from there on out. The clicks for the Mysterious Ones video continued to climb, and the attention they received made them kings of the internet. Due to the viral nature of the video's appeal, their popularity only grew over the next series of weeks, with the boys appearing in multiple news articles, thought pieces, TV interviews, and podcasts. A recorded press conference was even held to answer all the familiar questions about the video once the school year was drawing to a close and they had more time to field such appearances.

Question: So what led you to the woods that night?

Tyler: Uh... My friend, Ashton, and I were staying at a local hotel, and there was a message on the wall written in blood—

Question: I'm sorry—you said the message was written in blood?

Tyler: Uh, yeah.

Ashton: Yes.

Question: Who put the message there? The message that was—

Tyler: It was written by this psychic gypsy girl who was... Apparently, she was possessed by a wraith?

Question: And how did you know this girl?

Ashton: She was friends with a witch.

Tyler: A teenage witch.

Ashton: A teenage witch who drew us a map that showed us where to search the woods for them.

Question: For the Mysterious Ones?

Tyler: She and her stepbrother... They were occultish types.

Ashton: Correct.

Question: You also claim these entities were connected to the events leading up to the Salem witch trials.

Ashton: All the information's on our website, bro.

Tyler: Yeah, that's Ghostbros.net. If you wanna bookmark that. We actually had a conversation with the ghost of a witch from that period. What was her name?

Ashton: Sarah Good? Or—

Tyler: Yeah. Unfortunately, paranormal interference corrupted that piece of evidence. Shit happens.

Question: Back to these "Mysterious Ones." What are they?

Tyler: Nobody knows exactly what they are. But there are rumors. Rumors they were summoned into existence with a magic book.

Ashton: Black magic.

Question: And you believe in that. In black magic?

Tyler: Fuck. Yes.

Ashton: Definitely.

As their popularity soared, Tyler relished the attention, finally achieving the fame and glory he always desired. The fawning adoration was almost enough to make him abandon his regrets for never hooking up with a certain dishy redheaded enchantress who still invaded his thoughts on a regular basis. But Ashton had an entirely different reaction, becoming increasingly withdrawn as the weeks went on. It wasn't the glowing fame and celebrity that was bothering him—it was the fact that his girlfriend had gone missing.

To anyone who knew him, Ashton's stormy change of mood was apparent. Tyler knew his friend to be the type of person who usually kept his feelings close to his chest, so it wasn't unexpected that several weeks after returning from Little Salem, Ashton still had yet to open up to him about all the guilt he was harboring for being absent when his girlfriend had vanished. However, something else seemed to be bothering him, and things all came to a head at a party being thrown in celebration of their video reaching half a billion clicks.

The party was like any all-out college rager with drunken hormone-fueled college kids packed inside Tyler's frat house, everybody drinking and getting rowdy to a DJ playing bass-heavy party jams in the main room. Girls were twerking, guys were breaking; for the frat house, it was one for the record books. And Tyler was feeling like royalty, basking in the center of the riotous festivities from his place on a couch overlooking the packed dance floor, sipping from a red solo cup while surrounded by a doting group of pretty co-eds.

"So then I start running through the forest, and I'm, like, 'Ashton! Ashton!'"

Tyler was describing the now infamous encounter like an old war story when he glanced up to see his fellow ghost hunter wandering the room. Ashton seemed immune to the infectious energy that surrounded him and was roaming the party like the living dead.

"Yo, Ashton! Grab a seat, bro!"

Despite his friend's enthusiasm, Ashton showed no interest. Similar to his behavior at the press conference, he displayed little desire for socializing and gave Tyler a hard look before continuing on his gloomy way.

Under normal circumstances, Tyler would have ignored the cold shoulder and left his friend to sort out his personal business at his own speed. But Ashton's behavior was starting to worry him and needed some serious addressing at some point, with the party serving as good a time as any. Tyler also had a pretty good buzz going and didn't think he'd be able to enjoy himself if his best buddy wasn't also digging the whole scene.

"Uh, excuse me, ladies. Don't go anywhere!"

Tyler pushed his way through the crowd until he finally reached his sullen amigo, grabbing him by the arm and flashing a boozy smile.

"Dude, what's with the pity parade? Our video just hit half a billion clicks! We've got groupies here, fangirls here—whole place is popping off like Mardi Gras! This is what we always dreamed!"

Ashton cast a harsh glance at him.

"You really have to ask?"

"Dude, I know. You're thinking about Mercy. She disappeared, and it's totally crazy. But it happens! People disappear all the time!"

"Dude, you did not just say that. What's wrong with you? Did your mother drop you as a kid?"

"Look. All I'm saying is I know you loved her and thought the world of her. But there is a first-year psyche major named Tiffany sitting *right there*. And she'd make you forget your own name if you just got to know her a bit."

Ashton glanced at the couch to the group of girls Tyler had been sitting with, noticing a buxom sorority girl smiling flirtatiously—apparently the aforementioned "Tiffany." But he couldn't be less interested, glaring at Tyler with contempt before plowing a stubborn path through the crowd.

"Dude!" Tyler yelled in frustration. "Why you gotta be such a buzzkill?"

Things only continued to decline in the boys' friendship from there on out. Later that night, Tyler caught Ashton leaving the party looking even more rattled. But when he tried to ask him what had just happened, Ashton only screamed that he wanted to be left alone. In the days that followed, Tyler continued to have difficulty with getting a hold of him, and it quickly began to feel like he was being shut out of his friend's life completely.

Tyler did feel a genuine sense of concern for Ashton, but in the end, he kept his distance. If his fellow Ghost Bro needed some space to deal with things, he would give it to him—and he kept up with this arrangement until the final week of school when he forced an encounter with the hopes that a special surprise would heal the widening rift between them.

"Ashton! Hey!"

Ashton had just left the lecture hall for his American History class, his enduring pain and suffering masked behind a stony expression. In the distance, he spotted Tyler approaching with a well-dressed professional-looking woman, whose name he learned was Olivia Wallace after a quick introduction.

With the formalities all taken care of, the woman made her intentions clear: She discussed her enthusiasm for their footage of the Mysterious Ones and her desire to set the boys up with their very own TV series.

"That video you shot in Little Salem? I don't know if that was real, but it scared the bejeezus out of me! If you can deliver more content like that, then I think we're in business."

His fellow Ghost Bro was beaming with pride, but Ashton only stared blankly at the woman. He thanked her for the offer and turned to Tyler, face void of emotion.

"It's over."

Ashton started walking away, leaving Olivia and Tyler stunned. Tyler wasn't about to let his friend walk out on a moment of a lifetime opportunity only to regret it later. He immediately chased after him, at a loss for words.

"Over? Ashton! Dude, what are you—?"

"It's over. 'Ghost Bros,' the TV thing."

"Ashton—Hey, listen—"

"I mean, sure. It was all a big laugh when we were just two brain-dead bros horsing around. But then spring break happened, and all that crazy witch stuff happened. And then I come back home to discover my girlfriend is a missing person?"

"Ashton, please. I didn't mean—"

"And maybe..." Ashton got up close to Tyler's face. "Maybe because she was *my* girlfriend—maybe that's why I'm taking all this a little more personally. Because, between the two of us, am I really the only one who doesn't have so much vast empty space between the ears to see that all this shit is connected?"

Tyler was like a deer trapped in the headlights as he stood there with Ashton now yelling at the top of his lungs, all the brimming anger burning inside of him rising to the surface.

"Are you really that stupid? How can you not see it? *How can you not see it?*"

Ashton shook his head with disappointment, trying to shake off the noxious emotions before heading on his way.

"Ashton. Ashton, hey!" Tyler glanced weakly at Olivia before pressing forward. "Ashton, I'm listening. Really. Just tell me how all of this ... how all of the... Just explain it to me, bro. I don't —"

"Explain it to you? Why bother? I mean, God damn it. What were we doing being friends in the first place? You're just so clueless."

Tyler noticed Olivia, his ticket to the big time, was walking away. But none of this mattered; his sole focus was to salvage what was left of his precious friendship before it was damaged beyond repair.

"Ashton. Don't do this," Tyler begged. "This isn't you."

Ashton turned to face him. "Do you think I care about any of this? All I want is my girlfriend. That trip was a mistake."

After this, he continued on his way, leaving Tyler speechless, still not aware this would be the last time they would speak as friends.

At the time, Tyler was oblivious to the treacherous path his companion seemed to be heading toward, where Ashton's family history, his ominous dreams, and the warnings from Ada would all seem to collide. Ashton said that all of his recent experiences were connected. Not being able to figure out the whole puzzle on his own was bound to eat away at him; to pick at his brain like a scavenger and cause him to unravel further and further...

58

HAUNTED FOREVER

The rain was pouring down from the heavens when Ashton returned to his apartment following his bizarre and highly eventful week in Little Salem. As he entered with his luggage, shaking the damp from his hair, he called out to his girlfriend...but there was no answer. It was strange she wouldn't be there like she usually was. Still, it was easy for him to write this off—she could have been out with friends or studying for a class. Discovering all the power was dead was something a bit more unexpected.

"Hey, Mercy? Damn it. Hello?" Ashton still wasn't fully convinced he was all alone as he slowly felt his way through the darkness. "Did Max give you any trouble while I was gone? You are not going to believe the trip I had."

Maybe she's hiding, Ashton thought. Tucked around a corner somewhere, trying not to giggle as she waited to surprise him. Like when she pulled the whole "showing up with nothing under the trench coat" bit during the week leading up to his going away. He reminded himself it wouldn't have been unlike her to remain hidden before jumping out to startle him once he had let his guard down. But as he made his way into the apartment with flashes of lightning brightening the setting sporadically, nothing happened. And he noticed it was deathly quiet and something didn't feel right.

"Mercy? Are you there?"

Ashton dumped his luggage in the bedroom and started at the sound of a low growl...but he couldn't see his cat anywhere.

Feeling uneasy, he cautiously scanned the room before his eyes landed on the wall behind his bed, and a sudden burst of lightning briefly illuminated his surroundings. That's when he saw it: a large Algiz rune accompanied by the initials, "lol," spray-painted in black right above the headboard, knowing right then and there his apprehensions had been justified, and that during his weeklong absence, something had gone horribly wrong.

Over the next few days, it quickly became apparent that his girlfriend had disappeared. Ashton wasted no time in filing a missing person report, but the police investigation turned up nothing and things only proceeded to disintegrate in the days to come. During the weeks following the disappearance, the Mysterious Ones video continued going viral, and Ashton and Tyler were transformed into minor celebrities. But it was impossible for Ashton to truly enjoy the experience as his mind continued to remain fixated on the graffiti on the wall of his bedroom and the unknown purpose it had for being there when he returned back home.

It wasn't until the school year was drawing to a close when he would finally receive some answers to the maddening questions assaulting his brain ad nauseam—around the time the Mysterious Ones video hit half a billion clicks. He was attending the frat party, wondering why he had bothered to show in the first place, when he had his frustrating exchange of words with Tyler, who had the gall to scold him for wandering through the setting like a ghost. After leaving his callous drunken companion on the dance floor, he sought refuge in the kitchen, standing in the corner and staring gloomily into his drink. He was ignoring the buzzing din from the mass of revelers while wondering why he didn't just leave if he was already feeling so out of place when he suddenly sensed someone approaching him, seeing Miles of all people.

"Hey, Ashton. Do you remember me?"

The question seemed trivial. Of course he remembered him. The last thing he expected was to cross paths with someone from Ada's coven ever again.

"What are you doing here?" Ashton asked. "Is Ada with you?"

"No," Miles answered. The impeccably-dressed young man smiled regrettably. "No, I no longer—What I mean is, I don't know where she is."

Miles pursed his lips as if he was thinking about how best to express something before directing a piercing stare at Ashton and stating he thought that they should talk. Sensing the seriousness of the request, Ashton accompanied him to the backyard where there were fewer people around to hear them. He remained curious to learn what had happened to Ada and the others, and had no idea the subject Miles wanted to discuss was Mercy.

"After McAllister sent me to Boston, I ran into your girlfriend at a pep rally," Miles explained. "No one was more shocked than I was to hear that she disappeared." He looked Ashton in the eye, his face deathly serious. "I walked your girlfriend home that night. I might have been the last person to see her before she went missing."

Ashton was stunned, his face growing paler by the second.

"But there's more," Miles said. "I need to show you something."

His interest peaked, Ashton accompanied Miles to one of the frat house's upstairs bedrooms. Once they were alone, Miles removed a laptop from the black satchel he was carrying and began scrolling through the contents.

"The police weren't being very helpful, so I started doing some investigating on my own." Miles clicked on a video file and a grainy surveillance video began to play, showing an empty lobby that looked remarkably familiar.

Ashton's eyes narrowed.

"Is this...?"

"It's the security feed for your building. From the night she went missing." Miles gestured to the screen. "See? Right there."

And there she was: Mercy, entering the doors to the building; crossing the lobby and stepping onto the elevator.

Ashton clenched his fists while viewing the imagery. But Miles was only getting started and had a much bigger surprise in store.

"This is from five minutes later." Miles jumped ahead in the video to show another figure entering the building: a young woman with a waifish figure wearing a gray hoodie, black skirt, black stockings, and black boots. When she reached the elevator, she raised her head and he paused the video, revealing a pair of haunting blue-violet eyes staring at the surveillance camera.

Ashton leaned forward, jaw agape. "No..."

Miles gazed solemnly at the disturbed young man sitting beside him. "The night you went into the woods and shot that video... Do you know where Ada was? What she was doing?"

Ashton fidgeted in his seat, his body hit with a cold sweat as he stared at the eerie cherubic visage peering up at him from the screen.

"I left her at the reservation, and then... I didn't see her until..."

Miles waited for Ashton to complete his sentence, but he'd been rendered speechless. So many things had happened in Little Salem, and the timeline of events had grown fuzzy. There was definitely a long stretch of time where Ada's activities were a total mystery, meaning that what Miles was saying...

"You can't trust them, Ashton," Miles affirmed quietly. "Images don't lie."

After this event, Ashton quickly left the party, rushing outside to get some air and giving Tyler the cold shoulder before stumbling off in a daze. Over the next series of days, he chose to avoid Tyler and pretty much everyone else in his life and quit the Ghost Bros for good the next time he ran into him, essentially ending their friendship forever. Their paranormal adventures all seemed so insignificant in light of all that had happened, and Ada and Mercy were now consuming his daily reflections. His mind remained mainly devoted to Mercy, spending countless hours scrolling through photos and videos on his smartphone displaying the times they shared. But these cherished thoughts and remembrances would often become interrupted by his memories of Ada as he continued anguishing over how it was Ada who was responsible for the disappearance—even if this was something that didn't make sense.

Had she just been lying to him about who she was and what she was up to? What game was she playing? And something else was bothering him...

As Ashton sat on his bed one evening, scrolling through old photos and getting more emotional by the second, he eventually landed on the picture Tyler had taken at Sir Godfrey's: the bloody red circle hanging on the wall of the trophy room. The image brought back flashes of his recurring dream of his father and Mr. Frau, both of them laughing on the couch together, before giving way to memories of the monstrous city of flesh and bone.

Gritting his teeth and pressing his eyes tightly shut, Ashton let his smartphone fall to the ground. He grabbed his head in agony as he fought the stressful visions, all while his cat appeared to watch him from a place on the floor, frowning with concern.

Indulging in all of these conflicting thoughts and recollections was pressing him perilously past the borders of sanity. He knew he had reached the point where he had to do something to ease his troubled headspace before he was driven mad completely.

After forcing these turbulent visions aside, Ashton slowly rose to his feet and crossed to his closet, rummaging through the back until he found what he was searching for: a framed picture facing the wall. He removed it from its resting place and held it in front of him to observe the blood-red circle that was broken on one side, the colors dripping down the canvas.

The disquieting item was the gift he received in his dream, which hadn't been a dream at all. For Ashton, reality and his nocturnal world of supposed fantasies were one and the same—a painful pill to swallow if he wanted to get to the bottom of what was going on with him, what his experiences over spring break had been all about, and where his life was currently headed.

Standing frozen in place, acknowledging the distressing path that lay before him, he stared hard at the framed picture. His fingers tightly gripped the edges while his cat continued watching him, tail twitching anxiously.

Dark storm clouds enveloped the sky when Ashton returned to his college campus. From where he was parked, he could see Professor Emmanuel in his office, his desk positioned next to the window on one of the upper floors of the building. Emmanuel was still at work when Ashton arrived outside his door, knocking first and waiting for a response.

"Come in."

Upon his entry, Ashton received a hesitant smile, noting his professor could see he wasn't in the greatest shape at present. However,

Emmanuel remained as accommodating as possible, mentioning it was good to see him and asking if he was there to discuss his final paper—which was on the topic of forbidden magic in the early days of New England, coincidentally.

Scholarly matters couldn't have been further from Ashton's mind. He came to a halt a short distance from his professor, and his eyes were drawn to a framed piece of canvas containing a blood-red circle, hanging on the wall beside the desk.

"I need to speak to Ada. Where is she?"

Emmanuel stared at him unflinchingly, smiling like a shark.

"I assume you're referring to my wayward stepdaughter. I'm afraid we haven't been in contact for... Oh, heaven knows. Why must you speak to her?"

"I need answers."

"Do you? I don't believe she'd be able to give you any. Is this about your missing girlfriend?"

At the sudden mention of Mercy, Ashton's body went stiff. Flashes of his missing lover assaulted his fevered brain, the painful memories competing with images of Ada—something he was quick to recover from, but the tension in his limbs was now unbearable.

He had reached the end of his rope.

"It's about everything!" Ashton screamed. "Everything that's been happening since the day that I—*that I met that witch!* And long before that!"

Ashton glared at Emmanuel beseechingly. "I don't understand. What's happening to me? There are so many things that are happening that don't make any sense!"

"Perhaps I can be of assistance."

Ashton spun around to address the voice that had joined the conversation, startled to discover the sight of his father lounging on the couch behind him.

Upon making eye contact with his long-suffering progeny, the man rose to his feet while his estranged son glared back at him at a complete loss for words.

"Dad?"

"Good to see you, Ashton."

He crossed to the door and opened it.

"Please. Follow me."

While accompanying his father down the hallway, Ashton glanced back to notice that Emmanuel was joining them, following at a distance as he was led to a classroom. When he entered, he found a small group waiting for him, eyes all gazing at him unblinkingly. The group included Miles, a beautiful older woman dressed in all black, and about a dozen others; all of them Caucasian, mostly middle-aged, and smiling in a discomforting manner.

"I believe you already met Miles." Ashton's father gestured to the rest of the group. "This is Emmanuel's wife, Ursula—You'll be meeting the others soon. I'm also fairly certain you remember our mutual friend, Mr. Frau."

Ashton felt a cold chill as the man revealed himself from the back, looking every bit as irksome and skeletal as he did in his dreamscape—no, his memories—only now he was seeing him in the full light. He stared at the man's dusty old suit and his ever-present reptilian grin; at the intense bulging eyes boring into him while every nerve in his body seemed to be instructing him to get the hell out of there while he still had the beggar of a chance.

No. His quest for answers felt much too significant to abandon so prematurely. He balled his fists and stood his ground as his father joined the group and faced him, smiling majestically.

"Ashton, we are here today because we want to extend to you a personal invitation for membership into a very elite and exclusive group. A group made up of talented and distinguished individuals just like yourself. A group we have been grooming you to join since the day you were born."

In the blink of an eye, Ashton realized that Ada's prophecy was coming to fruition. He also recognized that, despite his original intentions, if he wanted to make a hasty getaway, he had reached his last opportunity.

"Please. Hear us out," his father requested, sensing his son's hesitation. "Then you will be more than free to leave us. Mr. Frau?"

The ever-smiling Mr. Frau began his slow approach, his eyes remaining fixed on Ashton's antsy, irresolute gaze as the young man trembled with anxiety.

"Hello, Ashton," Mr. Frau said to him. "I'm sure you recall all the pleasant visits we shared. Regrettably, I haven't brought our special book with me, as there is nothing left for me to read to you. Instead, I have brought you...a film."

It was at this moment that Ashton noticed the battered film projector at the back of the room, and his mind started spinning, wondering just who on earth all these people were and what was going on with this dubious meeting as everyone found a seat and faced the projection screen.

"I'm quite certain you will already be familiar with the story." Mr. Frau gestured for Ashton to join them. "Lights?"

As instructed, Emmanuel hit the lights, and the projector was switched from off to on. Ashton swallowed his hesitation, finding it curious that before the film even began, all who were present were gazing in front of them with deep reverence.

While watching the film, he found himself feeling restless and irritated. But over time, he started becoming enamored by all he was seeing: a parade of silent moving images that were both mysterious and mildly upsetting, all leading up to a terrifying climax that inspired a wave of conflicting emotions to churn through his system.

"So, as you can see," Mr. Frau explained, referring to the film as he sat grinning beside him, "our distinguished hero wanders into the night past accursed and desolate place and numerous formidable hardships before arriving at his fated destination: *The Golden City*."

This is when the horrifying visions hit Ashton full force, instantly eliciting all the usual symptoms: his eyes widened, his face turned pale, and his gaping jaw fell open as the sight of a living, breathing metropolis seared his addled vision.

And yet, the experience felt different. While reacting to all the familiar horrors, with the addition of the film playing in front of him, he began to process the disturbing imagery in a manner that was entirely new to him. The horrible images flashing in his mind were as disgusting and sickening as ever, but there was also a strange and frightening beauty attached to them. And he realized... He realized he was crying, a single tear rolling down his cheek.

It was all just so...beautiful.

59

ANGEL EYES

The wind was blowing violently and a full moon was shining overhead when Rudy returned to the roadside motel with a large shopping bag. The skinny miscreant had been situated at the gloomy half-star establishment for several weeks at this point—after being abandoned by Ada and left to fend for himself.

The day the New Lords fled Little Salem, the group stopped at the motel for a quick breather, and Rudy sat on one of the suite's ratty double beds, staring solemnly at the carpeting as he listened to Ada's wailing, torturous sobs bleed through the bathroom door. The assault against the witches happened so suddenly that Ada had never gotten the chance to mourn the death of her one true love, and in that harrowing moment, all the pain, along with the horrible sense of loss she was experiencing, was pouring out of her in a manner that was so heartrending he eventually had to leave the room. His valiant leader's unbearable anguish was devastating, and he felt riddled with scores of clashing emotions on account of his absolute powerlessness to do anything to console her.

"This is fucked. This is so fucked!" From where he stood at the edge of the lonely asphalt lot, Rudy could see that rain was on the horizon, dark storm clouds crowding the sky above him. "The diary's gone, McAllister's fucking dead..."

Several feet away from him, Agatha sat in the driver's seat of the convertible with Lucy sitting beside her, silently petting Ada's black kitten. Both girls looked drained of emotion, with Lucy likely saving whatever she had left to be there for Agatha once she was ready to enter her own period of mourning. For the time being, Agatha was letting her emotions simmer, feeling more angry about the situation and worried about Ada than anything. This left Rudy as the perennial "odd man out"—a role he was overly familiar with.

Rudy had always been the runt of the group. Being the last member to join Ada's coven until Lucy essentially replaced Izzy, he shared the least amount of history with everyone and lacked the strong bonds this history created. He was a year older than Ada and two years older than Izzy, but all of the girls in Ada's coven felt like older sisters to him; mainly because, unlike everybody else, he possessed no inherent magical gifts whatsoever.

Ada was always telling him that his talents when it came to working with technology made him a "tech wizard" of sorts, but his skills felt second-rate when compared to the amazing abilities his comrades were born with. Being a non-magical person in the company of naturally gifted magical people while living in a world where magic was definitely real—and a strong aspect of everybody's lives whether they knew it or cared to admit it—was something that filled him with a great deal of anxiety and insecurity. And no matter how hard he studied in order to, at the very least, possess a serious background in the occult sciences like McAllister did, who, like him, was also born with a lack of natural magical ability, this remained far out of reach, placing him at a disadvantage when it came to finding solutions to deal with the coven's problems and making him destined to always suffer a permanent inferiority complex because of this.

It was true that Ada did teach him the basics when it came to magic and witchcraft, and he enjoyed some minor successes in chaos magic and in situations where he could use his gifts with technology to his advantage. Rudy also possessed a thorough knowledge of all the various types of magic that were out there, so he could at least recognize certain dangers when he came across them. But there was nothing he could do when it came to helping Ada feel whole again; no potion or charm or spell would be sufficient in helping to stop the tears from flowing or put her back together in one piece. And when it came to the mission of defeating the Scarlet Council, he felt woefully unprepared for this as well. Everyone in the group had always relied on Ada to give them the winning edge in their battles. With the recent loss of McAllister and the discovery that Miles was a traitor, they were now in serious trouble, and Rudy felt even more pathetic and worthless due to his total lack of any tools that could be useful when it came to their present difficulties.

"We can't stay here," Rudy eventually said after pacing back and forth for several moments. "We can't stay!"

"We're not staying. You are."

The voice startled him—and not just because he was so caught up in his anxieties that the faintest outburst was bound to make him jumpy. The last person he was expecting to hear from was Ada herself; standing in the doorway to the motel room, her eyes red, face stained with tears as she clutched McAllister's copy of Austin Osman Spare's *Book of Pleasure* like a priceless totem, holding it close to her chest.

"*Me?*" Rudy saw his worst nightmare unfolding as Ada slowly approached him, her lips quivering and her voice becoming stronger and angrier and more hurtful with every word that was unleashed.

"Your *carelessness* in the company of others led Miles to the beach to murder McAllister," she said. "Your *negligence* at the asylum led to Izzy being possessed by a wraith. And your *cowardice* in the face of danger led you to hide like a rat while Agatha was being tortured within an inch of her life."

Ada stood in front of him, her eyes darkening as he cowered at the sight of her. "YOUR ACTIONS ARE A DISGRACE!" she shrieked. "You don't deserve my compassion! Or my friendship! Your journey ends here. Any minor semblance of a relationship between us is finished, and your membership with the New Lords has been revoked. Now do us all the courtesy of forgetting you ever knew us."

With that, Ada coldly turned her back on him; his bags were dropped at his feet, and the convertible took off in a cloud of dust. Rudy had been abandoned; left sullen, dejected and heartbroken in the motel lot. Ada, the truest friend he ever had, leaving him by the side of the road like nothing more than a common bag of trash.

Rudy thought about this moment a great deal—and the look on Ada's face. He thought about how, while she was screaming at him, he never felt so utterly powerless. Totally unable to defend himself from the witch's harsh and scornful criticism.

Maybe she had been right in her judgment.

But he was determined to have the last laugh.

Weeks had passed, and when Rudy shuffled into the hotel room, the TV was on, reporting on the strange weather patterns that had been popping up of late.

"Curious weather striking the Northeast this evening. We have heavy winds hammering one region in particular. This is the same region that was affected by that freak storm a few weeks ago—also unexplained."

The news report continued as he pocketed his key card and crossed to the bed.

"State officials are warning residents to be on the alert for rolling blackouts and unsafe—"

He flipped the TV off before removing his purchase from the shopping bag—a portable flatbed scanner—taking a deep breath before assembling the device next to his cluttered workspace, the motel table now featuring a large computer with various books on coding and advanced ceremonial magic piled next to it.

As Ada's former dependable "tech wizard," Rudy had the scanner set up in no time, attaching it to the CPU and plugging it into the power strip. He booted up the computer as he removed the crown jewel from his coat pocket: a folded piece of ancient parchment with a series of Enochian letters forming an unusual pattern at the center.

This rare and enigmatic item was the cipher from the back of the Engelander Diary; the rumored Forty-ninth Enochian Key. Rudy had pinched the object before McAllister retrieved the book to take it to the beach with him. At the time, he had no idea what he intended to do with the artifact, simply assuming that whatever had been written on it had to be significant. Since he had sticky fingers, he stole the item without thinking, resigned to try to figure out why it was so exceptional at a more convenient juncture. He'd been boning up on a lot of research ever since, trying his damnedest to become an Enochian master but quickly discovered that Enochian magic was way over his pretty little head. The learning curve for this material was overwhelming, and the preparations for an Enochian ritual were exceedingly complex. So much so that when it came to trying to contact the entities referenced in the material, it helped if you were someone who had a lot of experience with meditation and altered states of consciousness—two things he was horribly lackluster at.

Edward Kelley, for example, had been something of a born seer. During the Angelic Conversations, John Dee would spend extended lengths of time praying for the spirits to appear until Kelley would sense their presence and communicate with them. Likewise, when Crowley was employing the Enochian system during his experiments in Mexico and Algeria, he would work himself into a frenzy and use the Enochian Calls to place him in an altered state that would inspire strange luminous visions and dreams. Rudy tried both of these methods and failed miserably, and there were many periods over the past series of weeks where he felt like giving up altogether and doing his best to try to return to a normal life. But at the same time, he already knew that living a "normal life" would be impossible after all he had experienced with Ada and his former companions—especially after what he learned from her about who was really in charge of things and what the world they were living in was really all about.

It was during his moments of deep-seated insecurity, ironically, that Ada's "tech wizard" comment kept coming back to him. This is what inevitably gave him the idea for how he could decode the key, remembering the special program he showed to Tyler that revealed the secret mathematical formulae hidden in various Enochian ciphers. Rudy had been anticipating the experiment all day, and with all the proper tools at his disposal, he was feeling extremely anxious about going through with the experiment. Regardless, now wasn't the time for hesitation. Everything was all plugged in and ready to go; all that was left was for him to place the piece of parchment under the cover of the scanner and open up his computer program.

After scanning the item, Rudy brought an image of the Enochian table up on the screen. He still wasn't entirely sure what he was doing but was determined to give it a shot in hopes of proving to the world that he wasn't as much of a failure as Ada painted him out to be. With nothing left to lose, he held his breath and tensely clicked a menu item, and the cluster of Enochian letters began lighting up one by one. But while the program was running, the experiment was interrupted by a sudden power surge, with all the fixtures in the room getting much brighter right before everything turned to black.

Startled by the blackout and finding himself now sitting in total darkness, Rudy frantically looked around him. "Oh c'mon, c'mon."

He started clicking various keys on his computer, which was now apparently dead.

Great. So much for that.

After glancing around the room in frustration, he checked the power strip and all the plugs and outlets, searching for any sign of a problem, but everything appeared to be fine. He assumed the blackout must have been caused by the weather and that he would just have to try the experiment at a different time.

But then, the strangest thing happened. Without any assistance, the computer suddenly booted itself back up. When he emerged from under the table, a new program seemed to be running, and a message in white text on a black background was waiting for him on the screen:

Hello.

Body tense, Rudy sat up and leaned forward.

"What the...?"

He noticed the blinking cursor on the line below the greeting. Silently signaling to him, beckoning for a response.

Rudy paused, trying to remember his research.

For Dee and Kelley, after going through all the necessary preparations, they would often hear voices or see visions of the entities they contacted in the reflection of a black mirror. To Rudy, a computer screen was something that wasn't much different. In a way, the dark reflective surface did resemble a black mirror—or something like it. And if that was the case, could it mean...?

Still not quite sure what he was doing but determined to carry on with his project, he straightened his posture and placed his fingers on the keyboard, typing:

"Who are you?"

He hit the return key and waited. The blinking cursor below his answer simply stared back at him.

And so much for that, Rudy thought again. He was considering writing off the strange phenomenon entirely when suddenly...a new line of text appeared underneath his question:

We are the angels.

All the color drained from Rudy's face.

"We...are the angels," he muttered, his heart rate accelerating as he started typing away, his hands shaking.

Rudy's imagination was running wild, thinking of all the different possibilities for what could be happening and what this conversation could actually mean. Back in Little Salem, he confessed to Tyler that the identities of the Enochian Angels were a total mystery. Modern magicians frequently debated about where these "angels" came from and what they actually were. One of the arguments was that these strange beings had to be some form of high-functioning multi-dimensional intelligence. Powerful entities that had access to vast quantities of information about the past, present, and future; that had a special predilection for dark prophecy and forbidden wisdom and could be called upon to be granted knowledge that mere mortals typically lacked sufficient access to.

Being granted an audience with the "angels" was like hitting the occult lottery. But this was not without danger for Lord only knew their true intentions or what special use they saw in those they granted communications with.

"Can I speak with you? Can I use this program to speak to you?"

Rudy hit the return key, a cold sweat forming on his forehead. The blinking cursor sat below his petition for what felt like forever, and just when he felt like his heart might explode with anticipation, a new line of text appeared on the screen:

Yes. Ask us anything.

* * *

Several miles away from the motel, the Truegood family home was calm and peaceful. On the surface, it appeared that everything in Little Salem was back to normal: Wilbur and Nancy opened the frozen yogurt shop every day at the same time they always did, Mary Sue returned to school, and the household all enjoyed dinner together as a family every evening. Everything was back to being picture-perfect—although Mary Sue wasn't talking to her parents much and mainly kept to herself. When she returned to her room after dinner, she curled up in bed and started work on a drawing of the charming band of outsiders she developed an intense fascination with during the short but eventful time she had known them.

Ada, McAllister, Agatha, Rudy, and, of course, Izzy: The Lords of Light, all of them standing together, etched into her drawing pad in painstaking detail, like they could all come to life at any moment.

As Mary Sue gazed at the drawing, her eyes were drawn to the window. A violent wind was howling outside, and the dark of the night seemed much blacker and more treacherous.

Mary Sue's parents were both in bed fast asleep, but the tranquil moment was interrupted when Nancy's face suddenly started twitching. Her lips began issuing forth a string of words in a low monotone that sounded not entirely like her own. Like all the words were being forced out of her against her wishes.

"It's not over," Nancy mumbled. "It's not over. It will never be, never be..."

Her voice steadily grew louder.

"Never be over. Never be... Never be..."

The wind screamed against the window, and Nancy's eyes popped open—just in time to witness the wooden crucifix hanging across from her falling off of the wall and dropping to the floor with a dramatic thud.

This strange forceful breeze was also blowing through the forest that surrounded Little Salem, while standing on a hilltop overlooking the shimmering lights of the town below was a dark figure, humming the melody to "The End of the World," by Skeeter Davis.

The figure was a stranger to Little Salem, outfitted in a long black coat worn over a flattering but old-fashioned floor-length purple dress. A black wide-brimmed hat sat on top of her head, her long chestnut-colored tresses trailing out from underneath it. Dark circular sunglasses covered her eyes, the darkness of the glasses offering a fine contrast to her porcelain skin and blood-red lips.

As the wind continued howling, the figure stopped humming long enough to take a long drag on a brown clove cigarette. Her lips curled into a smirk as she stifled a spontaneous burst of laughter with only the faintest glimmer of a delirious cackle escaping into the atmosphere; no doubt in reaction to all the delightful shenanigans she intended to pursue now that the force of nature known as Dakota Crawford had arrived in Little Salem in the flesh.

60

SALEM'S BURNING

"Your friend said you know a lot about this place." Ashton was alluding to something that was mentioned at the tavern on the walk back to his hotel.

"I visited here with my family," Ada said. "Around five years ago. I found the trip to be very...meaningful. You only care about ghost stuff, right?"

"That's not all that I care about." His reply was rakish and somewhat flirtatious, but it was an honest comment. There were plenty of things he cared about besides the supernatural.

But Ada already knew this. Ashton may not have known it, but she'd been watching him for quite some time. Ever since McAllister phoned her from overseas, announcing his return and the plan he wished her to take part in upon their reunion in Little Salem.

Ashton's desire to visit the notoriously haunted locale was a stroke of luck actually. While observing his activities over the past series of days, Ada found the initial inception of the trip highly intriguing, proving her stepbrother's suspicions that the Council was trying to get their hooks into him and get him acquainted with what they were all about.

Ada witnessed many other fascinating aspects of the young amateur ghost hunter's daily life and regimen. She watched him break into a boarded-up home to perform an investigation, observed the frequent comings and goings of his girlfriend, Mercy—she was even close by when her stepfather recommended traveling to Little Salem and spied on him while he was researching the town in the school library. Ada had also been present in the middle of the night to witness the boys' arrival at their hotel and had been the one to lure Ashton out into the street so that Rudy could pick his pocket and lead him to the tavern where she would finally introduce herself.

Ashton remained ignorant about how much she already knew about him and why she arranged for their meeting in the first place. But it was still far from the most opportune time to reveal this.

She didn't want to scare the poor boy off after all.

Not when she had such big plans for him in the future.

Wearing a playful smile, Ada skipped somewhat as they walked down the sidewalk. "I really don't see what people find so terrifying about that stuff. Ghosts are just something you may or may not be able to see that may or may not be trying to communicate with you. What's so terrifying about all that?

"Uh, you don't see how that might be a little bit creepy?"

She leaned against a wall and smiled coyly.

"I think you like things that scare you."

"I'm not scared of anything."

Ada suppressed a chuckle, and her lips curled into her token impish smirk. "Perhaps you just have a limited imagination," she suggested and started on her way again.

"Whoa—hey now. Are you trash-talking me?"

Ada predicted the comment would get a rise out of him. It was funny—the boy really knew so little about his place in the world and what he was a part of. For Ashton, ghosts and a little demon or two were about as dark or strange as things could get. But Ada knew much more about the hidden evils of the world and where his life was currently headed, which included some very dark and troubling places to say the very least.

It was no surprise she would know these things.

She was a witch, after all.

And Ashton's initiation into her world was only just beginning.

"'*There are more things in heaven and earth, Horatio, than are dreamt of in your philosophy,*'" Ada said.

"Right. Didn't Bill Shakespeare say that?" Ashton replied.

Ada smiled mysteriously, her otherworldly eyes sparkling in the moonlight while taking into account the precise placement of the moon and the stars, wondering if the odds were really in her favor for accomplishing all she was trying to achieve in the world.

Back on the ground stood all the same shops and businesses she remembered from her fateful visit five years earlier: the hardware store at one end of the quiet and empty main drag and the historic hotel on the other, with a sprinkle of eclectic family restaurants and boutique retail shops in between. There was a manicurist, a hair salon, an antique store, a convenience store, a couple of banks... The Truegoods' frozen yogurt shop was a new addition, but Little Salem possessed a certain time warp quality, changing very little over time. The community really went out of their way to try to preserve the hearty small-town flavor of the delightful setting. That's what made it so tragic that the simple townspeople seemed all too willing to bargain their souls away to maintain the whole façade.

"Well, let's hear a little about you," Ashton said after catching up with her. "What makes you tick?"

"I don't think you're ready to know that just yet."

"Seriously?"

Ada shrugged nonchalantly. "I'm just a simple, old-fashioned girl really. In town to get some kicks. See? We already have so much in common. Oh look, we're almost at your hotel."

The clever misdirection worked like a charm. But in a way, this was exactly how Ada saw herself, her words layered with extra meaning for those with the right ears to interpret them.

For instance, the reason why she saw herself as old-fashioned was that she practiced what witches called "the old religion." If Ashton had known what this truly meant, he wouldn't have had much more to ask her. In fact, there was a very good chance he would run the other way after learning this. And it was true that she was in town for a bit of mischief and hellraising and knew they shared various interests since he was someone with an exceptionally curious nature and was drawn to things that were highly unusual.

It was fortunate that McAllister had found a future pledge of the Council that was so easy to connect to. The fact that he was easy on the eyes was an added bonus. Ada enjoyed toying with Ashton and got a thrill out of playing the role of a secret agent, but what she was looking forward to more than anything was her reunion with the one who advised her to connect with the boy in the first place, her eyes lighting up and her whole body shivering just thinking about it.

Ada still had no idea when she would be seeing her so-called stepbrother, as silly as it was to find herself still thinking of him as such. So, for the time being, she stuck to the plan at hand.

When Ada and Ashton arrived at the hotel, they agreed to meet the following day so she could give him a tour of the town and various spooky sites of interest that might tickle his fancy. They said their goodbyes to one another and Ada set off back down the street, casting her smile at the "Season of the Witch" banner stretched across the boulevard and feeling cautiously optimistic for a change, the future looking much brighter than it had in quite some time. While her gaze was directed at the friendly moon and glittering cosmic canopy hanging above her, marveling at the intricate patterns of stars sparkling in the heavens as vivid, kaleidoscopic dreams danced in her head, she suddenly heard a faint mewing and turned to a nearby alleyway. There, an adorable black kitten was sitting all by its lonesome, the tiny furball's sleepy amber eyes gazing back at her.

"There you are," Ada said. She beamed brightly as she retrieved the precious feline and smothered her beloved mini-beast close to her face. "I've been looking for you all over..."

Where she obtained this pet and how she lost her in the first place is another story altogether, but reuniting with her darling familiar prior to her anticipated engagement felt like a good omen. Little did she know that danger was lurking close by—so close it was practically breathing down her neck.

As Ada continued her moonlit stroll back to the tavern with the purring black kitten now cradled in her arms, she remained blissfully unaware of two shadowy figures following her at a distance, stalking her like apex predators until they were only a few yards away.

"Hey! Freak Show!"

With her eyes wide as flying saucers, she spun around to discover two men wearing black business suits aiming guns at her. Based on their attire, she recognized them as assassins from the Scarlet Council, and given a chance to learn any more about the two fellows, she would have discovered that the one with the emo-core haircut was named Billy, and the one with the lumberjack beard was named Dave, and they were currently in town seeking vengeance for McAllister's little murder spree in Prague. Both men were glaring at her with intense bile and animosity, but the one named Billy looked especially menacing, no doubt savoring the opportunity to kill his victim in as cruel and heartless a manner as possible.

The two gunmen had caught Ada by surprise. As she froze in confusion, Billy cracked a sly grin.

"How many witches does it take to dodge a bullet?"

Without giving her time to answer, he pulled the trigger.

Bang!

Time seemed to slow down as the shot traveled toward her. But when the bullet was only inches away, it came to a halt in mid-air.

Ada cocked her head to the side, admiring the motionless object before watching it drop harmlessly to the ground. Her haunting, otherworldly eyes glanced at her two assailants as a wicked smile spread across her face.

"Lemme guess. One?"

Both men were flabbergasted. Dave started backing away as Billy stubbornly raised his weapon to fire again.

Tragically, for one person at least, Ada's attacker would never get the chance to pull off the shot. Ada lazily waved her arm and her enemies went flying in different directions before dropping hard to the ground. Without skipping a beat, she crossed to the groaning body of Billy, her heels clicking softly across the pavement as the young man struggled to rise to his feet, something primal deep inside of him urging him to rally himself before the very worst could happen.

Ada came to a halt and stared coldly at her opponent, a bare, unbridled ruthlessness shining in her eyes like starlight.

"Boys like you give me such a headache," Ada said, her black-nailed manicured fingers stroking the tiny black kitten cradled in her arms. As her unearthly eyes stared transfixed at her shameful would-be killer, he suddenly grabbed his temples and let out an agonizing scream—right before his head exploded, sending blood and brain matter flying everywhere.

The world seemed to stand perfectly still in that moment before Billy's hideous headless body slumped to the ground. With one vile and loathsome pest successfully exterminated, Ada turned her attention to Dave, his eyes staring aghast at the gruesome display.

"Anyone else want some?"

Dave didn't stick around to answer, taking off as fast as he could. As Ada watched after him, her face took on a weary expression before glancing at her clothes and grimacing.

"Aw man. I got blood all over my cool threads."

Disaster had been averted, but she couldn't let down her guard just yet. Alerted by the sound of slow clapping, her eyes darted over to observe a dark figure emerging from the shadows.

McAllister.

"Well now. I see my little stepsister's all grown up."

"Brother! You're back!"

It felt like ages since she had seen him, and Ada immediately embraced her long-lost companion, practically unable to believe he was there with her arms wrapped around him once more.

"It's been so long." Ada broke the embrace to observe all the familiar features that made her blood race. The dark eyes, the brash smile, the lean and wiry physique all draped up in nightmare black. "I never thought I'd see you again."

"You were a little girl when I last saw you," McAllister observed.

Ada giggled and did a dramatic twirl, showing herself off to him—no longer just a girl and very much a young woman and eager to have him accept her as such. It was true she had changed in other departments as well. Her dark and tangled hair was now much longer and much more wild and unruly, and she was also more confident and assertive with her tantalizing womanly charms.

But while admiring her dear "stepbrother," her face became more serious, taking account of all the marked differences since the last time she saw him.

"You've changed as well," Ada muttered softly. "Haven't you?"

This was something that was noticeably apparent. Ada's strange alien beauty may have amplified in her beloved cohort's absence, but for McAllister, the changes were a bit more unsettling. The portrait overall was similar, almost like he had barely aged a day, but his skin was now unnaturally pale, and his features were much sharper and more gaunt. There was also something different about his eyes; a cold harshness with a glint of madness in them (although she felt certain she saw love in there as well, possibly), and the tattered black military overcoat he was wearing made him look like he was ready for war and not intimidated by what battlefields lay in front of him.

During his time living in exile, McAllister's dark and dangerous mystique seemed to have intensified considerably—something Ada found a bit worrisome but also exhilarating—and it was plain to see that something dreadful had happened to cause so many changes in him. But it was also apparent that he intended to keep the details of his transformation a secret, and as his stony gaze examined her, she couldn't help but notice something resembling a faint tinge of regret lingering behind the eyes.

"Is everything going according to plan?"

Ada suppressed a nervous giggle and flashed her impish grin, more than willing to let him change the subject so their special reunion could continue.

"Would I ever let you down? Oh heavens, there's so much I have to tell you—"

"McAllister?"

Ada watched McAllister turn his head to address the voice calling out to him, locking eyes with Agatha, standing in the doorway of the black Victorian across the street from them. McAllister would be enjoying a special reunion with her as well at some point, Ada reminded herself, based on all she had learned about their steamy liaison before he was forced to flee for sanctuary overseas. She knew the shapely siren was deeply in love with him but wasn't quite sure of his own feelings, and she found herself praying he would remain by her side and resist abandoning her so prematurely.

Please, just a few more moments so I can enjoy this while it lasts, Ada silently wished. She anxiously awaited his next move, wondering if the spirits would acknowledge her, and felt her heartbeat quickening as McAllister cast a devilish smile at the redhead.

"Hey! Who's a guy have to lay to get a drink around here?"

The comment drew an excited and coquettish smile out of Agatha. After she headed back inside to attend to her lover's witty appeal, Ada's heart started beating faster and faster, steadily coming to realize that her wish had been granted, earning her a few extra moments with her heart's restless infatuation.

Moments later, when McAllister turned back to her, she knew for certain right then and there that their story had been unmistakably joined together when their eyes first met almost five years earlier.

It was unlikely that he would kiss her madly and take her in his arms just then, but she could see he was yearning to spend more time with her and have her in his company. And in just a few moments, he would playfully ruffle her hair and she would grab his hand in hers, fighting back goosebumps as they crossed the street together to their newly remodeled base of operations, all while Sanchez, still hard at work since that morning and in the process of making the finishing touches, removed the wooden boards from the windows to reveal a brand new sign for the establishment:

BLACK DEATH TAVERN.

In the meantime, with splatters of blood on her face and the kitten still cradled in her arms, Ada beamed up at her fated other half. Her haunting and bewitching eyes were practically glowing, thinking about all the wonderful mischief they'd be getting up to as he smiled fondly and said:

"So... Ready to party?"

About the Author: Brian McIlroy is a spider from Mars that lives in Los Angeles. He is a child of the underground and a friend to animals. *Hunting For Witches — Salem's Burning* is his first novel.

www.ingramcontent.com/pod-product-compliance
Lightning Source LLC
Chambersburg PA
CBHW060808120726
47909CB00006B/1829